PRAISE FOR Shriek: *An Afterword*

"With literary stylings, a complex, riveting plot, and ideas that lesser writers could not imagine, *Shriek: An Afterword* further establishes Jeff VanderMeer as the finest fantasist of his generation."
—*Austin Chronicle*

"VanderMeer explores brilliantly, penetratingly, the frail, evanescent intersection of human understanding and historical actuality.... In the telling, *Shriek: An Afterword* is an exceptional novel, a tapestry of fine writing, deep psychological insight, and acute narrative excitement.... a dark fantasy of tremendous distinction." —*Locus*

"Five stars! A stunning and very different fantasy novel from an author who should be turning heads in the 'serious' literary world. VanderMeer concerns himself with the life of a notorious historian whose investigations into a subterranean race known as 'grey caps' may hold the key to an ancient mystery. In reality, however, the book cleverly plays with the ways in which an author can manipulate an audience. But it's far less heavy and more entertaining than that makes it sound." —*BBC Focus* magazine

"It is, in short, exactly the sort of book which ought to be in contention for major literary prizes—except that it is set in an imaginary city beset by malevolent fungus, and non-genre award panels tend to get scared of such books. In this case, such fears are misplaced; *Shriek* is a fantastic book, and a fantastical one. For lovers of the uncomfortable and slightly unhealthy work of a Will Self, or the fractured cityscapes of M. John Harrison, *Shriek* is a delight." —*The Birmingham Post*

"Jeff VanderMeer's latest is as complicated, impressive, and exasperating as anything he has written.... VanderMeer makes no compromises with his readers, but *Shriek* is twisted, darkly funny, and ultimately rewarding."
—Jon Courtenay Grimwood, *The Guardian*

"A typical VanderMeer novel: clever, intense, and multi-layered. Four stars."
—*SFX* magazine

"Jeff VanderMeer's work opens a trapdoor in the world we think we know, into a realm as unforgettable and compelling as an opium dream, and as seductive. *Shriek: An Afterword* is a sinister and bewitching tour-de-force."
—Elizabeth Hand, bestselling author of *Mortal Love*

"Here is a desert island book, a tale you can lose yourself in for days, a novel of character in which the setting—the magnificently gritty city-state named Ambergris—proves as the light fails to be the finest character of all."
—Gene Wolfe, author of *The Wizard*

"There's a madness in Jeff VanderMeer's literary eye, and I would be a liar if I didn't admit it seems intimately familiar. VanderMeer envisions an outlaw literature of shrieks and shouts and a screaming across the sky, worth a thousand polite and respectable mutterings. I, for one, am listening."
— Steve Erickson, author of *Our Ecstatic Days* and editor of *Black Clock*

"Political, philosophical, many-textured, and multilayered, the history of fantasy's most intriguing city, Ambergris, is brought vividly to life. The perfect balance of conscientious invention and subtle, comic irony—VanderMeer fearlessly walks a tightrope to deliver an enthralling read."
— Jeffrey Ford, World Fantasy Award–winning author of *The Girl in the Glass*

"Bloody brilliant."   — Hal Duncan, author of *Vellum*

"*Shriek: An Afterword* is the first authentic twenty-first century fantastical writing. A masterpiece by any standard."   — Zoran Zivkovic, author of *Hidden Camera*

"An enthralling book which takes you into the vivid and superbly realized world of Ambergris. It is in turn unsettling, moving, and thrilling—with passages of writing that can be dryly funny on one page. . . and beautiful on the next."
— Clare Dudman, author of *98 Reasons for Being*

"Jeff VanderMeer is an extraordinary writer. His vision of Ambergris is passionate, beautiful, complex, terrifying. What is remarkable about *Shriek: An Afterword* is the way it combines such surreal imagery with intensely human feeling. He writes about real people—about the real world."
— Tamar Yellin, author of *The Genizah at the House of Shepher*

"Jeff VanderMeer is a realist of the surreal, a chronicler and bibliographer of the impossible city of Ambergris, which could only have been constructed in a collaborative dream between Charles Dickens and E. T. A. Hoffmann. It is a city of Dickensian scope and intricacy whose inhabitants are the lovers, the artists, the grotesques of German romanticism, and I sometimes suspect that VanderMeer himself is a fragment of the same dream. *Shriek* is a beautiful and maddening, and beautifully maddening, book. Go to Ambergris: lose yourself among its labyrinthine streets and the fabulous, deadly secrets that lie beneath them."
— Theodora Goss, author of *In the Forest of Forgetting*

Shriek:

An Afterword

Shriek:

An Afterword

❧

Jeff VanderMeer

A TOM DOHERTY ASSOCIATES BOOK ◆ TOR® NEW YORK

SHRIEK: AN AFTERWORD

Copyright © 2006 by Jeff VanderMeer

Hoegbotton logo © 2002 Eric Schaller
Appendix Photographs © 2006 Jonathan Edwards

Edited by Liz Gorinsky
Book design by Nicole de las Heras
Machine diagram rendering by Jim Kapp

A Tor Book
Published by Tom Doherty Associates, LLC
175 Fifth Avenue
New York, NY 10010

www.tor.com

Tor® is a registered trademark of Tom Doherty Associates, LLC.

Library of Congress Cataloging-in-Publication Data

VanderMeer, Jeff.
    Shriek: an afterword / Jeff VanderMeer.
        p. cm.
    "A Tom Doherty Associates Book."
    ISBN-13: 978-0-7653-1466-6
    ISBN-10: 0-7653-1466-5
    1. Title.
PS3572.A4284S57 2006
813'.54—dc22

                                        2005034500

First Hardcover Edition: August 2006
First Trade Paperback Edition: July 2007

Printed in the United States of America

0 9 8 7 6 5 4 3 2 1

for Ann

&

for
Howard Morhaim
who sold it

Jim Minz
who bought it

Liz Gorinsky
who edited it

No one makes it out.

—Songs: Ohia

⁂

If you live a life of desperation,
at least lead a life of loud desperation.

—Dorothy Parker

⁂

We dwell in fragile, temporary shelters.

—Jewish Prayer Book

⁂

The dead have pictures of you.

—Robyn Hitchcock

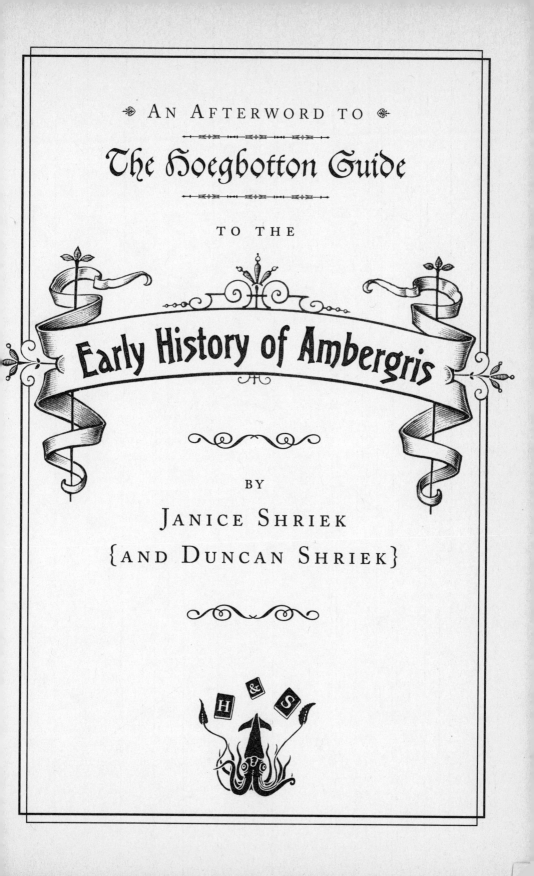

❖ AN AFTERWORD TO ❖

The Hoegbotton Guide

TO THE

Early History of Ambergris

BY

JANICE SHRIEK

{AND DUNCAN SHRIEK}

H & S

A NOTE FROM THE AUTHOR

The following is my account of the life of noted historian Duncan Shriek. This text was originally begun as a belated afterword to Duncan Shriek's *The Hoegbotton Guide to the Early History of Ambergris,* but circumstances have changed since I began the book.

Having begun this account as an afterword, ended it as a dirge, and made of it a fevered family chronicle in the middle, all I can say now, as the time to write comes to an end, is that I did the best I could, and am gone. Nothing in this city we call Ambergris lasts for long.

As for Mary Sabon, I leave this account for her as much as for anyone. Perhaps even now, as late as it has become, reading my words will change you.

Goodbye.

—JANICE SHRIEK

{When I found this manuscript, I contemplated destroying the entire thing, but, in the end, I didn't have the will or the heart to do so. And I found I really didn't want to. It is flawed and partisan and often crude, but it is, ultimately, honest. I hope Janice will forgive or forget my own efforts to correct the record. —DUNCAN}

Part 1

[Upon the altar, the Cappan Aquelus' men found an] old weathered journal and two human eyeballs preserved by some unknown process in a solid square made of an unknown clear metal. Between journal and squared eyeballs blood had been used to draw a symbol. . . . More ominous still, the legendary entrance, once blocked up, boarded over, lay wide open, the same stairs that had enticed Manzikert I beckoning now to Aquelus. The journal was, of course, the one that had disappeared with Samuel Tonsure 60 years before. The eyes, a fierce blue, could belong to no one but Manzikert I. Who the blood had come from, no one cared to guess.

—From Duncan Shriek's depiction of the Silence in
The Hoegbotton Guide to the Early History of Ambergris

❧ I ❧

MARY SABON ONCE SAID OF my brother Duncan Shriek that "He is not a human being at all, but composed entirely of digressions and transgressions." I am not sure what she hoped to gain by making this comment, but she said it nonetheless. I know she said it, because I happened to overhear it three weeks ago at a party for Martin Lake. It was a party I had helped put together, to celebrate the artist's latest act of genius: a series of etchings that illustrated *The Journal of Samuel Tonsure*. {One of many parties I have missed over the years. Maybe if I'd been there, everything would have turned out differently. Maybe it even would have affected the past portrayed in Mary's books.}

Sabon arrived long after Lake, a reticent and not entirely undamaged man, had left for the Café of the Ruby-Throated Calf. I had not invited her, but the other guests must have taken her invitation for granted: they clustered around her like beads in a stunning but ultimately fake necklace. The couples on the dance floor displayed such ambition that Sabon's necklace seemed to move around her, although she and her admirers stood perfectly still.

Rain fell on the skylight above with a sound like lacquered fingernails tapping on a jewelry box. Through the open balcony doors came the fresh smell of rain, mingled—as always in Ambergris—with a green dankness. As I hobbled down the wide marble staircase, into their clutches, I could pick out each individual laugh, each flaw, each fault line, shining through their beaded faces. There were names in that flesh necklace—names that should someday be ticked off a list, names that deserve to be more public.

At ground level, I could no longer see anything but patches of Sabon—a glimpse of red hair, of sallow cheek, the pink allure clumping, a flash of eye, the eyelashes overweighed with liner. The absurd pout of a lip. The crushing smell of a perfume more common to a funeral parlor. She looked so different from

the first time I had met her—lithe, fresh student—that I thought for a moment
she had put on a disguise. Was she in hiding? From what?

*"He is not a human being at all, but composed entirely of digressions and trans-
gressions."*

I admit I laughed at Sabon's comment, but I laughed out of affectionate
recognition, not cruelty. Because Duncan did digress. He did transgress. He
might well have dashed Sabon's living necklace to bead pieces with just as
amusing a phrase to describe Sabon, had he not disappeared, possibly forever, a
few days before the party. That was another thing—Duncan was always disappearing, even as a child.

Sabon's comment was amusing, but not, as one gentleman misidentified it,
"the definitive statement." A shame, because my brother loved definitive statements. He used to leap up from his chair at definitive statements and prick the
air out of them, deflate them with his barbed wit, his truculent genius for argument, his infinite appreciation of irony. {I think you both mock me here. Whatever I might have been in my youth—and I can't remember ever having been a
witty conversationalist—I'm long past any such trickery. Let the spores be
tricky. Let those who ignore them—from the Nativists on down—expend their
energy in fanciful phrasings, for all the good it will do them.}

⬦⬥⬦

I REALLY OUGHT TO START again, though. Begin afresh. Leave Sabon to
her admirers for now. There will be time to return to her later.

Duncan often started over—he loved nothing better than to start again in
the middle of a book, like a magician appearing to disappear—to leave the
reader hanging precariously over an abyss while building up some other story
line, only to bring it all back together seamlessly in the end, averting disaster. I
would be a fool to promise to duplicate such a feat.

For a time, Duncan sat next to the desk in my apartment—in an old comfortable yellow chair our parents had bought in Stockton many years before.
There he would sit, illumined by a single lamp in a twilight broken only by calls
to prayer from the Religious Quarter, and chuckle as he read over the transcript
of his latest chapter. He loved his own jokes as if they were his children, worthy
of affection no matter how slack-jawed, limb-lacking, or broken-spined.

But I best remember Duncan at his favorite haunt, The Spore of the Gray
Cap, a place as close as the tapping of these keys. {Favorite? Perhaps, but it was
the only one that would have me, at times. At the more respectable establishments,

I would walk in and be greeted with a silence more appropriate to the sudden appearance of some mythical beast.} Sober or drunk, Duncan found the Spore perfect for his work. Within its dark and smoky back chambers, sequestered from the outer world by myopic, seaweed-green glass, my brother felt invisible and invincible. Through a strange synchronicity of the establishment's passage-ways out of keeping with its usual labyrinthine aura, those who congregated at the altar of the bar could, glancing sideways down the glazed oak counter, see Duncan illuminated by a splinter of common space—at times scribbling in-spired on his old-fashioned writing pad, at times staring with a lazy eye out of a window that revealed nothing of the outer world, but which may, reflecting back with a green wink, have revealed to him much of the inner world. {The outer world came to me—at various times I entertained Mary, Sirin, Sybel, and, yes, even Bonmot, pillar of the community, in that place.}

He had become a big man by then, with a graying beard, prone to wearing a gray jacket or overcoat that hid his ever-evolving physical peculiarities. Sometimes he would indulge in a cigar—a habit newly acquired from his asso-ciation with the fringe historian James Lacond—and sit back in his chair and smoke, and I would find him there, gazing off into a memory I might or might not be able to share. His troubles, his disease, could not touch him in those moments.

I much prefer to remember my brother in that space, calm and at the center of himself. While he was there, many regular taverngoers referred to him as the God of the Green Light, looking as he did both timeless and timeworn. Now that he is gone, I imagine he has become the Ghost of the Green Light, and will enter the annals of the Spore as a quiet, luminescent legend. Duncan would have liked that idea: *let it be so.*

❧❦❧

BUT I *DO* CHOOSE TO begin again—Duncan, after all, often did. Like the shaft of green light shooting down the maze of passageways at the Spore, each new shift of attention and each new perspective will provide only a fraction or fracture of the man I knew, in several senses, not at all.

If there is a starting point in Duncan's life, it would have to be the day that our father, Jonathan Shriek, a minor historian, died at our house in Stockton, a town some hundred miles south of Ambergris, on the other side of the River Moth. Unexpected reversal ripped through Dad and destroyed his heart when I was thirteen and Duncan only ten. I remember because I was seated at the kitchen table doing my homework when the mailman came to the door. Dad heard the bell and hopped up to answer it. "Hopped" is no exaggeration—Dad was a defiantly ugly man, built like a toad, with wattles and stocky legs.

I heard him in the hall, talking about the weather with the mailman. The door shut. The crinkle of paper as my father opened the envelope. A moment of silence, as of breath being sucked in. Then a horribly huge laugh, a cry of joy or triumph, or both. He came into the kitchen and barreled past me to the open hallway that led to the back door.

"Gale," he was shouting. "Gale," my mother's name. Out into the backyard he stumbled, me right behind him, my homework forgotten, beside myself with suspense. Something marvelous had happened and I wanted to know what it was.

At the far end of the lawn, Duncan, ten and still sandy-haired, was helping our mother with the small herb garden. My father ran toward them, into the heart of the summer day. The trees were lazy in the breeze. Bees clustered around yellow flowers. He was waving the letter over his head and yelling, "Gale! Duncan! Gale! Duncan!" His back to me. Me running after him, asking, "What, Dad? What is it?" {I remember this with the same kind of focused intensity as you, Janice. Dad was running toward us. I was smiling because I loved seeing Dad's enthusiasm. I loved seeing him so euphoric, so unselfconscious for once.}

He was almost there. He was going to make it. There is no doubt in my mind, even today, that he was going to make it. But he didn't. He stumbled. He fell into the sweet, strange grass. {"Mottled with shadows from the trees," I wrote in my journal later. It is those shadows I remember most from that day— the dappling and contrast of light and dark.} The hand with the letter the last to fall, his other hand clutching at his chest.

I stopped running when I saw him fall, thought he had tripped. Looked up across the lawn at my mother and brother. Mom was rolling her eyes at her husband's clumsiness, but Duncan's face was pale with horror. Duncan knew our father hadn't fallen, but had been *made* to fall. {I don't know how I knew, just remember the way Dad's smile flattened and his face took on a sudden pallor and sadness as he fell, and know he knew what was happening to him.} A moment later, Mom realized this, too, and all three of us ran-to-him converged-on-him held-him searched-for-a-pulse called-for-the-doctor, and sat there crying when he did not move, get up, say it had all been a joke or accident. {Even now, the smell of fresh grass is the smell of death to me. Was there, even then, a sentinel in the shadows, peering out at us?}

It was Duncan who took the letter from Dad's hand and, after the doctor had gone and the mortician had removed the body, sat down at the kitchen table to read it. First, he read it to himself. Then, he read it to us, Mom staring vacant-eyed from the living room couch, not hearing a word of it.

The letter confused Duncan in ways that did not occur to my mother, to me. It bent the surface of his world and let in a black vein of the irrational, the il-logical, the nonsensical. To me, my father was dead, and it didn't matter how or why, because he was dead regardless. But to Duncan, it made all the difference. Safely anchored in place and family, he had been a madly fearless child—an ex-plorer of tunnels and dank, dark places. He had never encountered the brutal dislocation of chance and irony. Until now. {Did it make a difference? I don't know. My resolve has always seemed something fiercely internal.}

For our father, Jonathan Shriek, minor historian, had died in the grasp of a great and terrible joy. The letter, which bore the seal of the Kalif himself, con-gratulated him "for having won that most Magnificent Award, the Laskian Historical Prize," for a paper published in the *Ambergrisian Historical Society Newsletter*. The letter asked my father to accept an all-expenses paid trip to the Court of the Kalif, and there study books unread for five centuries, including the holiest-of-holies, *The Journal of Samuel Tonsure*.

The letter had become a weapon. It had rescued our father from obscurity, and then it had killed him, his blood cavorting through his arteries at a fatal speed. {I couldn't get it out of my head that he had died due to something in his research, as irrational as that might seem. It instilled in me a kind of paranoia. For a while, I even thought it possible that the letter had been poisoned in some way by the Kalif's men, that Dad had been too close to the solving of some his-torical mystery the Kalif would prefer remain unsolved.}

The funeral that followed was farce and tragedy. We attended the wrong cas-ket and were shocked to be confronted by the visage of a young man, as if death had done my father good. Meanwhile, another family with a closed casket had buried our father.

"Death suited him." It didn't matter that it wasn't true—it seemed true. That he had gone into death old and come back young. And more comforting still— the idea that there had been a mistake and he was alive somewhere.

Of us all, Duncan stared the longest at that young man who was not our fa-ther, as if he sought the answer to a mystery for which there could be no solution.

⁂

FOUR YEARS LATER, WE MOVED from Stockton to Ambergris, there to live with our mother's side of the family in a rheumy old mansion with a flooded basement. Set against the banks of the River Moth, remote from much of Ambergris, the place could hardly be called an improvement over the house we had grown up in, but it was less expensive, and our mother had come to realize that with her husband dead nothing much remained to keep her in Stockton. Thus, we shared space with an ever-changing mob of aunts, uncles, cousins, nephews, nieces, and friends of the family. {Although, over the years, this cacophony of distant relations reduced itself to just our mother, which is probably how she would have preferred it from the beginning.}

We came to Ambergris across the thick sprawl of the muddy River Moth, by ferry. I remember that during the journey I noticed Duncan had a piece of paper in his shirt pocket. When I asked him what it was, he pulled it out and showed it to me. He had kept the letter from the Kalif to our father; as far as I know, he has it still, tattered and brittle. {I do have it—or the remains of it, anyhow. I don't dare open it anymore, for fear it will turn to dust.}

"I don't want to forget," he said, with a look that dared me to doubt his loyalty to our father.

I said nothing, but the thought occurred to me that although we might be traveling to a new place, we were still bringing the past with us.

Not that Ambergris didn't have a rich past of its own—just that we knew much less about it. We knew only that Ambergris played host to some of the world's greatest artists; that it was home to the mysterious gray caps; that a merchant clan, Hoegbotton & Sons, had wrested control of the city from a long line of kings; that the Kalif and his great Western Empire had thrice tried to invade Ambergris; that, once upon a time, some centuries ago, a catastrophe called the Silence had taken place there; and that the annual Festival of the Freshwater Squid often erupted into violence, an edgy lawlessness that some said was connected to the gray caps. The gray caps, we learned from helpful relatives seeking to reassure us, had long since retreated to the underground caverns and catacombs of Ambergris, first driven there by the founder of the city, a whaler despot named Manzikert I. Manzikert I had razed the gray caps' city of Cinsorium, massacred as many of them as he could, and built Ambergris on the smoldering ruins. {It all sounded incredibly exciting and exotic to us at that age, rather than horrifying.}

Of artists, we found ample evidence as soon as we arrived—huge murals painted onto the sides of storehouses—and also of the Hoegbotton clan, since we had to pay their tariffs to leave the docks and enter the city proper.

As for the gray caps, as our relatives had promised, we discovered scant initial trace of this "old, short, indigenous race," as the guidebooks called them. They were rarely seen aboveground during the day, although they could be glimpsed in back alleys and graveyards at dusk and during the night. We knew only what we had gleaned from Mom's rare but unsettling bedtime stories about the "mushroom dwellers of Ambergris," and a brief description from a book for children that had delighted and unnerved us simultaneously:

Fifty mushroom dwellers now spilled out from the alcove gateway, macabre in their very peacefulness and the even hum-thrum of their breath: stunted in growth, wrapped in robes the pale gray-green of a frog's underbelly, their heads hidden by wide-brimmed gray felt hats that, like the hooded tops of their namesakes, covered them to the neck. Their necks were the only exposed part of them—incredibly long, pale necks; at rest, they did indeed resemble mushrooms.

Of the Silence, we had heard even less—a whisper among the adults, a sense that we should not ask about it. Even in Stockton, so far from what had happened—separated by both time and geography—there seemed to be a fear that, somehow, the event might be resurrected by the most casual of comments. No, I discovered Silence much later—only learned during my brief attendance at the Hoegbotton School for Advanced Studies, for example, that the annotations in Ambergrisian history books {A.S. and B.S.} stood for After Silence and Before Silence. Of Samuel Tonsure's journal, so inextricably linked to the Silence, I heard not even a whisper until Duncan educated me. {I may have given you the most personalized and eccentric education on the Silence in the history of Ambergris!}

We did not learn much about any of this from Mom. For a good portion of our youth in Ambergris, rare was the day that she rose before noon. Sometimes we barely saw her. She had so many rooms to hide in in that house. Her internal clock, her rhythms, became nocturnal and erratic. She continued to paint, but sometimes we would return home to find that instead of a canvas she had painted the wall of an unused room in a welter of dissonant colors. Until the basement began to flood with river water every time it rained, she loved to sit down there in the damp and read by an old oil lamp we'd brought with us from Morrow, an heirloom dating back to the time of the pirate whalers. {When she was there, Janice and I would sometimes join her. We'd pull up chairs and listen to the whispering gasp of the river water as it tried to get in through the floor-boards, and we'd read our books or do our homework. Mom rarely said any-thing, but there was something about being together in the same room that felt comfortable. I think she enjoyed it, too, but I don't know for sure.}

I do remember that in our mother's absence one of my aunts tried to help orient us to the city, telling us, "There's a Religious Quarter, a Merchant Quarter, and an old Bureaucratic Quarter, and then there are places you don't go no matter what. Stay out of them." Faced with such vague warnings, we had to dis-cover Ambergris in those early days by exploring for ourselves or asking our classmates.

The move to Ambergris changed my relationship with Duncan. Before the move, Duncan had been the annoying shadow, the imitator who always had to do what I was already doing. When I started a rock collection at the age of eight, inspired by the exposed granite on the hillside near our house in Stock-ton, Duncan started one, too, even though he didn't understand why. No mat-ter how I shooed him away, Duncan had to follow me up the hill. A cautious distance away from my irritated mumblings, he would squat in his wobbly way and run his hand through the pebbles, looking for the shiniest ones. Over time, he would squinch closer and closer, waddling like a duck, until before I knew it we were looking for stones together and my collection became our collection.

When I became entranced by the children's stories of mammalogist Roger Mandible, Duncan not only stole the books from my room but colored in them and scrawled his name, handwriting as neat as a drunken sailor's, across many of the pages.

By the time I'd reached the age of fourteen or fifteen, I'd realized he copied me because he loved me and looked up to me. {I didn't look up to you for long—you stopped growing after you turned fourteen, I believe.}

But by then the death of our father and the move to Ambergris had trans-formed me into something more than Duncan's sister. There was something in the connection Dad and Mom had that had energized them both—that had made them both more than they had been alone. Because without Dad, Mom lost, or forgot, how to take care of us. I'm certain if Mom had died instead that Dad would have behaved the same way. He was no more practical than our mother. He was as apt to fall over and stub a toe putting on his pajamas as she was to cut herself chopping up carrots. They shared a general absentmindedness that Duncan and I, looking back on those years as adults, found endearing. Dad searching for the newspaper he held in the crook of his arm. Mom looking for the earrings she'd just put back in the jewelry case. Somehow, together, though, they muddled through and managed to disguise their individual incompetence at the job of parenting.

With Dad dead and the move to Ambergris having unmoored Mom from any last vestiges of parental regard, I became Duncan's mother in many ways. I made sure he got up in time for school. I made him breakfast. I helped him with his homework. I made sure he got to bed on time. He stopped copying me and started obeying me. {. . . Although with a smoldering disrespect for authority as embodied by my suddenly strict sister. But I'm lying. I welcomed it. I needed some structure. I needed someone to tell me what to do back then. I was still just a child. And a frequently scared one, despite all of my explorations. To take the lead while exploring seemed natural; to take the lead in everyday life was monstrously difficult.} Gone was the admiration, perhaps, but so too the corrosive disease of competition. At least, back then.

Somehow, despite our rough knowledge and this change in our roles, we managed to fit in, to get along, to come to feel part of Ambergris with greater ease than might have been expected. Much of it had to do with our attitude, I think. Duncan and I should have been upset about leaving our old school and friends behind, but we weren't. Not really. In a sense, it came as a great relief to escape the pity and concern others showed us, which trapped us in an image of ourselves as victims. Freedom from that meant, in a way, freedom from the moment of our father's death. This made up for the other dislocations.

{Dare I deprive the reader of that first glimpse of Ambergris? That first teasing glimpse during the carriage ride from the docks? That glimpse, and then the sprawl of Albumuth Boulevard, half staid brick, half lacquered timber? The dirt of it, the stench of it, half perfume, half ribald rot. And another smell underneath it—the tantalizing scent of fungi, of fruiting bodies, of spores entangled with dust and air, spiraling down like snow. The cries of vendors, the cries of the newly robbed, or the newly robed. The first contact of shoe on street out of the carriage—the resounding solidity of that ground, and the humming vibration of coiled energy beneath the pavement, conveyed up through shoe into foot, and through foot into the rest of a body suddenly energized and woken up. The sudden hint of heat to the air—the possibilities!—and, peeking from the storm drains, from the alleyways, the enticing, lingering darkness that spoke of tunnels and sudden exploration. One cannot mention our move to Ambergris without setting that scene, surely! That boulevard

became our touchstone, in those early years, as it had to countless people before us. It was how you traveled into Ambergris, and it was how they carried
you out when you finally left.}

❦

BUT AS FASCINATED AS DUNCAN would become with Ambergris, he went
elsewhere for his education. At our mother's insistence, in one of her few direct
acts of parenting, Duncan received his advanced degrees in history from the
Institute of Religiosity in Morrow {or as historians often call it, "that other
city by the River Moth," a good hundred miles from Ambergris}, his emphasis
on the many masters of the arts who had been born or made their fortune in
Ambergris, as well as on the Court of the Kalif—for he saw in these two geo-
graphical extremes a way to let his interests sprawl across both poles of the
world. He could not study the artists of Ambergris without studying the very
anatomy of the city—from culture to politics, from economics to mammalogy.
And because Ambergris spread tentacles as long and wide as those of the old-
est of the giant freshwater squid, this meant he must study Morrow, the Aan,
and all of the South. Study of the Kalif, which I always felt was a secondary
concern for him, meant mapping out all of the West, the North. {Early on, I
had no idea what constituted a "secondary concern." Anything and everything
could have been useful. The important thing was to accumulate information,
to let it all but overwhelm me.}

In that Duncan was never what I would call religious, I believe that this
monumental scope represented his attempt to re-place himself within the
world, to discover his center, lost when our father died, or to build himself a
new center through accumulation of knowledge. In a sense, History was *always*
personal to Duncan, even if he could not always express that fact.

To say Duncan studied hard would be to understate the ardor of his quest
for knowledge. He devoured texts as he devoured food, to savor after it had
been swallowed whole. He memorized his favorite books: *The Refraction of
Light in a Prison, The Journal of Samuel Tonsure, The Hoegbotton Chronicles, Aria:
The Biography of Voss Bender.* Years later, he would delight me, no matter how
odd the circumstances of our meetings, with dramatic readings, in the imagined
pitch and tone of the authors, him still so passionate in his love of the words
that I would forever find my own enthusiasm inadequate.

In short, Duncan became overzealous. Obsessed. Driven. All of those
{double-edged} {s}words. He did not allow for his own human weakness, or

his need to feel connected to the world through his flesh, through interactions with other human beings. Better, I am sure he felt, to become the dead hand of the past, to become its instrument.

Duncan did not make friends. He did not have a woman friend. When I visited him, during breaks in my own art studies at the Trillian Academy, at his rooms at the Institute, he could not introduce me to a single soul other than his instructors. Duncan must have appeared to be among the most pious of all the pious monks created by History. {I *had* friends. Your infrequent trips to visit meant your idea of my life in that place was as narrow as that sliver of emerald light in the Spore that you keep going on about. I needed to converse with people to test out my theories, to gauge dissent and to begin to realize what ideas, when expressed to others in the light of day, evaporated into the air.}

Recognizing both his genius and his desire for lack of contact, the Institute, its generosity heightened by the small scholarship our father had endowed it with as well as the memory of him walking its hollowed halls, had, by the second semester, isolated Duncan in rooms that expanded with his loneliness. My brother's only window looked out at the solid, unimaginative brick of the Philosophy Building, giving him no alternative to his vibrant inner life. {This was, after all, the point of the Institute—to focus on the unexamined life. Nothing wrong with that.}

As if to embody the complexity and brittle joy of his inner life in the outer world, Duncan slowly covered the walls of his rooms with maps, pictures, diagrams, even pages torn from books. Ambergrisian leaders stared down impishly, slightly crooked, half-smothered by maps of the Kalif's epic last battle against the infidel Stretcher Jones. Bark etchings by the local Aan tribespeople shared space with stiff edicts handed down by even stiffer Truffidian priests. James Alberon's famous acrylic painting of Albumuth Boulevard formed the backdrop for a hundred tiny portraits of the original Skamoo synod. The bewildering greens and purples of Darcimba's "The Kiosks of Trillian Square" competed with the withered yellows of ancient explorers' maps, with the red arrows that indicated skirmishes on military schemata.

Duncan devoted one dark, ripe little corner to the "changing facade of Ambergris," as he called it. At first, this corner consisted only of overlapping street plans, as if he were building an image of the city from its bones. The stark white paper, the midnight black veins of ink, contrasted sharply with everything else in his rooms. The maps were so densely clustered and layered that the overall effect reminded me of a diagram of the human body. Or, perhaps more metaphorically accurate, like a concentrated forest of intertwining vines {recalling the forests of my youth in Stockton}, through which no one could possibly travel, even armed with a machete. {My first great accomplishment— a way of cross-referencing dozens and dozens of seemingly unrelated phenomena so that, in a certain light, in a certain darkness, I could begin to see the patterns, the connections. Later, I would use this same technique, on a vastly different scale, at the Blythe Academy.}

With each visit, I noticed that the forest had grown—from a dark stain, to a presence that variously resembled in shape a mushroom, a manta ray, and then some horribly exotic insect that might kill you with a single sting. Gradually, in an inexorable invasion through both time and space, Ambergris came to dominate his rooms, and then layer itself to a thickness greater than the walls, or so it often seemed, sitting in my chair, looking over a manuscript.

The stain had become the wallpaper, and the last remnants of non-Ambergris materials had become the stain. Looking back on those earliest diagrams and montages on his walls, could he have guessed how far they would lead him? How far he would travel, and at what price? {Underneath, any astute observer could have found a wealth, a riot, of new information. You had only to peel away a corner and there, revealed, the secret obsession: the ghosts of the Silence, the gray caps, and much else. "I'm going underground," it all said. For those who could read it.}

"Your wall has changed. Has it changed your focus?" I asked him once.

"Perhaps," he replied, "but it still doesn't make sense."

"What doesn't make sense?" I asked.

"They're the only ones who could have done it. But why? And how?"

I looked at him in confusion.

"The Silence," Duncan said, and a shiver, a resonance, passed through me.

The Silence and the gray caps.

More than two hundred years before, twenty-five thousand people had disappeared from the city, almost the entire population, while many thousands had been away, sailing down the River Moth to join in the annual hunt for fish and freshwater squid. The fishermen, including the city's ruler, had returned to find Ambergris deserted. To this day, no one knows what happened to those twenty-five thousand souls, but for any inhabitant of Ambergris, the rumor soon seeps through—in the mottling of fungi on a window, in the dripping of green water, in the little red flags they use as their calling cards—that the gray caps were responsible. Because, after all, we had slaughtered so many of them and driven the rest underground. Surely this was their revenge?

I had only learned about the Silence the semester before; it was frightening how adults could keep the details of certain events from their children. It came as a revelation to me and my classmates, although it is hard to describe how deeply it affected us.

"It keeps coming back to the Silence," Duncan said. "My studies, Dad's studies. And Samuel Tonsure's journal."

Tonsure, Duncan had told me, was one of those who pursued the gray caps underground during the massacre that had preceded the founding of Ambergris. He had never returned to the surface, but his journal, a curious piece of work that purported to describe the gray caps' underground kingdoms, had been found some seventy-five years later, and subsequently pored over by historians for any information it might impart on the Silence or any other topic related to the gray caps. They were studying it still, Duncan included.

"You're not Dad, Duncan," I said. "You could study something else."

Even then, before he was employed by James Lacond, before he met Mary, I sensed the danger there for Duncan. Even then, I knew somehow that Duncan was in peril. {We're all in peril from something. I count myself lucky not to have succumbed to the usual perils, like addiction to mushrooms or alcohol.}

But Duncan just stared at me as if I were stupid and said, "There's nothing else to study, Janice. Nothing important."

I remember the inevitable progression of the images on his walls with the clarity of dream. However, beyond the few words reproduced above, our conversations have faded into the oblivion of memory.

❦

DUNCAN EMERGED FROM THOSE ROOMS with a degree and good prospects {an exaggeration; I perhaps had the prospect of a brief flash of fame, followed by an urgent need to make a living in a profession other than the one I had chosen as my passion}, but even then he was different from the other students. I watched his professors circle him at the various graduation parties. They treated him with a certain worried detachment, perhaps even fearfully, as if he had grown into something they could no longer easily define. As if they dared not develop any emotional attachment to this particular student. {Mom, who had continued to recede into her memories, did not come up for the ceremony—and we rarely went to see her, now that we were grown.}

Later, Duncan told me that he had never known solitude, never known loneliness, as he did in those few hours after graduation when he walked like a leper through gilded rooms tabled with appetizers and peppered with conversations meant for everyone but him. The tall towers of senior professors glided silent and watchful, the antithesis of Mary Sabon and her quivering, eager necklace of flesh. {Everyone feels isolated at those types of events, no matter how good the party, or how scintillating the conversation, because you're about to be expelled into the world, out from your own little piece of it.}

Yet out of his zeal, his loneliness, his passion that had literally crawled up the walls of his rooms, Duncan had already created something that might take the place of the silence or at least provide an answer to it. He had written a book entitled *On the Refraction of Light in a Prison.*

Despite countless exams, essays, and oral presentations, Duncan had found the time to write a groundbreaking tome that analyzed the mystical text *The Refraction of Light in a Prison* {written by the imprisoned Monks of Truff from their high tower in the Court of the Kalif}. It will not surprise anyone that this was one of the subjects our father had meant to tackle prior to his sudden death. {How could I not tackle it before going on? It was like completing my father's life in some small part. I remember looking at the finished book, with the inscription, "To my father, Jonathan Shriek," and thinking that I had resurrected him for a time, that he was alive again in my book. When I sent the book to our mother, she broke from her usual stoic silence to write me a long letter relating stories about Dad she had never felt comfortable telling me before.}

I had the privilege of reading the book {and helping to edit it, in your incendiary way} in manuscript form on one of my trips to Morrow. By then, my own education in Stockton and Ambergris had reached its somewhat disappointing end, and I was torn between pursuing a career in art or diving into art history. I had done much advanced research and encountered much in the way of genius, but I remember even then being astounded by the brilliant audacity of my brother's conclusions. At the same time, I was concerned that the book might be too good for its intended audience. Perhaps my brother was destined for obscurity. I admit to a sting of satisfaction in the thought, for nothing is more savage than sibling rivalry.

In any event, Duncan found a publisher in Morrow after only three months: Frankwrithe & Lewden, specialists in reference books, odd fictions, and histories. Frankwrithe & Lewden was an ancient publisher, rumored to have been established under the moniker "Writhelewd" during the last century of the Saphant Empire. Then, as the Empire collapsed into fragments not long after "Cinsorium" became "Ambergris," they transplanted their operations to Morrow, their name mangled and transformed during the long trek upriver in flat-bottomed boats. Who better to publish Duncan's esoteric work?

Frankwrithe & Lewden published fifteen thousand copies of *On the Refraction of Light in a Prison*. By barge, cart, and motored vehicle, the book infiltrated the southern half of the continent. Bookstores large and small stocked it. Traveling book dealers purchased copies for resale. Review copies were sent out with colorful advance blurbs from the dean of the Institute and the common man on the street {a badly-conceived F&L publicity stunt, soliciting random opinions from laypeople that resulted in blurbs like, " 'Not as good as a bottle of mead, but me and the missus quite enjoyed the bit about monk sex.' —John Tennant, plumber"}.

At first, nothing happened. A lull, a doldrums of no response, "as if," Duncan told me later, "I had never written a book, never spent four years on the subject. In fact, it felt as if I, personally, had never existed at all." Then, slowly, the book began to sell. It did not sell well, but it sold well enough: a steady drip from a faucet.

The critical response, although limited, did give Duncan hope, for it was, when and where it appeared, enthusiastic: "After an initial grounding in cold, hard fact, Shriek's volume lofts itself into that rarefied air of unique scholarly discourse that distinguishes a good book from a bad book" {Edgar Rybern, *Arts & History Review*}. Or, this delicious morsel: "I never knew monks had such a difficult life. The overall sentiment expressed by this astonishing book is that monks, whether imprisoned or not, lead lives of quiet contemplation broken by transcendental bursts of epiphany" {the aforementioned James Lacond, Truff love him, with a rare appearance in the respectable *Ambergris Today*}.

The steady drip became stronger as the coffers of the various public and private libraries in the South, synchronized to the opinions of men and women remote from them {who might well have been penning their reviews from a lunatic asylum or between assignations at a brothel}, released a trickle of coins to reward words like "rarefied air," "good," and "astonishing."

However, even the critics could not turn the trickle into a torrent. This task fell to the reigning head of the Truffidian religion, the Ambergris Antechamber himself, the truculent {and yet sublime} Henry Bonmot. How dear old Bonmot happened to peruse a copy of *On the Refraction of Light in a Prison* has never been determined to my satisfaction {but it makes me laugh to think of how he became introduced to us}. The rumor that Bonmot sought out blasphemous texts to create publicity for Truffidianism {because the rate of conversions had slowed} came from the schismatic Manziists, it was later proved. That Duncan *sent* Bonmot a copy to foment controversy demonstrates a lack of understanding about my brother's character so profound I prefer not to comment on it.

The one remaining theory appears the most probable: Frankwrithe & Lewden conspired to place a copy on the priest's nightstand, having first thoughtfully dog-eared those pages most likely to rescue him from his impending slumber. Ridiculous? Perhaps, but we must remember how sinister F&L has become in recent years. {Once upon a time, in a still-distant courtyard, I did ask Bonmot about it, but he couldn't recall the particulars.}

Regardless, Bonmot read Duncan's book—I imagine him sitting bolt upright in bed, ear hairs singed to a crisp by the words on the page—and immediately proclaimed it "to contain uncanny and certain blaspheme." He banned it in such vehement language that his superiors later censured him for it, in part because "there now exists no greater invective to be used against such literature or arts as may sore deserve it." {It was my good fortune that he turned to my explication of Chapter One of *The Refraction of Light in a Prison*, "The Mystical Passions," which in its protestations of purity manages to list every depraved sexual act concocted by human beings over the past five thousand years. It was my theory, and Dad's, that this was the monks' method of having it both ways. It didn't help that I included Dad's mischievous footnote about the curious similarity between the form of certain Truff rituals and the acts depicted in the chapter.}

Luckily for Duncan, the darling {and daring!} Antechamber's excellent imitation of a froth-mouthed dog during his proclamation so embarrassed the more practical administrative branch of the Truffidian Church—"them what pay the bills," as an artist friend of mine once put it—that they neglected to impose a sentence or a penalty. Neither did the Truffidian Church exhort its members to "stone, pummel, or otherwise physically assault" Duncan, as occurred some years later to our soon-to-be editor Sirin, who had decided to champion a book on the "cleansing merits of interreligious romantic love." {Sirin, alerted by a sympathetic typesetter, managed to change both the decree and the flyers created by it, causing the designated Truffidian Voice, the Antechamber standing by his side, to read a decree in front of the famous porcelain representation of the God Truff and all others in the Truffidian Cathedral that called for the Antechamber's stoning, pummeling, and much worse. I teased Bonmot about this event many times.}

The ban led to the predictable upswing in sales, lofting the book into the "rarefied air" that distinguishes an almost-bestseller from a mediocre seller. {F&L took advantage of the ban to an uncanny degree, I must say, but it is not true that they had ten thousand copies of a new edition printed two nights before the announcement with "Banned by the Antechamber!" blaring across the cover in seventy-two-point bold Nicean Monk Face.}

Suddenly, Duncan had something of a reputation. Newspapers and broadsheets, historians and philosophers, decried and debated, lauded and vilified both the book and Duncan—on unusually obscure elements of Duncan's argument {for example, whether or not the Water People of the Lower Moth Delta had ever been exposed to the teachings of Truff}. Meanwhile, the Court of the Kalif denied it still held the monks who had written the original *The Refraction of Light in a Prison* and declared the new book to consist of a vast, sprawling fiction built on the foundation of *another* vast, sprawling fiction. {The Kalif also revoked father's prize, an action I never forgave.}

But no matter what position a particular commentator took, it was always with the underlying assumption that *On the Refraction of Light in a Prison* contained ideas of substance and scholarship. Duncan was asked to contribute articles to several major and minor historical journals. Inasmuch as the fate of the monks had become a political issue, and thus one of interest to many people, he was invited to more parties peopled by the Important than he could have stomached on his most extroverted day . . . and yet did not reply to a single invitation.

What made him reluctant to savor his new-found notoriety? The fear of the consequences of the ban did not make him a recluse, nor did his innate distress in social situations. The true answer is hinted at in his journal, which I have beside me now for verification purposes. Scrawled in the margin of an entry from this era, we find the words "Is this how Dad felt?" Remembering the fate of our father, dead at the zenith of his happiness, Duncan truly believed he too would die if he partook of too much joy—if not by heart attack, then by some other means. {Your theory may be correct on a subconscious level, but on the conscious level, I was merely obsessed and somewhat paranoid. Obsessed with the possibilities of the next book. Paranoid about how people would continue to receive my studies. Worried about how I would do on my own, so to speak, without Dad's research notes to prop me up.}

Of course, I did not understand this until much later. At the time, I believed his shyness had led him to squander perhaps his only opportunity to take up a permanent place in the public imagination. On this, I turned out to be wrong. Debate raged on for a while regardless, perhaps fed by Duncan's very absence.

Then, to compound the communal mystification, Duncan disappeared from sight—much as he would several decades later in the week before Martin Lake's party. His rooms in Morrow {which the Institute had let me keep for a year following graduation} were untouched—not a sock taken, not a diagram removed from the walls. . . . Duncan simply wasn't there.

I walked around those rooms with the school's dean, and it struck me as I stared at the crowded walls that Duncan's physical presence or absence meant nothing. Everything that comprised his being had been tacked or glued or stabbed to those walls, an elaborate mosaic of obsession.

Clearly, the school understood this aspect of Duncan, for they made a museum out of the rooms, which then became the physical location for discussions of Duncan's work. Much later, the "museum" became a storehouse, crumbled over time into a boarded-up mess, and then a broken-down safety hazard; such is the staying power of fame. {I never expected it would last as long as it did, to be honest.}

As we walked together, the Dean made sympathetic sounds, expressed the hope that Duncan would "soon return to his home." But I knew better. Duncan had emerged from his cocoon. The wallpaper of plans, photographs, diagrams was just the husk of his leaving, the remains of his other self. Duncan had begun to metamorphose into something else entirely.

That is, assuming he was still alive—and without the evidence of a dead body, I preferred to believe he was. {I was. As you know. Such melodrama!}

❧❧

NOW I SHOULD START AGAIN. Now I should skip six months of worry. Now I should tell you how I came to see Duncan again. This is such a difficult Afterword to write. Sometimes I am at a loss as to what to put in and what to leave out. Sometimes I do not know what is appropriate for an Afterword, and what is not. Is this an Afterword or an afterwards? Should I massage the truth? Should I maintain an even tone? Should I divide it all into neat, easily digestible chapters? Should I lie? {Dad, in his notes on writing: "A historian is half confidence artist and half stolid purveyor of dates and dramatic re-creations."}

❧❧

DUNCAN REINTRODUCED HIMSELF TO ME six months later with a knock on my door late one night in the spring. The prudent Ambergrisian does not eagerly open doors at night.

I called out, "Who is it?" and received, in such a jubilant tone that I could not at first place the voice, the response, "Your brother, Duncan!" Shocked, relieved, perplexed, I opened the door to a pale, worn, yet strangely bulky brother wrapped in an old gray overcoat that he held closed with both hands. Comically enough, a sailor's hat covered his head. His face was flushed, his eyes too bright as he staggered past me, pieces of debris falling from him onto the floor of my living room.

I locked the door behind him and turned to greet him, but any words I might have spoken died in my throat. For he held his overcoat open like the wings of some great bird, and what I saw I could not at first believe. Just brightly colored vest and pants, I thought, but protruding, like barnacles on a ship's hull. How unlike my brother to wear anything that outlandish. I took a step closer. . . .

"That's right," Duncan said, "step closer and really *see*."

He tossed his hat onto a chair. He had shaved off his hair, and his scalp was stippled and layered in a hundred shades of blue, yellow, green, orange.

"Mushrooms. Hundreds of mushrooms. I had to wear the overcoat and hat or every casual tourist on Albumuth Boulevard would have stared at me." He looked down at his body. "Look how they glow. What a shame to be rid of them." He saw me staring unabashedly. "Stare all you like, Janice. I'm a dazzling butterfly, not a moth . . . well, for another hour or two." {A butterfly could not compare. I was magnificent. Every part of my body was *receiving*. I could "hear" things through my body, feel them, that no human short of Samuel Tonsure could understand.}

He did not lie. From the collar of his shirt to the tips of his shoes, Duncan was covered in mushrooms and other fungi, in such a riot and welter and rash of colors that I was speechless. I walked up to him to examine him more closely. His eyelashes and eyebrows were lightly dusted with purple spores. The fungi had needled his head, burrowed into the skin, forming whorls of brightness that hummed with fecundity. I took his right hand in mine, examined the palm, the fingers. The palms had a vaguely greenish hue to them. The half-moons of his fingernails had turned a luminous purple. His skin was rubbery, as if unreal. Looking up into his eyes, I saw that the spark there came from pale red ringing the pupil. Suddenly, I was afraid. {To be honest, to dull the pain a bit, I'd had a few drinks at a tavern before stumbling to your door. That might have contributed to the condition of my eyes.}

"Don't be," he said. "Don't be afraid," scaring me even more. "It's a function of diet. It's a function of disguise. I haven't changed. I'm still your brother. You are still my sister. All of this will wash away. It's just the layers added to me the past three months. I need help scraping them off."

I laughed. "You look like some kind of clown . . . some kind of mushroom clown."

He took off his overcoat, let it fall to the floor. "I agree—I look ridiculous."

"But where have you been? How did this happen?" I asked.

He put a finger to his lips. "I'll answer your questions if you'll help me get rid of this second skin. It itches. And it's dying."

❧

SO I HELPED HIM. IT was not as simple as having him step out of his clothes, because the mushrooms had eaten through his clothes and attached themselves to his poor pale skin. A madness of mushrooms, mottling his skin— no uniform shape or variety or size. Some pulsed a strobing pink-blue. Others radiated a dull, deep burgundy. A few hung from his waist like upside-down wineglasses, translucent and hollow, the space inside filled with clusters of tiny button-shaped green-gold nodules that disintegrated at the slightest touch. Textures from rough to smooth to rippled to grainy to slick. Smells—the smells all ran together into an earthy but not unpleasant tang, punctuated by a hint of mint. The mushrooms even made noises if you listened carefully enough—a soft *pough* as they released spores, an intermittent whine when left alone, a *pop* as they became ghosts through my rough relocations.

"Remember BDD when you three had to wash all that mud and filth off of me?" he asked, as we worked with scrubbing implements and towels in the bathroom.

"Of course I do," I said.

Before Dad Died, BDD, a grim little acronym meant to help us remember when we had been a happy family. If we had arguments or bouts of depression that threatened to get out of control, one of us would remind the others that we had all behaved differently before Dad died. We held BDD time in our heads as a sanctuary whenever our anger, our loss, became too great.

Once, Duncan, his usual mad, exploring, BDD self, had managed to get stuck in a sewer pipe under our block and we had had to pull him out after a frantic half hour searching for the source of his pathetic, echoing voice. Then Mom, Dad, and I spent another three hours forcing the black-gray sludge off of him, finally standing back to observe the miracle we had wrought: a perfectly white Duncan, "probably as clean as he's ever been," as Dad observed.

I wonder, Mary, if Duncan ever shared memories like this with you, while the lights flickered outside his apartment windows?

"Remember BDD. . . ."

Duncan's remark made me laugh, and the task at hand no longer seemed so strange. I was just helping clean up Duncan after another BDD exploration mishap, while Duncan looked on half in relief, half in dismay, as the badges of his newly gained experience fell away, revealed as transitory. {I was losing sensation with each new layer peeled off—reduced to relying on old senses. I knew it had to be done, but I felt as if I were going blind, becoming deaf, losing my sense of smell.}

Me, I felt as if I were destroying a vast city, a community of souls. On one level, I lived with the vague sense of guilt every Ambergrisian feels who can trace their family's history back to the founding of the city. Even for me, even come late to Ambergris, a mushroom signifies the genocide practiced by our forefathers against the gray caps, but also the Silence and our own corresponding loss. Can anyone not from Ambergris, not living here, understand the fear, loss, guilt, each of us feels when we eradicate mushrooms from the outside of our apartments, houses, public buildings? *The exact amount of each emotion in the pressure of my finger and thumb as I pulled them from their suction cup grip on Duncan's skin.*

It took five hours, until my fingertips were red and my back ached. Duncan looked not only exhausted but diminished by the ordeal. We had moved back into the living room, and there we sat, surrounded by the remains of a thousand mushrooms. It could have been a typical family scene—the aftermath of a haircut—except that Duncan had left behind something more profound than his hair. Already the red brightness had begun to fade from his eyes, his hands less rubbery, the half-moons of his fingernails light purple.

I had opened a window to get the smell of mushrooms out and now, by the wet, glistening outdoor lamps, I could see the beginning of a vast, almost invisible spore migration from the broken remains at our feet, from the burgundy bell-shaped fungi, from the inverted wineglasses, from the yellow-green nodules. Like ghosts, like spirits, a million tiny bodies in a thousand intricate shapes, like terrestrial jellyfish—oh what am I trying to say so badly except that they were gorgeous, as they fled out the window to be taken by the wind. In the faint light. Soundlessly. Like souls.

In that moment, almost in tears from the combination of beauty, exhaustion, and fear of the unknown, I think I caught a glimpse of what Duncan saw; of what had created the ecstasy I had seen in him when he had stumbled into my apartment five hours before. A hundred, a thousand years before. {I tried so hard to capture this for Mary, and yet I couldn't make her see it. Maybe *that* is where the failure occurred, and maybe it is *my* failure. Not all experiences are universal, even if you're in the same room when something miraculous occurs. I suppose it was too much to ask that she take it on faith?}

"Look," I said, pointing to the spores.

"I know," my brother said. "I know, Janice."

Such regret in that voice, mixed with a last, lingering joy.

"I'm less than I was, but I've captured it all here." He tapped his head, which still bore the scars of its invaders in the vague echo of color, in the scrubbed redness of it. "The spores are part of the record. They will float back to where I've been, navigating by wind and rain and by ways we cannot imagine, and they will report to the gray caps. Who I was. Where I was. What I did. It will make it all the more dangerous next time."

I sat upright in my chair. Next time? He stood there, across the room from me, dressed in the rags of his picked-apart clothes, surrounded by the wreckage of fungal life, and he might as well have been halfway across the city. I didn't understand him. I probably never would. {I didn't need you to understand what I myself saw but dimly. I wanted you to *see*—and you saw more than most, even then. Mary saw it all, by the end, and she stitched her eyes shut, stopped up her ears, taped her mouth.}

"Yes, well, Duncan, it's been a long night," I started to say, but then his eyes rolled up in their sockets and he fell to the soft floor, dead asleep. I had to drag him to the couch.

There he remained for two days. I took time off from my job at an art gallery to watch over him. I went out only for food and to buy him new clothes. He slept peacefully, except for five or six times when he slipped into a nightmare that made him twitch, convulse, cry out in a strange language that sounded like bird-song. I remember staring down at his pale face and thinking that he resembled in texture and in color nothing more or less than a mushroom.

❧❧

DUNCAN HAD NO BELIEVABLE EXPLANATION for his enfeebled state when he finally awoke on the third morning. As I fed him toast and marmalade at the kitchen table, I tried to get some sense of what he might have endured in the six months since I had last seen him. Although I had swept away the remains of the mushrooms, their presence haunted us.

Elusiveness, vagueness, as if a counterpoint to the terrible precision of his writing, had apparently become Duncan's watchwords. I had never known him to be talkative, but after that morning, his terseness began to take on the inventiveness of an art form. I had to pull information out of him. {I was trying to protect you. Clearly, you still don't believe that, but I will give you this: you're right that I should have found a way to tell you.}

"Where have you been?" I asked him.

He shrugged, pulled the blanket closer around him. "Here and there. Mostly *there*," and he giggled, only trailing off when he realized he had lapsed into hysteria.

"Was it because of the Truffidian ban?" I asked.

He shook his head. "No, no, no. That silliness?" He raised his head to stare at me. His gaze was dark and humorless. "No. Not because of the ban. They never published my picture in the newspapers and broadsheets. No Truffidian outside of Morrow knows what I look like. No, not the ban. I was doing research for my next few books." He rolled his eyes. "This will probably all go to waste."

"Did you only go out at night?" I asked. "You're as pale as I've ever seen you."

He would not meet my gaze. He wrenched himself out of the chair and walked to the window, hands in his pockets. "It was a *kind* of night," he said.

"Why can't you just tell me?"

He grinned. "If you must know, I've been with Red Martigan and Aquelus, Manzikert and Samuel Tonsure." A thin smile, staring out the window at some unnamable something.

A string of names almost as impenetrable as Sabon's necklace of human beads, but I did recognize the names Manzikert I and Tonsure. I knew Duncan had continued to study Tonsure's journal.

"I found," Duncan said in a monotone, as if in a trance, "something in Tonsure's journal that others did not, because they were not looking for it. . . ."

Here I mix my memories of the conversation with a transcript of the account found in my brother's journal, which I am lucky enough to have in a trunk by my side along with several other things of Duncan's. {It's something of a shock to find you rifling through my papers and notebooks. Usually, it takes a person years to develop the nerve to attempt outright theft. For a moment, I was upset, even outraged. But, really, Janice, I'd rather you quote me than paraphrase, since the meaning becomes distorted otherwise.}

I found something in Tonsure's journal that others did not, because they were not looking for it. Everyone else—historians, scholars, amateurs—read it as a historical account, as a primary source to a time long past, or as the journal of a man passing over into madness. They wanted insight into the life of Tonsure's captor, Manzikert I. They wanted insight into the underground land of the gray caps. But although the journal can provide that insight, it is also another thing entirely. I only noticed what was hidden because I had become so accustomed to staring for hours at the maps and diagrams on the walls of my rooms at the Institute. I fell asleep to their patterns. I dreamed about their patterns. I woke up to their patterns.

When I finally began to read Tonsure's journal, I was alive with patterns and destinations. As I read, I began to feel restless, irritable. I began to feel that the book contained another level, another purpose. Something that I could catch only flashes of from a copy of the journal, but which might be as clear as glass or a reflecting mirror in the original.

As I reached the end of the journal—the pages and pages of Truffidian religious ritual that seem intended to cover a rising despair at being trapped belowground—I became convinced that the journal formed a puzzle, written in a kind of code, the code weakened, diluted, only hinted at, by the uniform color of the ink in the copies, the dull sterility of set type.

The mystery ate at me, even as I worked on *On the Refraction of Light in a Prison,* especially because one of the footnotes added to *The Refraction of Light in a Prison* by the editor of my edition contains a sentence I long ago memorized: "Where the eastern approaches of the Kalif's empire fade into the mountains no man can conquer, the ruined fortress of Zamilon keeps watch over time and the stars. Within the fortress, humbled by the holes in its ancient walls, Truffidian monks guard the last true page of Tonsure's famous journal."

That the love of a woman might one day become as mysterious to Duncan as a ruined fortress, that he could one day find the flesh more inexplicable than stone, must have come as a shock.

After the discovery, my curiosity became unbearable. I could not fight against it. As soon as I graduated, I began to make plans to visit Zamilon. These plans, in hindsight, were pathetically incomplete and childish, but, worse, I didn't even follow the plans when I finally made the journey.

One night, as I stared at the maps on my walls, the pressure grew too great—I leapt out of bed, put on my clothes, took my advance money from Frankwrithe & Lewden from the dresser, peeled a map of the eastern edge of the Kalif's empire from the wall, and dashed out into the night.

Without a thought for my peace of mind, or our mother's. Typical. How many times should we have to forgive Duncan just because he was always the eccentric genius in the family? {Surely this doesn't reflect your feelings now, but only your emotions at the time? Not with everything you've seen since? I refuse to defend myself on this count, especially since we would have need to forgive you many times over in the years to come.}

The wanderings and mishaps of the next two months are too strangely humorous for me to bother relating, but suffice it to say that my map was faulty, my funds inadequate. I spent as many days earning money as traveling to my destination. I became acquainted with a dozen different forms of transportation, each with its own drawbacks: mule, mule-drawn cart, mule-powered rolling barge, leaky canoe, the rare smoke-spitting, back-farting motored vehicle, and my own two slogging feet. I starved. I almost died from lack of water. Once, when I had had the good fortune to earn some money as a scribe for an illiterate local judge, I was robbed within minutes of leaving the accursed town. I survived a mudslide and a hailstorm. My feet became thick, insensate slabs. My senses sharpened, until I could hear the stirrings of a fly on a branch a hundred feet away. In short, in every way I became more attuned to the details of my own survival.

Nor were the monks of Zamilon more understanding than the elements of nature or the vagaries of village dwellers. It took an entire week to convince the monks that the rag-clad, unshaven, stinking stranger before them was a serious scholar. I stood in front of Zamilon's hundred-foot gates, upon the huge path cut out of the side of the mountain, the massive stone sculptures from some forgotten demonology leering at me from either side, and listened while the monks dumped down upon me, like boiling oil, the most obscure religious questions ever shouted from atop a battlement.

However, eventually they relented—whether because of my seriousness or the seriousness of my stench, which was off-putting to other pilgrims, I do not know. But when I was finally allowed to examine the page from Tonsure's journal, all my suffering seemed distant and unimportant. It was as I had suspected: the original pages, the supposed idiosyncrasies found upon them, created a pattern intended as a map for anyone lucky enough to decipher it. I only had access to one page—and would never see the rest, imprisoned as it was by the Kalif along with the authors of *The Refraction of Light in a Prison*—but that was enough to parse a fragmented meaning of the whole.

I wrote down my findings—and, indeed, a first account of my journey—on a dozen sheets of paper, forced myself to memorize the evidence before I left Zamilon, and then burned my original scribblings. The knowledge seemed too precious and too personal to commit permanently to paper. It frightened me. With what I had learned, I could now, if I dared, if I desired, access the gray caps' underground kingdom . . . and survive.

I thought about at least two things on my long journey to Ambergris from Zamilon. {I had no intention of returning to Morrow.} First, to what extent had Tonsure corrupted his own journal in order to transmit this secret code— or had he corrupted it at all? In other words, did the coherent elements of the journal accurately reflect events and Tonsure's opinions of those events, or had he, to create a book that was also a map, sacrificed reality on the altar of symbolism?

Further, I was now convinced that Tonsure had written the entire journal *after* he followed Manzikert I belowground. He had encrypted it in the hope that even if he never made it back to the surface, the gray caps might preserve the journal, not realizing it posed a threat to their secrets. This revelation, if supportable, would change the entire nature of discourse surrounding the journal, render obsolete a hundred scholarly essays, and not a few whole books besides. The battered journal returned to the surface by the gray caps had not been the half-coherent ramblings of a mind slowly going insane, but a calculated risk taken by a man all too aware of his predicament.

What followed from this conclusion is simply this: Another, earlier version of the journal must have, at one point, existed, whether a polished product or a loose collection of notes. And from this earlier version, Tonsure had created a facsimile that contained the map, the schematic, for navigation of the gray caps' underground strongholds. Something even the gray caps had not been able to decipher. Something that would be Tonsure's secret and his alone.

Second, and most important, my head was filled with the grandeur of Tonsure's design, the genius of it, which I had seen but a fragment of and which our father had glimpsed only in the potential for research revealed by the letter that had killed him.

When I finally made my way back to Ambergris and strode down Albumuth Boulevard, I had only one thought. It ran through my mind over and over, like a challenge, like a curse: Did I have the courage to act on what Tonsure had given me? Could I live with *not* acting on that knowledge?

I found out that my courage outweighed my fear. Perhaps because I could not let Tonsure's supreme act of communication go to waste. The thought of him reaching out from beyond his own death only to be thwarted by my cowardice . . . it was too much to bear. More's the pity.

So I found my way down among them and back again without being disfigured or murdered. It was easy in a way. With Tonsure as my guide, I could not miss this sign here, that symbol there, until even the vaguest scratch in muddied rock, the slightest change in temperature or fruiting bodies alerted me to the next section of the path. It was a strange, dark place, and I was afraid, but I was not alone. I had Tonsure with me.

Do I understand most of what I saw down there? No. Does the memory of seeing things I do not understand help me, do me any good at all? No. For one thing, who would believe me? They would say I am having visions. I'm not sure I believe it all myself. Thus, I have become no better off than Samuel Tonsure, except that I may move above- and belowground at will.

When Duncan related portions of this to me in person, he ended with the lines, "And now you will have to believe me when I say that I cannot tell you anything else, and that it will do no good to press me for information or ask more questions. This is for your own protection as much as anything else. Please trust me on this, Janice."

Such a sense of finality informed his words that it never occurred to me to probe further. I just nodded, thinking about the mushroom spores floating out the window three nights before, from a room that now seemed so gray and empty. I was still trying to absorb that image. Unhappily, Duncan's journal entries are no more revealing than our conversations {You didn't think I'd leave *both* of my journals aboveground, did you?}, but at the time, I was secretly glad he didn't tell me more—his experience was so remote from mine that the simplest word sounded as if spoken in another language.

"I'm just glad you're safe again, and home," I said.

"Safe?" he said with a bitter little laugh. "Safe? Look at my hands." He held them out for my inspection. The half-moons of his fingernails shone a faint green. Along the outer edge of both hands a trail of thin, fern-like fungi followed a rough line down to the wrists. Perhaps, in certain types of light, it might be mistaken for hair.

"That will go away in time," I told him.

"No," he said. "I don't think so. I think I've been branded. I think I will always have these marks, no matter how they manifest themselves."

Duncan was right, although the manifestations would not always be fungal: for decades, he would carry everywhere a reproduction of Tonsure's journal, the pages more worn with each passing year, until finally I began to feel that the diary of the madman had become Duncan's own. And he would add more marks to the book, nearly silent scars that would leave their own strange language on his skin. Unspoken. Unwritten. But there.

Until only in the dim green light of the Spore would he feel truly comfortable aboveground.

❧ 2 ❧

CAN I START AGAIN? WILL you let me start again? Do you trust me to? Perhaps not. Perhaps all I can do is *soar* over. Perhaps we'll fly as the crow flies—on night wings, wind rattling the delicate bones of the rib cage, cold singeing feathers, gaze scouring the ground below us. The landscape will seem clear but distant, remote yet comprehensible. We will fly for ten years straight, through cold and rain and the occasional indignant sparrow certain we've come to raid the nest. Ten years shall we fly across before we begin our slow, circling descent to the cause of Duncan's calamity. Those ten years brought five black books flapping their pages. Five reluctant tombstones. Five millstones round my brother's neck. Five brilliant bursts of quicksilver communication. Five leather-clad companions for Duncan that no one can ever take away. {Five progressively grandiose statements that stick in my craw.}

We fly this way because we must fly this way. I did not see much of Duncan during those ten years. The morning after my conversation with him, he borrowed money from me against expected book royalties and left my apartment. He rented a small one-bedroom at the east end of Albumuth Boulevard in one of the several buildings owned by the legendary Dame Truff. Did he delight in living so close to the Religious Quarter, to know that he, the blasphemer, slept within a few blocks of the Antechamber's quarters in the Truffidian Cathedral? I don't know. I never asked him. {I delighted in the dual sensations of normalcy and danger, something you, Janice, always craved, but was new for me. To wake up every morning and make eggs and bacon with the full knowledge that my dull routine might be swiftly shattered by the appearance of the Antechamber's goons.}

While Duncan published, I perished half a dozen times. I shed careers like snakeskins, molting toward a future I always insisted was the goal, not merely an inevitable destination. Painter, sculptor, teacher, gallery assistant, gallery owner, journalist, tour guide, always seeking a necklace quite as bright, quite as fake, as Mary Sabon's. I never finished anything, from the great sprawling canvases I filled with images of a city I didn't understand, to filling the great sprawling spaces in my gallery. I've never lacked energy or drive, only that fundamental secret all good art has and all bad art lacks: a healthy imagination. Which, as I look back, is intensely ironic, considering how much imagination it took to get to this moment with my sanity intact, typing up an afterword that, no matter how sincere, will no doubt be as prone to accusations of pretense and bombast as any of my prior works.

✖

I DID MY BEST TO keep in contact with Duncan, although without much enthusiasm or vigor. The long trek to his loft apartment from mine often ended in disappointment; he was rarely home. Sometimes, curious, I would sneak up to the door and listen carefully before knocking; I would look through the keyhole, but it revealed only darkness.

My reward for spying usually took the form of a rather echoing silence. But more than once I imagined I heard someone or something scuttling across the floor, accompanied by a dull hiss and moan that made me stand up abruptly, the hairs rising on my arms. My tremulous knock upon the door in such circumstances—whether Duncan Transformed or Duncan with Familiars, I wanted no part of that sound—was usually enough to reestablish silence on the other side. And if it wasn't, my retreat back into the street usually changed from walk to run. {I heard you sometimes, although I was usually engrossed in my work and thought it best that you not enter. Ironically enough, a couple of times, I thought you were *them*, graycapped sister.}

I imagine I looked rather pathetic in front of his apartment—this thin, small woman crouched against a splintery door, eagerly straining for any aural news of the interior. I remember the accursed doorknob well—I hit my head on it at least a dozen times.

Thwarted, I gained any news of Duncan from rare interviews in the newspapers, which usually focused on writing technique or opinions on current events. For some reason, people are under the deluded impression that a historian—blessed with hindsight—can somehow illuminate the present and the future. Duncan knew nothing about the present and the future. {I knew nothing about the present and the immediate past. I would argue, however, that I began to glean an inkling of the future.}

The biographical notes on the dust jackets of his books were no help—they crackled with a terseness akin to fear: "Duncan Shriek lives in Ambergris. He is working on another book." Even by investigating the spaces between the words, those areas where silence might reveal a clue, could anyone ever "get to know" the author from such a truncated paragraph? More importantly, no one would ever *want* to know the author from such a paragraph.

Only in the fifth book did more information leak through, almost by accident, like a water stain on a ceiling: "Shriek intends to write a sequel to his best-selling tome, *Cinsorium*."

By then, Duncan's luck had run out, and all because of a single book we must circle back to, a delighted Sabon as raptor swooping down to observe over our feathered shoulder—Mary's presence doubling, trebling, the scope of the disaster, because it was she who turned Duncan into fodder for her own . . . what shall we call it? Words fail/cannot express/are not nearly enough. {Triumph. Unqualified. You must give her that. Bewitching eyes and the pen of a poet.}

Gliding, wheeling, we circle back through the windstream and let the titles fall in reverse order so that we might approach the source by a series of echoes or ripples: *Vagaries of Circumstance and Fate Amongst the Clans of the Aan; Mapping the Beast: Interrogatories Between the Moth and Those Who Travel Its Waters; Stretcher Jones: Last Hope of the West; Language Barriers Between the Aan and the Saphant Empire.* And the first book, sprawling out below us in all of its baroque immensity: *Cinsorium: Dispelling the Myth of the Gray Caps.* This maddening book, composed of lies and half-truths, glitters beneath us in all of its slivers and broken pieces, baubles fit for our true crow-self.

What is it about even half of the truth that can tear at the fabric of the world? Was it fear? Guilt? The same combination of emotions that flickered through my thoughts as I extinguished the welter of mushrooms from Duncan's poor pale body?

I don't mean to speak in riddles. I don't mean to fly too high above the subject, but sometimes you have no choice. Still, let me land our weary crow and just tell the story. . . .

PERHAPS DUNCAN SHOULD HAVE REALIZED what he had done after Frankwrithe & Lewden's reaction to the manuscript. {I realized it when I read over the first draft and saw the thousand red wounds of revision marks left by my second editor—lacerations explaining in their cruel tongue that this book would either behave itself or not be a book at all.}

A month after submission of the book, Duncan's editor, John Lewden, summoned Duncan to F&L's offices in downtown Morrow. The journey from Ambergris took Duncan two grueling days upriver by barge, into the heart of what proved to be a glacial Morrow winter. Once there, Duncan found that his editor was "on vacation" and that F&L's president, Mr. L. Gaudy, would talk to him instead.

A secretary quickly escorted Duncan into Gaudy's office, and left immediately. {I remember the office quite well. It was "resplendent," with a rosewood desk, a dozen portraits of famous F&L authors, and an angry, spitting fireplace in the corner opposite the desk.}

Gaudy, according to Duncan's journal, was "a bearded man of indeterminate age, his gaunt flesh wrapped across sharp cheekbones." He sat behind his desk, staring at the room's fireplace. {His eyes were like blue ice, and in his presence I smelled a certain cloying mustiness, as if he spent most of his time underground, or surrounded by hundred-year-old books.}

Duncan moved to sit, but Gaudy raised one hand, palm out, in abeyance. The calm behind the gesture, almost trancelike, made Duncan reluctant to disobey the man, but "also irritated me intensely; I had the feeling he knew something I did not, something I wanted to know."

They remained in those positions, respectively sitting and standing, for over five minutes. Duncan somehow sensed that just as he should not sit down, he also should not speak. "I began to think this man held some power over me, and it was only later that I realized something in his eyes reminded me of Dad."

When Gaudy finally lifted his bespectacled face to stare at Duncan, the flames reflected in the glass, Duncan saw an expression of absolute peace on the man's face. Relieved, he again moved to sit down, only to again be told, through a gesture, to remain standing.

Duncan began to wonder if his publisher had gone insane. "At the very least, I wondered if he had mistaken me for someone else."

As the fire behind them began to die, Gaudy smiled and broke the silence. He spoke in a "perfectly calm voice, level and smooth. He stared at the fireplace as he spoke, and steepled his fingers, elbows on the desk. He appeared not to draw a single extra breath."

He said:

"You need not sit and thus defile my perfectly good chair because it will take no time at all to say what needs to be said to you. Once I have said what I am going to say to you, I would like you to leave immediately and never return. You are no longer welcome here and never will be welcome again. Your manuscript has performed the useful function of warming us, a function a thousand times more beneficial than anything it might have hoped to accomplish as a series of letters strung together into words, phrases, sentences, paragraphs, and chapters. The fire has purified it, in much the same manner as I would like at this moment—and will desire at all moments in the future—to purify *you*, were it not outside of the legal, if not moral, boundaries placed upon us by the law and society in general. By this time it ought to be clear to you, Mr. Shriek, that we do not intend to buy the rights to your 'book'—and I use the word 'book' in its loosest possible sense—nor to its ashes, although I would sooner buy the rights to its ashes than to its unblemished pages. However, on the off chance that you still do not comprehend what I am saying to you, and allowing for the possibility that you may have entered a state of shock, I shall continue to talk until you leave this room, which happy event I hope will take place before very much longer, as the sight of you makes me ill. Mr. Shriek, as you must be aware, Frankwrithe & Lewden has a history that goes back more than five hundred years, and in that time we have published our share of controversial books. Your first book—which, by the way, you may be fascinated to know is as of this moment out of print—was the forty-first book to be banned by the various Antechambers of Ambergris over the years. We certainly have no qualms in that regard. Nor have we neglected to publish books on the most arcane and obscure topics dreamt of by the human brain. As you are no doubt aware, despite the fact that many titles no longer have even a nostalgic relevance, we keep our entire, and considerable, backlist in print—*Pelagic Snail Rituals of the Lower Archipelago* comes to mind, there being no such snail still extant, nor such an archipelago; still, we keep it in print—but we will make an exception for your first book, which shall be banished from all of our catalogues as well. As I would have hoped you had guessed by now, although you have not yet left this office never to return, we do not like your new book very much. In fact, to say I do not like your book would be like calling a mighty tree a seedling. I loathe your book, Mr. Shriek, and yet the word 'loathe' cannot convey in even a thousandth part the full depths of my hatred for this book, and by extension, you. But perhaps I should be more specific. Maybe specifics will allow you to overcome this current, potentially fatal, inertia—tied no doubt to the aforementioned shock—that stops you from leaving this office. Look—the last scrap of your manuscript has become a flake of ash floating above the fireplace. What a shame. Perhaps you would like an urn to collect the ashes of your dead newborn? Well, you can't have one, because not only do we not have an urn, but even if we did, we would not allow you to use it for the transport of the ashes, if only from the fear that you might find some way to reconstruct the book from them—and yes, we do know it is likely you have a copy of the manuscript, but we will feel a certain warmth in our hearts if by burning this copy we can at least slow down your reckless and obstinate attempt to publish this cretinous piece of excrement. Returning to the specifics of our argument against this document: your insipid stupidity is evident from the first word of the first sentence of the first paragraph of your acknowledgments page, 'The,' and from there the sense of simple-minded, pitiable absence of thought pervades all of the first paragraph until, by the roaring crescendo of imbecility leading up to the last word of the first paragraph, 'again,' any possible authority the reader might have granted the author has been completely undermined by your inability to in any way convey even an unoriginal thought. And yet in comparison to the dull-witted pedantry of the second paragraph, the first paragraph positively shines with genius and degenerate brilliance. Perhaps at this point in our little chat, I should repeat that I don't very much like this book."

Gaudy then rose and shouted, "YOU HAVE BEEN MEDDLING IN THINGS YOU KNOW NOTHING ABOUT! DO YOU THINK YOU CAN POKE AROUND *DOWN THERE* TO YOUR HEART'S CONTENT AND NOT SUFFER THE CONSEQUENCES?! YOU ARE A COMPLETE AND UTTER MORON! IF YOU EVER COME BACK TO MORROW, I'LL HAVE YOU GUTTED AND YOUR ORGANS THROWN TO THE DOGS! DO. YOU. UNDERSTAND. ME??!"

What other rhetorical gems might have escaped Gaudy's lips, we will never know, for Duncan chose that moment to overcome his inertia and leave Frankwrithe & Lewden's offices—forever.

"It's not so much that he frightened me," Duncan told me later. "Because after going belowground, really, what could scare me? It was the monotone of his delivery until that last spit-tinged frothing." {I was terrified, Janice. This man was the head of an institution that had been extant more than five hundred years ago. And he was telling me my work was worthless! It took a month before I even had the nerve to leave my apartment in Ambergris. I rarely visited Morrow again, and kept a low profile whenever I did.}

Later, during the War of the Houses {as it came to be called}, we realized that Gaudy, for political reasons, could hardly have reacted any other way to Duncan's manuscript. But how could Duncan know that at the time? He must have been shaken, at least a little bit. {Yes. A bit.}

Undaunted, Duncan found a new publisher within six months of Gaudy's strange rejection. Hoegbotton Publishing, a newly created and over-eager division of the Hoegbotton & Sons trading empire, gave Duncan a contract. In every way, the book struck Duncan's new editor, Samuel Hoegbotton—an overbearing and inconsequential young man with hulking shoulders, a voice like a cacophony of monkeys, and severe bad breath {who would never find favor in the eyes of his tyrannical father, Henry Hoegbotton}—as "A WORK OF GENIUS!" Duncan was happy to agree, bewildered as he might have been, unaware at the time that Samuel had transferred from the Hoegbotton Marketing Division. Samuel had not set foot in a bookstore since his twelfth birthday, when his mother had presented him with a gift certificate to the Borges Bookstore. {"Promptly traded in for its monetary value," Sirin, our subsequent editor, mused disbelievingly some years later.} That Samuel died of a heart attack soon after publishing Duncan's fifth book surprised no one. {Except me!}

The book, published with the full {perhaps crushing} weight of the Hoegbotton empire behind it, was called *Cinsorium: Dispelling the Myth of the Gray Caps.* It became an instant bestseller.

Despite this success, *Cinsorium* signaled the beginning of Duncan's slide into the obscurity I had previously wished upon him. If he had dreamt of a career as a serious historian—the sort of career our father would have died for—he should have suppressed the book and moved on to a new project. Samuel Hoegbotton, contributing to the disaster, ordered the printing of a banner across the top of the book {almost, but not quite, obscuring my name} that proclaimed: "At Last! The Truth! About the Gray Caps! All Secrets! Revealed!"

I bought the book as soon as it came out, not trusting Duncan to send me a copy. {I would have, if you'd asked.} It disappointed me for contradictory reasons: because it showed little of the scholarly care displayed by *On the Refraction of Light in a Prison,* and because it never mentioned, even once, Duncan's underground journey. I had already accepted the irritation of waiting to read about the trip along with everyone else. This I could have tolerated, even though it indicated a lack of trust. But not to mention it at all? It was too much. {I did mention Zamilon, though. Wasn't that enough? To start with?}

The book did not "reveal" all secrets. It obscured them. Duncan tantalized readers with incredible images he claimed had come from ancient books, the existence of which most scholars discounted. Mile-high caverns. Draperies of fungi that "undulated in time to a music conveyed at too high a pitch for the human ear." Mushrooms that bleated and whined and "talked after a fashion, in the language of spores." {Yes, perhaps I obscured some deeper truths, but nothing was made up.}

In typical Duncanesque prose, it tried with almost superhuman effort to hide the paucity of its insight:

> Although the inquisitive reader may wish for further extrapolation regarding this aspect of Tonsure's journal, such extrapolation would be so speculative as to provide a poor gruel of a meal indeed, even for the layperson. Some mysteries are unsolvable.
>
> {One part fear, I suppose. One part truth. Some mysteries *are* unsolvable. Just when you unearth the answer, you discover another question.}

A beautiful sword, but blunt, the book relied on quotations from "unnamed sources" for the bulk of its more exotic findings. Although claiming to know the truth about the gray caps, Duncan instead spent most of the book combining a history of fungi with historical suppositions that made me laugh:

> Could it be that the rash of suicides and murders in the Kalif's Court fifty years before the Silence were the result of emanations from a huge fungus that lay under the earth in those parts? Might much of the supposed "courtly intrigues" of the period actually have more to do with fruiting bodies? Might this also reveal the source of the aggression behind so-called "bad Festivals" in Ambergris?

The book, in short, violated most rules of historical accuracy and objective evidence. Duncan mentioned that he had journeyed to examine the page of Tonsure's journal, but he gave no specifics of location or content. Certainly nothing like the detail and "local color" provided by his own journal. {I admit *Cinsorium* was hardly my finest hour, although I had my reasons for writing it at the time. My thoughts turned to Tonsure and his encryptions. My need for encryption was not as urgent as his, or as profoundly solitary, but I still felt a certain danger. Not just from the gray caps, but from those who might read the unexpurgated truth and . . . reject it. And reject it violently. Couldn't I, I reasoned—falsely—allude to and suggest that truth so that, perhaps, even if in just a thousand minds, my suspicions might harden into certainty? It is a question I wrestled with even later, working with James Lacond, although by then I had come to realize that the best I could hope for was a hardening certainty in a mere handful of souls.}

The most daring idea in *Cinsorium* was the theory that Tonsure had rewritten the journal after completing it, which alienated dozens of influential scholars {and their followers, don't forget} who had based hundreds of books and papers on the conventionally accepted chronology. {I don't think it alienated them—most of them lacked the resources or the knowledge to verify or deny the discovery. I didn't feel like an outcast, at first. Besides, is it fair to chastise me for both poor scholarship and unique ideas?}

As I read, I became struck by the way that half-truths wounded Duncan's cause more seriously than outright lies. He stumbled, he faltered throughout the book, but continued on anyway—persevering past the point where any reasonable person might have given up on such a hopeless trek.

Oddly, it made me love him for being brave, and it almost made me cry as well. I knew that he held our father in his head as he wrote, running toward him across the summer grass. That, I could respect. But by not revealing all, he became lost in the *land between,* where lies always sound like lies, and so does the truth. He could not protect the gray caps *and* satisfy serious readers without betraying both groups. {The gray caps needed no protection, only the readers. Janice, you may now be beyond protection, but there are still things that can be done for those aboveground.}

In part due to these defects, *Cinsorium* had a peculiar publication history. It became an instant bestseller when the Kalif's Minister of Literature, rather than ban the book, had his operatives buy all available copies and ship them off to the Court. Readers in the South bought most of the second printings, the Kalif distracted by warfare with the Skamoo on his northern border. However, despite the sale of more than fifty thousand copies, Hoegbotton refused to go to a third printing.

Certainly the strange and curious silence created by the book must be seen as a reason for Hoegbotton's reluctance to reprint *Cinsorium.* This silence occurred among those most raucous of vultures, critics. In the superheated atmosphere that is the Southern book culture, such omissions rarely occur. Even the most modest self-published pulp writer can find space in local book review columns. {Fear. It was fear.} This lack of attention proved fatal, for although many journals noted the book's publication in passing, only two actual reviews ever appeared, both in a fringe publication edited by James Lacond. Lacond, a passing acquaintance of Duncan's even in those days before the war, wrote that, "Subtle subjects require subtle treatments. For every two steps back, Shriek takes three steps forward, so that in the circular but progressive nature of his arguments one begins to see this pattern, but also a certain truth emerging." Perhaps. Perhaps not. {At least someone was prepared to accept it!}

But none of these events concerned me, not in light of what I thought the book told me about Duncan. The book, I felt, was an argument between Duncan and Duncan, and not about any of the surface topics in the book. Duncan did not know what, exactly, he had seen while underground. He had only a rudimentary understanding of the gray caps. {This is true—I didn't know what I'd seen. But I couldn't keep what I didn't know to myself. How could I? I saw too many things that might shake someone's worldview.} This kept alive Duncan's compulsion to do what I most feared: return to the underground until he felt he understood . . . everything.

❧❦

PERHAPS IT SHOULD NOT HAVE surprised me that Duncan's next four books settled back into the realm of acceptable accomplishment. Duncan reverted to the scholarship that had been his trademark. It was too late, of course. It didn't, and couldn't, matter, because the cowardly critics who had refused to review *Cinsorium had* read it. And so Duncan's scholarly style steadily lost readers seeking further crass sensationalism, while critics savaged later books, most of them omitting any reference to *Cinsorium*. It hung over Duncan's work like a ghost, an echo. The reviews that did appear dismissed Duncan's work in ways that made him appear a crank, a misfit, even a heretic. {I've always blamed Gaudy for this, although for a long time I had no proof, or even a coherent theory. But I now believe Gaudy used his connections to blacklist me in typical F&L fashion—with the underhanded compliment, the innuendo, the insinuation. Did Gaudy do more than meet with a few influential journal editors? Perhaps not, but that might have been enough.} They appended the story of his banning by Bonmot in harmful ways: "This, the latest offering from the author who blasphemed against the Truffidian Church, concerns . . ." It did not matter what it concerned.

Shortly after the publication of *Vagaries of Circumstance and Fate Amongst the Clans of the Aan,* Hoegbotton announced that Duncan had been dropped from their stable of writers. Gaudy must have been laughing from behind his rosewood desk in Morrow. No other publisher of note would prove interested in Duncan's sixth book. None of his books would long remain in print. For all practical purposes, Duncan's career as a writer of historical books had come to an end, along with any hopes of serious consideration as a historian. At the age of thirty-three.

It would only get worse after he met Sabon, who would spend much of her time chipping away at Duncan's respectability, so that his books no longer contained anything but metaphorically shredded pages.

❧

ODD. IT STRIKES ME FOR the first time that Duncan has been preparing me for this moment all of my life. There's a green light shining upon the typewriter keys, and maybe it's the light that allows me to see so clearly. Must we always be blind to those we are close to? Must we always fumble for understanding? Duncan never mistrusted me. He just didn't want me to implode from the information he had—he wanted to dole it out in pieces, so that it would not be such a shock to my system. And yet it would have been a shock, no matter how gradual. I don't see how it could be otherwise.

If Duncan feared losing me, he must have also feared losing his audience.

Which reminds me. I should ask: Am I losing you? Have I lost you already? I hope not. There's still a war to come, for Truff 's sake.

Maybe the only solution is to start over.

Should I? Perhaps I should.

$\twoheadrightarrow$ 3 $\twoheadleftarrow$

WE DON'T SEE MANY THINGS ahead of time. We usually only avoid disaster at the last second, pull back from the abyss by luck or fate or blind stupid chance. Exactly nine years before Mary Sabon began to destroy my brother like an old house torn down brick by brick, Duncan sought me out at my new Gallery of Hidden Fascinations. How he found me there, I still don't know {a mundane story, involving broadsheet adverts and luck}. I had just bought the gallery—a narrow place off of Albumuth Boulevard {I remember when it was a sweets shop that also sold mood-altering mushrooms—a much more honest trade}—with the help of a merchant loan against our mother's property along the River Moth. {*That* took some persuading!}

Outside, the sky was a blue streaked with gold, the trees once again threatening to release their leaves, turning yellower and yellowest. The smell of burning leaves singed nostrils, but the relief of slightly lower temperatures added a certain spring to the steps of passersby.

Half the proposed gallery lay in boxes around my feet. Paintings were stacked in corners, splashes of color wincing out from the edges of frames. Piles and piles of papers had swallowed my desk.

I was happy. After years of unhappiness. {It's easy to think you'd been unhappy for years, but I remember many times you were invigorated, excited, by your art, by your studies. The past isn't a slab of stone; it's fragmented and porous.} By now I had given up my dream of a career as a painter. Rejection, rejection, rejection. It had made the part of me that wanted to paint wither away, leaving a more streamlined Janice, a smoother Janice, a less creative Janice. I had decided I would do better as a gallery owner, had not yet realized I was still traveling toward remote regions marked on maps only by terms such as "Art Critic" and "Historian." {You were traveling toward me, Janice. That's not such a bad thing.} Only later did I come to see my initial investment in the gallery as a form of self-torture: by promoting the works of others I could denigrate my own efforts.

❦

THIS TIME, DUNCAN HAD A haunted look about him, the joy of his previous underground adventures stripped away, leaving behind only a gauntness akin to death. The paleness that had taken over his features had blanched away any expression, any life, in his limbs, in his movements. He:

Beard like the tendrils of finely threaded spores.

Swayed in the doorway like a tall, ensanguinated ghost, holding the door open with one shaking, febrile arm.

Shoes tattered and torn, as if savaged by a dog.

Muttered my name as if in the middle of a dream.

Clothes stained everywhere with spores, reduced to a fine, metallic dust that glittered blackly all around him.

Trailed tiny obsidian mushrooms, trembling off of him at every turn.

Eyes embedded with black flecks, staring at some nameless vision just beyond me.

Clutched something tightly in his left hand, knuckles pale against the dark coating of spore dust.

❦

HE STAGGERED INSIDE, FELL TO the floor amid the paintings, the curled canvases, the naked frames vainglorious with the vision of the wall behind them. The gallery smelled of turpentine, of freshly cut wood, of drying paint. But as Duncan met the floor, or the floor met Duncan, the smells became one smell: the smell of Duncan. A dark green smell brought from deep underground. A subtle interweaving of minerals and flesh and fungus. The smell of old water trickling through stones and earth. The smell of lichen and moss. {Flesh penetrated by fungus, you mean—every pore cross-pollinated, supersaturated. Nothing very subtle about it. The flesh alive and prickly.} The smell, now, of my brother.

I locked the door behind him. I slapped his face until his gaze cleared, and he saw me. With my help, he got to his feet and I took him into the back room. He was so light. He might as well have been a skeleton draped with canvas. I began to cry. His ribs bent against my encircling arm as I gently laid him down against a wall. His clothes were so filthy that I made him take them off and put on a painter's smock.

I forced bread and cheese on him. He didn't want it at first. I had to tear the bread into small pieces and hold his mouth open. I had to make him close his mouth. "Swallow." He had no choice. He couldn't fight me—he was too weak. Or I was, for once, too strong.

Eventually, he took the bread from my hands, began to eat on his own. Still he said nothing, staring at me with eyes white against the dust-stippled darkness of his forehead and jutting cheekbones.

"When you are ready, speak," I said. "You are not leaving here until you tell me exactly what happened. You are not leaving here until I know why. Why, Duncan? What happened to you?" I couldn't keep the anguish from my voice.

Duncan smiled up at me. A drunkard's smile. A skeleton's smile. My brother's smile, as laconic as ever.

"Same old sister," he said. "I knew I could count on you. To half kill me trying to feed me." {To help me. Who else would help me back then?}

"I mean it. I won't let you leave without telling me what happened."

He smiled again, but he wouldn't look at me. For a long time, he said nothing as I watched him.

Then the flood. He spoke and spoke and spoke—rambling, coherent, fragmented, clever. I began to grow afraid for him. All these words. There was already less than nothing inside of him. I could see that. When the last words had left his mouth, would even the canvas of his skin flap away free, the filigree of his bones disintegrate into dust? Slowly, I managed to hear the words and forget the condition of the one who spoke them. Forget that he was my brother.

He had gone deeper into the underground this time, but the research had gone badly. He kept interspersing his account with mutterings that he would "never do it again." And, "If I stay on the surface, I'm safe. I should be safe." At the time, I thought he meant staying physically aboveground, but now I'm not so sure. {Be sure.} I wonder if he also meant the surface of his mind. That if he could simply restrain himself from the divergent thinking, the untoward analysis, that had marked some of his previous books, he might once again be a published writer. {Who knows? I might have given up on myself if forced to listen to my own ravings. I might have even become a respectable citizen.}

As he spoke, I realized I wasn't ready for his revelations. I had made a mistake—I didn't want to hear what he had to say. I needed distance from this shivering, shuddering wreck of a man. He clung to the edges of the smock I had given him like a corpse curling fingers around a coffin's lining. The look on his face made me think of our father dying in the summer grass. It frightened me. I tried to put boundaries on the conversation.

"What happened to the book you were working on?" I asked him.

He grimaced, but the expression made him look more human, and his gaze turned inward, the horrors reflected there no longer trying to get out.

"Stillborn," he gasped, as if breaking to the surface after being held down in black water. He lurched to his feet, fell back down again. Every surface he touched became covered in fine black powder. "Stillborn," he repeated. "Or I killed it. I don't know which. Maybe I'm a murderer. I was . . . I was halfway through. On fire with ancient texts. Bloated with the knowledge in them. Didn't think I needed firsthand experience to write the book. Such a web of words, Janice. I have never used so many words. I used so many there weren't any left to write with. And yet, I still had this fear deep in my skull. I couldn't get it out." {I still can't get it out of my head, sometimes. Writing a book and going underground are so similar. That fear of the unknown never really goes away. But, after a while, it becomes a perverse comfort.}

He relinquished his grasp on the object in his hand, which I had almost forgotten.

It rolled across the floor. We both stared at it, he as astonished as I. A honey-and-parchment-colored ball. Of flesh? Of tissue? Of stone?

He looked up at me. "I remember now. It needs moisture. If it dries, it dies. Cracks form in its skin. It's curled into a ball to preserve a pearl of moisture between its cilia."

"What is it?" I said, unable to keep the fear from my voice.

He grinned in recognition of my tone. "Before Dad died," he said, "you would have found this creature a wonderful mystery. You would have followed me out into the woods and we would have dug up fire-red salamanders just to see their eyes glow in the dark."

"No," I said. "No. There was no time when I would have found this *thing* a wonderful mystery. Where did you find it?"

His smirk, the way it ate up his face, the way it accentuated the suddenly taut bones in his neck, made the flesh around his mouth a vassal to his mirth, sickened me.

"Where do *you* think it came from?"

I ignored the question, turned away, said, "I have a canteen of water in the front, near my desk. But keep talking. Keep telling me about your book."

He frowned as I walked past him into the main room of the gallery. From behind me, his disembodied voice rose up, quavered, continued. A thrush caught in a hunter's snare, flapping this way and that, ever more entangled and near its death. His smell had coated the entire gallery. In a sense, I was as close to him searching for the canteen as if I stood beside him. Beyond the gallery windows lay the real world, composed of unnaturally bright colors and shoppers walking briskly by.

"So I never finished it, Janice. What do you think of that? I couldn't. Wouldn't. I wrote and wrote. I wrote with the energy of ten men each evening. All texts I consulted interlocked under my dexterous manipulations. It all made such perfect sense . . . and then I began to panic. Each word, I realized, had been leading me further and further away from the central mystery. Every sentence left a false trail. Every paragraph formed another wall between me and my thesis. Soon, I stopped writing. It had all been going so well. How could it get so bad so quickly?

"I soon found out. I backtracked through the abyss of words, searching for a flaw, a fissure, a crack in the foundation. Perhaps some paragraph had turned traitor and would reveal itself. Only it wasn't a paragraph. It was a single word, five pages from the end of my silly scribblings, in a sentence of no particular importance. Just a single word. I know the sentence by heart, because I've repeated it to myself over and over again. It's all that's left of my book. Do you want to hear it?"

"Yes," I said, although I wasn't sure. I was still searching for the canteen under all the canvases.

"Here it is: 'But surely, if Tonsure had not known the truth then, he knew it after traveling underground.' The word was 'truth,' and I could not get past the truth. The truth stank of the underground, buried under dead leaves and hidden in cold, dry, dark caverns. The truth had little to do with the surface of things.

"From that word, in that context, on that page, written in my nearly illegible hand, my masterwork, my beautiful, marvelous book unraveled syllable by syllable. I began by crossing out words that did not belong in the sentence. Then I began to delete words by rules as illegitimate and illogical as the gray caps themselves. Until after a week, I woke up one morning, determined to continue my surgical editing of the manuscript—only to find that not even the original sentence had been spared: all that remained of my once-proud manuscript was that single word: 'truth.' And, truth, my dear sister, was not a big enough word to constitute an entire book—at least not to me." {Or my publishers, come to think of it. If there had been any publishers.}

I had found the canteen. I came back into the room and handed it to him. "You should drink some. Rinse out the lie you've just told."

He snorted, took the canteen, raised it to his lips, and, drinking from it, kissed it as seriously as he would a lover.

"Perhaps it is in part a metaphor," he said, "but it is still, ironically enough, the truth."

"Don't speak in metaphors, then. How do you tell truth from lies otherwise?"

"I want to be taken literally."

"You mean literarily, Duncan. Except you've already been taken literarily—they've all ravished you and gone on to the next victim."

"Literally."

"Is that why you brought this horrible rolled up ball of an animal with you?"

"No. I forgot I had it. Now that I've brought it here, I can't let it die." {Actually, Janice, I did bring it with me on purpose. I had just forgotten the purpose.}

He sidled over to the golden ball of flesh, poured water into his hand.

He looked up at me, the expression on his face taking me back to all of his foolish explorations as a child. "Watch now! Watch carefully!"

Slowly, he poured water over the golden ball. After a moment the gold color blushed into a haze of purple-yellow-blue-green, which then returned to gold, but a more vibrant shade of gold that flashed in the dim light. Duncan poured more water over the creature. It seemed to crack apart, fissures erupting across its skin at regular intervals. But no—it was merely opening up, each of its four legs unfurling from the top of the ball, to settle upside down on the floor. Immediately, it leapt up, spun, and landed, cilia down, revealed as a kind of phosphorescent starfish.

Duncan dribbled still more water over it. Each of its four arms shone a different glittering shade—green-blue-yellow-purple—the edges of the blue arm tinged green on one side, yellow on the other.

"A starfish," I said.

"A compass," he said. "Just one of the many wonders to be found belowground. A living compass. North is blue, so if you turn it like so," and he reached over and carefully turned the starfish, "the arm shines perfectly blue, facing as it does due north."

Indeed, the blue had been cleansed of any green or yellow taint.

"This compass saved me more than once when I was lost," he said.

I stared at my ungainly, stacked frames. "I'm sick of wonders, Duncan. This is just a color to me, just a trick. The true wonder is that you're still alive. No one could have expected that. You suffer what may have been a mental breakdown, go down below, return with a living compass, and expect me to say . . . what? How *wonderful* that is? How *awed* I am by it all? No. I'm appalled. I'm horrified. I'm angry. I've failed at one career after another. I'm about to open my own gallery. I haven't seen you in almost ten years, and you shamble in here, a talking skeleton—and you expect me to be impressed by a magic show? Have you *seen* yourself lately?"

I can't remember ever being so furious—and out of nowhere, out of almost nothing. My hands shook. My shoulders had become rigid blocks of stone. My throat ached. And I'm not even sure why. {Because you were scared, and because you were my sister, and you loved me. Even when you were mad at me, I was your family.} I almost want to laugh, typing this now. Having seen so many strange things since, having been at peace lying on a floor littered with corpses, having accepted so much strangeness from Duncan, that starfish seems almost mundane in retrospect, and my anger at Duncan self-indulgent.

He scooped up the starfish, held it in his hands. It lay there as contentedly as if in a tidal pool. "I don't expect anything, Janice," he said, each word carefully weighed, wrapped, tied with string before leaving his mouth. "I have no one else to tell. No one else who saw me the last time. No one else who might possibly believe anything I saw. Starfish or no starfish."

"Tell Mom then. Mom would listen. If you speak softly enough, Dad might even pick up a whisper of it. Did you meet him down there?"

He winced, sat back against the wall, next to a leering portrait by a painter named Sonter. The shadows and the sheen of black dust on his skin rendered him almost invisible.

Coated by the darkness, he said, "I'm sorry. I didn't mean to—I didn't realize . . . But you know, Janice, you *are* the only one who won't think me crazy."

The starfish had begun to explore the crook of Duncan's arm. Its rejuvenated cilia shone wetly, a thousand minute moving jewels amongst the windless reeds of his arm hairs.

"It's so hard," he said. "Half of what you see seems like a hallucination, or a dream, even while you're living it. You are so unsure about what's real that you take all kinds of stupid risks. As if it can't hurt you. You float along, like a spore. You sit for days in caverns as large as cities, let the fungi creep up and devour you. The stars that can't be stars fall in on you in waves. And you sit there. An afternoon in the park. A picnic for one.

"*Things* walk by you. Some stop and stare. Some poke you or hit you, and then you have to pretend you're in a dream, because otherwise you would be so afraid that nothing would stop you from screaming, and you'd keep screaming until they put a stop to you."

He shivered and rolled over on his side. "Sorry, sorry, sorry," he whined, the starfish on his shoulder a golden glimmer.

"Was it worth it?" I asked him, not unkindly. "Was it?"

"Ask me in fifty years, Janice. A hundred years. A thousand." {It didn't take that long. Within five years, I began to recognize that my sojourn underground was akin to one more addict's hit of mushrooms. It took ten years of these adventures for me to realize that I could only *react* to such journeys, never *predict*. Always *absorbing*, but mostly in the physical sense.}

He twisted from side to side, holding his stomach.

"I thought I could get it out of me if I talked about it," he said. "Flush it from my brain, my body. But it's still in there. It's still in me."

Again, he was talking about two things at once, but I could only bear to talk about what I might be able to help him with right then.

"Duncan," I said, "we can't wash it off of you this time. I think it's inside of you, like some kind of poison. Your pores are clogged with black spores. Your skin is . . . different."

He gasped. Was he crying? "I know. I can feel it inside of me. It's trying to change me."

"Talk about it, then. Talk about it until you talk it all out."

He laughed without any hint of humor. "Are you mad? I can't talk it out of my skin. I can't do that."

I joined him along the wall, moving Sonter's portrait to the side. The starfish had splayed itself across the side of his neck like an exotic scar.

"You're due north," I said. "Its arm is blue. And you're right, Duncan. It's beautiful. It's one of the most beautiful things I've ever seen."

He moved to pull it off, but I caught his arm. "No. Don't. I think it's feeding on the spores embedded in your skin." It left a trail of almost-white skin behind it.

"You think so?" His eyes searched mine for something I'm not sure I've ever been able to give.

In that moment before he began to really tell me his story, to which all of this had been foolish, prattling preamble—in that moment, I think I loved my brother as much as I ever had in all the years since his birth. His face shone darkly in my doomed gallery, more precious than any painting.

WE LAY SIDE BY SIDE, silent in the semi-darkness of the back room, sur-rounded by dead paint. The now-reluctant glare from the main room meant the sun had begun to fade from the sky. The starfish flinched, as if touched by the memory of light, as it continued its slow migration toward the top of Duncan's head.

I could remember afternoons when Duncan and I would sit against the side of the house in Stockton, out of the sun, eating cookies we'd stolen from the kitchen while we talked about school or the nasty neighbor down the street. The quality of light was the same, the way it almost bent around the corner even as it evaporated into dust motes. As if to tell us we were never alone—that even in the stillness, with no wind, our fingers stained by the grass, we are never really outside of time.

Duncan began to talk while I listened without asking questions or making comments. I stared at nothing at all, a great peace come over me. It was cool and dark in that room. The shadows loved us.

But memory is imperfect, incomplete, fickle. It tells us the exact shade of our mother's blouse the day our father died, but it cannot accurately recall a conver-sation between siblings decades after that. Thus, I resort, as I already have through most of this afterword, to a much later journal entry by Duncan— clearly later because it is polluted by the presence of Mary Sabon; so polluted that I could not easily edit her out of it. {You can't erase the past just because you wish it hadn't happened.}

Does it make any difference now to Duncan who sees it? None. So why not steal his diary entry and spill his innermost thoughts like blood across the page, fling them across the faces of Sabon's flesh necklace in a fine spackle of retreat-ing life. I'll let Duncan tell us about his journeys underground. {Do I have a choice? But you're right—it doesn't matter anymore. I will not edit it, or any-thing else, out, although I may protest from time to time. I haven't decided yet if you're a true historian or one step removed from a gossip columnist.}

Tonsure got parts of it right—the contractions of spaces, small to large, and how mysterious perspective becomes after long periods underground. The way the blackness picks up different hues and textures, transformed into anti-color, an anti-spectrum. The fetid closeness and vastness, the multitude of smells, from the soothing scent of something like mint to the putrid stench of rotting fungi, like a dead animal . . . and yet all my words make of me a liar. I struggle to express myself, and only feel myself moving further from the truth. No wonder Mary thinks me a fool. No wonder she looks at me as if I am much stranger than the strangest thing she has ever seen. I caught a glimpse of her soft white breast when she leaned down to pick up a book. I'd be rougher than nails to her skin. The thought of being close tantalizes and yet makes me sick with my own clumsiness.

That is one thing I prefer about the underground: the loss of self to your environment is almost as profound as orgasm or epiphany, your senses shattered, rippled, as fragmented and wide as the sky. Time releases its meaning. Space is just a subset of time. You cease to become mortal. Your heartbeat is no longer a motion or a moment, but a possibility that may someday arrive, and then pass, only to arrive again. It's the most frightening loss of control imaginable.

For me it was still different than for Tonsure. He had no real protection, no real defenses, until he adapted. At least I had the clues Tonsure left behind. At least I knew how to make myself invisible to them, to lose myself but not become lost. To become as still as death but not dead. Sometimes this meant standing in one place for days. Sometimes it meant constant, manic movement, to emulate the frantic writhing of the *cheraticaticals* [no known translation].

I found the standing still worse than the walking and running. I could disguise myself from the gray caps, but not from their servants—the spores, the parasites, the tiny mushroom caps, fungi, and lichen. They found me and infiltrated me—I could feel their tendrils, their fleshy-dry-cold-warm pseudopods and cilia and strands slowly sliding up my skin, like a hundred tiny hands. They tried to remake me in their image. If it had been you, Mary, I would not have minded. If you had found me, I would have given up my identity as easily as a wisp of cloud.

I drifted and drifted, often so in trance that I did not have a single conscious thought for hours. I was a pair of eyes reporting to a brain that had ceased to police, to analyze, the incoming images. It all went through me and past, to some place other. In a way, it was a kind of release. Now, it makes me wonder if I had learned what it feels like to be a tree, or even, strike me dead, a gray cap. But, that cannot be so—the gray caps are always in motion, always thinking. You can see it in their eyes.

Once, as I stood in one of my motionless trances, a gray cap approached me. What did he do? Nothing. He sat in front of me and stared up at me for hours, for days. His eyes reflected the darkness. His eyes had a quality that held all of me entirely, held me against my will. Mary holds me, but not against my will—her eyes and my will are in accord. Her eyes: green, green, green. Greener than Ambergris. Greener than the greenest moss by a trickling stream.

After a time, I realized the gray cap had gone, but it took me weeks to return to the surface of my thoughts, and months to find the real surface, and with it the light. The light! A weak trickle of late afternoon gloom, presage of sunset, and yet it pierced my vision. I could not open my eyes until after dusk, fumbling my way along the Moth riverbank like some pathetic mole. The light burned into my closed eyelids. It seemed to crack my skin. It tried to kill me and birth me simultaneously. I lay gasping in the mud, writhing, afraid I would burn up.

I took a long sip from the canteen at this point, if only to assuage Duncan's remembered heat. The starfish now served as an exotic, glowing ear, eclipsing flesh and blood. It hummed a little as it worked. A smell like fresh-cut orange surrounded it.

I offered Duncan the canteen. He used the opportunity to pour more water on his pet. I was about to prod him to continue when he pulled the starfish from his ear, sat up, and said, looking down at the compass as it sucked on his fingers, "Do you know the first sentences of the Truffidian Bible?"

"No," I said. "Do you?" Our parents had treated religion like a door behind which stood an endless abyss: better not to believe at all, the abyss revealed, than have it be closed over, falsified, prettied up. {And yet, there is something in my skin now, after all these years, that hums of the world in a way that predicts the infinite.}

"Yes, I do know them. Would you like to hear them?"

"Do I have a choice?"

"No. Those words are 'The world is broken. God is in exile.' Followed shortly thereafter by 'In the first part of creation, God made light and made vessels for the light. The vessels were too fragile: they broke, and from the broken vessels of the supernal lights, the material world was created.'"

Something very much like a void opened up inside me. A chill brought gooseflesh to my skin. Each word from my mouth sounded heavier than it should have: "And what does the creation of the world have to do with the gray caps?"

He put a finger to his lips. His face in the sour light gave off a faint glow, pale relative to the illumination of the starfish. His skin winked from behind the mushroom dust. He looked so old. Why should he look so old? What did he know?

He said: "A machine. A glass. A mirror. A broken machine. A cracked glass. A shattered mirror."

I remember now the way he used the phrases at his disposal. Clean, fine cuts. Great, slashing cuts. Fractures in the word and the world.

"Some things should not be articulated. Some words should never be used in exact combination with other words." My father said that once, while reading a scathing negative review of one of his essays. He said it with a tired little sigh, a joke at his expense. His whole body slumped from the words. Weighed down with words, like stones in his pocket.

A machine. A glass. A mirror. Duncan's journal, with the advantage of distance, described his discovery much more gracefully. . . .

But it doesn't work right. It hasn't worked right since they built it. A part, a mechanism, a balance—something they don't quite understand. How can I call it strictly a machine? It is as much organic as metallic, housed in a cavern larger than three Truffidian Cathedrals. You feel it and hear it before you see it: a throbbly hum, a grindful pulse, a sorrowful bellow. The passageways rumble and crackle with the force of it. A hot wind flares out before it. The only entrance leads, after much hard work, to the back of the machine, where you can see its inner workings. You are struck by the fact of its awful carnality, for they feed it lives as well as fuel. Flesh and metal bond, married by spores, joined by a latticework of polyps and filaments and lazy strands. Wisps and converted moonlight. Sparks and gears. The whole is at first obscured by its own detail, by those elements at eye level: a row of white sluglike bodies curled within the cogs and gears, eyes shut, apparently asleep. Wrinkled and luminous. Lacking all but the most rudimentary stubs of limbs. But with faces identical to those of the gray caps.

You cannot help but look closer. You cannot help but notice two things: that they dream, twitching reflexively in their repose, eyelids flickering with subconscious thought, and that they are not truly curled within the machine—they are curled *into* the machine, meshed with it at a hundred points of contact. The blue-red veins in their arms flow into milk-white fingers, and at the border between skin and air, transformed from vein into silvery wire. Tendrils of wire meet tendrils of flesh, broken up by sections of sharp wheels, clotted with scraps of flesh, and whining almost soundlessly as they whir in the darkness.

As you stare at the nearest white wrinkled body, you begin to smell the thickness of oil and blood mixed together. As the taste bites into your mouth, you take a step back, and suddenly you feel as if you are falling, the sense of vertigo so intense your arms flail out though you stand on solid ground. Because you realize it isn't one pale dreamer, or even a row of them, or even five rows of five hundred, but more than five thousand rows of five thousand milk-white dreamers, running on into the distance—as far as you care to see—millions of them, caught and transfixed in the back of the machine. And they are all dreaming and all their eyelids flicker in unison, and all their blood flows into all the wires while a hundred thousand sharpened wheels spin soundlessly.

The hum you hear, that low hum you hear, does not come from the machinery. It does not come from the wheels, the cogs, the wires. The hum emanates from the white bodies. They are humming in their sleep, a slow, even hum as peaceful as they are not—how can I write this, how? except to keep writing and when I've stopped never look at this again—while the machine itself is silent.

The rows blur as you tilt your head to look up, not because the rows are too far away, but because your eyes and your brain have decided that this is too much, this is too much to take in without going mad, that you do not want to comprehend this crushing immensity of vision, that if comprehended completely, it will haunt not just your nightmares for the rest of your life—it will form a permanent overlay upon your waking sight, and you will stumble through your days like a blind man, the ghost-vision in your head stronger than reality.

So you return to details—the details right in front of you. The latticework of wires and tubes, where you see a thrush has been placed, intertwined, its broken wings flapping painfully. There, a dragonfly, already dead, brittle and glassy. Bits and pieces of flesh still writhing with the memory of interconnection. Skulls. Yellowing bones. Glossy black vines. Pieces of earth. And holding it all together, like glue, dull red fungus.

But now the detail becomes too detailed, and again your eyes blur, and you decide maybe movement will save you—that perhaps if you move to the other side of the machine, you will find something different, something that does not call out remorselessly for your surrender. Because if you stand there for another minute, you will enmesh yourself in the machine. You will climb up into the flesh and metal. You will curl up to something pale and sticky and embrace it. You will relax your body into the space allowed it, your legs released from you in a spray of blood and wire, you smiling as it happens, your eyes already dulled, and dreaming some communal dream, your tongue the tongue of the machine, your mouth humming in another language, your arms weighed down with tendrils of metal, your torso split in half to let out the things that must be let out.

For a long time, you stand on the fissure between sweet acceptance of dissolution and the responsibility of movement, the enticing smell of decay, the ultimate inertia, reaching out to you . . . but, eventually, you move away, with an audible shudder that shakes your bones, almost pulls you apart.

As you hobble around to the side of the machine, you feel the million eyes of the crumpled, huddled white shapes snap open, for a single second drawn out of their dreams of you.

⚘

There is no history, no present. There are only the sides of the machine. Slick memory of metal, mad with its own brightness, mad with the memory of what it contains. You cling to those sides for support, but make your way past them as quickly as possible. The sides are like the middle of a book— necessary, but quickly read through to get to the end. Already, you try in vain to forget the beginning.

⚘

The front of the machine has a comforting translucent or reflective quality. You will never be able to decide which quality it possesses, although you stand there staring at it for days, ensnared by your own foolish hope for something to negate the horrible negation of the machine's innards. Ghosts of images cloud the surface of the machine and are wiped clean as if by a careless, a meticulous, an impatient painter. A great windswept desert, sluggish with the weight of its own dunes. An ocean, waveless, the tension of its surface broken only by the shadow of clouds above, the water such a perfect blue-green that it hurts your eyes. A mountain range at sunset, distant, ruined towers propped up by the foothills at its flanks. Always flickering into perfection and back into oblivion. Places that if they exist in this world you have never seen, or heard mention of their existence. Ever.

You slide into the calm of these scenes, although you cannot forget the white shapes behind the machine, the eyelids that flicker as these images flicker. Only the machine knows, and the machine is damaged. Its thoughts are damaged. Your thoughts are damaged: they run liquid-slow through your brain, even though you wish they would stop.

⊱⊰

After several days, your vision strays and unfocuses and you blink slowly, attention drawn to a door at the very bottom of the mirror. The door is as big as the machine. The door is as small as your fingernail. The distance between you and the door is infinite. The distance between you and the door is so minute you could reach out and touch it. The door is translucent—the images that flow across the screen sweep across the door as well, so that it is only by the barely perceived hairline fracture of its outline that it can be distinguished beneath the desert, ocean, mountains, that glide across its surface. The door is a mirror, too, you realize, and after so long of not focusing on anything, letting images run through you, you find yourself concentrating on the door and the door alone. In many ways, it is an ordinary door, almost a nonexistent door. And yet, staring at it, a wave of fear passes over you. A fear so blinding it paralyzes you. It holds you in place. You can feel the pressure of all that meat, all that flesh, all the metal inside the machine amassed behind that door. It is an unbearable weight at your throat. You are buried in it, in a small box, under an eternity of rock and earth. The worms are singing to you through the rubble. The worms know your name. You cannot think. Your head is full of blood. You dare not breathe.

There is something behind the door.
There is something behind the door.
There is something behind the door.

The door begins to open inward, and *something* fluid and slow, no longer dreaming, begins to come out from inside, lurching around the edge of the door. You begin to run—to run as far from that place as you possibly can, screaming until your throat fills with the blood in your head, your head now an empty globe while the rest of you drowns in blood. And still it makes no difference, because you are back in that place with the slugs and the skulls and the pale dreamers and the machine that doesn't work that doesn't work that doesn't work thatdoesn'twork hat doesnwor atdoeswor doeswor doewor dowor door . . .

This entry about a defective "machine" built by the gray caps is the strangest part of my brother's journal. By far. In its pure physicality I sense a level of discomfort rare for Duncan. As if, from fretful tossing and turning, he woke, reached for pen and notepad from the nightstand, and wrote down his first impressions of a fading nightmare. He appears at first anxious to record the experience, and then less so, the use of second person intended to place the burden of memory on the reader, to purge the images from his head. {It is more that I could not find words to accurately convey what I saw, and so I tried to describe how I *felt* instead—in a sense presaging Ambergrisians' reaction to the recent Shift.}

If Duncan had, in the gallery that afternoon, told me about the machine with the calm madness of that journal entry, a silence would have settled over us. Our conversation would have faded away into a nothingness made alive and aware by his words. Thankfully, Duncan told his story with less than brutal lucidity. He used stilted words in rows of sentences crippled by fits and starts—a vagabond, poorly-rehearsed circus of words that could not be taken seriously. He focused on the front of the machine with its marvelous visions of far-distant places. He dismissed the back of the machine with a single sentence. Somehow, I could not reconcile his vision with my memory of the spores floating out of my apartment window.

Even so, an element of unreality entered the gallery following his revelation. I remember staring at him and thinking that his face could not be composed of flesh and blood, not with those words coming from his mouth. The light now hid his features, but his hands, lit by the starfish, glowed white.

"The door in the machine never fully opens," Duncan said in a distant tone.

"What would happen if it did?"

"They would be free. . . ."

"Who?" I asked, although I knew the answer.

"The gray caps."

"Free of what?"

Pale hands, darkened face, gray speech. "I think they care nothing for us one way or the other, Janice. They have only one purpose now. The same purpose they've had for centuries."

"In your unconfirmed opinion, brother," I said, and shivered at the way the mushroom dust on his face still glittered darkly.

"What do you know about the Silence?"

"The gray caps killed everyone in the city," I said.

He shook his head. Forgetting the starfish in his hands, he stood abruptly. The starfish fell to the floor and began to curl and uncurl in a reflexive imitation of pain. Now Duncan was stooped over me. Now he was crouched beside me. If there were ever a secret he truly wanted to tell me, this was the secret. This was the cause of it. We had returned to the last survivor of his sixth book, alive amid all of the suicides: the truth. As my brother saw it.

"You learned it wrong," he told me. "That's not what happened. It didn't happen like that. I've seen so many things, and I've thought a lot about what I've seen. They disappeared without a single drop of blood left behind. Not a fragment of bone. No. They weren't killed. At least not directly. Try to imagine a different answer: a sudden miscalculation, a botched experiment, a flaw in the machine. All of those people. All twenty-five thousand of them. The men, the women, the children—they didn't die. They were *moved.* The door opened in a way the gray caps didn't expect, couldn't expect, and all those people—they were *moved* by mistake. The machine took them to someplace else. And, yes, maybe they died, and maybe they died horribly—but my point is, it was all an *accident.* A mistake. *A terrible, pointless blunder."*

He was breathing heavily. Sweat glistened on his arms, where before the black dust had suppressed it.

"That's crazy," I said. "That's the craziest thing I have ever heard in my life. They've killed thousands of people. They've done terrible things. And you have the nerve to make apologies for them?!"

"Would it be easier to accept that they don't give a damn about us one way or the other if we hadn't massacred them to build this city? What I think is crazy is that we try to pretend they are just like us. If we had massacred most of the citizens of Morrow, we would expect them to seek revenge. That would be natural, understandable, even acceptable. But what about a people that, when you slaughter hundreds of them, doesn't even really notice? That doesn't acknowledge the event? We can't accept that reaction. That would be incomprehensible. So we tack the idea of 'revenge' onto the Silence so we can sleep better at night—because we think, we actually have the nerve to think, that we understand these creatures that live beneath us. And if we think we understand them, if we believe they are like us in their motivations, then we don't fear them quite as much. If we meet one in an alley, we believe we can talk to it, reason with it, communicate with it. Or if we see one dozing beneath a red flag on the street during the day, we overlook it, we make it part of the scenery, no less colorful or benign than a newly ordained Truffidian priest prancing down Albumuth Boulevard in full regalia."

"You're crazy, Duncan. You're unwell." Anger again burned inside of me. The idea of the Silence reduced to a pathetic mistake enraged me. The idea that my own brother might utter the words that made it so seemed a betrayal of an unspoken understanding between us. Before this moment, we could always count on sharing the same worldview no matter what happened, even when we saw each other at wider and wider intervals.

"It's more complicated than you think," he said. "They are on a journey as much as we are on a journey. They are trying to get somewhere else—but they can't. It doesn't work. With all they can do, with all they are, they still cannot make their mirror, their glass, work properly. Isn't that sad? Isn't that kind of sad?"

I slapped him across the face. My hand came away black with spores. He did not move an inch.

"Sad?" I said. "Sad? Sad is twenty-five thousand lives snuffed out, not a broken machine. Not a broken machine! What is happening to you that you cannot see that? Regardless of what happened. Not that I believe you. Frankly, I don't believe you. Why should I? For all I know, you've been in the sewers for the past few weeks, living off of rats and whatever garbage you could get your hands on. And all you've seen is the reflection of your own filthy face in a pool of scummy water!"

Duncan smiled and pointed at the starfish. "How do you explain that?"

"Ha!" I said. "It was probably groveling for garbage along with you. It definitely isn't proof of anything, if that's what you mean. Why didn't you bring something substantive, like a gray cap willing to corroborate your statement?"

"I did bring a gray cap," he said. "Several, in fact. Although not by choice. Take a good look through the doorway, out the front window, to the left. I doubt they would corroborate anything, though. I think they'd like to see me dead."

"Don't joke."

"I'm not. Take a look."

Reluctantly, I raised myself, my left leg asleep—even less impressed by Duncan's story, apparently, than I was. I peered around the doorway. Sheathed like swords by the fading light, more sharp shadow than dream, three gray caps stood staring in through the window. They stood so still the cobblestones of the street behind them seemed more alive. The whites of their eyes gleamed like wet paint. They stared at and through me. As if I meant nothing to them. The sight of them sent a convulsive shudder through me. I ducked back, beside Duncan.

"Maybe we should leave by the back door," I said.

A low, humorless laugh from Duncan. "Maybe they came for your gallery opening."

"Very funny. Follow me. . . ."

In a pinch, I still trusted my brother more than anyone else in the world.

❧❦

Every human being is a puppet on strings, but the puppet half controls the strings, and the strings do not ascend to some anonymous Maker, but are glistening golden strands that connect one puppet to another. Each strand is sensitive to the vibrations of every other strand. Every vibration sings in not only the puppet's heart, but in the hearts of many other puppets, so that if you listen carefully, you can hear a low hum as of many hearts singing together. . . . When a strand snaps, when it breaks for love, or lack of love, or from hatred, or from pain . . . every other connected strand feels it, and every other connected heart feels it—and since every strand and every heart are, in theory, connected, even if at their most distant limits, this means the effect is universal. All through the darkness where shining strings are the only light, a woundedness occurs. And this hurt affects each strand and each puppet in a different way, because we are all puppets on strings and we all hurt and are hurt. And all the strings shimmer on regardless, and all of our actions, no matter how small, have consequences to other puppets. . . . After we are dead, gone to join the darkness between the lines of light, the strands we leave behind still quiver their lost messages into the hearts of those other puppets we met along the way, on our journey from light into not-light. These lost strands are the memories we leave behind. . . . Magnify this effect by 25,000 souls and perhaps you can see why I cannot so lightly dismiss what you call a mistake. Each extinguished life leaves a hole in many other lives—a series of small extinguishments that can never be completely forgotten or survived. Each survivor carries a little of that void within them.

This is part of a letter I wrote to Duncan—the only attempt following our conversation to express my feelings about the Silence to him. One day I came home to my apartment early to find Duncan gone on some errand. For some reason I had been thinking about the Silence that day, perhaps because two or three new acquisitions had featured, in the background, the shadowy form of a gray cap. I sat down at my desk and wrote Duncan a letter, which I then placed in his briefcase full of papers, expecting he'd come across it in a week or a month. But he never mentioned it to me. I never knew whether he had read it or not until, going through his things after this final disappearance, I found it in a folder labeled simply "Janice." {I did read it, and I cried. At the time, it made me feel more alone than I had ever felt before. Only later did I find it a comfort.}

Duncan stayed at my apartment for nearly six months. By the fifth month, he appeared to have made a full recovery. We did not often speak of that afternoon when he had told me his theory about the Silence. In a sense, we decided to forget about it, so that it took on the hazy lack of detail specific only to memory. We were allowed that luxury back then. We did not have Sabon's glittering necklace of flesh to set us straight.

The starfish lasted four months and then died in a strobe of violent light, perhaps deprived of some precious nutrient, or perhaps having attained the end of its natural life cycle. Its bleached skeleton on the mantel carried hardly more significance than a snail's shell found by the riverbank.

❧ 4 ❧

TIME TO START OVER. ANOTHER dead white page to fill with dead black type, so I'll fill it. Why not? I've nothing better to do, for now anyway. Mary's still holding court at the bottom of that marble staircase at Lake's party, but I think I'll make her wait a little longer.

Especially since it strikes me that at this point in the narrative, or somewhere around here, Duncan would have paused to catch his breath, to regroup and place events in historical context. {If it were me, I would have skipped "historical context" and returned to that marble staircase, since that's really the only part of this story I don't know already.} *Years passed. They seem now like pale leaves pressed between the pages of an obscure book.*

Oddly enough, I don't give a damn about historical context at the moment. I can see the sliver of green light becoming dull, indifferent—which means the sun is going down outside. And we all know what happens, or can happen, when the sun goes down, don't we? Don't answer that question—read this instead:

The death of composer/politician Voss Bender and the rise of the Reds and Greens, who debate his legacy with knives: a civil war in the streets, which the trader Hoegbotton uses to solidify control of the city. I witness a man die right outside my gallery, hit in the head with a rock until his skull resembles a collection of broken eggshells dripping with red-gray mush. No art to it that I could see. No reason, either. Followed by: defeat of the Reds, disbanding of the Greens, the tossing of Bender's ashes in the River Moth—only, the wise old river doesn't want them, according to legend, and blows them back in the faces of the assembled mourners; thus dispersing Bender all across the city when the mourners go home. Scandal in the Truffidian Church—boring as only a Truffidian scandal can be: oh my goodness, the Antechamber Henry Bonmot, whom I still miss terribly, has been caught taking money from the collection plates! At the same time, the River Moth overflows its banks for a season and takes a sizable portion of our mother's property with it, making us officially heirs of Nothing but an old, rotting mansion. The Kalif of the Western Empire chokes on a plum pit, replaced by another faceless bureaucrat. Meanwhile, infant mortality continues to decline, along with the birth rate, while old people die in droves from a heat stroke that withers even the hardiest southern trees. A slight upswing in the fortunes of motored vehicles due to an influx of oil from the Southern Islands is offset by a plummet in the availability of spare parts. Voss Bender's posthumously produced opera, *Trillian,* reaches the two-year mark of its first run, its full houses unscathed by the dwindling tourist trade {no one likes to die while on holiday, whether by heat stroke or by gray cap}. Other composers and playwrights, who could really use the Bender Memorial Theater as a venue for their own drivel, gnash their teeth and whine in the back rooms of bars and taverns: Bender, dead, still lives on! Three Festivals of the Freshwater Squid pass by without so much as a pantomime of real violence—what is wrong with us as a people, I ask you, that we have become so passive? Are we not animals? Perhaps this squalid, shameful peace has something to do with the introduction of the telephone, at least for the well off, which allows Ambergrisians to call up total strangers and breathe at them, make funny noises, or vent our rage at the string of flat, bloodless festivals. The telephone: come to us from the Kalif, his empire, a domesticated beast, taken to colonizing through commerce rather than warfare; the ghost of the rebel Stretcher Jones, as Duncan might have put it, would never have recognized this temporarily toothless Empire, slumped back on its haunches. Inexplicably, guns arrive with the telephone. Lots of guns. In all types and sizes, mostly imported through Hoegbotton & Sons. Hoegbotton's armed importer-exporters, now doing a brisk trade in bandages, tourniquets, and bolted locks, are respected and feared the length and breadth of the River Moth— except by the operatives of Frankwrithe & Lewden, who continue their quiet infiltrations of Hoegbotton territory. More festivals, replete with the sound of gunplay. More years of *Trillian* and its vainglorious blather; will Voss Bender *never* die? Yes, this really is a historical summary of which my brother would be proud. {Not really, but think anything you like.}

Meanwhile, everything Duncan had told me about his underground adventures began to recede into the distance as "real life" took over again, for both of us. A retreat of sorts, you could call it—me from what Duncan had said, Duncan from what he had done. Perhaps he needed time to absorb what had happened to him. Perhaps he had been exhausted by what he had seen, and he couldn't physically undertake another journey so soon. Whatever the reason, he would become, in a sense, a religious man, while I would take a different path entirely. {I never became any more or less religious than I'd always been, or do you mean this as a joke? What I became was more aware of the world, the texture and feel of it, the way it changed from day to day, minute to minute, and me with it. And I did continue with my work, although I don't blame you for not noticing.}

If I gave Duncan's life less attention in those years after the starfish, it was because my fortunes waxed unexpectedly. Martin Lake—an arrogant, distant prick of a man—rose to prominence through my gallery, his haunted haunting paintings soon a fixture next to the telephones in the living rooms of the city's wealthiest patrons of the arts. {And who can say, in the long run, which was the worthier work—Lake's bizarre melancholia or the telephone's febrile ring.}

My gallery sparked a nameless, shapeless, and unique art revolution that soon became labeled {pinned like one of Sirin's butterflies} "the New Art." The New Art emphasized the mystical and transformative through unconventional perspective, hidden figures, strange juxtapositions of color. {It would be most accurate to say that the New Art *opened up* to include Martin within its ranks, and that he devoured it whole.}

As soon as I saw the change in Lake's art—he had been, at best, uninspired before whatever sparked his metamorphosis—I sought out anything similar, including the work of several of Lake's friends. Within months, I had a monopoly on the New Art. Raffe, Mandible, Smart, Davidson—they all displayed their art with me. Eventually, I had to buy the shop next door as an annex, just to have enough space for everyone to come see my art openings.

I had begun to experience what Duncan had known briefly after the publication of his first book: fame. And I hadn't even had to create anything—all I had had to do was exploit Lake's success, and build on it. {You're too modest. You made some brilliant decisions during that time. You were like one of the Kalif's generals, only on the battlefield of art. Nothing escaped your attention, until much later. I admired that.}

Suddenly, the local papers asked for my opinion on a variety of topics, only a few of which I knew anything about, although this did not stop me from commenting.

I have some of the clippings right here. In the *Ambergris Weekly*, they wrote, "The Gallery of Hidden Fascinations lives up to its name. Janice Shriek has assembled a group of topnotch new artists, any one of whom might be the next Lake." *The Ambergris Daily Broadsheet,* which Duncan and I would one day work for, noted, "Janice Shriek continues to build a dynasty of artists who are determining the direction of the New Art in Ambergris." The clippings are a bit faded, but still readable, still a source of pleasure. {As well they should be— you worked hard for your success.} I can remember a time when I kept such clippings in a jacket pocket. I'd pull them out and make sure they still said what I thought they had said, that I hadn't imagined it.

However, the New Art soon became about something other than artistic expression. A kind of tunnel vision set in whereby a painting was either New Art or Not New Art. Those works identified as Not New Art were dismissed as unimportant or somehow of lesser ambition. I admit to participating in this mindset, although for the ethically pure reason that I wanted my gallery to make money. So I would do my best to label whatever I had hanging there as "New Art," from the most experimental mixing of media to the most hackneyed scene of houseboats floating idyllically down the River Moth.

"That's an ironic New Art statement," I would say of the hackneyed houseboats, mentally genuflecting before the latest potential customer. "In the context of New Art, this painting serves as a condemnation of itself in the strongest possible terms."

I have to say, I loved the sheer randomness of it all—there is nothing more liberating than playing an illogical game where only you understand all of the rules.

❦

MY GALLERY GREW FAT ON Lake's leavings, even after he left me, while Ambergris continued to prosper even as it headed ever deeper into complete moral and physical collapse or exhaustion. As the city's fate, so my own—and it took so little time. This is what, looking back, I marvel at—that I could discover so many new appetites, vices, and affectations in so short a time. Four years? Maybe five? Before beginning the inevitable plummet. These things never last—you ride them, you live inside of them, and then, almost without warning, you are flung to the side, spent, used up. {Although you must admit that, in this case, you flung yourself to the side.}

Most nights, I would be at a party until close to dawn. If not a party, then permanent residency at the Café of the Ruby-Throated Calf, drinking. I wore the same clothes for three or four days, no longer able to distinguish between dawn and dusk. It was one continuous swirling spangle of people and places in which to revel in my fame ever more religiously.

I met many influential or soon-to-be-influential people during that time {unsurprising, as you *were* one of those people, Janice}, Sirin being a prime example.

My first memory of Sirin, our enigmatic future editor, has me slouched in a chair at the café and feeling someone slide into the chair next to me. When I opened my eyes, a slender, dark-haired man sat there. He held his head at a slight angle. He smelled of a musky cologne. His mouth formed a perpetual half-smile, his eyes bright, penetrating, and reflectionless. The man I saw reminded me of old tales about people who could shape-change into cats. He looked like a rather smug, perhaps mischievous, feline. {He was the most exasperating, talented, maddening genius I've ever met. My initial reaction to meeting him was to want to simultaneously punch him, hug him, shake his hand, and throw him down a dark well. Instead, I generally stayed clear of him and let Janice serve as my intermediary, as she saw mostly his charming side.}

"Janice Shriek," he said. It was not a question.

"Yes?"

"Sirin," he said. He handed me a card.

Still struggling with context {with alcohol, you mean}, I looked down. The card gave his address at Hoegbotton & Sons, on Albumuth Boulevard.

"I like what you do," he said. "Come find me. I may have a use for you."

Then he was gone. At the time, Sirin was a great womanizer, attending parties and cafés just to identify his next victims. I wasn't sure what "use" he might have for me, and I was skeptical.

Sirin's fame as an editor and writer had begun to spread by that time. He had, like the mythical beast he took his name from, generic yet universal qualities. He brought to his editing the same sensibilities found in his writing. He could mimic any style, high or low, serious or comedic, realistic or fabulist. It sometimes seemed he had created the city from his pen. Or, at least, made its inhabitants see Ambergris in a different light. That he thought too much of himself was made tolerable by the depth and breadth of his talent. It never occurred to me that he would want me to write for him.

People like Sirin would come out of the haze of lights and nights, and I would receive them with a gracious smile, an arm outstretched, to indicate, "Sit. Sit and talk awhile!" I was very trusting and open back then. {Trusting? Perhaps. But can you be trusting or suspicious when you are not yourself? I came to some of those all-night sessions at the café, Janice, but most of the time you were in such an altered state that you didn't recognize me. And that conversation you recall so fondly? Your end of it was often, I hate to say it, a garbled warble of slurred speech and mumbled innuendo. Although it probably didn't matter, because only rarely were the people you spoke to any better off. I don't mean to reproach, but I must bring a sense of reality to this glorious, decadent age you write of with such wistful fondness. I became so bored that I stopped coming to the café. It wasn't worth my time. I'd rather be underground, off on the scent of some new mystery.}

Sybel—luminous, short, sweet Sybel—was one of those people I met during this time. He had a thick rush of dirty blond hair exploding off the top of his head like waves of pale flame, clear blue eyes, a grin that at times appeared to be half grimace, and he wore outrageous clothes in the most impossible shades of purple, red, green, and blue. He rarely sat still for very long. In those early years, he had the metabolism of a hummingbird. A coiled spring. A hummingbird. A marvel.

The first thing Sybel said to me was, "You need me. New Art will soon be dead. The newest art will be whatever Janice Shriek decides it is. But you still need me." Which made me laugh.

But I did need him. Sybel had explored every crooked mews in Ambergris. A courier for Hoegbotton, he also knew everyone. A member of the Nimbly-tod Tribes, he had an affinity for tree climbing that no one could match, and a cut-bark scent that clung to him as if it was his birthright. His only pride revolved around his knowledge of the streets, and his well-tended, lightweight boots, which had been given to him by his tribe when he had left for the city. He couldn't have been more than eighteen years old when I met him for the first time.

"I'm quick and good," he said, but did not specify good at what. "I'm eyes and ears and feet, but I'm not cheap," he told me, and then named a large monthly fee.

I suggested a smaller amount, but added, "And you can stay at my apartment whenever you like." After all, I was rarely there, except to catch up on three or four hours of sleep.

So it was that I acquired a roommate I rarely saw. I know he welcomed the refuge, though: his tumultuous love life meant he was continually getting kicked out of some woman's bed.

I soon found I had chosen well. From careful observation at Hoegbotton—when he was not out all night cavorting with painters and novelists, sculptors and art critics—Sybel had learned how to run a business, something I never did well. Over time, he became my gallery assistant—on and off, because he had a habit of disappearing for several days at a time. But I was hardly punctual myself, and I loved his energy, so I always forgave him, no matter what his transgressions. I used to imagine that every once in a while, Sybel got the urge to return to his native forests, that he would fling off his clothes and climb into the welter of trees near the River Moth, soon happily singing as he leapt from tree to tree. But I'm sure his absences had more to do with women. {Actually, Sybel's absences had a myriad of causes, because he led a myriad of lives, some of which he did not tell you about. I cannot remember exactly when I entered into one of those lives, but I do remember many a morning when, having emerged from yet another dank hole in the ground, grimy with dirt and sweat, I would stand exhausted by the banks of the River Moth beside a particular tree chosen in advance, inhabited by a certain member of the Nimblytod Tribe.

{Sybel always smiled down at me from that tree. I don't know if he liked the dawn or liked the tree or liked me, but it always made me smile back, no matter how grim the context of my emergence.

{Our meetings had a practical purpose, though. The Nimblytod were renowned for their natural cures, using roots, bark, and berries. Sybel made a considerable amount of money on the side selling various remedies. You had to go to him, though, and that meant appearing at a particular tree by the river-bank at a particular time.

{For me, he did two things—sold me a tincture of ground bark and leaves for fatigue and, if I thought it was warranted, snuck a rejuvenating powder into your tea, Janice, to balance the effects of your debauchery.

{"If she ever found out, she'd be furious," Sybel told me once.

{"Better that than dead," I said.

{"She's much stronger than you think," Sybel said. "She can go on this way for a long time. So can I." He was looking at me with some measure of amusement— me in my fungal shroud, giving every appearance of being on my last legs. Who was I to lecture anyone about these things?

{I just stared back at him and said, "I want my tincture. Where's my tincture, tree man?"

{He never left that damned tree during any of my meetings with him there. Not once. Just tossed my cure down to me.}

Sirin and Sybel were the only men I didn't sleep with during that time—for, suddenly, I had dozens of lovers. I slept with more men than there were paint-ings on the walls of my gallery, my nights a blurred fantasy of probing tongues, stroking hands, and hard cocks. I slept, quite a few times under the stars, with Lawrence, with John, with James, with Robert, with Luke, with Michael, with

George . . . and the list goes on without me, intertwined with the sound of drums and a line of dancers. About as interesting, in retrospect, as Sabon's necklace. I'm sure Duncan rolled his eyes behind my back whenever I mentioned a new "boyfriend," since the longevity of my boyfriends was akin to that of a mayfly. I can hardly remember their names. {Since I was actually paying attention during that period, I remember them. There was the painter James Mallock, whom you called "old hairy back"; and the sculptor Peter Greelin—too clutchy, you said; and the theater owner Thomas Strangell, who had trouble getting it up on opening nights; and so many more—"an endless parade of erotic follies," as you used to typify it. In an odd sense, it didn't bother me, Janice. At least you were enjoying yourself. I don't know if you ever realized this, but before that you rarely seemed to enjoy yourself.}

I became addicted to anonymous sex, sex without love, sex as an act. I loved the feel of a man's chest against my breasts, the quickening of his breath while inside me, the utterly sublime slide of skin against skin. Each encounter faded from memory more quickly than the last, so that I only became more ravenous. Before, I had been starving; now, I felt as if I could never be satiated.

In other words, I began, under the steady, orgasmic pressure of fame, to become someone totally different than I had been. Can I blame me? It felt marvelous. It felt so good I thought I would die from ecstasy. I was successful for the first time ever. For the first time ever, it was me, not Duncan, who commanded respect. If our father had been alive, he wouldn't have ignored me—he couldn't possibly have ignored me. {He never ignored you, Janice. No one ignored you. You just couldn't see them looking at you, for some reason.}

And still I consumed and consumed and consumed. I could not stop. Even in the midst of such carnality, a part of me remained distant, as if I were pulling the strings of my own puppet. I used to walk through a crowd of people, most of whom I knew intimately, and feel utterly alone. I had written that letter to Duncan about the golden threads and yet forgotten everything it meant.

Even Sybel had his doubts about my philosophy of life, despite how perfectly it fit in with the New Art ideal. We'd sit on the steps leading into the courtyard at Trillian Square, eating fruit that Sybel had plucked from some trees near the River Moth.

"How do you think everything is going?" Sybel would ask, a typical way for him to start a conversation if concerned about me.

I'd reply, "Great! Wonderful! Spectacular! Did you see that new painting? The one by Sarah Sharp? And it only cost us half of what it should have. If I can sell it, there are twenty more where that one came from. And after that there will be twenty more from somewhere else and then before you know it another gallery and after that, who knows. And that reminds me, did you see the mention in the *Broadsheet*? You need to make sure the theater owners see that—free advertising for us both. We have to maximize any leverage we get."

And I couldn't. Stop. Talking. And Sybel would eat his fruit and sometimes he'd put his hand on my shoulder and he'd feel that I was trembling and that I couldn't control it, and that touch would become a firmer grip, as if he were steadying me. Righting me.

Despite this, I didn't stop. I refused to stop—I wanted to eat, drink, and screw the world. Each new party, each new artist, each new day, started the process anew. With what glittering light shall we drape the new morning? Starved for so long, I now became the Princess of Yes. I. Simply. Could. Not. Say. No.

❧❦❧

IT IS BECAUSE I COULD not say no, ironically enough, that I became involved in so many projects for Sirin at Hoegbotton Publishing—and inadvertently provided the catalyst for the clandestine {and erratic} second career of Duncan, my by then thirty-six-year-old brother.

This new secret history he would carry with him was only one of many. He already brought with him the labyrinth beneath the city. He already brought with him a secret understanding of his own books—and a personal history increasingly intertwined with Ambergris'. For Duncan had discarded his public self; he had returned to the facelessness from which he had come. {What freedom there can be in this! Unfettered from all of the distractions, finally and forever. Yes, I would long for, pine for, legitimate publication many times—but then I felt that first rush of anonymity after the last book went out of print, and with it fled any obligation to anything other than tracking the mystery of the gray caps.}

To become . . . someone else. I was learning that lesson every day as *Janice Shriek* remade herself into a hundred different images reflected from store windows and mirrors and the approving or disapproving expressions on other people's faces. No longer jailed by expectations—of himself or anyone else. No longer anything but himself.

And yet, even then, he was beginning a slow slog back toward the printed page, from a different angle—a forced march with no true destination, just a series of way stations. At first, it must have seemed more of a trap than an opportunity. . . .

Duncan could publish nothing with Hoegbotton, at least directly. The last meeting with his editor had ended with a violent shouting match and an overturned desk. {For the record, I had nothing against either my editor or the desk—especially the desk. My reaction to the rejection of what would have been my sixth book for Hoegbotton was a delayed reaction to L. Gaudy's calm diatribe several years earlier in the offices of Frankwrithe & Lewden. All my editor at Hoegbotton said was, "I'm very sorry, Duncan, but we cannot take your latest book." Yet I found myself doing what I should have done to Gaudy—trying to beat his silly, know-nothing head against a desk. I'm lucky he didn't have me detained by Hoegbotton's thugs.}

But as I have written, Hoegbotton offered me more opportunities than I could possibly accept, and I did not turn them down. With the result that I had no choice but to enlist Duncan's help. Duncan took to it easily enough. {What choice did I have?} He was even eager for it. In fact, I can now reveal that the entire series of seventy-five travel pamphlets Hoegbotton published, one for each of the Southern Islands, was written by Duncan, not me. He would take my feverish, indifferent research, fortify it with his less-frenzied studies, and try to mimic my prose style, codified in many an art catalog:

> *Archibald With Earwig,* by Ludwig Poncer, Trillian Era, oils on canvas. This tititular crenellation of high and low styles, by virtue of its unerring instinct for the foibles of both the human thumb and the inhuman earwig, has delighted generations of art lovers who pine for the shiver of dread up the spine even as their lips part to offer the sinister white of a smile.

Blah blah mumble mumble and so forth and so on yawn yawn.

Duncan also wrote, under the pseudonym "Darren Nysland," the three-hundred-page *Hoegbotton Study of Native Birds* {which included my lovely, poetic entry on the plumed thrush hen}, still in print and often referenced by serious ornithologists. {As well it should be. It came into existence with excruciating slowness over many months. I soon wished a pox upon the entire avian clan. I never want to see another bird, unless eggwise, sunny-side up on my breakfast plate, or simmering in some sort of mint sauce.}

When, much later, I could not complete an essay on Martin Lake for the *Hoegbotton Guide to Ambergris,* Duncan did an admirable job of presenting my {crackpot, or at least unsupportable} ideas in good, solid prose. {And doing what you would not—protecting the identity of Lake's real lover. I wonder if you noticed. That and the peculiar "messages" I embedded in the text.} As if this was not confused enough, my work sometimes appeared under pen names, and thus when this work was actually written by Duncan, he appeared in print twice removed from his words.

I loved helping Duncan in this way. I loved that his style and my style became entangled so that we could not between us tell where a Janice sentence began and a Duncan sentence ended. For this meant I was very nearly his equal. {No comment.}

It was during this period that the Spore of the Gray Cap first became his favorite haunt. He had begun to put on a little weight, to grow a mustache and beard, which suited him. He even began to smoke a pipe. Thus outfitted, he would spend a few hours a day at the Spore, sitting in the {this very} back room, where he could keep a friendly eye on the bar's regulars and yet not have to speak to them. The bartenders loved him. Duncan never made a fuss, tipped well when he could, and added a sense of authentic eccentricity that the Spore needed. {These were not the only or even the primary reasons I spent so much time here. At some point, Janice, you will have to abandon suspense for a fully dissected chronology, will you not? Or perhaps I can help. It just so happens that below the back room of the Spore lies the easiest portal to the gray caps' underground kingdom.}

This deception continued for over three years, to the continued glorification of Janice Shriek, with rarely even the warmth of reflected light for poor Duncan. Hoegbotton did pay very well, and I dutifully gave Duncan sometimes as much as three-fourths of our earnings. {H&S could afford to pay well—not only were its trading activities booming, but it had managed to make inroads into the Southern jungles, and to consolidate control of almost all trade entering Ambergris. This was no benevolent organization, but perhaps being an anonymous thrall was better than the alternative.}

I suppose for this reason alone Duncan would have continued to supply his work for my byline. But we eventually put a stop to it anyway. I believe it was because my own instability made him yearn for stability of his own. When your sister continually looks pale as death, throws up on a regular basis, introduces you to a new boyfriend every other week, and is given to uncontrollable shaking, you begin to wonder how long it will be before people stop assigning her freelance work. {Not true—you flatter yourself. There were two reasons. First, I was sick of writing fluff. You try writing seventy-five articles on vacation opportunities in the Southern Islands and you will have written a new definition of boredom.

Vomiting would be the least of your worries. Second, freelancing did not appeal because there was no set schedule, and I could never know when you might have work for me. Third, I began to see that this facile copy writing was taking a lot of energy away from my underground inquiries, which became more urgent the more it seemed that the symptoms I'd manifested after coming aboveground were not going away.}

Besides, Sirin, now my editor at Hoegbotton, had published all manner of pamphlets early in his career, passing off fiction as nonfiction and nonfiction as fiction; when his readers could not tell the difference between the two, it filled him with a nonsensical glee. Several times, he wrote an essay in a periodical, a scathing review of it under a pen name, then a letter to the editor under yet another pen name, this alter-alter ego defending Sirin's original point. In short, Sirin was as apt to ape a novel in his essays as to mummify a treatise in his fancies. He was also a scrupulous rewriter of other writers' work, always sensitive to a change in tone or style, and drove Duncan to near insanity with his relentless line edits. With such an editor, it would not have been long before Sirin sniffed out the hoax. {I'm sure he sniffed out the hoax from nearly the beginning but chose not to say anything. What did it matter to him who wrote what so long as someone wrote it?}

For these reasons {and more, too tedious to, etc., etc.}, the arrangement did not last. One day I came to Duncan with an assignment {the abysmal task of creating an "upbeat" listing and description of funeral homes and cemeteries in Morrow; it made me suspicious—had Sirin come up with that to torment me?} and Duncan told me he couldn't do it. No, Duncan had taken a "regular" job.

My brother, Duncan Shriek, the fearless explorer, had finally accepted everyday reality as his own—just as I had begun to reject it. Joined the humdrum, wash-the-dishes, take-out-the-garbage, go-to-bed-early, get-up-and-go-to-work life shared by millions of people from Stockton to Morrow, Nicea to Ambergris. My shock only amused him. {Actually, dear sister, it was your squinty-eyed, sallow face, the way your pupils seemed ready to rise up into your head as your jaw, as if in balance, dropped. You looked, in short, as if we had traded places, sunshine for the subterranean. At least one of us was taking out the garbage.}

What job had Duncan taken? A teaching job at Blythe Academy, a minor Truffidian religious school. Blythe might have been best known for its longevity—it had been established some years before the Silence, although it had wandered from place to place, finally coming to rest a few blocks from the

Truffidian Cathedral. In a bit of irony I'm sure they had thought made good sense, Blythe's library had been superimposed on the ruins of an old gray cap library. {It wasn't ever a library. It was more of a marker for the Machine.} In the center of their main reading room, the circular nubs of that former structure remained, looking cold, remote, and threatening.

Blythe had a pointed history of accepting as many students from "artistic" or "creative" parents as possible, especially those of a certain social status—regardless of whether they believed in Truffidianism. I suppose the founders believed that the rote, compulsory weekly religious services in the small chapel behind the school might eventually permeate the brains of their charges—or at the very least instill the kind of guilt that in later years results in large sums of money being sent in to support new buildings, philosophies, or styles of teaching.

Blythe had also had famous teachers from time to time—Cadimon Signal for a few years, and even some of the Gorts who had gained such fame from the statistician Marmy Gort's controversial findings. Certainly, there was no shame in attending as a student or teaching at the school. However, as Duncan soon found out, greater shame could be found in those serving as headmaster, or Royal, to the school.

Imagine Duncan's shock the first day, arriving in starched collar and suffocating tie, to find his interviewer, the Vice Royal of Blythe Academy, joined by the Royal himself, who turned out to be none other than the former Antechamber, Bonmot. His features, already naturally condensed into a look of continual bemusement by the circumstances of his fall from grace, had attained a sublime parody of surprise {did anything really surprise him anymore?} as he looked up at Duncan and slowly realized who he was.

"Ironic, isn't it?" Duncan said with a toothy grin, as Bonmot nodded like a man in dream.

❦

FOR A SHORT WHILE, DUNCAN once again disappeared from my life, although this was a much gentler disappearance: his ghost remained behind. Postcards fluttered into my mailbox with alarming regularity, for him—at least one every two weeks. Duncan wrote in tiny letters, fitting long-winded, philosophical diatribes on them. {Not long-winded. Just, perhaps, impractical for the allotted space.} I would respond with postcards that teased him in the language of fashions and gossip—although, truth be told, sometimes I had Sybel write them when I was too busy. {It was no secret. Sybel told me, and his handwriting was markedly different from yours. He used to apologize to me for you when I collected my remedies from him. It was no secret, but also no sin. Still, I must admit to exasperation at the few times Sybel asked for advice on what he should write to me about!} From the evidence of the postcards alone, we might have been the two most uniquely different people in the world.

But the postcards were a way to remind each other of our existence, and those things most important to us at the time. Could I help it that my mind concerned itself with the ephemeral, the weightless, the surface, while Duncan continued to plunge into the depths?

On the corporeal level, the postcards meant nothing. What is a scrawl of letters next to that infinity of physical details that makes up a face? So I dropped by the Blythe Academy for lunch whenever I could find the time—at least once a month, depending on what demands Sybel and my ever-expanding gullet of a gallery made on me.

⁂

I SHARED THE GHOST OF Duncan, this Serious Man seemingly more concerned about his students than his life's work {so it might have seemed, I'll admit} with Bonmot, for the Antechamber and my brother had become friends. {Good friends? Great friends? I honestly don't know. The dynamic of our relationship was transformed day by day. On some level, despite our affection for one another, I think there was a certain caution, a certain wariness. He may have felt my obsession with the gray caps would lead me to discoveries that might bring dishonor to his faith in God. I know I was afraid that his religion might somehow infect my studies, change me in a way that I did not want to be changed.}

Without question, these lunches became the high point of my days. Whether in the sleepy cool heat of spring, the hot white light of summer, or the dry burnt chill of fall and winter. By the carp-filled fountain. They laughed so much!

I'd never seen Duncan laugh without bitterness or sarcasm since Before Dad Died. It almost felt like we were huddled around the dinner table in the old house in Stockton again, with Dad telling us some obscure fact he'd dug up in his research. Usually, he would mix in some lie, and the unspoken assumption was that we'd try to ferret it out with our questions. Sometimes, the truth was so outrageous that finding the lie took awhile. He would sit back in his chair, eyebrows raised in a look of innocence—something that always made Mom laugh—and answer us with a straight face. {I always knew when Dad wasn't telling the truth, because the faintest lilt or musical quality would enter his voice—as if the joy of constructing the story was too much for him to contain.}

These lunches with Bonmot formed pockets of time and space separate from the stress and rigor of my responsibilities {or lack thereof}. Where everything else blended together in a blur of faces and cafés and alcohol, that sun-filled courtyard with its rustling willows, light-soaked dark wooden benches, and aged gray stone tables riven with fissures still remains with me, even in this place. And Bonmot was one with the benches and tables: weathered but comfortable, solid and stolid both. His hands felt like stone hands, his two-fisted greeting like having your skin encased in granite. He had been a farmer's son before he found his calling, and his hulking physique remained intact, along with a startling openness and honesty in his light brown eyes. Nothing in him indicated a propensity for clerical crimes. {The honesty didn't come easily to him. He had earned his reform, and it had transformed him.} His speech rippled out like liquid marble, strong and smooth. He was, in all ways, a comfort.

As for Bonmot and Duncan, they pulled back far enough from the rift that was Duncan's long-ago banned book to find they shared many interests, from explorations of history and religion to a taste for the same music and art. More than once, I would walk into that blissful place carrying sandwiches bought from a sidewalk vendor to find the two men deep in conversation, Bonmot's wrinkled face further creased with laugh lines, his melon-bald head bowed and nodding as Duncan hammered home some obscure point, Duncan's hands heavy with the weight of knowledge being expressed through them. Two veterans of exile, reborn in the pleasure of each other's company. {Which isn't to say we didn't argue—we argued, sometimes viciously. We knew where we stood with one another.}

Early on, Duncan dispensed with politeness and pressed Bonmot about his faith. Duncan's journal relates one such discussion, over an early lunch I wasn't at:

Bonmot irritates me with his faith sometimes, because it seems based on nothing that is not ephemeral. And yet my own faith, misdiagnosed as "obsession," cannot incite such blind obedience or trust.

"What I don't understand," I said to Bonmot today, "is how you went from corrupt Truffidian Antechamber to beatific Blythe Academy Royal."

I supposed I was interested because of my own "scandal," even if it was just the ignominious fate of being out of print. Perhaps I could re-create Bonmot's path.

But Bonmot laughed and dispelled any hope of true explanation by saying, "Better to ask how I became corrupt in the first place. But, really, to answer your question, I had no choice. It just happened. When you are inside a situation like that, you see the world in a way that allows you to rationalize what you are doing. When you lose that perspective, you wake up."

"Are you saying that no trigger, no incident, brought you to the realization?"

"No," Bonmot said. "I literally woke up one day and had the distance to realize that I had gotten onto the wrong path and I had to change."

"Very convenient," I said, which made Bonmot emit one of his rare belly laughs, doubled over for a moment or two.

{Did the disappointed look on my face amuse him? No, he was too kind for that. Was he laughing at something else entirely—some cosmic personal or religious joke? I couldn't tell at the time, but I thought about it often, because it confused me. Now, if I had to guess, I would say that Bonmot was laughing at the memory of his own foolishness, laughing too at the sheer luck of having escaped it.}

"Ah, Duncan," he said, wiping a tear from his cheek. "I admit it is convenient. That I should have been redeemed so easily. Such a pat revelation. But the good news is, the same may happen for you one day, if you have need of it."

"I do need a few revelations," I said.

"Maybe you need God," Bonmot said, though with a lilt to his voice that let me know he might be teasing. "Do you think maybe that's why you've come to me?" His tone made it so. I hadn't come to him for that reason, and yet I was almost open to it in a strange way.

"You have faith in something you cannot see," I said. "I can understand that, but I can't believe in it."

He shrugged. "'There is no speech, there are no words; the song of the heavens is beyond expression.' Not just some*thing*, but some*one*."

"Someone, then," I said. "So tell me—why are we so different? I also believe in something or someone I cannot see. It just happens to live underground." I said it casually, and it came out like a joke, but my breath quickened, and I think that on some level, I really wanted a profound answer. I wanted an answer of some kind, at least—one that would help me understand why I could not stop pursuing *my* mystery.

"There's a difference," Bonmot said, although I've wondered ever since how he could know such a thing, without having seen what I've seen, down there.

"What is the difference?"

"Your unseen world only exists inside your head," he said, in as gentle a way as he could—he even reached out across the table with his huge hands, as if, for a second, he meant to console me. "My unseen world, however, *is* the truth. It is truth that convinces and the divine that gives the gift of true faith."

I've always had a problem with Truth and those who espouse Truth, no matter how much I might love and respect them. Faith, on the other hand, has never been an issue for me. But, I said, because I could: "I thought it might be a question of *scale*. Of the *number* of souls infected with the delusion."

Bonmot wasn't smiling anymore. "No, it's not a matter of scale."

{But *of course* it was a question of scale. That's why I failed. You must infect the minds of hundreds of thousands to get anything done, to make an impact. You can't live out your days presenting your theories to a hundred souls at a meeting of a discredited historical society. It doesn't make a difference.}

"What, then?"

Bonmot said, "I told you already. But you aren't ready to listen. You have to know the truth—have something worth believing in. Over time. Over centuries. Something so important people are willing to form their whole lives around it. To live, and, yes, die for it. And that means it must be much bigger than anything imaginable. 'Silence with regard to You is praise,'" he quoted. "'The sum total of what we know of You is that we do not know You.'"

I leaned closer, across the table. "What if you *could* know, though? Would that diminish it? If you could see what I have seen. I think it might change your mind." {And, toward the end, didn't he change? And didn't I wish then that I'd never tried to see him uncertain.}

"'The angels of darkness, whose names I do not know,'" Bonmot said. "You must take care to resist the false light."

The false light. I shivered. Samuel Tonsure had written that once in his journal. But Tonsure hadn't known about the Machine, about the door. There was, I had become convinced, a *real* door, not just an illusion or a delusion or a mirror. A door. And here Bonmot was talking about not letting in a false light. For a moment, just a moment, I asked myself if he might have some insight into the same truth I sought. {After all, Bonmot often professed to be an expert on Zamilon, a place I had become convinced held, in some time period, the answer to the mystery of the Machine. But the tough old bastard never imparted what he knew, no matter how I tried to pry that knowledge from him. And then it was too late.}

I pulled away, sat up straight on the bench, felt the lacquered rough-smoothness of its grain against my palms. Felt the sun against my face. Felt the breeze. Wondered at how I could get so lost in a conversation that I forgot the world around me.

I started again. I don't know why I tried. Bonmot couldn't convince me and I couldn't convince him. "It *is* that important to me, Bonmot. It's a religion to me."

"I've no doubt of your sincerity," Bonmot said. "I'm just not sure what you want from me."

"To say my theories are not incompatible with your beliefs," I said.

"But your theories are impossible. Nor are they truly relevant to the larger world."

This made me angry for an instant. "Relevant? Relevant. How about this—our future survival in Ambergris. A second Silence. Is that relevant enough for you?"

Bonmot sighed. It was like stone or solid earth sighing. "That's what Truffidianism is all about, my friend. Exactly that—you should read our texts more closely in future. 'The same fate is in store for everyone, pure and impure, righteous and wicked, the good and the sinners.'"

"'No one makes it out,' as Tonsure once wrote," I said. "But what if that fate is coming sooner to all of us than it should?"

Bonmot shrugged. "I don't believe in what you believe."

But I knew that, faced with the reality of it, he would not be so calm or accepting. I knew that the reality of what might one day happen would trump the imaginations of even those who had the capacity to believe in an all-powerful being that had never once manifested in the flesh to Bonmot or, to the best of my knowledge, anyone else.

{I once had a conversation about Faith and Truth with Sybel while waiting for him to relinquish a tincture. "What's the attraction of Truffidianism? Of a *single* Truth, Sybel?" I asked. "It's simple," he replied. "You don't have to *search* anymore. You can just *be*." "So can a tree, Sybel," I said, which was probably the wrong thing to say.}

Conversations like this one usually ended amicably on both sides—for Duncan because he found much about Truffidianism compelling {that may be wish fulfillment on your part, Janice} and for Bonmot because he had been too flawed in his past to judge the disbelief of others too harshly. And still they went back and forth, sometimes comically.

Duncan: "I've seen a kind of a god. It lives underground."
Bonmot: "The Silence was more about sin than mushrooms."
Duncan: "But rats, Bonmot? Why do you have to worship rats?"
Bonmot: "The ways of God are mysterious, Duncan. And, besides, you
        are coming perilously close to blasphemy . . . only some of us
        worship rats. I do not worship rats."
Duncan: "Rats, Bonmot? Rats?"

We talked about serious subjects, yes, but we also told dirty jokes and teased each other mercilessly. I shared wicked stories about the outrageous behavior of my artists, while Bonmot shared tales from his days at the religious academy in Morrow. {My personal favorites concerned the exploits of the head instructor, Cadimon Signal.} Rarely were our conversations revelatory. That's not the point. These were people I loved and came to love. For me, some months, it saved me to be in such company. It took me out of the self-destructive spiral of my own thoughts in a way that even Sybel couldn't. For Bonmot, I think our lunches allowed him to relax in a way he had not relaxed since he entered the priesthood. {And I had fun, too. But, really, Janice, you make it all sound so perfect. It was fun, but it wasn't perfect.}

I should have been envious of the way Duncan and Bonmot talked, but the truth is, it made me happy for them both: the hulking giant and my relatively "dainty" brother. When I approached them with my sandwiches, I often felt guilty for taking them from their collective world of words and ideas, twinned heads turning to look up at me, bewildered—who was this intruder?—followed by recognition and a gracious acceptance into their company. {This is a subtle piece of misdirection that allows you to keep your own emotional intimacy with Bonmot secret, I think. As I had Lacond later, so you had Bonmot, in a way I didn't. *I* was often the intruder, Janice. You two took so easily to one another it was remarkable. But if you don't want to share such details here, I won't make you.}

I still remember how Bonmot's generous drum of a laugh, deep and clear, often drew disapproving looks from the students studying nearby. And yet even then, during what I considered retreats from the exhausting carnality of my "normal" life, Mary Sabon was with us, folded into the pages of the grade book Duncan kept with him. There never really is a finite beginning, is there? No real starting point to anything. Beginnings are continually beginning. Time is just a joke played by watchmakers to turn a profit. Through memory, Time becomes conjoined so that I see Mary as a physical presence at those lunches, leaning against Duncan, trying to get his attention.

She is everywhere now. I am, almost literally, nowhere.

❧ 5 ❧

CAN A CHILDHOOD MEMORY BE misconstrued as starting over? I don't think so. Not if I tell it this way:

The forests outside Stockton remain as real to me as the humid, fungi-laden streets of Ambergris, maybe more so. The dark leaves, the mottled trunks, the deep green shadows reflected on the windows of our house, as of some preternatural presence. All sorts of trees grew in Stockton, but the difference between the staid oaks that lined our street and the misshapen, twisted, coiled welter of tree limbs in the forest seemed profound. It both reassured us and menaced us in our youth: limitless adventure, fear of the unknown.

Our house lay on the forest's edge. The trees stretched on for hundreds of miles, over hills and curving down through valleys. Various were the forest's names, from the Western Forest to the Forest of Owls to Farely's Forest, after the man who had first explored the area. Stockton had been nestled comfortably on its eastern flank for centuries, feeding off of the timber, the sap, the animals that took shelter there.

By the time I had turned thirteen and Duncan was nine, we had made the forest our own. We had colonized our tiny corner of it—cleared paths through it, made shelters from fallen branches, even started a tree house. Dad never enjoyed the outdoors, but sometimes we could persuade him to enter the forest to see our latest building project. Mom had a real fear of the forest—of any dark place, which may have come from growing up in Ambergris. {I never had the sense that growing up in Ambergris had been a trauma for her—she lived there during very calm times—but it is true she never talked about it.}

One day, Duncan decided we should be more ambitious. We had made a crude map of what we knew of the forest, and the great expanse labeled "Unknown" irked him. The forest was one thing that could genuinely be thought of as his, the one area where he did not mimic me, where I followed his lead.

We stood at the end of our most ambitious path. It petered out into bushes and pine needles and the thick trunks of trees, the bark scaly and dark. I breathed in the fresh-stale air, listened to the distant cry of a hawk, and tried to hear the rustlings of mice and rabbits in the underbrush. We were already more than half a mile from our house.

Duncan peered into the forest's depths.

"We need to go farther," he said.

Back then, he was a mischievous sprout, small for his age, with bright green eyes that sometimes seemed too large for his face. And yet he could effortlessly transform into a little thug just by crossing his arms and giving you an exasperated look. Sometimes he'd even sigh melodramatically, as if fed up with the unfairness of the world. His shocking blond hair had begun to turn brown. He liked to wear long green shirts with brown shorts and sandals. He said it served as a kind of camouflage. {Camouflage or comfort—I don't remember.} I used to wear the same thing, although, oddly enough, it scandalized Mom when I did it. Dad couldn't have cared less.

"How *much* farther?" I asked.

I had become increasingly aware that our parents counted on me to keep watch over Duncan. Ever since he'd gotten trapped in a tunnel the year before, we'd all become more conscious of Duncan's reckless curiosity.

"I don't know," he said. "If I did, it wouldn't be much of an adventure. But there's something out there, something we need to find."

His expression was mischievous, yes, but also, somehow, *otherworldly*. {Otherworldly? I was nine. There was nothing "otherworldly" about me. I liked to belch at the dinner table. I liked to blow bubbles and play with metal soldiers and read books about pirates and talking bears.}

"But there's all that bramble," I said. "It will take ages to clear it."

"No," he said, with a sudden sternness I found endearing, and a little ridiculous, coming from such a gangly frame. "No. We need to go out exploring. No more paths. We don't need paths."

"Well . . . ," I said, about to give Duncan my next objection.

But he was already off, tramping through the bramble like some miniature version of the Kalif, determined to claim everything he saw for the Empire. He had always been fast, the kind to set out obstinately for whatever goal beckoned, whatever bright and shiny thing caught his eye. Usually, I had control over him. Usually, he wanted to stay on my good side. But when it came to the forest, our relationship always changed, and he led the way.

So off he dashed into the forest, and I followed, of course. What choice did I have? Not that I hated following him. Sometimes, because of Duncan, I was able to do things I wouldn't have done otherwise. And, such a relief, when I followed him, the weight of being the eldest lifted from me—that was a rare thing, even BDD.

The forest in that place had a concentrated darkness to it because of the thick underbrush and the way the leaves and needles of the trees diluted the sun's impact. To find a patch of light in the gloom was like finding gold, but those patches only accentuated the surrounding darkness. The smell of rot caused by shadow was a healthy smell—I didn't mind it; it meant that all of the forest still worked to fulfill its cycle, even down to the smallest insect tunneling through dead wood. It did not mean what it would come to mean in Ambergris.

Duncan and I fought our way through stickery vines and close-clumped bushes. We felt our way over fallen trees, stopping in places to investigate nests of flame-colored salamanders and stipplings of rust-red mushrooms. The forest fit us snugly; we were neither claustrophobic nor free of its influence. The calls of birds grew strange, shrill, and then died away altogether. {As if we had gone through a door to a different place, a different time, Janice. I could not believe, sometimes, while in the forest, that it existed in the same world as our house.}

At times, the ground rose to an incline and we would be trudging, legs lifting for the next step with a grinding effort. The few clearings became less frequent, and then for a long time we walked through a dusk of dark-green vegetation under a canopy of trees like black marble columns, illuminated only by the stuttering glimmer of a firefly and the repetitive clicking of some insect. A smell like ashes mixed with hay surrounded us. We had both begun to sweat, despite the coolness of the season, and I could hear even undaunted Duncan breathing heavily. We had come a long way, and I wasn't sure I could find the route back to our familiar paths. Yet something about this quest, this foolhardy plunge forward, became hypnotic. A part of me could have kept on going hour after hour, with no end in sight, and been satisfied with that uncertainty. {Then you know how I have felt my entire adult life—except that we're told there is no uncertainty. *No one makes it out,* we're told, from birth until our deathbed, in a thousand spoken

and unspoken ways. It is just a matter of when and where—and if I could discover the truth in the meantime.}

The sting, the burn, of hard exercise, the doubled excitement and fear of the
unknown, kept me going for a long time. But, finally, I reached a point where
fear overcame excitement. {You mean common sense overcame excitement.}

"Duncan!" I said finally, to his back. "We have to stop. We need to find our
way home."

He turned then, his hand on a tree trunk for support—a shadow framed by
a greater gloom—and I'll never forget what he said. He said, "There is no way
to go but forward, Janice. If we go forward, we will find our way back."

It sounded like something Dad would have said, not a nine-year-old kid.

"We're already lost, Duncan. We have to go back."

Duncan shook his head. "I'm not lost. I know where we are. We're not *there*
yet. I know something important lies ahead of us. I know it."

"Duncan," I said, "you're wearing *sandals*. Your feet must be pretty badly cut
up by now."

"No," he said, "I'm fine." {I wasn't fine. The brambles had lacerated my feet,
but I'd decided to block out that discomfort because it was unimportant.}

"There's something ahead of us," he repeated.

"Yes, more forest," I said. "It goes on for hundreds of miles." I thought about
whether I had the strength to carry a kicking, struggling Duncan all the way
back to the house. Probably not.

I looked up, the long trunks of trees reaching toward a kaleidoscope of
wheeling, dimly light-spackled upper branches, amid a welter of leaves. In
those few places where the light was right, I could see, floating, spore and dust
and strands of cobweb. Even the air between the trees was thick with the decay
of life.

"Trust me," Duncan said, and grinned. He headed off again, at such a speed
that I had no choice but to follow him. In the shadows, my brother's thin, wiry
frame resembled more the thick, muscular body of a man. Was there any point
at which I could convince him to stop, or would he stop on his own?

Another half-hour or so—just as I could no longer identify our direction, so
too I had begun to lose my sense of time—and a thick, suffocating panic had
begun to overcome me. We were lost. We would never make it home. {You
should have trusted me. You will need to trust me.}

But Duncan kept walking forward, into the unknown, the thick loam of the
forest floor rising at times to his ankles.

Then, to my relief, the undergrowth thinned, the trees became larger but spread farther apart. Soon, we could walk unimpeded, over a velvety compost of earth covered with moist leaves and pine needles. A smell arose from the ground, a rich smell, almost like coffee or muted mint. I heard again the hawk that had been wheeling overhead earlier, and an owl in the murk above us.

Duncan stopped for me then. He must have known how tired and thirsty I was, because he took my hand in his, and smiled as he said, "I think we are almost there. I think we almost are."

We had reached the heart—or a heart—of the forest. We had reached a place that in a storm would be called the eye. The light that shone through from above did so in shafts as thin as the green fractures of light I can see from the corner of my eye as I type up this account. And in those shafts, the dust motes floated yet remained perfectly still. Now I heard no sound but the pad of our feet against the earth.

Duncan stopped. I was so used to hurrying to keep up that I almost bumped into him.

"There," he said, pointing, a smile creasing his face.

And I gasped, for there, ahead of us, stood a statue.

Made of solid gray stone, fissured, splashed with light, overgrown with an emerald-and-crimson lichen, the idol had a face with large, wide eyes, a tiny nose, and a solemn mouth. The statue could not have been taller than three or four feet.

We walked closer, in an effortless glide, so enraptured by this vision that we forgot the ache in our legs.

Iridescent beetles had woven themselves into the lichen beads of its smile, some flying around the object, heavy bodies drooping below their tiny wings. Other insects had hidden in the fissures of the stone. What looked like a wren's nest decorated part of the top of the head. A whole miniature world had grown up around it. It was clearly the work of one of the native tribes that had fled into the interior when our ancestors had built Stockton and claimed the land around it. This much I knew from school.

"How?" I asked in amazement. "How did you know this was here, Duncan?"

Duncan smiled as he turned to me. "I didn't. I just knew there had to be something, and if we kept looking long enough, we'd find it."

At the time, while we stood there and drank in the odd beauty of the statue, and even as Duncan unerringly found our way home, and even after Mom and Dad, waiting in the backyard as the sun disappeared over the tree line, expressed their anger and disappointment at our "irresponsibility"—especially mine—I never once thought about whether Duncan might be crazy rather than lucky, touched rather than decisive. I just followed him. {Janice, I lied to you, just a little. It's true I didn't know exactly where to find the statue, but I had already heard about it from one of the older students at our school. He'd given me enough information that I had a fairly good idea of where to go. So it wasn't preternatural on my part—it was based on a shred, a scrap, of information, as are all of my wanderings.}

❧

JUST AS DUNCAN PUSHED ME and himself farther than was sane that day, so too Duncan pushed Blythe Academy. It was not only the impending matter of Mary Sabon—it was the clandestine way in which Duncan used the Academy to further his primary lifelong interest: the gray caps and their plans.

I've no inkling about Duncan's ability to teach {thanks a lot}. I never sat in on his classes. I never even asked him much about the teaching. I was too busy. But I do know he discovered that he enjoyed "drawing back the veil of incomprehension" as he once put it {jokingly}. The act of lecturing exercised intellectual muscles long dormant, and also exorcised the demons of self-censorship by letting Duncan speak, his words no longer filtered through his fear of the reading public. {Not to worry—I never had a real reading public, or I'd have continued to find publication somewhere. But, yes, I was fearful that I might one day develop one. Just imagine—someone actually reading those thick slabs of paper I spent years putting together.} He could entertain and educate while introducing his charges to elements of the mysterious he hoped might one day blossom into a questioning nature and a thirst for knowledge.

But was it all innocent education? Was there, perhaps, something else beneath it?

An examination of his lesson plans reveals a pattern not unlike the pattern formed by the poly-glut documents, maps, illustrations, and portraits that had once lined Duncan's room at the Institute of Religiosity. {I never told you, but I received word only a year ago that, at Cadimon Signal's request, the entire display had been lovingly preserved under glass, framed, and spirited away to some dark, vile basement in Zamilon for a prolonged period of zealot-driven dissection. What they hope to find amongst my droppings, I don't know, but the thought of their clammy hands and ratty eyes pawing through my former wall adornments is a bit much.}

While Duncan could not, and would not, divulge the essence of his underground journeys, he taught a stunningly diverse series of social, economic, religious, cultural, psychological, geographic, and confessional texts intended to re-create a complete context for the formation of the early Truffidian Church. The course centered around *The Journal of Samuel Tonsure*—ostensibly to give them a feel for Truffidian twaffle, pamp, and circumglance—and included a number of supporting elements, such as Truffidian folklore, study of the mushroom dwellers, and scrutiny of transcripts of conversations between Truffidian priests around the time of Tonsure's adventures.

I have, in this trunk of Duncan's papers that I have half dragged, half had dragged here, some of his lesson plans. For example:

SPRING SEMESTER

PRIMARY TEXTS

· *Cinsorium*: teacher's copy; to be loaned, three days each student
· *The Journal of Samuel Tonsure* by Samuel Tonsure
· *Red Martigan: A Life* by Sarah Carsine
· *The Relationship Between the Native Tribes of Stockton & the Gray Caps* by Jonathan Shriek: thesis paper; copies to be distributed
· *The Refraction of Light in a Prison* by the Imprisoned Truffidian Monks
· *Zamilon for Beginners* by Cadimon Signal: in preparation for next semester

AREAS OF STUDY

· *Samuel Tonsure's Journal*: The Apparently Impossible Spatial Perspective Expressed in the Sections on the Underground. {I've since come to understand that the problem lies with the limitations of human senses, not Tonsure's account.}
· *Evidence of the Gray Caps in Morrow*: A Selection of Texts, including a cavalryman's diary from the period of the Silence. {Alas, this now appears to have been at worst a hoax, at best bad research.}
· *An Examination of Fungi Found on Religious Structures*: Field trip.
· *Guest Lecture by James Lacond* {Oddly, Lacond and I did not converse much during that first face-to-face meeting. He was polite but not inquisitive, gave his lecture on his own theories about the gray caps, and left. This was the first and only time Bonmot met Lacond. They circled

each other warily, looking at each other as if two creatures from vastly different worlds. A muttered pleasantry or two, and they set off in opposite directions, literally and figuratively, Bonmot not staying for the lecture. Yet, how similar they were in many ways.}

Alas, Duncan either did not preserve his accompanying private notes or did not include them with these plans. However, after a careful review of all of the lesson plans—most too tedious to replicate here—I believe Duncan had more on his mind than teaching students. I believe he sought independent verification of his own findings. He thought that, subjected to the same stimuli, his students—maybe only one or two, but that would be enough—would one day vindicate him of historical heresy. How ironic, then, that his efforts would instead lead one of his students to *convict* him of historical heresy.

{Janice, enough! You had ample opportunity to *ask* me about any and all of this, and would have received a more honest answer than the one generated by your suppositions. We may be siblings, but you cannot see into or through my mind. You have gotten it half-right—which means you have gotten it all wrong. I did seek to educate my students first and foremost. This did require a varied and wide approach, primarily because few existing texts interwove the complexity of historical issues with a thorough cross-disciplinary approach. Why do you think I had to create that "document" on my wall back at the Institute in the first place? So I taught them, and taught them well. The subtext of my teaching—yes, there was a subtext, I admit it—had nothing to do with hoping my students would replicate my work. The only true way any of them could replicate my work would be to follow me underground, and, as you well know, I made that mistake only once.

{No. What you fail to see are the truly diabolical intentions behind my approach. You underestimate me. Validation? Hardly. *Three hundred* students could validate my findings and still not a soul would believe them, or me. No, my plan concerned *additional* research. With plucking the half-formed thoughts like plums. With growing another thirty or forty brains and limbs each semester, to become this multi-spined creature that might, in its flailing, lurching way, accomplish more than a single, if singular, scholar, ever could. Each text I made them read, every essay question answered, every research paper written, corresponded to a section of the grid in the incomplete map of my knowledge. *They* taught *me* in many cases. They didn't have the scars I had, or the foreknowledge; they were unblinkered, unfettered by my peculiar brand of orthodoxy. I used to watch them, heads bowed, heavy with knowledge, working on the latest test, each swirling loop of letter from their pens on paper signifying a kind of progress—this permutation, that permutation, forever tried, discarded, yielding nothing, and yet valuable for that fact alone. Discount *this*, and you can begin testing *that*. Sabon was part of it at first, certainly—she bought into it, and may even have understood what I was doing.

{When one puzzle piece—and a semester of thirty students might fill in a single puzzle piece, at best—had been locked into position, we would move on to the next. A careful observer might have noticed that my curriculum began to resemble cheese cloth. Much of it was useless, much of it redundant, much of it insanely boring and obscured by lazy or talentless students. But they did receive a relatively full education from me. And keep in mind that I was not their only teacher.

{In time, the game did outgrow its original boundaries. At every opportunity, I would murmur in the ears of my fellow instructors, like an echo of their own desires, hints of scholarship and glory if they only turned their attention to this or that ignored corner of history. "I wonder if anyone has ever compared the version of Nysman's report on the Silence stored at Nicea with the version stored at Zamilon. I am told they diverge in ways that speak to issues of authenticity in Samuel Tonsure's journal." Casually, off-the-cuff, as if it fell outside my area of expertise, but should be pursued by someone, with great rewards for any enterprising scholar. In all of this, Bonmot was an interesting factor. He guessed what I was up to rather early on, I think, but never did anything to stop me. Raised an eyebrow, gave me a penetrating stare, but that was it.

{And so, by the fourth year of my employment at Blythe Academy, I had built my own machine, fully as terrible and far-reaching as the Machine I had encountered underground. You understand now, I hope? I had managed to subvert and divert the resources of an entire institution of higher learning to the contemplation of a single question with many branches. The diagram I drew to exemplify this question was based on Tonsure's account and deliberately resembled the gray caps' most recurrent symbol, which had been drawn on walls, on cobblestones, but never explicated.

{Intentionally incomprehensible to outsiders, the diagram helped me see the relationships between various people and concepts in a new way. Manzikert I had triggered the Silence, I felt certain, with his actions in founding Ambergris. Samuel Tonsure had somehow catalogued and explained the gray caps during his captivity underground. Aquelus, a later ruler of Ambergris, had suffered

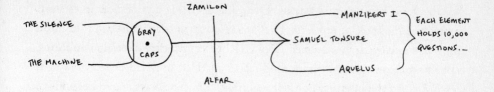

Manzikert's same fate, but survived to return aboveground. As Zamilon held some answer, so too did Alfar, the ruined tower to which Aquelus' wife had retired prior to the Silence, thus ensuring her survival. And then there were the Silence and the Machine. How did they connect? And how did it all tie back in to the gray caps? These were the perhaps unanswerable questions I struggled with, and the structure through which I examined them.

{Although this is perhaps the least of what I unearthed during that time, it still represents an impressive experiment in collective unconsciousness, in beehive mentality. Did more than a few of those brains set diligently upon the course plotted for them ever suffer a tremor, a tickle of an inkling of my manipulation? I doubt it. I'm too proud of my work, perhaps, but I did little harm and much good. Several instructors published papers in prominent journals without ever knowing I had color-coded their innocent discoveries into a vast pattern of conspiracy and misdirection. They stood in their sunlit lecture halls turning their ideas over and over in their hands—brightly colored baubles for their students to applaud, confident they had solved a complete puzzle rather than assembled a single piece. The students, meanwhile, became specialists sensitive to the rhythms of synergy, analysis, and synthesis. Tuning forks for knowledge, they vibrated prettily, their shiny surfaces one by one catching the light. I admit, I derived great satisfaction from all of this. To have such a measure of control made me nearly ecstatic at times, fool that I was. And still, I wasn't gathering enough knowledge fast enough. I felt frustrated, twice-removed from where I needed to be: underground. Ironic that, aboveground, I felt much as James Lacond once described Tonsure underground:

Most of the time [Tonsure] walks in the darkest night. Now and again, a wavering finger of light flutters across the darkness, teasing him with the outline of a path. Hopeful, he runs toward it, only to find himself in another maze. The hope that night must give way to day allows him to continue, and he tries to guess where a more permanent light might break through—a crack, a crevice, a hole—but the end of night never comes.}

Early on, I met these students, Duncan's unwitting accomplices in esoteric, possibly meaningless, research. They made no particular impression on me: a formless row of fresh-scrubbed faces attached to identical dark blue uniforms. The eyes that populated those ruddy faces sparkled or flared or reflected light according to the intensity of their ambition. Some students stared defiantly at you. Some let you stare *through* them. Still others looked away, or down at their feet—every foot hidden by proper white socks, sheathed in black, brightly polished shoes. They smelled like soap and sweat. Their voices cracked and buzzed and sang out with equal innocence and brashness. In their uniformed rows, I could not tell the poor from the rich, the smart from the stupid. Thus did Blythe Academy serve as an equalizer of souls.

Never once did I think to challenge that semblance of equality, to search for that one variant, that one mimic cleverly made up to resemble the others, but actually of a different species altogether. {She was just another student in so many ways. You shouldn't think that she was other, or different. I was the mimic, if anyone was. I threw off the balance in that place.}

❧❦❧

MARY'S PRESENCE, WHEN I LOOK back, first resonated as a faint music vibrating through the strings of my golden metaphor: a resonance neither sinister nor angelic. In that respect, she reminds me of a character in a novel by Sirin. She exists on the edges of the pages, in the spaces between the words, her name unwritten except in riddles: a woman's green-and-gold scarf on Duncan's apartment desk, sudden honeysuckle in a glass in his school office, a puzzling hint of cologne during lunch. A half-dozen passive yet sensual details a jealous wife might hoard—or that a sibling might half-remember with amusement, but later revisit harshly.

Duncan never mentioned Mary during that time. {She was my student, for Truff's sake! Why would I mention her? You make this all sound so tawdry yet ethereal. Is it possible she just escaped your myopic powers of observation? Is it possible you were so continually drugged and drunk that you noticed no one? You should strike all of this from the record. There's no reason for it and no one cares. I don't even care anymore, except the now-dulled sting that you tried to undermine my relationships rather than support them.} Curiously, though, Duncan's postcards began to contain more personal information than our lunchtime conversations, possibly because of Bonmot's presence.

Sometimes the postcards consisted of odd lines that told me he had re-opened his investigations well beyond Blythe Academy:

Even the flies have eyes, Janice. Eyes for them. There is no corner of this city they cannot see in some form. But it's too much information. They cannot review it all at once. I imagine them down there, in the fungal light, review-ing intelligence gathered a decade ago—awash in information, none of it useful to them because it overwhelms them. And yet—why? Why attempt to gather it?

If Dad had actually studied Tonsure's journal, I wonder if he would have found what I found. Even more important—what would he have done with the knowledge?

Sometimes they gather around my door. Sometimes they burrow up from below. When they get in—which isn't often; I've learned some of their tricks—they watch me. Observe. It is more unnerving than if they were to hurt me.

Either he, in a sense, hoped to distance himself from such knowledge by physically sending it away from him on postcards or, intensely involved in his studies, cast off these postcards in the fever of scholarship, like heat lightning. Anyone other than his sister would have thought these notes the ramblings of a madman. {Actually, Bonmot and I discussed "personal information," as you call it, quite often, and he never thought I was mad. I admit to writing most of the postcards during bouts of considerable pain caused by my diseases. Sometimes they reflected my research. Sometimes they simply reflected my agony. Even the starfish had been unable to remove the source of the infection. I was changing, and I was changing my mind to come to terms with that fact.} More alarmingly, Duncan changed his living quarters with insane frequency, sending dozens of change-of-address postcards to the {newly renamed but still comfortingly inept} Voss Bender Memorial Post Office before finally giving up and listing the Academy as his mailing address. He refused to live at the Acad-emy, although he would sleep in a guest room on nights when he worked late. Even after he met Sabon, Duncan moved from apartment to apartment. He never signed a lease of more than six months. He never took a ground floor apartment. He always moved up—from the second floor, to the third, to the fourth, as if fleeing some implacable force that came up through the ground. {Yes—bad plumbing. Not to mention gray caps.}

Clearly he was hiding from something, but why should his plight affect me? After all, he had been stumbling into danger even BDD. Yes, I had written him the note about golden threads, the way our lives touch each other, but do you know how hard it is to keep that in mind from day to day? You'd have to be a priest or a martyr. So I let him go his separate way, confident that, like the time we had gotten lost in the forest, he would find his way out again.

Besides, I was distracted. By then, I had ascended to the very height of my powers. I led a council of gallery owners. I wrote withering and self-important reviews for *Art of the Southern Cities*. I had lunch with Important People like Sirin and Henry Hoegbotton at such upscale restaurants as The Drunken Boat.

For two years running, my stable of artists had received more critical attention and created more sales than the rest of the city's galleries combined. A word from me could now cripple an artist or redeem him. Utterance of such words became almost sexual, each syllable an arching of the back, a shudder of pleasure. Even when Martin Lake moved his best paintings to his own gallery, leaving me only his dregs, I told Sybel not to worry, for surely a thousand Lakes waited to replace him.

"Are you sure?" he asked me. "I expected the world to leave Lake behind, which hasn't happened. That we could deal with. But his leaving *you* behind could cause you damage."

I dismissed his concerns with a wave of my hand. "There are more where he came from."

I should have taken heed of his astonished look. I had yet to realize that my power had limits—that it could recede like the River Moth during drought.

The sheer opulence of my life disguised the truth from me. Not content with attending parties, I had begun to host parties. I entertained like one of Trillian's Banker-Warriors from the old days, my parties soon so legendary that some guests were afraid to attend. Legendary not just for the food or music or orgies, but how all three elements could be artfully combined in new and inventive ways. Outside of the incessant, unceasing rumors that they were "squid clubs" {a euphemism for the more sadomasochistic sex parlors, so named for the old squid-hunter habit of tying up their catch and delivering it alive to the buyer}, nothing could diminish the allure of my parties.

Sybel was a great help in this arena—he took to party planning as if he had found his true calling. Under his artful administration, we staged many delightful debacles of alcohol and drugs. Each weekend, we would move to some new, more exotic, location—the priests of the Religious Quarter, in their greed, would rent to me their very cathedrals. Or Sybel would hire "party consultants" to scout the burnt-out Bureaucratic Quarter for suitable locations. Then, to the surprise of the homeless and the criminal element, some blackened horror of a building—say, the former Ministry of Foreign Affairs—would, well after midnight, erupt with light and mirth and the loud confusion of alcohol-aided conversations. The artists so *elsewhere* that they stood in corners talking to statues, coat racks, and desks. Morning revealed as grainy light touching pale bodies that in turn touched each other casually amongst the random abandoned divans and couches and makeshift beds crusted with cake and cum.

I remember waking up once, in the middle of the night, my cold sweat moistening the bedsheets, my skin crawling with a nameless dread. Sybel sat in a chair beside my bed, snoring.

I woke him up in a complete panic, chest tight, lungs heavy. I couldn't bear to be alone with my thoughts. "How long can we keep this up? How long can we keep going like this?"

Poor, beautiful, sly Sybel rubbed his eyes, looked up at me, smiled a sleepy smile, and said, "As long as you tell me to."

I hit him in the shoulder. The smile never left his face. "What does that mean?" I asked.

Sybel's gaze sharpened and he sat up in the chair. "Forever, Janice. Or close enough. This is just the beginning."

Poor stupid me. I believed him.

❧❧

THIS IS JUST THE BEGINNING. And so it was. But the beginning of what? The beginning of the end, really. The one time Janice Shriek's life significantly impacted Duncan Shriek's life. I became addicted to hallucinogenic mushrooms. Little purple mushrooms with red-tinged gills. So tiny. So cute. They magnified the minute and humbled the magnificent, and I couldn't get enough of them. I'd have a meeting with Sirin while on them and watch as his head became bigger and bigger, eclipsing his body. I would eat one while in the middle of another all-night drunken escapade and suddenly the noise and confusion around me would: stop. I would see the glittering detail of a streetlamp light shining off of the water in the gutter, and that sudden moment would become as large as the world. A comfort, really. A solace. {A plague. A way for you to escape the world.}

Sybel called them Tonsure's Folly, and I can't really complain, because I asked him to get them for me. And I can't even blame the mushrooms for everything that happened next. I was wandering further and further from the golden threads of my note to Duncan. I was becoming more and more unhappy, even though I was filling myself with so many substances and preying off of enough new people, new experiences, that my distress was for the longest time just an echo of an ache in my belly. {No, you can't blame the mushrooms. But those mushrooms, over time, make the user more and more depressed. And you were already in a fragile state. I'm afraid I'd lost the thread of your life, caught up in my own problems, or I would have insisted that Sybel intervene.}

The parties I still remember with fondness, although the only one I've really come close to describing happened ages afterward—the Martin Lake party I was asked to help organize recently. The first party I'd been to for years, and haunted by the ghosts of other, grander parties. These ghosts lingered long enough to laugh at the staid properness of Janice Shriek in her old {c}age. No guests rolling naked over the carpet. No fruit served from the delicious concavities of the lithe bodies of young men and women. Not even the simple pleasures to be found in bowls of mushroom drugs. Just guests, music, light dancing, and lighter punch, not even spiked. Oh, what humiliation!

⊰❧⊱

"DO YOU THINK SHE CAN see us from in there?"

"Naw—she's busy."

"She's deep in thought, she is—but what could she be thinking *about,* do you think?"

"About the next word she puts her hard finger to."

Distractions abound. Sometimes they become part of the story. Anyway:

The careful reader will remember that when I last left off the story of my final confrontation with Mary Sabon and her necklace of flesh—which, if you will remember, consisted, before the metaphor came to life and lurched forward, of two dozen of those social climbers who had become convinced she was the best historian since my brother—I was walking down the marble stairs in their direction.

I descended to the foot of the stairs. The marble shone like glass; my face and those of the others reflected back at me. The assembled guests slowly fell apart into their separate bead selves. Blank-eyed beads wink-winking at me as they formed a corridor to Sabon. Smelling of too little or too much perfume. Shedding light by embracing shadows. A series of stick-figures in a comedy play.

"What can she be typing so furiously?"

"How long's she been in there?"

"At least five days. I bring her food and drink. I take it out again. She's enough paper in there to last another week."

"Do *they* mind?"

"What? *They?* Haven't seen them here for weeks. They'll not be around again."

Mary Sabon. We are approaching Sabon now. Or I am, now that I've made it down the marble staircase. I suppose I must conjure her into existence before I can banish her. . . . Red hair. Massive long locks of red hair, forest-thick and as uncivilized. Emerald eyes—or, perhaps, paste pretending to be jewel. A figure that. A voice which. A smile of.

I'm afraid I cannot do her the justice Duncan did in his journal entries, so I will stand aside to let him speak, even if he does stutter, enraptured by a schoolgirl-smell, white-socks fantasy with as much reality to it as a paper chandelier.

Mary Sabon. Sabon, Mary. Sabon. Mary. Mary. Mary Sabon. Sabon. Sabon. Sabon. The name burns like a flame in my head like her hair burns like her name burns like a flame in my head. She burns in my head. She burns in my head. I am delirious with her. I am sick with her. Blessed infection. I think of nothing but her. Walking home today, I could sense that the trees lining the boulevard contained her. I see her features when I stare down at the pavement upon which I tread. She is half-formed in the air. The faint smell of Stockton pine needles and incense. As of her. As of an echo of her. Her form a flame in the world that burns through everything, and there is nothing in the world but her—the world revealed as paper that burns away at the first hint of her. Above and below, a flame in my head. I cannot get her out. I am not sure I want to get her out. Rather banish myself from myself than to banish her from me.

❦

"DOES SHE TIP WELL?"

"Well enough. I don't mind her. She's no trouble. Not like you lot."

"That's a rough thing to say."

They are beginning to annoy me. I cannot keep them out of the text.

Everything around me is going into the text—every dust mote, every scuff upon the floor, the unevenness of this desk, the clouded quality of the windows. I cannot keep it out right now.

Flame or not, at my party, Mary Sabon wore dark green. She almost always wore dark green. She might as well have been a shrub or a tree or a tree trunk.

Ignoring my presence—something she would have done at her peril in the old days—she said, "Duncan Shriek? Why, Duncan is not a human being at all, but composed entirely of digressions and transgressions. Assuming he is still alive, that is."

As she said this, she turned and looked right at me.

I stared at her for a moment. I let her receive the venom in my eyes. Then I walked up to her and slapped her hard across the face. The impact shone as red as her hair, as flushed as the gasp from the necklace of flesh. It lit up her face in a way that made her look honest again. It spread across her cheek, down her neck, swirled between the tops of her breasts, and disappeared beneath her gown.

If the world is a just place, that mark will never leave her skin, but remain as a pulsing reminder that, at some point in the past, she hurt someone so badly that she hurt herself as well.

But I was not done. Not by half. I had just begun.

What did I do? You'll find out soon enough. Jump pages. Jump time. Skip through the rest as if it were a park pathway on a Sunday afternoon, and you eager to feed the ducks at the far end, in Voss Bender Memorial Square. But I haven't written the path yet, and you'd get lost without it—and, paper cuts aside, I'll find ways to make you wait. Waiting is good. I've been waiting for over five days now. I know something about waiting. And afterwords.

"I say again: What's she typing in there? Clack-clack-clack—it's disturbing my peace of mind."

"Wasn't her brother the writer?"

"Obviously not the only one in the family."

"You must be new to this conversation."

"What's she writing, do you think?"

"The story of your life, Steen. A history of the Cappans. How should I know?"

"Whatever it is, it must be important. To her."

Pickled eyes in pickled light. A glimpse of cheddar-wedge nose.

"Funny. It's like an echo. It falls away when we stop talking."

. . .

"See. No typing. Do you think she's . . . ?"

She's what? Typing your inane speech, perhaps? Why not? You've become my companions after a fashion. Although I've never talked to them, I've shared this place with them for days now. I ought to feel grateful for their interest. I ought to get out of this dank back room and go over and suggest a game of darts.

"Naw—she's not typing us. Hasn't got anything to do with us."

I think I'll go for a walk. I'm going to go for a walk. My hands are cramping. My stomach growls. The clock on the wall tells me I've been here much longer than I thought.

Even ghosts can take a walk, so why not me?

❧ 6 ❧

I WAS BEGINNING TO SOUND like a character in a book. I had to escape the relentless pressure of the words. I had to get away. From the typewriter keys. From my wrinkled hands, which prove my brain lies to me about my age. From the faces staring through the green crack where the corridors synchronize into a fracture of seeing. From the feeling that I had begun to *parrot* on these pages, blandly resuscitating facts. {Janice, once you start a project like this, it's impossible to tell what is truly important or who will find what the most interesting, so it's no use second-guessing your decisions, no matter how I may have protested against some of them.}

I went for a hobbling walk, leaning heavily on my cane every step of the way. But when you've lived in a place this long, no walk can occur solely in the present. Every street, every building, appears to you encrusted with memories, with perspectives that betray your age, your cynicism, your sentimentality, or your lack of feeling where you *should* feel something. Here, the site of a quick fuck, a fumbling moment of ecstasy. {"Lover's tryst," Janice, is, I believe, the preferred term; once again your style slips from Duncanisms to gutterisms.} There, a farewell to a departing friend. A fabled lunch with an important artist. The dust-smudged window of a rival gallery, still floundering along while you are forever out of business. A community square, where once you held an outdoor party, strung with paper lanterns. And if this were not enough—not relentless enough, not humbling enough—that unspeakable vision overlaying all of it, had you only the glasses to see: the mark of the gray caps on the city in a thousand secret signs and symbols.

It is not an easy thing for me to walk through Ambergris these days, but there is also comfort: why, she said, her heart breaking a little, there are so many friends to visit, even if they are all in the ground.

But at first I just hobbled down Albumuth Boulevard in the late afternoon light, letting my path be decided by the gaps between supplicants and pilgrims. Happy that everything appeared normal, that evidence of the Shift was hidden, or so minute that I didn't notice it. {Or maybe you didn't notice it because you had become so used to it.}

I took deep breaths, to catch all the smells in this most beautiful and cruel of all cities: passionflower and incense, lemon trees and horse flop, rotting meat and coffee grounds. For a few minutes I tried to pretend to be a tourist, a passerby, an incidental part of the city. It didn't work. How could it? I am Janice Shriek.

⤞⬥⬤⬥⬠

MY LEG WAS ALREADY BEGINNING to ache, but I thought I might feel more optimistic if I headed for the site of my greatest triumphs. I hadn't visited it in ages, so I went despite the discomfort. After a good half hour, I finally stood in front of what had once been the Gallery of Hidden Fascinations. A flower shop and a bakery stood to either side, but the part of the building that had housed the gallery lay empty as if cursed. The shadow where the hand-painted sign had once hung had been branded into the wall by years of hard weather. Beyond the cracked windows lay dust, moldy frames, and darkness. No paintings. No paint not peeling. Just seasons and seasons of neglect. The smell of stale bread, rotting wood. Layers of purple fungus had taken root in the closest wall. Passersby hardly spared the place a second glance. It should have been a monument, or at least a memorial. It had housed dozens of famous paintings and painters. Conversations that shaped all aspects of the art world had taken place there. Much of the art mentioned in the Hoegbotton tourist guides, the descriptions of the New Art movement, had started with my gallery. *I* had started there. Everything I have been since came from my gallery. This dump. This husk of broken timbers. Even my memories of it—saturated in the marinade of all five senses and as sharp as yesterday—could not bring it to sudden life. I might as well have never left the typewriter. I was still trapped in an afterword.

I headed into the Religious Quarter, immediately calmed by the sound of bells—bells from steeples and cathedrals, from alcoves and altars, which I could never quite find the source of, which lingered at the edge of hearing.

I disturbed a boy in the act of lighting a candle in the recess that marked the northernmost corner of the Church of the Seven-Edged Star. He looked up at

me, his face whiter even than his white robes against the tousle of black hair, his
eyes a glistening green, his mouth forming a half-conscious "O," the long
match held with divine grace in his slightly upturned right hand. The white of
his revealed wrist sent a shudder through me, but he smiled and the image of
grace returned.

He was right to light the candle, for the Quarter at that hour had not only
distant bells but distant light, the dusk so strong it might as well have been a
smell, a musk, that slid over the unprotected surfaces of cobblestones, windows,
and walls, leaving behind the chaos of rippling illuminations that remain in the
Quarter after dark. Priests shuffled past, murmuring mouths and bare feet.
Truffidians, Manziists, Menites, Cultists? Doubtless Duncan the historian
would have known. No matter how Ambergris Shifted, we could count on the
rituals of the Quarter remaining the same.

Moving on, I walked to the edge of the Religious Quarter—by now an act
of will, as my leg really hurt—past the stern-looking Truffidian Cathedral, and
by way of a flurry of alleys soon found myself in front of Blythe Academy. The
dark covered the Academy comfortably, content to linger at the outskirts of
lamps and torches.

Even from the street I could see directly into the courtyard, and beyond the
courtyard into the student apartments, here and there a window illumined with
golden light. In the foreground, the pale willow trees rustled in the breeze. {As
pale willow trees are wont to do.} The stone benches and tables were solid, dark,
strangely comforting masses. A monk strode across the courtyard. Another followed, cowl hiding his face. The sweet, pungent scent of honeysuckle wound itself around me.

I do not know how long I stood there, remembering those long-ago conversations, but as I did, an unbearable sadness came over me. Nothing I can type on
these pages can convey—truly—what I felt as I looked into the darkened courtyard where Duncan, Bonmot, and I had sat and talked. And, if I am truthful,
that place I stood in front of, which meant so much to me, no longer had any
more to do with me than the Borges Bookstore. The moment, the spirit, had
passed out of it and it was just a place once more. Duncan no longer taught
there. Bonmot no longer sat behind the desk in his office, listening to the imagined miseries of yet another homesick student. Duncan had disappeared. Bonmot had died more than twelve years ago.

What strange creatures we are, I thought as I stood there. We live, we love,
we die with such random joy and grief, excitement and boredom, each mind as

individual as a fingerprint, and just as enigmatic. We make up stories to understand ourselves and tell ourselves that they are true, when in fact they only represent an individual impression of one individual fingerprint, no matter how universal we attempt to make them.

I stood there, mourning the death of that place, even though it had not really died, even though it had since spawned a thousand stories to join the millions of stories that comprised the city, and then I walked back here, to the typewriter, to continue my epic, my afterword, so consumed by what? By emotion. That my hands are shaking. They are shaking right now. What shall stop them? Perhaps a dose of the dead past.

⊰⊱

AT BONMOT'S FUNERAL, SOME TWELVE years ago, men and women who would not have dared visit him while he was alive circled around the polished oak coffin like impatient iridescent flies. The day held a hint of rain in the gravel sky, the air moist and cool. The smell of mold was everywhere.

Outside the Truffidian Cathedral, Martin Lake dourly limped about on his polished cane, stopping to mutter grim Lakeisms to friends such as Merrimount and Raffe, all of whom avoided me as if I embodied a disease they might one day become. That's how far I had fallen. I limped like Lake by then. I had a cane like him. But I was not enough like him, especially now that he had passed from "successful" to that ethereal realm where one's fame will always outlive the fading mortal body.

The Morrow ambassador to the House of Hoegbotton—newly renamed to reflect the aftermath of war—presented a dapper sight in slick black tuxedo and tails, at least until he managed to slide in a patch of mud created by overzealous grave diggers and groundskeepers. A general from the Kalif's army, a supposed friend of Bonmot's in his youth, looked out of place in turban and gold-and-red glittery uniform, his presence barely tolerated by a city that so frequently had been bombarded by his masters.

Dozens of priests arrived from the Religious Quarter, from orders as diverse as the Cult of the Seven-Edged Star and Manziism. They all wore variations of black-on-white and somber stares. They all had guards with them. Ever since the War of the Houses, no one trusted anyone else. Hoegbotton's men were out in force as well, armed with guns and with knives. Some of them stood in motored vehicles, in well-heeled clumps, staring.

Business leaders also arrived to pay their bemused respects. The newly ascendant Andrew Hoegbotton, a weaselly stick figure of a man with large, liquid eyes, shared uneasy space with Lionel Frankwrithe, a smug middle-aged man who kept snapping out his pocket watch in sudden motions that kept wretched Andrew flinching. Truces between House F&L and House H&S rarely lasted very long anymore.

At the edges, surrounding these dim luminaries, stood beggars, prostitutes, and the working poor, all of whom Bonmot had helped at some period in his life, whether as Antechamber or as the Royal of Blythe Academy. As *The Ambergris Daily Broadsheet* noted:

> Every element of Ambergrisian society turned out yesterday to grieve the death of a man most had abandoned in his exile and which, happy coincidence, they now remembered as the hour of heartfelt high-profile memorial speeches grew near. {Janice, you know I wrote this.}

The procession from the cathedral to Bonmot's final resting place was silent. The flags of the Religious Quarter lay limp against the breezeless sky. As we walked, our procession grew larger and more diverse. More and more people left their homes or temples to join us. I remember thinking that this wasn't just a funeral for Bonmot—it was a funeral for the city. So much uncertainty faced us now. We'd been shaken out of our preconceptions by the War and its aftermath. We'd been roused from our blindness—or so we hoped.

The procession ended with an interminable parade into and through Trillian's cemetery. They say Trillian populated the cemetery with the victims of his bloody merchant wars. But within its walls, I have always felt a theme of renewal and peace rather than death. Its massive oak trees, its giant, curling green ferns, its elegant stone houses for the departed—they all conspired to make the visitor think of woodland walks and primordial forests rather than decay. That day, the graveyard seemed more alive than the insensate, gangrenous city surrounding it.

The trio of violinists abruptly stopped playing. The coffin was lowered into its final resting place, a headstone to be added later. The grave diggers who would fill in the dirt stood leaning on their shovels next to the mound of earth, their stares flat and steady. In front of them, the current Antechamber began to give the final speech of the afternoon, a few hollow words about his predecessor, couched in platitudes and numbing repetition.

"Give back to this earth this good man, O Lord," he said, much to the grumbling dismay of several Manziists present, who missed their traditional rat-festooned funeral ceremony. "Give back to this good man the earth, O Lord," he said again, like a man who, having missed his memorized mark, has to start over in the correct order. "And let you, O Lord, serve as a light to him, for we are imperfect vessels and we platitude simile extended metaphor with barely any pauses followed by more repetition. Period. Comma. Stop. Start. Here I go again about God and the dirt and wait: another platitude, quote from the Truffidian Bible everyone's heard a thousand times before, and even though I once actually knew Bonmot when I was a junior priest, not a single personal anecdote about the man because the scandal of his long-ago departure as Antechamber might somehow still cling to me like a fetid stench. Amen."

While they buried our friend, I watched a glossy emerald beetle, carapace age-pocked and mossy, fend off an attack by a dozen fuzzy ants, their red thorax glands releasing tiny jets of bubbly white poison. This drama took place in a leafy alcove while storks flew against the rapidly darkening sky and moth wings muttered on mottled tree trunks, the world in constant rebellious motion against the stark silence within the coffin.

Duncan came, of course, his face ever more deeply lined with the weight of secret knowledge {or maybe I had just stayed out too late the night before}, his gaze settling upon the assembled rabble in search of one perfect, elusive face . . . but Mary did not come. Parties, lecture series, concerts, readings, she attended, even during wartime. Funerals, however, never made Mary's agenda. She did not like funerals. People, for her, did not die, and places never became disenfranchised from those moments that made them important. Both became entombed in her books and, until placed there, never failed to behave as less than caricature or puppetry.

"Duncan," I said. "She's not coming. She never was going to come. Not for you. Not for Bonmot." She would be writing, or doing something equally destructive to Duncan's {lack of a} career.

He would not answer me. He would not look at me. As the Antechamber tossed a clot of earth on Bonmot's coffin, Duncan stared at it, too downcast at Sabon's absence to utter a word.

Time had made no difference. Whether minutes after the dissolution of their relationship or years after, Duncan was the same. Even when increasingly attacked and hounded by the words like knives from her various books, he allowed her to control his heart.

As we left the funeral, Duncan was still searching the crowd for any sign of Mary.

{Janice, I accepted your dressing down, which you conveniently dilute and misremember, because I knew you hurt from Bonmot's death as much as I did. But please do not mistake my silence for agreement with your reading of my thoughts. If I surveyed the crowd, it wasn't to search for Mary. I knew she wasn't coming. My gaze was blind—I saw nothing, but always looked inward to my memories of Bonmot. While the procession lurched toward the cemetery, while the Antechamber gave his depressing speech, even while you lashed out at me, I was nowhere near that place. I was where you should have been—in the courtyard, sitting on a bench beside Bonmot and talking. Besides you, our mother, and Lacond, Bonmot was one of the only people keeping me above-ground. I never really bought into religion, but I believed in Bonmot, and because he had faith, I had faith through him. And I was heartbroken for missed opportunities, because it had been so many years since I'd had a personal conversation with him.

{You congratulate yourself on being sensitive to my thoughts, but you barely knew them at times. It stung that you saw what no one else could—that the fungus had continued to colonize my skin, that even as I stood there and watched them pour dirt over Bonmot's coffin my body fought a thousand battles more vigorous than those between beetle and ants—and yet you could not understand why I might be distracted. That my mind was consumed by another attempt to stand firm against the invasion of my own body on the most basic levels, like pissing black blood or sweating out green liquid fungus.}

DUNCAN AND MARY. FOR A time, long before that horrible day in the grave-yard, they were inseparable. And yet: Never a more unlikely couple, a pair less paired, less suited for suitability. Would that I could provide a complete chronicle of the misshapen event. Alas, I cannot tell this part of the story through Duncan's journal. I am embarrassed to report that Duncan's journal entries on these matters prove nearly incomprehensible in their extremes of love, despair, lust, and, yes, love again, repetitious and maudlin. I will spare the reader the full scope of their sexual senility by only providing excerpts. I suggest you fill in any blanks with applicable entries from your own diary. . . .

It was, as they say, a beautiful spring day when Duncan first recorded his utter surrender. Outside, the willow trees breathed gently from side to side under a merciful sun, and street vendors danced joyously in anticipation of Duncan's ardor, and the birds stopped in midair to witness the innocence that was Duncan's lust, and the gray caps came aboveground to gift all citizens of the city with garlands of sweet-smelling fungus, and I must stop before I make myself sick. {I'm already sick. This whole section will make me sick, I think.}

Inside the Academy, Duncan breathed gently on the neck of the woman child {she was already twenty-one!} he had kept after class for "further instruction":

Today Mary wore a white blouse, and as I pointed out a relevant passage in Tonsure's journal, she stood next to me, our clothes just touching. I felt a pressure between us, as if she held me up or I held her up, and if the tension was broken, one of us would fall. I turned my head into the blindness of that endless white as she stood beside me, and every inch of my body knew the certainty of her generous hips where the blouse disappeared into her skirt and the reckless knowledge of her soft neck above the blouse, the face shining above the neck. All of these elements destroyed me more than what I saw, which was just the blouse, filled with her. The stitching on the blouse. The texture of the fabric itself. The soft curving caress of her breast beneath. So near. The nearness of her made me tremble. The smell of her, the smell of clean, firm skin. All I would have had to do was incline my head forward a fraction of an inch and my lips would have kissed her through the fabric. Time was extinguished by the tension between giving in, feeling her breast against my mouth for what might be only a second before her mutiny, and staying in position, forever teased by the possibility. Teetering on the edge of an abyss, where to fall was to fall was to fall into bliss, bliss, bliss; but torment, too. . . . And yet what if the action met not with outrage or rejection, but with a sigh of acceptance? Would that not be worth the risk? Would it not be worth the cost to remove the torment by attempting to consume it? To extinguish the flame by joining it?

For all of his wretched fumbling for words—I hope he didn't fumble that way with her bra strap!—I could have defined his condition for him with one word: lust. Why, I had become a world-renowned expert on lust by then, seeing the problem firsthand from several dozen different positions. I could have helped Duncan, except he didn't ask my advice; instead, he wrote it all down in his journal. {Not fair. I knew you would have advised me against it, and this I could not bear the thought of. I must say—I do appreciate you baring *my* soul in *your* afterword.}

I was destroyed by this. Destroyed. How can I describe the heaviness of her body next to me? The rich physicality of her, the smell of her skin, the way her body eclipsed my senses. She annihilated my dream of her—even flame too light a metaphor. Confronted by the reality of her, I was tormented by the urgency of a choice I could not make. I shuddered and drew back, so over-come with desire that I shivered and said nothing, even though an awkward pause had descended over our conversation, her gaze upon me.

Had Duncan taken lovers before Sabon? Rarely. He had no time for love with so much mucking about in underground tunnels ahead of him. I'll tell you the distasteful truth: he lost his virginity to a prostitute the night he graduated from the Religious Institute in Morrow. {One begins to wonder if you really have my best interests in mind.}

I remember it quite well. She arrived at the Institute much earlier than Dun-can intended, before I had left for my own quarters. He made her wait in the cloakroom while he finished getting dressed; I felt like asking him why he bothered.

She and I had nothing to talk about, although I looked her over as thor-oughly as if she had been meant for me. She seemed as respectable as anyone from Sabon's necklace of flesh, which is to say: not at all. Her blond hair had streaks of brown in it, and her face was too pale. Her hastily applied makeup encircled her eyes with too much blue. She looked ghostlike, waiflike, her dress a size too big. She wore it bravely nonetheless, struggling not to be lost in the greens of it.

Duncan came out then, his entrance accompanied by an expression of such utterly pathetic excitement that I found myself forgiving him, almost envying him. How could I pass judgment knowing how alone he had been? . . . But that wasn't all: as I closed the door, I saw them standing there in front of his wall of oddities, and the stare of recognition that passed between them, the alone meeting the lonely, carried with it a level of comprehension much deeper than anything I ever saw between Duncan and Mary; as deep as if they had been lovers for twenty years {the truth was, you spent about as much time with that prostitute as you did with Mary over the years, so how could you know?}.

The deliciousness of that moment, my intent almost exposed to Mary by my silence, lingers with me still, and I wonder if the consummation of this feel-ing could ever compare to the sheer, excruciating sweetness of this tension that binds me to her and her to me in this enclosed space of memory—my mouth so close to her blouse, which I must either kiss or tell her how I burn, and yet can do neither. There is no time in such a place, only thoughts and flesh transposed. The white of her blouse. The white of her beneath the white. And in my thoughts, where I can enslave everyone and everything, I cross the space between our bodies. I place my mouth upon her breast. She expresses neither surprise nor shock, but only sucks in her breath, moans, and slowly places her soft hands behind my head, drawing me into her, her hands so cool on my hair, her body soft soft soft.

I think I am going mad.

Mad? What did my poor, deluded brother know about going mad? I find it somewhat pathetic that my brother, the great historian, could not tell the difference between going mad and falling in love. The difference, as I know from bitter experience, is that when you go mad, you go mad utterly alone. Quite perfectly alone. That is the only difference.

How do I know this? I know this because one afternoon, while Duncan wrestled with an entirely different sort of madness, I entered my apartment, turned on the lights, and went into the bathroom, never intending to come back out again. . . .

✤ 7 ✤

START AGAIN. START OVER. HOW am I supposed to get through this part? I could ignore it, I suppose, but it wouldn't go away—it would be a huge, gaping hole in this afterword. A few snapped golden threads. An unrealized opportunity. Did I become more of Duncan's life then, or did I become a shadow to him?

Release my breath. Breathe in again. Imagine a courtyard with stone benches and willows and the scent of honeysuckle and sweet, good conversation.

I remember Bonmot asked me about death once when Duncan was off grading papers. I don't recall the context, or who had broached the subject.

"Are you afraid of death?" he asked me.

"I'm afraid of not knowing," I said. "I would like to know. I would like to know when I am going to die."

Bonmot laughed. "If you knew, you might relax too much. You might think, 'I've got twenty years. Today, I don't need to do a thing.' Or you might not. I don't know." He took a bite of his sandwich.

"Duncan's not afraid of death," I said.

Bonmot looked at me sharply. "What makes you think that?"

"The way he courts it. The way he puts himself in the path of death."

Suddenly, I felt as if Bonmot was angry with me.

"Duncan is afraid of death, trust me. Sometimes, I think he is more afraid of death than anyone I've ever met. Do you understand why I say that?" {I'm not afraid of death—I'm afraid of dying too soon.}

At the time, I didn't. I didn't understand at all. Now, I do understand. It is all too clear now.

✤✤✤

A COURTYARD. STONE BENCHES. WILLOW trees. Honeysuckle.

Bonmot: "You needn't be afraid of death. If you believe, you will come back."

Me: "Believe in what?"

Bonmot: "Anything. It doesn't matter what."

But I'm not there. I am here, and I know that we die. We die and we don't come back. Ever. Why should it matter that I tried to hasten the process—to go further than Duncan, to beat him to the beginning of the race, to fall between the glistening strands and keep on falling through the darkness? {I had my watchers on you by then. I would never let you fall between the strings—me, yes, but not you.}

I'm sorry. I've tried so hard to stick to a *sophisticated* style, something I thought Duncan would recognize and appreciate, even if he is gone forever. But the truth is, I can't keep on this way. Not all the time. The green glass glares at me. The hole in the floor is opening. I defy anyone under these circumstances to smile and dance and prattle on as if nothing had gone wrong.

We die. We die. It shrieks at me from an empty cage. Let my future editor, strange beast that he is, earn his wages and edit me. Edit all of me. Edit me out if necessary. By then I won't care. The flesh necklace can glitter with its scornful laughter and, laughing, shiver to pieces.

But where was I? It feels strange to type the words "But where was I?" but it helps orient me when I am truly lost. There's a loud gaggle of musicians—some might call them a "band," but I wouldn't—out there now, and although I glimpse only frenetic slices of them, the sound distracts me. Sometimes, I wonder if the lyrics infiltrate my own words, change them or their meaning. Sometimes, I wonder if my words fly off the page and into their mouths, to infiltrate their lyrics, change them as they are changing me. Surely this is how Duncan became misunderstood. {No, my dear sister—I became misunderstood because everyone was terrified of understanding me.}

So if you can hear me through all of this noise, lean close, listen, and I will tell you a kind of truth that once made sense to me and may again, in time, undergo that startling transformation from madness to the purest form of sanity: If you are feeling low. If you are so full of poison that you can find no light within you. If everywhere you look you see only bitterness or despair. If all of these conditions and situations apply to you, I recommend a refreshing suicide attempt. No matter what the so-called experts might say, a suicide attempt will clean you right out. True, it will also squeeze from your body the last remnants of the last smile, the last laugh, the last scrap of hope, of any small, shy, but still-bright part of you that ever cared about *anything*. Nothing will remain. Not

religion. Not friends. Not family. Not even love. A carcass picked clean and lying forgotten by the side of Albumuth Boulevard. A hollowed-out statue. A
wisp of mist off the River Moth.

But that doesn't last—how could it?—and at least it drains the poison so that
even in your isolation from yourself, you feel . . . gratitude. Which fades in turn
because at the end you don't even feel numb, because to feel numb implies that at
some point you were not numb, and so you feel like you don't really exist
anymore—which is the truest sort of truth: after a suicide attempt, you *don't* really exist anymore, just the images of you in other people's eyes.

Later, as I stared at the blood welling up from an accidental pen puncture
{how could they let you have a pen, with all the money I was paying them?!},
absent-minded and remote from the pain, I was amused at how concerned doctors get about such things; one would have thought a gardening convention had
blossomed around the fertile flower bed of my body for all the quick consterna-
tion they displayed at this pinprick.

Which belonged to a different world than my poor wrist, sliced to the bone.
I could see the bone wink through at me the night I did it, as if it shared the
joke in a way the blood could not. The blood wanted only to escape, but the
good, solid bone—it ground against the knife, made me reconsider, if only for a
moment, the bravery, the honesty, of pain. Craven, quivering flesh. Foolish
blood. And the bone winking through. I wish I could remember what it said to
me. I remember only fragments: the roar of blood as it raced away, drowned out
the murmur of the bones. Besides, I was preoccupied: I was laughing because
my hand flopped off the end of my wrist in a way I found hilarious. I was shaking so hard that I could not hold the knife to cut my other wrist. This was simply the most stunning miscalculation I had ever made! I flopped around like a
half-dead fish, unable to finish what I had started, but had no one to help me
out. Even funnier—and I almost tore myself apart with laughter over this
one—I was not enveloped in a warm hum of numbness. Not so lucky, no. The
pain blazed through me as intensely as if my blood were boiling as it left me. So
intense my laugh became a scream, my scream something beyond even the vo-
cal cords of an animal. Death, it seemed, wasn't all that much fun after all, especially when I became vaguely aware that someone had smashed in the door
and was carrying me out of the apartment, and he was weeping louder than I
was. . . . {That was me, Janice. When I saw you like that, your eyes so blank,
blood everywhere, I couldn't take it. Nothing affected me like that. Not the
underground. Not the disease taking over my body. But you, crumpled in the

bathtub, half-dead. You looked as though, without ever going underground, you had suffered all the terrors to be found there.}

So you can imagine my amusement over the doctor's concern about my thumb prick. The pricks should have been more concerned about where I found the pen—and where they had made me stay, and whose company I'd been keeping.

For you see, the Voss Bender Memorial Mental Hospital is not what I would call the most hospitable of accommodations. I will not be recommending it to my friends and family. I will not be tipping generously. Indeed, I will not even be stealing the bath towels or the little soaps from the shower. {I did think about putting you in Sybel's care—having him take you to live with the Nimblytod Tribes amid the thick foliage of tall trees. You would drink rainwater from the cups of lilies and feast on the roasted carcasses of songbirds. But then I remembered the casual nonchalance with which Sybel provided anyone who asked with the tinctures/powders/substances of their choice, and knowing of your addictions, I could not take the chance. Thus, you wound up in the Voss Bender Memorial Mental Hospital instead.}

Strange light, strange life, to end up in a place like that: an ivy-shrouded fortress of cruel stone and sharp angles, and gray like the inside of a dead squid, gray like a gray cap, gray like a thunderstorm, but not as interesting. Little windows like crow-pecked eyes, not even round or square sometimes, but misshapen. Had former inmates chiseled at them, attempting to escape? If you looked at the gray stone up close, you could see that it wasn't just stone—a type of gray fungus had coated those walls. It fit over the stone like skin; you could almost see the walls breathing through their fungal pores.

Smells? Did I mention smells? The smell of sour porridge. The smell of rotting cheese. The smell of unwashed *others*. Stench of garbage, sometimes, wafting up from the lower levels. Oil, piss, shit. All of it covered by the clean smell of soap and wax, but not covered well enough.

Intertwined with the echo of smells came the echo of sounds—screams so distant behind padded walls that I sometimes thought they came from inside my own head. The panting of inmates like animals in distress. A low screeching warble for which I could never find a source.

The hallways were like corridors to bad dreams. They rambled this way and that with no order, no coherence. You might find your destination, or you might not. It all depended on luck. I remember that once I turned a corner, and there was a dandelion growing out of a clump of dirt on the floor. After that, I wouldn't have been surprised if the lower levels were vast swamps or brambles, through which inmates thrashed their way to open space. Once, I swear I even saw a gray cap in the distance, running away from me, toward a doorway. But I was not particularly stable; who knows what I really saw. {You're exaggerating. It wasn't *that* bad. I wouldn't have sent you there if it was a torture chamber.}

All of this—this grand design, this palace—was run by a man they called only Dr. V, as if his last name were so hideous or so forbidden that even saying "Dr. V" aloud might lead to some arcane punishment. I had the impression that the man's name was very long. All I know is, I never saw him, not once, during my stay in those glorious apartments, those rooms fit for a king, or at least a rat king.

But as bad as the facilities might have been, I found my fellow inmates more disturbing. My new best friends were, predictably, all depressed, suicidal people. If you want to make a suicidal person even more depressed, keep them cooped up with several other suicidal people, that's what I always say.

My friends included Martha of the Order of Eating Disorders, who looked like a couple of wet matchsticks sewn together with skin; a writer who would not give his name and thought he had created all of us; Sandra, who suffered through experimental treatments, involving street lamps and an engine from a motored vehicle, that could have cooked a couple of hundred dinners; Daniel, who had reason to be devoid of hope—his deformity had fused his two legs into one stump that fed into his head, which had stuck to his shoulder in an unattractive way—and, of course, Edward.

Edward was different from the rest, and he stayed away from us. I would see him in the mornings, hunched in a corner. Short, dressed all in gray, with a large felt hat. Bright, dark eyes that peered from a pale, slack face. His hands had long dirty nails that looked as if they might snap off at the slightest suggestion of a breeze. A stale, dull, rotting smell came from his general direction, which I later discovered was due to the mushrooms he kept about his person. Sometimes, he made little chirping sounds, kin to the cricket that sang to me from outside my cell when the moon was full.

Edward, according to the experts, thought he was a gray cap. His misfortunes included losing his job as a bookbinder for Frankwrithe & Lewden; falling in love with a woman who could not love him back; the recent death of his grandfather, his only living relative; and not being taken seriously. {This last the fate of many of us.} He'd swallowed whole handfuls of poisonous mushrooms. The landlady had found him in time, but only because she stopped by to inquire about the lateness of the rent. He should have been grateful, but he was not.

In Edward, I seemed to have found someone who was distant cousins with Duncan. {I'd have been much like Edward if I'd let my obsession eat me. But I didn't want to *be* a gray cap, Janice—I wanted to *learn* about them.} I told Edward—with dull sunlight seeping through the dusty fungal filigree of the dull windows, in that dull common room with dull faded carpets and dull faded paint covered with lichen, while we and the other dull inmates sat in our stupid dull deck chairs—pulled off a Southern Isles vacation ship? or a Moth River ferry?—waiting to start another dull hopeless session of rehabilitation with a woman so cheerless and uninteresting that I cannot even conjure up a shadow of her name—I told him about the singing of the blood, the murmuring of the bone, and he agreed it sounded like a much superior method for a suicide attempt. The mushrooms he had taken had just made his body fall asleep. A knife wound, on the other hand, spoke to you in a myriad of voices. It told you how you really felt. He nodded like he understood. I nodded back as if *I* knew what I was talking about.

Edward only spoke to me using his chirps and whistles, and the occasional drawing. He always drew tunnels—crisscrossing tunnels, honeycombing tunnels, tunnels without end. He used black chalk or charcoal on butcher's paper. That was all we had in there to chart our creativity.

"I know," I told him. "I know. You want to go underground. Like my brother. My brother's been underground. Trust me. You don't want to go there."

Chirp, chirp, whistle. Huge eyes glistening from beneath his hat and his cowl.

"No, no—trust me, Edward. The world above ground holds more than enough for you, if you give it a chance," I replied, even though I didn't believe a word of it.

Some days I made fun of Edward. Some days I thought he was more in love with the whole idea of the gray caps than my brother. Some days I thought he *was* my brother. {I was never crazy, just committed.}

One day, on an impulse, I silenced his chirping with a hug. I held him tight, and I could feel his body shudder, relax, and melt into that embrace. I heard him whisper a word or two. I could not understand the words, but they were human. He did not want to let go. Something inside of him didn't believe in his own insanity. And suddenly, I found myself holding him tighter, and crying, and not believing in my insanity, either.

Soon enough, though, the guards pulled us apart, and we each returned to our separate madness.

❧❦❧

OVER TIME, THE DAYS TOOK on a sameness in that place. A crushing gray sameness. The only relief came in the form of Sybel, who visited two or three times. He let me know how my reputation fared in the outside world—not well—and brought with him "sympathy" cards from Sirin, Lake, and several others. Sirin had written his using letters cut from the wings of dead butterflies, while Lake had scrawled a sketch and an indecipherable message that appeared to be an attempt at a pun that had gone horribly wrong.

Startling proof of my former life running a gallery for unstable artist types, and yet that whole life seemed unreal, as if I had never lived it. I felt as if I were receiving messages from foreign lunatics.

"When are you coming back?" Sybel asked as he held my hand. I could see real sympathy in his eyes, not just pity.

I shrugged. "It depends."

"On what?" he asked.

"On when Duncan's money runs out. Where is Duncan anyway?"

"I don't know. I think he's gone underground."

The truth was, Duncan never visited me. I never asked him why. I didn't want to know. {I was too angry at you. And I had pressing matters to attend to underground.}

"How's the gallery?" I asked Sybel.

"As well as can be expected with Lake gone and you . . . recovering."

"Recovering. A nice word for it."

"What word would you like me to use?" Sybel asked. A glint of anger showed in his expression. It was the only time I angered him, or the only time I saw his anger.

"Any other word, Sybel," I said. "Any word that conveys just how fucked up I am."

Sybel laughed. "Just look at your sympathy cards. You're not the first and you won't be the last."

❧❦❧

I STAYED IN THAT PLACE for five months, until it became clear that I needed additional help, the kind that could not be provided at the hospital. At least they realized I would not try again. That madness was over with, although I had nightmares: *Their hunger was savage. They ate like wild animals, ate mushrooms and worse, drank and drank, fornicated in front of me, all against the backdrop of a city mad with fire.*

Two days before I left that place for a succession of other places, Edward told me he loved me as we played another ludicrous game of lawn bowling in the tiny interior courtyard around which the building curled like a half-open fist—me unable to hold the ball because of my traitorous wrist, him short-sighted and uncoordinated. Our legendary games lasted for brutal hours of incompetence while Martha, Daniel, the Nameless Writer, and Sandra watched with a kind of disinterested interest. This was the first time Edward had used recognizable human speech.

Applying the doctor's advice like a universal salve for any ill, I told Edward the truth: at the moment, I had no capacity for any kind of love. I did not love him back. I didn't love anyone back. I wouldn't have loved myself back if I'd walked past myself on a deserted street. . . .

The day before I left, Edward used a variation on the Janice Shriek Method to try to kill himself. He stood in his corner as usual, his hands hidden as he cut at his wrists with a piece of metal he'd loosened from the underside of one of the deck chairs. He slowly rubbed the skin and flesh off of his wrists until the blood came and his body trembled with the anticipation of stillness.

He stood there for at least half an hour, propped up by the wall, the blood hidden by his gray robes. He must have been very determined. I imagine the blood sang softly to him, comforting him. So I imagine. The truth must have a harder, sharper edge. It certainly did for those of us who had not noticed him in his corner, killing himself.

Luckily, or unluckily, an attendant discovered Edward's sin before it could claim him.

I swear I felt no guilt over the incident. It hurt terribly. No, it didn't. I cried for hours. No, I couldn't. He had bright, wide eyes, and he had a mind inside his body, a mind that could feel. I didn't have anything inside of me. My troubles looked so trivial next to his. Would it have hurt so much to say I loved him when I didn't? I couldn't even feel anger. Or despair. No despair for me today, thank you. Just an endless cool desert inside, and a breeze blowing and the sun going down, and this sense of calm eating at me. I only knew him for a few months and yet it hurt me terribly that memories of me would most likely be triggered every time he saw the scars on his wrists. {Do you get away with it that easily, Janice? Don't I have to forgive you, too? I was mad at you for a long time after that. There I was, lost in the tunnels under the city for days at a time, risking my life, and yet I never gave up the hope you abandoned all too easily.}

As it was, I never saw Edward again, or learned what happened to him or any of the other patients in that place. I had just been passing through.

❧❦

SO I LEFT THE HOSPITAL, but not for home—oh no. Duncan seemed to feel mental illness could only be cured by a great deal of travel at the disembarkation from which various "experts" poked and prodded various parts of your brain, only to prescribe more travel for the cure. From one end of Ambergris to the other, with Sybel my unwilling steward {you have no idea how much I was paying him—he *should* have been willing}, I spun like some poor gristle-and-yarn shuttlecock in a lawn tennis game.

Let me try to remember them all. Dr. Grimshaw tried some gentle water shock treatment that left me with a nervous tic in my left eye. Dr. Priott hypnotized me, which only made my tongue feel dry. Dr. Taniger tried night aversion therapy, but this only made me sleepy. Dr. Strandelson tried to make me believe that a life of severe and perfect nudity held the answer to my problems. Some tried religion, some science. None of them convinced me for even a moment. I rarely said anything. When I did, it was just to talk about Edward, the pretend gray cap.

When my brother had exhausted the restorative talents of over two dozen Ambergrisian quacks, he and Sybel contrived to transport my morbidly bored carcass to Morrow by the reincarnation of the locomotive engine: Hoegbotton Railways.

Hoegbotton & Sons, with their customary twinned avarice and industry, had unearthed vast coal deposits in the mountainous western reaches of the Kalif's empire, waged a private war to wrest the disputed area from the control of the Kalif's generals, and then, through a crippling act of sheer will, ripped the old steam engines from their deathlike slumber in Ambergris' metal graveyards, refurbished them, straightened and derusted by various unarcane means, and set them back on track. Like me, they had been resurrected. Like me, they resented it.

The view from the pretty paneled windows reminded me of a thousand respectable landscape paintings laid side by side and brought to sudden life. I amused myself by rating each landscape against the next until my vision blurred—sobbing uncontrollably and staring down at the rewelded floors of the compartment while wondering what rats and hobos had lived there before the exhumation, what myriad battles over bread or scraps of clothing or glints of loose change had taken place, and how much dried blood had been painted over, and was that a scar the workmen had been unable to remove in the shape of the gray caps' favorite symbol, and what was that stain/vein of green along the lower right side of the seats opposite—some fungus, some mold, some rot—and so just generally composing a long sentence in my head to keep out the emptiness, the sadness, and the plain old ordinary human embarrassment of what had occurred: waking up from my attempt to find Duncan and Sybel looking down at me with a mixture of pity and sorrow. {My look was not pitying—I was furious with you. Perhaps that is why I sent you to so many specialists. Here we had helped save you, and all you could do was scowl and scream at us. Do you wonder why we didn't visit much?}

⚓

IN MORROW I NEARLY DIED of boredom and the cold. Morrow is such a dry, dead town, a city of wooden corpses that talk and move about, but quietly, quietly. Morrow could never kill a soul with casual flair, as could Ambergris. Not instantly, snuffed out with a cruelty akin to the divine. No, Morrow would grind you down between its implacable wooden molars and create out of the resulting human-colored paste an acceptable, placid citizen who would marry, settle down, have children, retire, and die without a flicker of a flame of passion to warm/warn you on a cold winter night. In Morrow, a noise amongst the sewer pipes could never inspire fear, only conjure up a plumber. In Morrow, Duncan would have had to build tunnels or go mad and, sent to Ambergris to recuperate, have fallen in love with Her. No wonder Morrow was one of Mary's favorite cities; you're more than welcome to it, Mary—it deserves you.

Menite Morrow had always been—eternal heretics in the eyes of the Truffidians—and I soon discovered that the goal of the great, frozen Menite soul was to trudge on toward some ill-defined transition from unaccountable boredom to the responsible boredom of a transcendental bliss that would be enjoyed in the next life. Every doctor there was sensible to a fault, and not a one could help me because none of them had ever been where I had been. Relief came only in small doses; the bracing sense of embarrassment when Cadimon Signal, one of Duncan's more ancient former instructors, visited me: I could feel real warmth flood my face.

"Good," Cadimon said. "Shame is a good thing. It means you are alive, and you care what other people think."

Funny, I thought it was an involuntary reaction.

Another thaw quickly followed my bout of embarrassment: my curiosity returned as well, mostly due to frequent glimpses of the minions of Frankwrithe & Lewden from the window of my guarded room in an ice block of a hotel. With their sinister red-and-black garb, their aggressive sales tactics, their posters pounded into posts with straight nails, proclaiming forbidden books for sale—and their practiced street fights, their marching in closed ranks—they seemed better suited for Ambergris. As indeed they were destined, in time. They were preparing for the war—first with the ruler of Morrow and then anyone farther south who might get in their way.

One time, I even imagined I saw L. Gaudy watching his underlings from the shadow of an awning, smoking a pipe, nodding wisely. I wondered as I watched them at work if the town irritated them in the same way it irritated me. It made sense that they had to acquire Ambergris, if for no other reason than to escape Morrow. {Even then, I am sure, the emissaries of Hoegbotton & Sons haunted the streets, gliding through anonymously, eager for details, gossip, and trade.}

After two weeks of this foolishness, Duncan's attention wandered, no doubt due to Sabon's soft charms. The details of his well-intentioned plans for my imprisonment and rejuvenation became fuzzy and indistinct—as blurry as windows weighed down with sleet. I escaped from between the bars of a logic suddenly lost or nonexistent: doctor's bills unpaid, a nurse given no follow-up orders, a forgotten key languishing in a ready lock . . .

. . . and stepped out into the miserly heat of Morrow's sunrise, savoring and favoring my freedom. I had a sharp ache in the right wrist to remind me of my iniquities, and not a sign of a ticket home from my dear darling brother. {The nurse stole it, as I've told you dozens of times since.}

As I was lost, so too the light that lingered seemed lost as it stole gingerly across the snow in tones of dappled gold. It crept up my legs, purred its warmth across my face. Revealed: fir trees, two-story wooden houses, belching factories, thoroughfares full of hard-working hard-living quack psychologists. Morrow. I tried to love her in that last glance before I set off for the docks, a pathetic suitcase in hand. But failed. The light had revealed two truths: I was free, and rather than return directly to my former life, I had decided to visit my mother. . . .

※

HERE'S A TALE FOR YOU. . . .

Once upon a time, a woman decided to tell a story about how she tried to kill herself. Her brother saved her at the last second—and then sent her north to be dissected by various disciples of empirical religions. Until one day, when her brother's attention wandered, she escaped, and made her way south, back to her mother's home in the fabled city of Ambergris. She felt so hollow inside that she could no longer bear to think of herself as "I."

The bitter cold of the north followed her south to Ambergris. She could see her breath. The drone of insects faltered to an intermittent click of surprise, a sleep-drenched distress signal.

She first saw her mother's house again through a flurry of snow, flakes sticking to the windshield of the hired motored vehicle. As they lurched down the failed road that led to the River Moth and her mother, the driver cursing in a thick Southern accent scattered with Northern cold, the dark blue muscles of the river came into view, and then three frail mansions hunched along the river bank amongst the tall trees. The river was silent with cold and snow.

The mansions were silent, too: Three weary debutantes at a centuries-long ball. Three refugees of a bygone era. Three memories.

The force and pull of the past glittered from the wrought-iron balconies, from the hedge gardens sprinkled with snow. The faded appeal of the weathered white roofs that disappeared as the vehicle drove nearer, even the slender, hesitant windows reminding her of the tired places she had just left, with their incurable patients, their incurable boredom . . . the same lived-in appeal as the unstarched dress shirts her father used to wear, the white fabric coarse and yellow with age.

They drove through the remnants of faeryland—the frozen fountains in the brittle front yards, the pale statuary popular decades ago, the ornately carved doors with their tarnished bronze door knockers—until the vehicle came to a rest half-mired in snow, and for a heartbeat they watched the quiet snow together, she and the driver, content to marvel at this intruder: a strange incarnation of the invasion the Menites had long promised the lascivious followers of Truff.

Then, the moment over, the woman who had undergone a reluctant resurrection, exhumed while still living, paid the driver, picked up her suitcase, opened the door to the sudden frost, and trudged up the front steps of her mother's house. The driver drove away but she did not look back; she had no inclination to make him wait. She had resolved to stay in that place, and in her present state of mind she could not hold alternatives in her head without her skull breaking loose and rising, a bony balloon without a string, into the fissures of the cold-cracked sky. *What if?* had frozen along with the rose bushes.

Her mother's house. What made the middle mansion different from the other two aside from the fact that her mother lived there? It was the only inhabited mansion. It was the only mansion with the front door ajar. Icicled leaves from the nearby trees had swept inside as if seeking warmth, writing an indecipherable message of cold across the front hallway.

An open door, the woman thought as she stood there, suited her mother as surely as a mirror.

She stepped inside, only to be confronted by a welter of staircases. Had she caught the house in the midst of some great escape? Everywhere, like massive, half-submerged saurians, they curled and twisted their spines up and down, shadowed and lit by the satirical chandelier that, hanging from the domed ceiling, mimicked the ice crystals outside as it shed light that mingled in a delicate counterbalance with the frozen leaves.

Even there, in the foyer, the woman could tell the mansion's foundations were rotting—the waters of the Moth gurgled and crunched in the basement, the river ceaselessly plotting to steal up the basement steps, seeping under the basement door to surprise her mother with an icy cocktail of silt, gasping fish, and matted vegetation.

Having deciphered the hollow, grainy language of the staircases, the woman strode down the main hallway, suitcase in her hand. The hallway she knew well, had seen its doppelganger wherever her mother had lived. Her mother had lined both sides with photographs of the woman's father, father and mother together, grandparents, uncles, aunts, nieces, nephews, cousins, friends of the family, followed by paintings in gaudy frames of ancestors who had not had the benefit—or curse—of the more modern innovations. Most relatives were dead, and the others the woman hadn't seen for years.

She could feel herself progressing into a past in which every conceivable human emotion had been captured along those walls, frozen into a false moment. {The predominant expression, her brother would later point out, whatever the emotion behind it, was a staged smile, the only variation being "with teeth" or "without teeth." Perhaps, he would say to her later, parenthetically, outside the boundaries of frozen fairytale-isms, that she should understand the main reason he didn't like to visit their mother: he had no wish to draw back the veil, to exhume their father's corpse for purposes of reanimation; wasn't it bad enough that he died once?} Soon, it was difficult not to think of herself as a photograph on a wall.

The woman found her mother on the glassed-in porch that overlooked the river, her back to the fireplace as she sat in one of the three plush velvet chairs she had rescued from the old house in Stockton. The view through the window: the startling image of a River Moth swollen blue with ice, flurried snowflakes attacking the thick, rise-falling surface of the water, each speck breaking the tension between air and fluid long enough to drift a moment and then disintegrate against the pressure from the greater force. Disintegrate into the blue shadows of the overhanging trees, leaves so frozen the wind could not stir them.

Her mother watched the river as it sped-lurched and tumbled past her window, and now, from the open doorway, her daughter watched her watching the river as the flames crackled and shadowed against the back of her chair.

The daughter remembered a far-ago courtyard of conversation, a question posed by a gravelly-voiced friend of her brother: "And how is your mother? I know all about your father. But what about your mother?" The glint of his eye— through the summer sun, the crushed-mint scent from the garden beyond, and she, with eyes half-closed, listening to his voice but not hearing the question.

Her mother. A woman who had collapsed in on herself when her husband died, and was never the same happy, self-assured person again. Except. Except: She *had* provided for them. She just hadn't *cared* for either of them.

The woman had not seen her mother for five years, and at first she thought she saw a ghost, a figure that blurred the more she focused on it. Wearing a white dress with a gray shawl, her mother sat in half-profile, her thin white hands like twin bundles of twigs in her lap. Smoke rose from her scalp: white wisps of hair surrounding her head. The bones of her face looked as delicate as blown glass.

The daughter could see all of this because she was not actually in that room in the past, but in another room altogether, and as she typed she could see her own reflection in the green glass of the window to her left, since she had always been the mirror of her mother, and now looked much as her mother had looked, sitting in a chair, watching the river tumble past her window.

The daughter stood there, staring at her mother, clearly visible, *and her mother did not see her. . . .*

Dread trickled down the woman's spine like sweat. Was she truly dead, then? Had she succeeded and all else been a bright-dull afterlife dream? Perhaps she still lay on the floor of her bathroom, a silly grinning mask hiding her face and a bright red ribbon tied to her right wrist.

She shuddered, took a step forward, and the simple touch of the wooden door frame against her palm saved her. She was alive, and her mother sat in front of her, with delicate crow's-feet at the corners of her wise pale blue eyes—the mother she had known her whole life, who had tended to her ills, made her meals, put up with youthful mistakes, helped her with her homework, given her advice about boys and men. Somehow, the sudden normalcy of that revelation struck her as unreal, as from a land more distant than Morrow or the underground of Ambergris.

The woman dropped to her knees, facing her mother, saw that flat glaze flicker from the river to her and back again.

"Mother?" she said. "Mother?" She placed her hands on her mother's shoulders and stared at her. As if a thaw to spring, as if a mind brought back from contemplation of time and distance, her mother's eyes blinked back into focus, a slight smile visited her lips, her hands stirred, and she wrapped her arms around her daughter. Her light breath misted my cold ear.

"Janice. My daughter. My only daughter."

At my mother's words, a great weight dropped from me. A madness melted out of me. I was myself again as much as I ever could be. I hugged her and began to sob, my body shuddering as surely as the River Moth shuddered and fought the ice outside the window.

{What is it about distance—physical distance—that allows us to create such false portraits, such disguises, for those we love, that we can so easily discard them in memory, make for them a mask that allows us to keep them at a distance even when so close?}

❧❦

IT WOULD BE NICE TO report that my mother and I understood each other with perfect clarity after that first moment of affection, but it wasn't like that at all. The first moment proved the best and most intimate.

We talked many times over the next two weeks, as she led me up and down the rotting staircases in search of this or that memory, now antique, in the form of a faded photograph, a tarnished jewelry case, a brooch made from an oliphaunt tusk. But while some words brought us closer, other words betrayed us and drew us apart. Some sentences stretched and contracted our solitude simultaneously, so that at the end of a conversation, we would stand there, staring at each other, unsure of whether we had actually spoken.

I fell into rituals I thought I had abandoned years before, arcs of conversations in which I chided her for not pursuing a career—she had rooms full of manuscripts and paintings, but had never tried to sell them. For me, to whom creativity came so hard—each painting, each sculpture, each essay a struggle, a forced march—the easy way in which our mother created and then discarded what she created seemed like a waste. {Which begs the question, Janice: why didn't you sell her paintings in your gallery? It wasn't just because she didn't want you to have them; they also weren't very good.} She, meanwhile—and who could blame her?—chastised me for my lifestyle, for abusing my body. She had not missed the blue mottlings on my neck and palms that indicated mushroom addiction, although I had inadvertently kicked the habit in the aftermath of my attempt.

And so I slowly worked my way toward talking about the suicide attempt, through a morass of words that could not be controlled, could not be stifled, that meant, for the most part, nothing, and stood for nothing.

One day, as we watched the River Moth fight the blocks of ice that threatened to slow it to grimy sludge, we talked about the weather. About the snow. She had seen snow in the far south before, but not for many years. She sang a lullaby for the snow in the form of a soliloquy. At that moment, it would not have mattered if I were five hundred miles away, knocking on the doors of Zamilon. Her gaze had focused on some point out in the snow, where the river thrashed against the ice. The ice began to form around my neck again. I could not breathe. I had to break free.

"I tried to kill myself," I told her. "I took out a knife and cut my wrist." I was shaking.

"I know," she said, as casually as she had commented about the weather. Her gaze did not waver from the winter landscape. "I saw the marks. It is unmistakable. You try to hide it, but I knew immediately. Because I tried it once myself."

"What?"

She turned to stare at me. "After your father died, about six months after. You and Duncan were at school. I was standing in the kitchen chopping onions and crying. Suddenly I realized I wasn't crying from the onions. I stared at the knife for a few minutes, and then I did it. I slid down to the floor and watched the blood. Susan, our neighbor—you may remember her?—found me. I was in the hospital for three days. You both stayed with a friend for a week. You were told it was to give me some rest. When I came back, I wore long-sleeved shirts and blouses until the marks had faded into scars. Then I wore bracelets to cover the scars."

I was shocked. My mother had been mad—mad like me. {Neither of you were mad—you were both sad, sad, sad, like me. I didn't know Mom tried to take her own life, but thinking back, it doesn't surprise me. It just makes me weary, somehow.}

"Anyway," she said, "it isn't really that important. One day you feel like dying. The next day you want to live. It was someone else who wanted to die, someone you don't know very well and you don't ever want to see again."

She stood, patted me on the shoulder. "There's nothing wrong with you. You'll be fine." And left the room.

I didn't know whether to laugh or cry, so I did both.

Did I believe her? Was it true that you could leave your old self behind so easily? There was an unease building in me that said it wasn't true, that I would have to be on my guard against it, as much as Duncan was on guard against the underground. {You misunderstand me—I *embraced* the underground. It fascinated me. There was no dread, only *situational dread*—the fear that came over me when I clearly *did not* fit in underground, when I thought the gray caps might no longer suffer my presence.}

⊰❦⊱

AFTER THAT, WE AVOIDED THE subject. I never discussed my suicide attempt with my mother again. But we did continue to talk—mostly about Duncan. Duncan's books. Duncan's adventures. Duncan's early attempts at writing history papers.

We shared memories we both had of Duncan. Back in Stockton, sometimes, after breakfast, Duncan would sit by Dad's side and scribble intensely, a stern look on his face, while Dad, equally stern, wrote the first draft of some paper destined for publication in *The Obscure History Journal Quarterly*. Mother and I would laugh at the two of them, for Dad could not contain the light in his eyes that told us he knew very well his son was trying to imitate him. To become him.

It seemed safe, to talk about Duncan in such a way. Or at least it did, until I discovered my mother had one memory of him I did not share with her.

Something "your father would have been able to tell better," she said. We were in the kitchen preparing dinner—boiling water for rice and preparing green beans taken from the deep freezer in the basement. Outside, the river stared glassily with its limitless blue gaze.

"You know," she said. "Duncan saw one when he was a child—in Ambergris. Your father went there for research and he took Duncan while I took you to Aunt Ellis' house for the holidays. You can't have been more than nine, so Duncan was four or five." {Yet I remember this trip as if it had happened this morning.}

"What do you mean he 'saw one'?" I asked.

"A gray cap," she said, snapping a bean as she said it.

The hairs on my neck rose. A sudden warm-cold feeling came over me.

"A gray cap," I said.

"Yes. Jonathan told me after he and Duncan came back. He definitely saw one. Your father thought it might be fun to go on an Underground Ambergris tour while in the city. They still offered them back then. Before the problems started."

"Problems." My mother had a gift for understatement. The tours to the tunnels beneath the surface stopped abruptly when the ticket seller to one such event popped downstairs for a second, only to run screaming back to the surface. The room below contained no sign of the tour guide or the tourists—just a blood-drenched room lit by a strange green light, the source of which no one could identify. Much like the light I write by at this very moment. {Apocryphal. Most likely, they closed up shop because they were losing money due to their poor reputation. The gray caps have often been bad for certain types of business.}

"They bought their tickets," my mother continued, "and walked down the stairs with the other tourists. Your father swears Duncan held on to his hand very tightly as they went down into a room cluttered with old Ambergris artifacts. They went from room to musty old room while the tour guide went on and on about the Silence and Truff knows what else . . . when suddenly Jonathan realizes he's not holding Duncan's hand anymore—he's holding a fleshy white mushroom instead."

Our Dad stood there, staring at the mushroom, paralyzed with fear. Then he dropped it and began to run from room to room. He was shaking. He had never been so scared in his entire life, he told my mother later. {Where was I? One minute I was holding my father's hand. The next . . . }

He started to shout Duncan's name, but then he caught a blur of white from the next room over. He ran into the room, and there was Duncan, in a corner, staring at a gray cap that stood right in front of him, staring right back. { . . . I was staring at a gray cap. Just as my mother said. I wish I knew what happened between those two points in time.}

"It was small," my mother said. "Small and gray and wearing some sort of shimmery green clothing. There was a smell, Jonathan said—a smell like deep river water trickling through lichen and water weeds." {It smelled like mint to me. It opened its mouth and spores came out. Its eyes were large. I felt a feeling of unbelievable peace staring at it. It immobilized me.}

Our father screamed when he saw the gray cap—and he knows he screamed, because the other tourists came running into the room.

But it was as if Duncan and the gray cap were deaf. They continued to stare at each other. Duncan was smiling. The look on the gray cap's face could not be read. {Later, I became aware that we had stood there, watching each other, for a long time. At that moment, in that moment, it seemed like seconds. I felt as if the gray cap was trying to tell me something, but I couldn't understand what it was saying. I don't know why I thought that—it never made a sound. And yet that's the way I felt. I also felt as if I had been somewhere else part of the time, even if I could not remember it. Somewhere underground. I had a taste of dirt and mud in my mouth. I felt dirt under my fingernails as if I'd been digging, frantically digging for hours. But, later, when I checked them, my fingernails were clean.}

Then, as the other tourists entered the room, two things happened.

"First, the gray cap pulled a mushroom out of its pocket. Then it blew on the mushroom, softly."

A thousand snow-white spores rose up into Duncan's face, "and then the gray cap disappeared."

The gray cap, my father said, melted into, blended in with, the wall and *wasn't there anymore.* Although he knew this couldn't have happened, although he knew there must be something—a secret passageway, a trapdoor in the floor—to explain it. . . .

Duncan, awash in the milk-white spores, turned at the sound of his father's voice—which he could finally hear—and smiled so broadly, with such delight, that our father, for a moment, smiled back. {It's true. When the gray cap disappeared, a feeling of utter well-being came over me, and of wonder. Again, I can't say why. I don't know why. I was too young to know why. The gray caps and the underground have rarely since provided me with anything approaching a sense of calm.}

"Jonathan took Duncan to the doctors right away, but they couldn't find anything wrong with him. Duncan was the same as he ever had been, even if Jonathan wasn't. Jonathan was shaken by what had happened. It even changed the nature of his research. Suddenly, he became interested in *The Refraction of Light in a Prison* instead of the rebellion of Stretcher Jones against the Kalif.

The Refraction of Light led him to the monks of Zamilon, and from there to the Silence. {Much as it led me there. The key may still be in Zamilon, but not at this time.}

"I never told you because I didn't know how to explain it. It sounded absurd. It sounded dangerous."

They never found anything wrong with Duncan, although they took him to doctors frequently over the next year. Gradually, they forgot about it, buried the memory alongside other memories because, in their hearts, it terrified them. {There were several times I thought about telling you, Janice. I would open my mouth to tell you and the image of the gray cap standing silent in front of me would come to me, and somehow I couldn't say anything. After a while, it was no longer possible to tell you without it being clear I'd kept it from you. I still don't know why I felt such a compulsion against telling you. Was I protecting you? Was I protecting myself? I was so young, perhaps I just couldn't express what I'd seen.}

"What terrified Jonathan the most," my mother said, "was not the gray cap, or the spores, but the happy smile on your brother's face."

The beans were in the pot. The rice was on the boil.

I asked, "So Duncan wasn't changed by the event? No nightmares? No insomnia?"

My mother shook her head. "Nothing like that."

She paused, put her hand to her throat, her gaze distant. "There was one change, although I'm sure it's just that he was growing up. A year after he came back, he began to explore the drain tunnels near the house. Before that, I remember he hated dark places. But then he just . . . lost the fear." {Is it possible my encounter had been an invitation? That the point had been to invite me to explore?}

Old mysteries, brought home to me in a new way. I kept thinking back, trying to remember my impressions of Duncan at the age of four or five. There was precious little. I remembered him smiling. I remembered him blowing out the candles on a birthday cake, and the time I made him cry by pinching him because he'd pulled apart one of my dolls.

My mother's story gnawed and gnawed at me, even though I could not see the greater significance of it. {What were you meant to see, do you think? That I've been an agent of the gray caps my entire life? What, exactly, are you trying to say, Janice?}

Suddenly, it no longer seemed so safe to talk about Duncan. For the first time, I felt the urge to return to Ambergris, to my gallery, to my life. So I left the very next day, surprising myself as much as I surprised my mother. Even by then, though, we had slowly grown apart, so that I am sure that she, like me, in that awkward moment by the front door, with the motored vehicle waiting, thought that five years until my next visit might be no great hardship.

❧ 8 ❧

NOTHING WAS THE SAME WHEN I came back.

It's night here, as I type, and hot, and I don't know if it's a normal kind of heat or something related to the Shift. Something is gnawing away at the wood between the ceiling of this place and the roof. I find it almost relaxing to listen to the chewing—at least, I'd rather listen to that than to the sounds I sometimes hear coming from below me. It does not bear thinking about, what may be going on below me. Really, this afterword has been the only thing saving me from too many thoughts about the present. The green light is ever-present, but the clientele is not. It's late. They've gone home. It's just me and the lamp and the typewriter . . . and whatever is chewing above me and whatever is moving below me. And I feel feverish. I feel like I should lie down on the cot I had them bring in here. I feel like I should take a rest. But I can't. I have to keep going on. Despite the heat. Despite the fact that I'm burning up. I have some mushrooms Duncan left behind, but I'm not sure I should eat them, so I won't. They might help, but they might not. {Good decision! Those are weapons. If you'd eaten them, it would've been like eating gunpowder.}

So, instead, to stave off burning up, I'll write about the snow. I'll write about all of that wonderful, miraculous snow that awaited me on my return to Ambergris. Maybe the gnawing will stop in the meantime. Unless it's in my mind, in which case it may never stop.

❧

I RETURNED TO AN AMBERGRIS transformed by snow from semi-tropical city to a body covered by a white shroud. Every street, alley, courtyard, building, storefront, and motored vehicle had succumbed to the mysteries of the snow.

Ambergris was not suited to white. White is the color of surrender, and Ambergris is unaccustomed to surrender. Surrender is not part of our character.

At first, the city appeared similar to dull, staid Morrow, but underneath the anonymous white coating lay the same old city, cunning and cruel as ever. Merchants sold firewood at ten times the normal price. Frankwrithe & Lewden, in a hint of the strife to come, raided a warehouse of Hoegbotton books and distributed the torn pages as tinder. Beggars contrived to look as pathetic as possible, continuing a trend that had been refined since before the advent of Trillian the Great Banker. Thieves took advantage of the icy conditions to make daring daylight purse-pinchings on homemade ice skates. Priests in the Religious Quarter preached end-of-the-world hysteria to boost dwindling congregations. Theaters rushed a number of "jungle comedies" and other warm-weather fare into production, finally dethroning Voss Bender's *Trillian,* that play's six acts too long for most theater admirers, frozen bottoms stuck to icy seats. Swans died shrieking in ice that trapped their legs. Lizards shrugged philosophically and grew fur. Sounds once dulled by a species of heat intense enough to corrode even hearing were now bright and brassy.

But I remember most the smell, or lack of it. Suddenly, the ever-present rot-mold-rain scent was missing from the air, replaced by the clean, boring smell of Morrow. It was as if Morrow had colonized a vital element of the city, presaging the war.

{Not to mention the fungi, which adapted almost as if the gray caps had planned the change in the weather. There was something unreal about seeing mushroom caps in jaunty bright colors rise through the snow cover, unaffected by the cold.}

❧❦

SYBEL FORCED ME TO GO back to the gallery. I would have stayed in my apartment for weeks, if I'd had the choice, conveniently ignoring a few blood-stains my brother had missed when cleaning up. I no longer felt hollow, but I did feel weak, sluggish, indecisive. I didn't have any of the normal props that used to stop me from thinking about . . . everything.

Sybel looked like he always looked—a faint half-smile on his face, eyes that stared through you to something or somewhere else, presumably his future.

On the way to the gallery, walking through the frozen streets, Sybel turned to me, and said, "You don't know who your friends are, do you?"

I stared at him for a second. "What are you trying to tell me?"

We were only a few minutes from the gallery at that point.

"You gave keys out to people," he said.

"Gallery keys."

"Yes."

"And I shouldn't have."

"No. How could I stop them when they had keys of their own?"

I sighed. "Let me guess."

❦

INSIDE THE GALLERY, THE ONLY element that remained the same was my desk, with its two dozen bills, five or six contracts, and a litter of pens obscuring its surface. The rest had been stripped bare. Those paintings least popular, hung for several months, had left the beige shadow of their passing, but otherwise, I might as well have been starting up a gallery, not losing control of one. Everyone had abandoned me, as if I were whirling so fast toward oblivion that, at some point, they were simply flung clear by my momentum.

"When did this happen?"

"Gradually, over months," Sybel said, throwing the gallery keys on the desk and sitting in a chair. "They were pretty thorough, weren't they?"

"They?"

"The artists. I'm fairly certain it was the artists."

I looked around. The gallery had, in its emptiness, taken on aspects of my life. What was I to do?

"I couldn't be here day and night," Sybel said. Unspoken: *I had parties to plan. I had a suicidal boss to worry about.*

A sudden anger rose up inside of me, though I had no reason to be angry at Sybel. What could he have done?

"You just let them take all of their art?"

He shook his head. "David let them in. David's the one who started it. . . ."

David. Former boyfriend. A not-unpleasant memory of David and me escaping into the gallery's back room to make love.

"Oh." The anger left me.

Sybel stared up at me. "There's nothing left to manage, Janice. There's no gallery. I wish there were. But," and he stood, "there's nothing here for me to do. I'm not a rebuilder, I'm a manager. If you need help in the future, let me know."

I would need help in the future. A lot of help, but he couldn't know that now. He couldn't know how quickly everyone's fortunes would change.

"What will you do now, Sybel?"

Sybel shrugged. "I'll take some time off. I'll climb trees. I will enjoy the feel of the sun on my face in the morning. I will swim in the River Moth." {Right. And after about thirty minutes, when he was done gamboling about in the sunlight, Sybel would go on providing people with whatever they most desired. Specifically, providing *me* with what I most desired—whatever could get me through the night.}

I smiled and put a hand on his shoulder. "Take me with you."

"You wouldn't like it," Sybel said, somewhat wistfully, I thought. "You would be bored."

I nodded. "You're probably right."

At the door, Sybel turned to me one last time and said, "I'm glad you made it back. I really am. But you'll find it's changed out there. It's no longer the same place."

"What do you mean, it's changed?"

"There is no New Art anymore."

⁂

LATER, A SHORT INVESTIGATION WOULD prove Sybel right. While everyone's attention had been on the New Art, real innovation had been occurring outside of our inbred, self-congratulatory little circle. Real imagination meshed with real genius of technique had been bypassing and surpassing the New Art, sometimes with a chuckle and a condescending nod. This was the era during which Hale Jargin first displayed his huge "living canvases," complete with cages for small creatures to peep out from shyly. Sarah Frayden began to create her shadow sculptures, too. But neither of these qualified as New Art, in part because the galleries they showed in had no connection to the New Art.

By the time those of us associated with the New Art realized New Art was Old Art—my only excuse being my forced absence from the scene—the only one who had the option of escaping the death of the term was the only one who had never uttered the words in the first place: Martin Lake.

If they hadn't fled my gallery, I would have been stuck with a long line of has-beens who, squinting, had emerged from their corridor of tunnel vision to realize that, far from being on the frontier, they'd been in a backwater, as obsolete as the first generation of Manzikert motored vehicles the factories had trundled out over a hundred years ago.

"There is no New Art anymore," Sybel said, and then was gone, leaving me in my empty gallery, wondering what to do.

⁂

WHAT COULD I DO? I needed to find my brother—and find him I did, amid the tinkling rustle of the frozen willow trees outside of Blythe Academy. I think he knew I was coming. I think he knew I was looking for him. There he was in a long coat, sitting at a stone table and smiling at me. {Grimacing, actually. I experienced a lot of pain during the early days of my transformation. I was still changing.} He had regained his customary thinness.

"Hello, helpless helping brother," I said, smiling back as I sat down across from him. Behind him, the Academy was just waking up. It was a beatific morning—the sun lit the snow and ice into a fractured orange blaze.

"Hello, suicidal sister," he said, his gaze clear, focused on the present, on me.

"You should use more careful language," I told him. "I could do it all over again, and you'd have to send me on another tour of the world."

Duncan grinned. His teeth revealed an underlying rot, despite his apparent health: they were stained a gray-black along the gums.

"Not likely," he said. "I've already sent you to every head doctor within three hundred miles. If you were going to do it again, you would have done it while listening to the seventh or eighth as he droned on about your disturbed dream life."

"But I am fragile," I insisted. "I've been without drugs for weeks. I've been getting lots of sleep. I've been eating well. I could suffer a mental collapse at any moment."

{To see you that way, tired but whole, made me happy. A few months before I had had no idea if you would survive, or if you'd be the same person afterwards. It didn't matter that you were thin or drawn, just that you seemed sane once more.}

"The city is falling apart, not you. The snow. Look—it's snowing again."

He was right—thin, small flakes had begun to drop out of the sky.

"It hasn't really stopped snowing," I reminded him.

"I think the gray caps . . ."

I rolled my eyes to cut him off. "You think they're responsible for everything." {Because they are, Janice!}

He shrugged. "Aren't they?"

"Actually, no," I replied. "I brought the snow with me from Morrow—the most heartless, boring, terrible place you could possibly have sent me to."

Anger, rising up. It felt good. It felt right. It was the only thing I'd felt besides pain and sorrow in a long time.

"I saved your life," he said. "You'd be dead otherwise."

"Maybe I wanted to be dead," I replied. "Did you ever think of that?"

"No," Duncan said, shivering, "I don't think you wanted to be dead. I think you didn't want to feel. There's a difference. And I know all about not wanting to feel."

All the air went out of me with a single sigh. The truth was, it took too much energy to talk about such things.

A thought occurred to me. "How did you know I'd be here?"

Duncan grimaced, as if from some physical pain. {*As if?* Every time I moved, I could feel them all over me, burrowing into my skin.}

He looked away. "I have . . . friends . . . who tell me things. That's all. It's the same reason I found you in time."

I laughed, said, "Friends! I can only guess what kinds of friends. Do they have legs or spores? Do they walk or do they float?"

Duncan stared down at the snow. Now I could see, where the light caught his cheek, the side of his neck, that a faint black residue, insubstantial as smoke, had attached itself to his skin.

"Why did you do it?" he asked me.

I stared at him, the anger boiling over. What could I say to him? Why should I say anything to him?

"What kind of answer would you like?" I asked him. "Would you like me to say the pressure was too much? That I couldn't handle it? Do you want me to say I was under the influence of drugs? Do you want me to say my relationships all failed and I was lonely?"

My voice had risen with each new question until I was shouting. I stopped. Abruptly. While Duncan stared at me, concerned.

I realized I didn't know why I had done it. Not really. Every reason I could dredge up seemed ridiculous. I had written lots of notes about it, true. All the doctors wanted me to write things down, as if they could pull it out of me through ink applied to paper. I wrote nonsensical sentences, pompous things like:

I have finally figured it out. We are redeemed, if at all, by love and by imagination. I had imagination enough to realize I was not receiving enough love, and so I allowed myself to be seduced by those who did not love me, and whom I did not love. And then convinced myself, in my imagination, that I did love them, and that they did love me.

Or, on another scrap of paper I saved as a testament to my foolishness:

I spent my youth gripped in the fear of a sudden exit—like that of my father. I too might run across the sweet, strange grass only to fall prematurely inert at someone's feet. {"Sudden exit"? "prematurely inert"? For someone who wanted to die you have a real aversion to the word death.} And yet as an adult I have tried my best to run to meet that exit anyway, despite all of those careful steps. Driving my gallery into ruin. Driving my relationships into ruin with excess and promiscuity. Overindulging in drugs and sex.

And, finally, dredging up the distant past:

My dad was a hard man to love. He lived for his work, and anyone who did not live for that work would receive very little love. Not a bad man, or a man who could be intentionally cruel. Not a man like that, no, but a man who could ignore you with an imperiousness that could burn into your soul. Duncan rarely saw that side of our father. Duncan was protected by his interest in the mysteries of history. Me, I couldn't have cared less about history growing up. I was interested in many things—painting, reading, singing lessons, boys; in that order—but not history. I never could see the personal side to history until I started living it. Until Mary and Duncan showed me what history could mean. And by then it was too late: Dad was dead, and nearly me as well.

The doctors had made me do it—had made me feel like a political prisoner of the Kalif, forced to recant my beliefs and spout pseudo-personal parody to regain my freedom. {And yet, Janice, some of it rings true. I wish I could say it didn't.}

"I don't need an answer," Duncan said quietly. "I just thought I'd ask."

But I needed an answer, so I could stop it from happening again. Why had I done it?

I don't recall what I said to Duncan next, sitting in the freezing cold outside of Blythe Academy, students beginning their groggy paths across the courtyard to their classes. I don't remember any of the rest of our conversation. {We talked about the past, Janice. We talked about what Bonmot had been up to at the Academy. You told me about Mom and the condition of that old mansion. I told you about the research I had my students doing on Zamilon. Nothing you needed to remember.} I'm sure it didn't satisfy him. It didn't satisfy me.

I could remember, however, the night of the attempt—a night that seemed to epitomize the parties, the drugs, the lack of direction, the stretched, unreal quality of my existence. The late, late nights merging into days, the black of the sky, the hunt for yet another bar.

I had blown half of my remaining money on what I now realize was a suicide banquet—so much food, so many bodies, so little restraint. The pale white of people in a corner of the room, in a writhing orgy of legs and arms and torsos. The leering smiles of the onlookers. The smell of wine, of rot, of decay, of sex. But it wasn't enough for me, even then. We kept going *elsewhere*.

We were in a café. We were inside a burned-out building. We were on the street, giggling under a streetlamp. It was all merging together into one place, one time. I didn't know where I was. Sybel was there, then he wasn't there, then he was.

Finally, we came to the steps of an abandoned church. Sybel stood on one side and David, the cipher I was sleeping with at the time, stood on the other. I floated between them, staring at the huge double doors of the church, the old oak bound in iron and carved with flourishes. I could hear people talking loudly inside.

"Did I pay for this?" I asked. It had become my standard question over the past few months.

"No," Sybel said. "You didn't pay for this. You didn't like your own party."

"You wanted us to take you somewhere else," David said, an arm around my shoulders.

"From what I paid for?" I said.

Sybel laughed. "Yes, to something you didn't pay for. And you definitely didn't pay for this—this is a party sponsored by one of the new galleries."

"And somewhere else is something I paid for?"

"We thought it might be fun to spy," David added, ignoring me.

"In a church?" I said, incredulous, forgetting all of the blasphemous functions I'd sponsored inside even holier buildings.

David said, "It used to be for the Church of the Five Pointed Star, but they don't really exist anymore."

Obviously. The grass was high and the steps cracked with vines. The door was beginning to rot on its hinges.

"Lead the way," I said, giving up.

Sybel pushed open the door and we walked inside, the two of them practically carrying me—into the cacophony of music, the swirl of lights. We blended in perfectly. Same clothes. Same attitude. Within minutes, while Sybel and David looked on, I was carrying on a conversation with a young male artist who had the kind of pale waif look I find irresistible. It was crowded. I had to shout. I didn't know what I was shouting. I didn't know who I was rubbing up against. Sybel and David tried to act as my bodyguards; I ignored them. I was babbling.

At some point, I lost focus and stopped talking, trying unsuccessfully to nod as the young artist who I really didn't give a damn about rambled on about "the inspiration for my art." I was standing on a stool by then. I don't know who had provided the stool, but it gave me enough height to survey the crowd.

Off to the side, I could see the rival gallery owner, John Franghe, chatting up a couple of my clients, oblivious to my presence. I recognized darling Franghe's hand gestures. I recognized his body language. The odd combination of fawning flattery and absolute authority. He had a glass in his hand and was obviously drunk. He kept putting his hand on the arm of the prettier of the two artists and squeezing it, giving her a quick glance to catch her eye. There was nothing artful about it.

At some point while watching, I fell off my stool. My head was full of nails. My thoughts were coiled and frightened. David and Sybel came to my aid, set me down at a chair beside a table, beside two old veterans of the art movement. Bodies were swirling around me. The texture of the table even seemed to swirl, to become a whirlpool of wooden grain. I could smell the beer, the drugs, the sweat of all of those bodies in such an enclosed space.

At some point, I realized that none of it mattered, that none of it meant anything. I hated what I saw—the corrosion of fame, the accretion of falseness, the misuse of sex and desire. A strange dread came over me. I was alone in that church. I did not know who I was, or how I had come to this. I had become an observer in my own life.

I sent David and Sybel off on a mission to ask the hosts to find more of my favorite mushrooms. As soon as they had been swallowed up by the crowd, I stood up and snuck out of the church, through those rotting oak doors.

Stumbling, drunk out of my mind, I made my way down to a dirty little club at the dock-end of Albumuth Boulevard. Through the murmurous sounds of the River Moth, right outside, I listened to an old singer that someone said had once been famous.

As one will, I quickly became close friends with everyone at the bar, but even as I sat there joking and drinking with them, in the dark, I knew I was all alone. I knew the singer realized this, too. He seemed to sing for me and me only. No one else paid attention to him. It was horrible and wonderful at the same time. He would never reach the heights he had once known. One day, the people in the bar might not even recognize his best-known songs. But he sang them with a kind of terrible defiance. It wore me out to watch him. The empty laughter of the bar wore me out. All of it wore me out.

I sat there smoking a mushroom someone had given me and looking at the singer, but really staring past him into the distance, the foreground a blur, with not a thought in my head other than the melody of the song, the voice of the singer.

You become what you pretend to be. I could pretend that I was pretending when it came to the New Art, but eventually I had begun to believe the lies that justified the excesses.

Slowly, over time, a thought snuck past the music and the voice: that I could never be as brave as that singer, that I could never sing old songs to people who didn't care. {Though, ironically enough, some would say that is what you've wound up doing with this account.}

Is that a good reason? Would that have satisfied the doctors?

Because nothing else did.

❧

I LIED EARLIER, THOUGH. I do remember something else from my conversation with Duncan in the frozen courtyard. I remember that I smelled perfume on him. It brought me up short, changed the subject forever.

"What's her name?" I asked.

He smirked and said, "Mary Sabon."

❧

MARY SABON. SABON AND HER *necklace of liars. Where to start?*

Sybel was right—the New Art was dead. But it wasn't just the New Art that had died.

Before my "accident," I had lived almost exclusively within the secret history of the city—a history of moments, not events, a history that vanished as it came and lived on only in the shudder of remembered ecstasy. This secret history descends {transcends} through the bedrooms of a hundred thousand houses, in the dark, through the tips of our fingers as we learn that our bodies have a thousand eyes to feel with, a thousand ways to learn the true meaning of *touch*. From foreplay to orgasm, from first touch to last, everything we know is in our skins—this secret history that so few people will be part of. We don't talk about this history, although it made us and will make us and is the only way to get as close as we can to each other: an urgent coupling to close the space, to experience a pleasure that—excuse me as I stumble into this rapturous gutter {can we stop you?}—is on one level being filled or filling, but is also so much more. This is where I was and what I lived for before the accident. Afterwards, I gave it all up, even though it wasn't the problem.

I traded my secret history for another type of history altogether. I saw the backs of a lot of heads, sang a lot of songs, and had my fundament put to sleep by the hard wood I was sitting on on more than one occasion. Chanting, reading ancient books, fingering beads on a necklace much more humble than Sabon's. Always worried that this new dependency might end as the old one had, but willing to take the chance anyway.

But, in some great confluence of chance and destiny, as my erotic star fell, Duncan's rose, and shone all the more passionately, as his ardor—unlike mine—was directed toward one person: Mary Sabon.

I already knew Mary, although I did not realize it at the time. Duncan had talked about her for several months before the details of his attraction to her became clear. There was a potentially brilliant student in his class, he told me at lunch one day while Bonmot stared at both of us from beneath his bushy eyebrows. A student who absorbed theory like a sponge and immediately applied it to her own interests. A student who could, moreover, write, and write well. It was so obvious that this student should be in a more advanced class that at first he was undecided as to whether to let her go to some other school, but, finally, could not bring himself to suggest it.

"She does not have the necessary social maturity," I remember him saying. "She's still young. To go to the Religious Academy in Morrow, with much older students," he said, shaking his head. "She needs more time. Extraordinary student."

Bonmot frowned at that, gave Duncan a look that I didn't understand.

"Sometimes," he said to Duncan pointedly, "it's better to let them go. Better for the student and better for the teacher."

Duncan shook his head again. "No. She needs more time."

I should have known from the way he refused to use her name. Thank God I missed the courtship. Thank God I was trying to die.

For Duncan had, while hounding me from hospital to ward, ward to doctor's office, been displaying all the conjoined lust and random stupidity of a rabbit. He "succumbed to temptation," as he put it in his journal, when, one afternoon while tutoring Mary privately after class, his hand crossed that space between how-it-is and how-it-might-be . . . and found purchase on the other side.

"Tell me you don't love me and I will be glad to escape this fever, this vision," he wrote in his journal, and much else I cannot tell from the torn pages. "I've never been more naked," he tells her, apparently forgetting the night I scraped the fungus from his body, surely his most naked moment.

She did not leave him alone in his nakedness, for as he succumbed, and kept succumbing, without thought of the link between bliss and torment, she reciprocated, and continued to reciprocate. {Truly the driest account of making love I've ever read.} What promises they made to each other in those first few sweet, fumbling hours, I cannot tell you. Duncan has ripped those pages from his journal in such brutal fashion that even the pages surrounding that night are shredded—mangled words, mutilated phrases, quartered sentences. No one can read between lines that no longer exist.

Did he tear them out from anger later, or love before? {I'm not telling.} Did he premeditate their slaughter, or was it a crime of passion? For that matter, why would he rip out *those* pages as opposed to—for example—the pages about the gray caps' infernal machine? With the pages lost, and Duncan with them, we can only guess. {And yet, dear sister, here I am, editing your work, even after "death." Some things never change.}

All I have left as proof are a few short, unintentionally humorous letters from Sabon to Duncan, and from Duncan to Sabon—shaken out of Duncan's journal like dead moths.

Sabon: My love, last night was wonderful. I've never talked to anyone the way I've talked to you. You teach me so much. You make me understand things so well. You make me feel like I'm floating on a cloud, on a star, so light do

you make me feel. Until next time, I am sorrowful and sick. I will not sign
this letter, in case it is discovered, but you know who I am.

Duncan: Your skin is so smooth I want to lick it all day long. Your body makes
my body hum with pleasure. Your hair, your breasts, your small hands, your
ears, as delicate as the most delicate of fungi, your strong thighs, your elbows, your eyes, your kneecaps, even! I want all of you, again and again.

Sabon: My beautiful love—last night I felt I knew you better than before, if
that is possible. In the dark where we could not see each other, I still felt I
could somehow see you. {Humorously enough, there was, thinking back, a
certain glow to me back then, due to the colonization by the fungi.} The
way you talk to me—I don't know if I'm worthy of the love I hear in your
voice. But I will try.

Duncan: It is truly amazing, the way our bodies fit together like some kind of
perfect jigsaw puzzle. Yours makes mine feel so good. I hope I make yours
feel half as good. Every night I cannot come to you is agony. I can't think
of anything else—even in the classroom when I'm supposed to be teaching. And when you are near me then, I tremble. My hands, my legs, shake,
and I cannot hear anyone but you, and I want you there, then. This is a
craving I cannot satisfy.

Standard nattering romantic fare, uttered from the lips and pens of a thousand
lovers a year, although usually not in such a staccato point-counterpoint of ro-
mance/lust, romance/lust. {Not fair! That was early on, Janice! When I remained acutely aware that I was older and she was younger, and she worried
that she was too young and I was too mature. So we each tried to shed our age,
to reverse the expected. It might have been foolish, but it reflected concern, affection, care, for the other. Besides, we used to hide these letters in dozens of
places inside Blythe and on the grounds. Some never reached the intended recipient. Of those that did, I only kept a few of hers, and not all of mine were returned. Sometimes she was lustful and I was loving. Sometimes I would look
out across the Academy from my office and see nothing but a world of potentially hidden love letters, all for me or by me.}

Following that first contact and conquest, Duncan offered up a marvelous
spectacle to an unsuspecting potential audience of students, teachers, adminis-
trators, and five different orders of monks, none of whom would have sanc-
tioned the holiness of lust between teacher and student if they'd been awake to
see it. For more than two years, Duncan slunk, sneaked, crept, crawled, climbed,

and slithered past various obstacles to be with his beloved. The logistics of these lust-driven maneuvers were perhaps as complex as Duncan's perilous wanderings belowground, and almost as dangerous. If caught, Duncan would be fired and barred from teaching elsewhere in the city.

Having already exhausted the careers of respectable historian and pseudonymous writer-for-hire, I would have thought Duncan would be wary of ruining a third. And in a way, I guess he was—he took great care to be precise. His meticulousness took the form of a map to guide him in his strategic penetrations of Sabon's room. Each method of penetration had elements to recommend it. Some involved the excitement of speed, while others, in their lengthy explorations, yielded pleasures of a different kind. All, however, flirted with discovery; there would never be any safe way to enter Sabon's room. "Neither in the morning nor the night," Duncan wrote with a kind of unintentional poetry, "neither at noon nor at sunset." {Bonmot thought it showed a new level of devotion to the Academy, the way I would often trade the comforts of my apartment for a sad barren room on the premises.}

Complicating matters, Academy rules dictated that all students change rooms every semester, presumably to make trysts more difficult, although two or three girls got pregnant every year anyway. Therefore, Duncan had to readjust his perambulations every six months or so.

Duncan used three routes to Sabon's room during her sixth semester at the school. These routes constitute "love letters" in the purest sense of the term. Indeed, in his madness, in his missives to Sabon he even gave them names:

Route A: The Path of Remembering You. This path, this love, can never lead me to you fast enough and yet, cruelly, reminds me of you in every way—from the rough rooftops where we sat and watched the sky turn to amber ash, to the gardens where your walking silhouette would confuse my mind with your scent, with the sight of pale perfect legs sheathed in clean white socks. This path requires that I slip past all the male students who cannot have you as I have had you and, at the center of their snoring rooms, ascend the stairs to the roof. On the roof, I gaze out upon the line between the dormitory and the classrooms where I teach you things that no longer seem important. Then into the sometimes moonlit gardens, rushing through shrubbery as I throb for you—using the blind shoulder of the storage room to hide me from the night watchmen, only to arrive below your window, your outline ablaze against the curtain.

Route B: The Path of Naked Necessity. When I burn for you and I do not care for anything but you, I use this path, for it is as direct as my desire—past the Royal's sleeping quarters, past all teachers' rooms, on to the border, there to creep over unforgiving gravel below every student's dormitory window, not caring that an errant head might poke out between curtains after curfew and recognize me—and so once again, in the urgency of my need, I come to your window and you.

Route C: The Path of Careless Ecstasy. When my love for you quivers between caution and bravery, when I am too full of joy to be either brief or circum-spect, this is when I glide through the alley that separates dormitory from classroom and brazenly stride down the path past the cafeteria in time to dance with the night watchman at the front gate—zigzagging between entrances, climbing up the fence and back again, waiting in shadow as he walks by oblivious. And then down the wall that separates gardens and the second wing of classrooms—until, once again, breathless but happy, I am outside your window.

He alluded to them at the time, even seemed proud of himself, but I didn't dis-cover the full sad weight of his obsession until I read those descriptions in his journal. My favorite phrase is "rushing through shrubbery as I throb for you" {allow a love-besotted fool *some* latitude}. As Sabon wrote in her response to this letter, "I throb for you, too, dear-heart, especially rushing through the shrubbery." Sarcasm? Or gentle mockery? When, exactly, did Sabon's intent become treacherous? {Never, really. It was an incidental treachery.}

All rushing throbbery aside, this was dangerous work for Duncan. He used the paths not according to his mood, but according to the by now well-known and ritualistic bumblings of Simon and Jonathan Balfours, the two sixty-year-old night watchmen, twins of {in} habit{s}. He would also factor in the arrival of guests who might conceivably tour the academy at night and the random nocturnal walks of Bonmot. {However, by far the most dangerous person in all of Blythe Academy was Ralstaff Bittern, the gardener. What a tough old buzzard! Stringy as a dead cat, and twice as ugly. He had it in for me from the day I accidentally stepped on one of his precious rose bushes. He'd lie in wait for me at night, positioned strategically behind a willow tree, where he could see the entire courtyard. Many a night, I dared not brave his gaze.}

Indeed, Duncan came close to discovery every few weeks. The first time,

Duncan, using the Path of Naked Necessity and disguised as a priest, rounded a corner and came face to face with a fellow Naked Necessitator: a third-year boy, as petrified as Duncan, the two of them sneaking so noisily through the gravel that neither had heard the other coming.

Duncan wrote later:

If he had uttered a single sound, I would have lived up to my surname—I would have shrieked and begun a babbling confession. But his face in the moonlight reflected such a remarkable amount of fear concentrated in such a small space that I found my tongue first and, shaky but firm, let him know that this—whatever this was—would not be tolerated at Blythe Academy. Continuing on, as much from my own exquisite terror as anything else, I proceeded to drive the demons out of the boy with such overwhelming success that I believe he—certain he could never match the conviction and fervor of the mouth-frothing apparition he met that night—eventually abandoned the priesthood as a vocation and started a brothel on the outskirts of the Religious Quarter. Meanwhile, as he ran away from me, gasping over gravel right out of the Academy, I was shaking so hard my teeth ground together. How close I had come to discovery! What was I to do?

What Duncan did, cynically, was volunteer for "tryst duty" as much as possible, which meant that he joined the ceaseless wanderings of the old night watchmen, supposedly on the lookout for those lean and compact boys, their dark wolf eyes shining, who might defy curfew in hopes of bedding a female student. {I performed a valuable service, whether hypocritically or not. And much of the time, frankly, we caught female students sneaking into the boys' rooms.} This helped, but there were still unwelcome encounters with unexpected teachers or priests at unfortunate times—"Why, I was just checking the window to make sure it was securely locked"—and pricked buttocks from sudden jumps into rose bushes to avoid Bonmot, whom Duncan could not lie to. {The crushed bushes only made the gardener more relentless. Bittern complained to Bonmot several times, but Bonmot was not ready to believe him.} As his fellow history professor Henry Abascond once said to Duncan at a meeting of teachers, "A taste for the night life, have you? A taste for the dark, the shroud?" in typically pompous Abascond fashion. {And he wasn't joking about it, much as others thought he was referring to my area of study. I thought for one paranoid moment that he and Bittern had formed a conspiracy to ruin me, but there was only one genuine conspiracy: my conspiracy to ruin myself.}

Of course, nothing lasts forever, least of all desperate, ridiculous sexual melodrama, and Duncan would prove no exception to the cliché. But that day was as yet far off. In the meantime, Duncan reveled in his love for Sabon—you could see it in his distant enthusiasm at our lunches in the courtyard: a brightness to his eyes, a sheen to his skin that was impervious to rainy days or scholarly disappointments {or the more sympathetic interpretation, that it was the effect of the fungi}.

Still, I noticed that Bonmot scrutinized us both with a certain suspicion, no matter how pleasant our conversations. With me, I believe he was just worried—looking for signs of a despair that might lead me to again cut my wrists—and with Duncan, searching for something hidden that Bonmot could not quite, for all of his wisdom, figure out. {I am sure that if not for my secret studies, he would have found out about Mary much sooner. But rumors that I snuck around at night had, to his mind, more the feel of hidden tunnels and underground depths than of secret assignations with students. My prowess, in his eyes, was the prowess of research and obsession.}

I did not meet Sabon until ten months after I returned to Ambergris. Duncan did not seem eager for me to meet her—perhaps he was afraid Mary would know he had confided in me about their relationship, even if inadvertently; perhaps he was afraid something in our conversation might give him away to Bonmot. For whatever reason, for a long time I continued to hear about Sabon secondhand, through the mirror of Duncan's love for her.

For this first part of their relationship, I cannot bring myself to blame Sabon, not for their mutual seduction. She eventually ruined my brother in many different ways, but at first she made him see a different life—as if all these years there had been another Duncan Shriek, or the possibility of another Duncan Shriek, completely different from the person I knew as my brother. Because they could not be seen together, they devised complex ways of meeting in public. Mary would invite Duncan to one of her parents' parties along with all her other teachers, and then seek Duncan out for a "fatherly" dance or conversation.

Similarly, Duncan began to make the most of social functions at the Ambergris Historical Society by inviting his students to attend for "educational"

reasons. Most students would not show up, conveniently leaving Duncan required to escort Mary for the evening. {You can sneer all you want, Janice, but
that *was* the primary purpose. In fact, I also met other people there who were
useful to my career. I remet James Lacond there, for example, long before he
broke with the Society. You are suggesting I was not just incompetent, but ac-
tively sabotaging myself, which is not the case. It was coincidence that Mary
sometimes appeared at those events, which were so public that there could be
no chance of an assignation.} It was through his attendance at these events that
he had his first real conversations with James Lacond, an active member of
most of Ambergris' cultish "research" collectives—the beginning of a friendship
that would affect Duncan in many ways.

Duncan discovered that he didn't even mind dancing and that, "with a drink
or two in me," as he puts it in his journal, he could "endure chitchat and small
talk." He began to put on some weight, but it looked good on him, and his
new beard, prematurely shot through with gray, gave him a scholarly and respectable appearance. He discovered that people liked to hear him talk, liked to
hear his opinions, something that had only been true at the very beginning of
his career. Suddenly, he saw a future in which he might actually settle down
with Sabon.

Duncan's journal expresses no guilt for his AHS deception, or the many
other deceptions "forced" upon him over the next two years. {My journal could
not express such guilt—after all, my journal is an inanimate object, although
you are doing a fine job of forcing it, by tortuous miscontext, into confessions it
would not otherwise make.} Nor does Duncan's journal offer much in the way
of gray cap research over the next two years. Sabon might have inspired him,
but she also took up much of his time. {True, but by then I had other professors
unwittingly carrying out my research.} Sabon had so altered his perceptions
that a journal entry from the time reads:

All my research, even the gray caps themselves, seems remote, unconnected.
There might as well not be a Silence, a Machine, an underground. I feel as if
I have emerged from a bad dream into the real world. It does not seem possible that one person should be able to lead two such lives at the same time.
{And a third life, in a sense. I could not put aside my conversations with Bonmot. I could not find a way to completely discount the spiritual—not when, in
some sense, I was becoming so much a part of the world that, in the particles
of it that became the particles of me, I sometimes thought I sensed a kind of

presence. It maddened me—that I could not be certain of its relevance. That I could not be sure.}

But just because Duncan no longer believed that his life depended on the gray caps did not mean the gray caps no longer believed in Duncan, as he would soon find out.

❧ 9 ❧

THE SOUNDS FROM THE CEILING have stopped. The sounds from the hole leading underground have not stopped. Curiously, I am calm. I'm somehow glad, even though I can see Mary's necklace of admirers and the marble staircase, can see her books hovering like crows or bats in the green shadows of the ceiling. Age does that to you, I think. It makes it impossible to have a memory that is not colored by the future.

Still, during that time so many years ago, Duncan and Mary's romance progressed into its second year, randy and light-of-foot, although punctuated by awkward—but not fatal—events, such as a very tense parent-teacher conference during which Duncan almost fainted when Mary's father jokingly asked, "So what are your intentions with our daughter?"

Meanwhile, my gallery never fully recovered from my absence. Those artists who had not stolen their art from my walls deserted me in more subtle ways: a parade of apologetic or sniveling excuses is how I see them in my mind, usually delivered by proxy, the artist in question too cowardly or embarrassed to tell me in person. My little dance with death had been only one of several extreme actions that year: half a dozen writers and artists had died, either from their excesses, or from being murdered by rivals during the Festival. {Which, mercifully, you'd missed during your travels; I wish I had missed it as well. I had to work devilishly hard to protect the Academy from the gray caps that year.} The authorities, namely the family Hoegbotton, thought it wise to lay the blame for such maladies at the {comatose, oversexed, overdrugged} feet of the art community. Excess was "out," a new austerity—inappropriate for our great, debauched city, but completely appropriate to my new condition—was "in."

My suicide attempt had only placed an emphatic exclamation point on a year ruinous to all who enjoyed good, clean fun. {You forget the now-pervasive influence exerted by Frankwrithe & Lewden, which led to many of these mishaps. You should, historically, see this as an action by Hoegbotton & Sons against F&L, not against your friends.}

So my gallery stuttered on in an altered state, reduced to selling reproductions of reproductions of famous paintings, and unsubtle watercolors of city life created by people who would otherwise have made honorable livings as plumbers, accountants, or telephone salesmen.

Nearly broke, I had to find other sources of income. From time to time, Sirin still gave me article and book assignments—"My dear Janice," he would say, "come work for me full-time," a perilous agreement if ever there were one. I also received the leavings of Martin Lake, who sometimes gave me—as Sybel later put it— "the financial equivalent of a mercy fuck" in the form of preliminary sketches for paintings that Lake's new gallery, which Sybel had fled to when my fortunes faded, was selling for many times what I'd ever made off him. All in all, my attempt had killed me.

But it hadn't killed me physically—not as Duncan was being killed physically. That second year of his romance with Mary Sabon coincided with a definite worsening of his fungal disease. Sometimes it left him so weak and drained that he could not teach his classes—although this did not mean that if his disease went into remission by nightfall he would not take the Path of Hypocrisy right up to Mary's window. These symptoms varied with the seasons, as shown by a brief examination of the "symptom lists" he kept:

SPRING
Vomiting
Diarrhea
Cramps
Dry mouth
Shortness of breath
Violent mood swings

SUMMER
Dizziness
Blurred vision
Shivering

Profuse sweating
Excessive salivating
Violent mood swings

FALL
Vomiting
Diarrhea
Cramps
Violent mood swings

WINTER
Delirium
Blurred vision
Nausea
Violent mood swings

Duncan was convinced he had contracted these symptoms as a result of his encounter with the Machine. I was convinced the "violent mood swings" had nothing to do with his fungal affliction and everything to do with a malady known as "Mary Sabonitis."

Luckily for their relationship, which otherwise might have been punctuated by episodes more suited to a madhouse or a sick house than an institution of learning, the symptoms came and went like the summer storms that had always plagued Ambergris. {Ironic, that. Because now there is no slower turning to the world than with this disease, this gift in flux, in flow. I might as well be turning into a tree, putting down roots. The yearning in my flesh calls out to the yearning in the ground. Nothing can be made that is not a part of me, that will not eventually become me. "I want for nothing and hunger naught," as some crackpot old saint named Tonsure once said before they buried him underground.}

Admittedly, his disease sometimes brought with it great joy, no doubt also caused by the fungi. An episode during the second year of his affair with Mary best describes the extremity of effects that his body could force from him:

I felt a slight disorientation that morning when I woke in my teacher's quarters. A kind of half-hearted dizziness, a prickling in the skin: a harbinger of encroaching symptoms. However, the sensation faded, so I went to my classes anyway. I remember seeing Mary in the back row of my "Famous Martyrs" class at the exact second that my mouth went as dry as the blackboard. I remember thinking it was just her presence that had affected me. For the first twenty minutes I was fine, livening up my lecture by telling some old jokes about Living Saints that Cadimon Signal had related to me at the religious academy in Morrow. Then, suddenly, I could feel the spores infiltrating my head, my limbs—they clambered over my sinuses, got between me and my own skin. I couldn't breathe. I couldn't move. The spores began to seethe across my eyes, bringing a stinging green veil over my sight. I did the only thing I could do, the thing I have learned to do, still the hardest thing. I relaxed my arms, my legs, my neck, my head, so that I entrusted my balance to the fungi . . . and damned if I didn't stay up. Damned if I didn't continue to live, although I felt like I was drowning. I sweated from every pore. I felt nauseous, disoriented, dizzy. I felt as if the gray caps were searching for me across a vast distance—I could feel their gaze upon me, like a black cloud, a storm of eyes . . . and still the tendrils spread across my vision, blinding me . . . and then, as soon as they had finished their march from east and west, meeting somewhere around the bridge of my twitching nose, all of the discomfort faded and I could . . . breathe again. Not only could I breathe, but I was *flying*, soaring, my body as light as a single spore, and yet so powerful that I felt as if I could hold up the entire Academy with one hand. A fierce joy leaked into me, sped from my feet to my waist to my arms, my head. I could not have been happier had I been the sun, shining down on everyone from on high. And in that happiness, I did not even really exist, except as a connection, a bridge, an archway, linked with a hundred thousand other archways that extended up and down my body in a perfect crisscrossing pattern of completeness. And I cannot help feeling, even as the spores just as suddenly relinquished their hold and left me gasping and white, that what radiated into me was a thank-you from the thousands that comprise the invisible community that has become my body. {Later, Mary told me that I had kept talking through the entire episode, albeit with slurred speech.}

Do I believe him? I've seen too much not to. But, then, Sabon saw exactly what I saw, and she couldn't be bothered to take the leap. She decided, somewhere along the way, to ignore, to miss, to go blind, to *see through*.

After Duncan had recounted some of these "episodes" to me, it was hard to laugh when he began to sign his infrequent postcards, "Your Brother, the Fungus Garden." {But I was—I was a transplanted fungal garden torn from the subterranean gardens of the gray caps. As the seasons came and went, I was the end of the journey for a great exodus, a community of exiles that colonized me and tried to observe the same seasonal rituals—to bloom and ripen and die in accordance with their ancestry. They were homesick, but they made do with what they had: me. And I, poor sap, was in turn able to experience with each season some new explosion of fertility, selfish enough in my pleasure to endure the counterbalanced pain—and to only hope that when in remission my affliction was not contagious. In this way, I remained connected to the underground even though absent from it. One day I will dissolve into the world, will become a gentle spray of spores, will settle on the sidewalk and on trees, on grass and soil, and yet still *be*—watchful and aware.}

Perhaps more disquieting was that, unknown to me, each week brought Sabon's flesh necklace, and thus Duncan's final humiliation, closer.

I had an intimation of the future when, two years into her relationship with Duncan, Sabon finally visited me at my gallery, probably at Duncan's request. {No—she decided to do that on her own. You were my only family besides Mom. She was curious. It's your guilt showing through here—that you weren't supportive, that you were so negative despite never having met her. It strikes me now, Janice, that as much as we talked over the years perhaps we never talked about the right things.} You might well ask why she waited so long, why I waited so long, but I think she must have realized how deeply I disapproved of my brother sleeping with a student. {I'll grant you this now: you seem to have a sixth sense for impending tragedy. At the time, it just seemed like pettiness on your part.}

By then, I had begun to shed even my less respectable artists. But my gallery still maintained an aura of the respectable. I kept it Morrow-clean and replaced each departed painting with some admirable imitation. After that strange cold winter, the weather in Ambergris had been near-perfect for more than eighteen months. Good weather meant more walk-ins, and more walk-ins meant more sales. A few more tourists and I might again be as green as mint-scented, tree-lined Albumuth Boulevard.

So at first I saw Mary Sabon as only another potential buyer. Besides, from Duncan's feverish descriptions, I would have expected someone taller, wiser, more voluptuous. She was short but not slight, her frame neither fat nor thin, and from her shiny red hair to her custom-made emerald-green shoes, from the scent of perfume to the muted red dress that hung so naturally off of her shoulder, she radiated a sense of wealth and health. {She *dressed up* for you, Janice, in her Truffidian Cathedral best.}

She nodded to me as she came in and wandered from wall to wall, glancing at the paintings with nervous little turns of her head. Her hands, held behind her back, clutched a purse. She had not yet attained the artful guile of poise and positioning that would someday make her the center of attention. The necklace had not yet begun to form.

"Can I help you?" I asked, half rising from my desk. I remember wondering if I might interest her in one of the pathetic landscapes that had come to fill my walls—indeed, whether the listed prices were high enough to match her wealth. I had, at that time, some masticated and mauled views of Voss Bender Memorial Post Office—popular since Lake's success—as well as some nicely watered-down panoramas of the docks and the River Moth. All made respectable by the nearby presence and divine quality of two Lake sketches of fishermen cutting apart the carcass of a freshwater squid.

She turned to face me, smiled, and said, "I'm Mary Sabon." Despite her nerves, she carried herself with an assurance I have never had. It rattled me.

"Mary Sabon," I said.

She nodded, looked down at her shoes, then up at me again. "And you, of course, are Janice. Your brother has told me a lot about you." And laughed at her cliché.

"Yes. Yes, I am," I said, as if surprised to learn my own identity. "So you're Sabon," I said.

"Indeed," she replied, her gaze fixed on me.

I said: "Do you know that what you're doing could get Duncan fired by the Academy?"

It just came out. I didn't mean to say it. Ever since the Attempt, I haven't had any tact. {Ever since? You've never had any tact!}

Sabon's smile disappeared, a look of hurt flashing across her face. In that hurt expression I saw a flicker of something from her past coming back to haunt her. I never found out what it was.

"We love each other, Janice," she said—and *there's* a surprise, a shock. Something unexpected brought to the surface by the clacking of keys against paper: she's just a girl. When we met that first time, she was just a girl, without guile. I am ashamed of something and I'm not sure what. She was young. I was older. I could have crushed her then, but did not know it. {Dead. It's all dead. It's all gone. Senseless.}

"We love each other, Janice," Mary said. "Besides, your brother is a historian. He teaches for now, but he's working on new books. . . . And, besides, I won't be a student forever."

I think now of all the things I could have said, gentle or cruel, that might have led away from a marble staircase, a raised hand, a fiery red mark on her cheek.

I sat down behind my desk. "You know he's sick, don't you?"

"Sick?" she said. "The skin disease? The fungus? But it disappears. It doesn't stay long. It isn't getting worse. It doesn't bother me."

But I could tell it did bother her.

"Did he tell you how he got the disease?" I asked.

"Yes. He's had it since he was a boy, when he went exploring. You know—BDD. It comes and goes. He's very brave about it."

Never mind the magnitude of Duncan's lie; it was the BDD that caught me. All the breath left my body, replaced by an ache. Before Dad Died was something between Duncan, my mother, and me. {And yet here you are, sharing it in a manuscript that might be read by any old drunk off the street.}

"Are you all right?" she asked.

There must have been a pause. There must have been a stoppage, a shift of my attention away from her.

"I'm fine," I said, leaning back in my chair. "As long as you know about it."

Yes, the fungus left his skin for weeks, sometimes months, but when it returned, it was always more insidious, more draining of his energy. How could I possibly explain to her about Duncan's obsession with the underground, especially now that he swore it no longer obsessed him?

She smiled, as if forgiving me for something. The simplicity of that smile charmed me for only a moment. Simplicity, where no simplicity should exist. She would always be complex, complicated, devious, in my mind.

"I want to buy a painting," she said.

I had a feeling this was her last-ditch effort to make nice. She would buy my friendship.

"A painting," I echoed as if I were a carpenter, a butcher, a priest, anything but a gallery owner.

"Yes," she said. "What do you recommend?"

This was a good question. I wanted to recommend that she never see Duncan again. That she leave Duncan alone before she hurt him irrevocably. That she never return to my gallery because . . . because . . . Did I say these things? No. I did not. I held my tongue and pointed out the most expensive items in my gallery: the two squid sketches by Lake called, perversely, "Gill" and "Fin."

She nodded, smiled, looked at them, then looked at me. "They're very nice. I'll take them," she said, and, turning, blanched as she noticed the price.

I let her buy them, although I could see they were too expensive even for her. {She didn't have much money. You made her spend two months' allowance on those paintings. I bought them from her afterwards so she'd have money to live on.}

We exchanged minor pleasantries. At the door, purchases in hand, she turned back to me, smiled, and said, "Maybe someday I can join you and Duncan for lunch with Bonmot."

For lunch. Under the willow trees. Just the four of us. How comfortable. How perfect. We would eat our sandwiches in the glare of the summer sun and talk of flesh necklaces and how they form and do not form in this forlorn city by the River Moth. Just now, even in remembering this suggestion, I feel that I am drowning.

A blackness grew inside of me, or the fungus overcame me, or any of a number of conditions or situations that you may, reading this, imagine for yourselves, and I said:

"I wonder. What route will Duncan take tonight? The Path of Remembering You or the Path of Forgetting You."

The painting of the Voss Bender Memorial Post Office actually looked quite striking in the light that pierced the windows and gave my humble gallery a golden hue. The details of that painting became etched in my memory as I stared at it until I could no longer feel the reproach of her gaze and I knew she had gone.

My gallery was empty again. I was alone again. And that was as it should be.

Although I *saw* Mary on Duncan's arm a dozen times after that, the next time I *spoke* to her directly was at the party where she stood waiting for me at the foot of the staircase, the dagger of her comment about Duncan held ready.

❧

IRONIC, REALLY. I HAVE REACHED out across time and space to construct a mosaic of her in a harsh light, only to find that now, when she shares a room with me, that light fails and finds her nearly . . . harmless.

Perhaps I have never really understood Sabon. Perhaps she remains the type of cipher who seems more remote the more words I devote to her. Fading into the ink, untouchable.

The fungus in this place has eaten into the typewriter ribbon. I'm typing in sticky green ink now, each word a mossy spackle against the keys. If I could turn off the light, no doubt my sentences would read themselves back to me in a phosphorescent fury—the indignation of creatures uncovered from beneath a rock. {Equipment failures should never be part of your narrative. That's the first lesson Cadimon Signal ever taught me.} My ink has defected to the cause of the gray caps; not so my blood.

I have made Mary Sabon, deservedly so, as much of a villain in this After-word as the gray caps, and yet I could as easily have offered her an escape—even a fragile excuse could have absolved her for the way my heart feels right now. If only she had offered up something of herself. But she never has: you could pore over her books for a hundred years and never find anything personal. Whether Duncan had a better idea of her true nature is debatable. It is debatable that *Sabon* knew her own heart. {No—she knew. She knew who she was more per-fectly than anyone I have ever met. I think that is why I loved her, and why she did what she did.}

At the party, after I had slapped her—even then she did not offer anything personal. All she did was wave back those who would have otherwise taken me away. She waved back the onrush of beads from her flesh necklace. They re-treated, gleaming and muttering.

"What is it you really want, Janice?" she said, smiling. "Would you like the past back? Would you like to be successful again? Would you prefer you weren't a washed-up has-been with so few prospects she had to agree to help out with a party for an artist she used to agent?"

I had an answer, but it wasn't what Sabon expected. No, it was far more than Sabon expected.

❧❧

BUT I SHOULD PROBABLY START over, even here, and step back into the role of brittle chronicler of that which I would have liked to influence. . . .

Dry facts, as dry facts will, have mushroomed and moistened in recent years, along with the popularity of her books, so that now I can enter any bookstore or library and discover information about her childhood—inspiration, education, perversions, diversions, etc.

Her books, their titles like curses—*The Inflammation of Aan Tribal Wars, The Limited Influence of Gray Caps Upon Ambergris, A Revisionist History of the City*—parrot each other when opened to the biographical note, with selective information added to the end of successive notes like the accretion of silt in the Moth River Delta. Why, I happen to have a couple of her books right here. Imagine that.

The notes from her third book, *Reflections on Ambergris History*, and her latest, *Confessions of a Revisionist: The Collected Essays of Mary Sabon*, differ only by degree. I have combined them below for ease of dissection.

ABOUT THE AUTHOR: Mary Sabon has lived in Ambergris for her entire life. During the War of the Houses, she received her history degree from the Blythe Academy, where her teachers included author Duncan Shriek. (1) Sabon has written 16 (2) books over her distinguished twenty-year (3) career, including *The Role of Chance in the History of the Southern Cities; Trillian as Reformer: The Influence of Pig Cartels on Ambergrisian History;* (4) *Magical Ambergris: The Legacy of Manzikert IX; Nature Studies with My Father; The Gray Caps' Role in Modern Literature: The Dilemma of Dradin, in Love;* (5) and *Cinsorium: Rethinking the Myth of the Gray Caps.* (6) At 47, (7) Sabon remains (8) the most vital and beloved of Ambergris' many historians, shedding light on history and her fellow historians alike. (9) Her early interest in nature studies no doubt arises from her parents David Sabon and Rebecca Verden-Sabon, the former a noted naturalist best-known for having coined the term "Nativism," and the latter a gifted nature illustrator. (10)

Perhaps my annotations can be of help regarding this reeling litany of Mary's accomplishments:

1) *. . . Blythe Academy, where her teachers included author Duncan Shriek.* Over the years, Sirin has decided whether to include Duncan based on two factors: (1) To what extent the book guts Duncan's theories, and (2) The level of Duncan's limited notoriety at the time of publication. If the book openly attacks a theory or theories in Duncan's work—at least half have—and makes that aggression its thesis, the phrase disappears from the sentence, a phantom limb waiting to be reattached. As for notoriety, now that Duncan has disappeared, possibly for good, I imagine he will magically reappear in the author's biography, trapped there for all time. {Or magically reappear *right here.*}

2) *Sabon has written 16 books . . .* Alas, the number continues to rise, each new eviscerating tome kept in print by a necromancy beyond my understanding, and each leading to a more complete flesh necklace. What is Sabon's appeal to readers? Why is she always more popular than Duncan? {And why should

the answer interest us? Get on with the underground adventures.} In page after page of exquisite prose, much of which I cannot bring myself to read, Sabon has, over the years, reassured her readers, made them feel intelligent, offered rational commonsense explanations for even the most miraculous and profound of events. {Although even she cannot explain away the Silence!} It doesn't seem to matter if her answers are wrong or incomplete. It does not matter that her answers often diminish the complexities of the world—leach it of its sorrow and its joy in favor of a comforting numbness, a comforting sameness: the husk of a starfish, not its living body. {And yet, you must admit, Sabon enlivens the corpses with wit and glamour.}

Duncan, conversely, liked to provoke his readers, poke them with a sharpened stick, to emphasize the supreme unknowable irony of the world and then, in marching toward the truth, unearth new mysteries, so that every so-called solution begged a hundred questions. The reader left Duncan's books shaken and unmoored from what he or she had always taken for granted.

In short, if reduced to a single point of punctuation, Sabon's work would have been a period {sometimes an emphatic exclamation mark!}, Duncan's a question mark. Closed doors. Open doors. All shrouded, all revealed. {It could just be that I wrote bad books.} The average reader likes to return home after a long journey, not be left stranded in the middle of nowhere, with dark coming on and the printed pages a desert devoid of comfort. {You make my books sound like mirthless lumps of coal hidden at the bottom of a dry well, Janice! I refuse to believe you didn't see the humor, the enthusiasm, in my books. Replace "desert" with "a mysterious foreign land," with all the danger and excitement that entails.}

3) . . . *over her distinguished twenty-year career.* Unfortunately, this number also continues to rise, although riddled with inaccuracy. Seven years after Sabon graduated from Blythe, the author's note read "ten." Ten years after her graduation, the note read "fifteen." Regardless, I'm sure Bonmot was always glad to see a mention of Blythe Academy bereft of any hint of scandal.

4) The Influence of Pig Cartels on Ambergrisian History . . . The most unintentionally humorous book I have ever read. At its core, Sabon's atrocity is based on Duncan's observation in an article for the Ambergrisians for the Original Inhabitants Society's *Real History Newsletter* that Trillian the Great

Banker fell from power due to his battle with the leader of a powerful pig cartel over the favors of a woman {you can't be sure my mention sparked her book—the anecdote is, more or less, common knowledge}, which prompted Sabon to devote a 175-page book to the futile task of trying to convince the reader that pig cartels have wielded immense power throughout Amber-grisian history—and all the sentences that *I* read at least, are as breathlessly long as this one. {I admit, the book did bewilder me, as did its popularity. But we're all entitled to one bad book. I'm sure the pig cartels were flattered, at the very least.}

5) The Gray Caps' Role in Modern Literature: The Dilemma of Dradin, in Love . . . The only dilemma, to my way of thinking, being how to dignify as "literature" such a collection of angst, stupidity, and old wives' tales. At least Sabon left my brother out of this one.

6) Cinsorium: Rethinking the Myth of the Gray Caps . . . I don't feel up to addressing this book for now. It requires more explanation than I have the strength to give it. Besides, Nativism was born from it, and that's too horri-ble to contemplate at the moment.

7) *At the age of 47* . . . Thankfully, this number also continues to rise. One day it, and she, will pass on to the Infinite. {As will we all, without a little bit of luck or planning. And then none of this will matter to anyone, not that it matters to many people at the moment, anyway.}

8) *Sabon remains* . . . "Remains" best describes the current content of her books: the remains of Duncan's theories, devoured and spat out by Sabon. {That's the way it often happens, although usually, I think, the author stolen from is already dead or senile. Still, the sting of it is there, I cannot deny it.}

9) . . . *shedding light on history and her fellow historians alike* . . . This latest ad-dition to the Sabon Canon {or cannon} at least begins to acknowledge that most of her books feast off of the carcasses of other historians.

10) This mention of Mary's parents reminds me that I have lied a little for the sake of dramatic tension, I think. There was one time I saw Mary before she visited my gallery. I just didn't realize it was her.

I saw her with her parents at Blythe Academy once, surrounded by the controlled chaos that is the start of the spring semester. A spray of sudden greenery from the trees, the clatter of shoes on walkways and stairs as students—nervous and excited—tried to find their classes. As I passed by on my way to visit Duncan, one family caught my eye by their very stillness. They stood in the center of the courtyard and also at the center of a kind of calm. The girl stood, legs slightly apart, staring down at the ground, schoolbooks held carelessly in one hand, a pensive look on her face. Her parents stood like towers to either side of her, the space between them containing a daughter not quite belonging to the same world.

Their unlined, unremarkable faces expressed no great joy or sorrow, or none that I could discern, and yet I could feel a tension there; the presence of some overwhelming emotion. I almost felt as if I were a witness to some kind of ritual or ceremony. Was the girl's head bowed in prayer? As I walked away, I turned to watch them, and it seemed as if they were receding from me at a glacially slow pace.

That must have been Mary's first year at the Academy, and I find it interesting that even then I noticed her, before Duncan ever pointed her out to me, before I even knew who she was.

When I read Sabon's biographical note in her various books, what I envision when I come across the sentence beginning "Her early interest in nature studies . . ." arises not from her gallery visit, but from that first glimpse: of twinned parents standing guard on either side of a daughter whose face is tilted toward the ground. Something about their wary stance still worries me now, even after my research has made of them more than silent statues.

In fact, my research has somehow lessened their pull on my imagination, for the facts do not particularly impress. {They impressed me!}

Given that David Sabon's most important contribution to natural history consists of helping to edit a revised edition of Xaver Daffed's classic *A History of Animals*, perhaps it would be best to simply note his presence and move on. However, his peculiar {dangerous!} attitude toward the gray caps, delivered in the form of speeches to many a meeting of the Ambergris Historical Society {smoky, jaundiced events punctuated by coughs, grunts, and unintelligible murmurings from octogenarian senilitians}, should be documented somewhere. Where better than an afterword?

David Sabon preached a *strain* of Nativism {otherwise known as "a good way to get yourself killed"}, although not quite the same one later popularized by Mary. David Sabon not only believed that gray caps possessed "no more natural intelligence than a cow, pig, or chicken" but that they should be treated "much as we treat other animals." As the transcript for one memorable speech reads, "Gray caps should be used to support our labors, for our entertainment, and for meat."

Although David Sabon later claimed that "and for meat" had appeared in the speech by mistake {transposed from a speech on the King Squid}, the cut-throat Ambergris newspapers had no qualms about printing headlines like DAVID SABON RECOMMENDS SNACKING ON GRAY CAP BEFORE DINNER and NEW "ARCHDUKE OF MALID," DAVID SABON, LIKES A NICE BIT O' GRAY CAP BEFORE BED. Surely Mary Sabon, lone seed of a loon's loins, became indoctrinated with her father's attitudes at a very early age, setting the stage for her own irresponsible theories. {Perhaps so, but Mary always seemed embarrassed by her father's activities.}

While David Sabon's forebears included no one more distinguished than a barber in Stockton and a minor judge in Morrow, Mary's mother, Rebecca Verden-Sabon, came from newly minted stock. Her father, Louis Verden, began his career as a jeweler but went on to illustrate a number of scientific texts, although his best work appeared in *Burning Leaves,* a creative journal he eventually art directed and to which I sometimes contributed when I had no work from Sirin. Verden also illustrated a series of paranoid {not paranoid enough} Festival pamphlets for Hoegbotton & Sons, including *The Exchange, Bender in a Box, Naysayer Mews, In the Hours After Death,* and *The Night Step* {all in collaboration with the darkly humorous, underrated writer Nicholas Sporlender, whom I once bumped into by mistake—underground, oddly enough}.

Rebecca became her father's apprentice and eventually took over editorial duties at *Burning Leaves,* although not until my gallery had turned to dust and ash. Before that, she specialized in illustrations for advertisements or to accompany scientific texts. In some ways, it could be argued that Rebecca's work for her daughter's first book, *The Inflammation of Aan Tribal Wars,* gave her more exposure than all of her previous work combined.

❧❦

DUNCAN'S PARENT-TEACHER CONFERENCES WITH DAVID and Rebecca continued for several semesters. I have this rather humorous vision of Duncan in his office, talking solemnly with Mary's parents and then, once he has smiled reassuringly and guided them out the door, frantically jumping out of his office window, on his way to a tryst with their daughter. {I honestly thought I was protecting her, and that she could make her own choices. After all, she was already a young adult. She knew her own mind.}

Apparently, the famed Naturalist suffered from a peculiar form of blindness: an inability to see anything under his nose unless it crawled or flew or swam or galloped, for that keen observer of the natural world never realized what Duncan and Mary had been up to until he was told by a third party.

"Thank you," he'd said to Duncan. "Thank you for taking such good care of our daughter."

And in his way he had, hadn't he?

❧ IO ❧

MARY AND DUNCAN, DUNCAN AND Mary. As with all utopias, especially those based on love, someone thankfully, always comes along to say, "No—this is not right. No—this should end." Why? Because the true path Duncan always took to Mary's window was the Path of Denial, a path with which I was familiar. For example, take my current situation. I have begun to run out of money, although the owner of this establishment doesn't know it yet. He believes I just haven't had a chance to go to the bank, what with all the typing. {Real life, intruding on the recording of real life. How odd.}

Besides, I'm akin to a curiosity—he makes a healthy living from letting loathsome types peek around the corner at me. "That's Janice Shriek. She used to be famous." Some slack-jawed gimp is peering from behind a glossy wooden beam right now. I am ignoring him—he will not receive even a sliver of my attention.

I do like the smell of beer and whiskey and smoke, however. I do like the busy times when they are all chattering away in there, happy as a bunch of click-clacking gray caps holding a half-dozen severed heads, as in "days of yore."

Duncan only started coming here again in earnest after he fell out with Bonmot. When it all came crashing down, he called the Spore of the Gray Cap his home once more; again became the Green God of the Spore. Many a beer was consumed here. I wonder sometimes if Duncan ever came back during those happy-unhappy hours and sat looking at the corner, where all that can now be seen is a hole.

Now why would Duncan fall out with Bonmot? Could it have been over love? Possibly. If we turn to Duncan's journal, to the entry where he recounts to Mary Bonmot's fateful discovery along the Path of Remembering You, we shall soon find out. The ink was not yet dry on his grief when he wrote:

Glimpsed. Detected. Surprised. Held. Ensnared. Ensnarled. Entrapped. Captured. Stricken. No hope of understanding. He'd caught on, grasped, and comprehended, with no hope of acceptance. If I could make a fence of these words to keep him from us, I would, but it's no use. It's over. I am no longer a teacher. You are no longer my student. In a sense, we are released from all of it—the hiding, the sneaking around, the lying, the delicious forbidden feel of your lips against mine.

{There I go, romanticizing it—putting words between myself and the hurt. I disgust myself sometimes.}

I took the Path of Remembering You well after dark. I don't remember anything about my trip, except the absent-minded scratches from a rose bush in the gardens and the frozen position of the stars. It was cold, and I was glad to pull myself up into your open window and into your smooth white arms. Your skin, as always, awakened my senses, and I trembled from the power of your eyes, the soft place at the base of your neck, the soap smell of you, the miraculous hollows on the inside of your thighs.

And, afterwards, intoxicated by the feel and scent of you, the taste of you on my hands, my lips, I swung happily back into the cold, certain I would see you the next night; even the sudden tight prickle on my left arm, my right foot, that presaged spore-pain only added a spark to my mood. The stars swam and spun, and the solid, cold buildings seemed to sway with this happiness in me that was you.

But, my love, no happiness ever went untested. No happiness ever lasted unchanged, untransformed. It doesn't mean happiness has to end, just that it takes on new patterns, new shapes.

It happened by the willow trees where I first saw you, that flickering shiver of a glimpse, and yet that red hair like a fire burning through the trees. It was by those trees, along the path where I walked a happy man, that the stone table where I spent my lunch hours came into view. It lay at the very heart of the willows like a black cave, not a stone at all, and the dark green leaves of the surrounding bushes glistened with reflected light. And, my love, someone sat at that table, and even in that uncertainty, I knew who it was and all of the life left my gait. I could tell my happiness was about to change.

Bonmot sat at the table, dressed in his most formal clothes, as a Truffidian priest would on sacrament day at the Cathedral. Glittering robes, with gold thread woven through them. Even in the dark, they glittered.

I looked into that dark and I could not see his eyes. "Bonmot," I said, "is that you, Bonmot?" Even though I knew already that it was him.

He said nothing, but motioned for me to sit beside him at the table. I didn't hesitate, Mary—I sat next to him willingly. Any excuses about the cold, the lateness of the hour, would have been crushed by the weight of the stone and that gaze. So I sat and made a joke and remarked on the cold and said, "Should we have a midnight snack, then, instead of lunch?" and trailed off because throughout my nervous monologue Bonmot had said nothing. He stared at me with no expression on his face, the staff leaning against the stone bench, the medallion hanging around his neck on a silver chain. I clutched the table so hard that the stone abraded my fingers.

Now, finally, he spoke, each syllable unbearably clear against the cold night air. This is what he said, my love. I can't forget it. I can't sleep tonight because of it. He said, "It's no use, Duncan. I know. Once I too had a secret that made every breath I drew a lie, and so it's no use for you to talk of other things. Because *I know*. You have compromised your student, Mary Sabon."

There was silence for a full ten seconds and then I began to talk. I could not stop talking. Every word was a denial of what he had said. Every word placed such a distance between you and me that it made me physically ill—and yet I did it because I thought it was the only way to save us. And so I babbled on— what was Bonmot talking about? How dare he? Didn't he know me better than that? I had just been out taking a late walk. Didn't he know I helped to keep boys *away* from female students? Didn't he realize I was a colleague, a professional, a person who would never do what he accused me of? After so many talks in the gardens at lunch—so many wonderful conversations—how could he possibly consider—why, it was an outrage—why, I had been a model teacher—why, I was a published historian—I was—I was . . . and, finally, at some point, I realized that he had heard none of what I had said, and that his look of sorrow had transformed his face from granite to skin and flesh and bone. And I stopped talking. I looked away from him. My body shook. I could already anticipate everything he was about to take away from me, and I thought it meant the end. Really, The End.

He said: "There are no more lunches under the willow trees for us. You are no longer a teacher at this academy. I expect you to gather your things now and be gone before dawn. As for Mary, she will finish out the next two semesters and earn her degree, but if you ever set foot in this place again, she will be expelled in a very public way. I have had my fair share of scandal, Duncan. I will not let friendship or anything resembling it destroy my good works at this school. Good night, Duncan."

I did not even notice when he left because I thought I had lost you. I thought those words meant not just the end of my career as a teacher, but the end of us. But now, as I tell you all of this, I realize it is not the end—it just signals a change. A change for the good. We've been desperate and in love, which can be a great thing. It lends an urgency to all we do and say. It means that we do not take lightly each other's bodies or our hearts. It means we love each other fiercely and with no artifice between us.

But this is not the only kind of love we can have—it's not the only kind of passion. What we have is a flame like your hair, but there's another kind of excitement in the freedom to admire each other in public, without fear. There is a charge that comes from sharing our lives through more than just mid-night trysts and frantic letters like this one. And this is why, finally, having lost everything tonight, I am still oddly hopeful, Mary. Mary. Your name is still such a revelation to me, your body always reminding me of the first time so that your touch makes me weak with the miracle of this thought: I am with Mary Sabon. I am loving Mary Sabon.

I am writing this by lantern light in my office. As dawn begins to gray the city, I can almost see your window from where I sit. The air is sweet and cool. I have two cases full of books and other personal belongings. In a few min-utes, I will leave this academy, perhaps forever. I will leave only two things behind me: in my desk, for you to take when you will, that copy of Cadimon Signal's *Musings on the Many Faces of Ambergris* that you so much wanted—it was supposed to be a birthday present—and this letter, protected by our fa-vorite hiding place. Please, if you have read this far, don't cry. Everything will be okay. I promise.

Please do not abandon me.

Love,
Duncan

Please do not abandon me, he writes in this journal entry that awkwardly tran-sitions into a letter that could have been written by a nineteen-year-old, which he rips out of his journal, signs, and leaves for her—only for it to return to him four years later to be reunited with its fellow pages. He did not tear out related pages and send them to her. He did not send her the page right after his tearful but triumphant farewell, the one that contained this passage: "I have lost one of my best friends. I have lost a friend because of my own stupidity. Who will understand now? Who will I be able to talk to?"

Who will understand now? Here's the heart of it, what began to eat at Duncan. He told Bonmot so many things—sometimes in abstract, sometimes nonspecific, but still with enough detail that Bonmot could respond with all of his training and intellect. Me, I was neither historian nor priest, neither artist nor subject of art. Mary? Too young, he must have known on some level. Fine for the physical, but not to discuss such mysteries with. {Not true, and unfair, and judgmental, and unworthy behavior, even from you. I did not discuss the underground, the gray caps, my disease with her to *protect* her. And, yes, because she was young, but not because I didn't think she could understand—but because I was afraid I would scare her. That she would think me a crackpot, a false prophet, a madman.}

In fact, he did not tear out the *first* draft of his second page, which is identical to the second draft, except for the speech he attributes to Bonmot:

There are no more lunches under the willow trees for us. You are no longer a teacher at this academy. I expect you to gather your things now and be gone before dawn. As for Mary, she's just a child. She is as much your victim as this academy. Have you ever thought how this might hurt her? And I don't mean your status as her teacher, but you, Duncan, you in particular. How many obsessions can you sustain in your life? How many masters can you serve? Survive?

Did he suppress this part to save Mary from hurt, to protect Bonmot from her resentment? Or to make himself look better? {It doesn't really matter *now*, does it? One would think you were more intent on defending Mary than destroying her. You should decide what your purpose is.}

※

I THOUGHT WRITING ALL OF this down would help me place events in their proper order and context. Instead, the sequencing grows hazy. I stand at the base of the stairs at Martin Lake's party, the scarlet imprint of my hand still warm on Mary's face, about to respond to her careless words. What did I say? I'm not sure it matters anymore. The harder I focus, the faster the sharpness I desire and deserve dissipates, as if it all happened at the same time, or backwards, and we only now approach a beginning.

Is there any real reason, other than bad luck and ill-timing, that Mary and Duncan could not still be together? Is there any reason it could not have been Mary and Duncan that I walked toward down the stairs, the flesh necklace/noose undone before it ever formed, its pieces resolved into smiling, appreciative faces? The imprint of my hand on Mary's face transformed into the loving touch of a sister-in-law? I might not be here now, the darkness of the ceiling muted only by the purple tiers of fungus that encroach at such speed. {No purple fungus ever grows with good intent in this city, Janice. You must have known that. It is a breed bred for spying, the source of myriad fragmented reports collected in the depths of the city's underground passages.}

But words will never persuade the past. Bonmot did fire Duncan. It did signal the beginning of the end {in one sense, but only in one sense} for my brother and Mary.

I remember that Bonmot told me about it during one of our sessions in the Truffidian Cathedral. I didn't have unbridled sex anymore, so I had, as you may have guessed, turned to "religion." That didn't last, either, because it had little to do with faith, but at least it gave me an excuse to spend time with Bonmot. We were standing in the very place where he later died, among the pews closest to the door.

"Janice," he said. "I've had to do something. I hope you won't hate me for it."

"I don't think I could hate you, Bonmot."

"You might. I've had to let Duncan go. Because of Mary. I think you already know what I mean?"

For a second, it was very quiet. I was shocked. Duncan hadn't had a chance to tell me. I hadn't seen him in days.

"Did you really have to?" I asked. I think I was worried, at first, as much about how it might affect my relationship with Bonmot as about Duncan.

"Yes. I had to."

He bowed his head, and we prayed.

※

HOW DID MARY RESPOND TO this news? For a long time—for longer than I might have expected—she stood by Duncan. Duncan told me a week later, an echo of passion in his voice, that Mary had smuggled a letter to him through her unsuspecting parents. {Bonmot had left it up to Mary to tell her parents, and she never did.} In it, she begged him to wait for her. Either Duncan's line of romantic blather had ensorcelled her or she found the general notion of separated lovers, forced to check their desires, tragically romantic.

"A year and I can be with her," Duncan told me. "We'll find an apartment. Settle down."

"Have some kids?" I said. "Find a respectable day job? Stop skulking around belowground?"

A bitter smile twisted his face, but he did not reply.

{It may have seemed bitter to you, but I was mostly aghast at your lack of faith. I truly thought back then that Mary and I shared the same beliefs about the underground. In my dreams, I led her through those tunnels as if I were still a boy of fifteen, her sense of adventure as acute as my own.}

Mary might beg him, but Bonmot's begging days were well behind him; the old priest would never forgive my brother. His superiors in the Truffidian hierarchy used the incident to further humiliate him within the church. Nor would the Academy as a collective of teachers forgive him. Although Bonmot made no attempt to spread the news beyond informing them that Duncan had left the staff, Duncan's fellow instructors found out. How could they not? Their lack of forgiveness would take many forms, the worst of which would further hound my brother to the outer edge of his chosen field. {I was more concerned about getting from them the data they'd collected while working unwittingly on my many projects.} Many {not so many; certainly not, I thought then, enough to scuttle any future career aspirations} of his former colleagues wrote for history journals, or edited them, or had written books. With them as gatekeepers, with their long memories, it became less and less likely that Duncan's theories would ever find print in respectable publications again. {Respectable? Disreputable, really. Hundreds of pages of print a year devoted to concealing or sidestepping the truth. *They* were on the fringe the entire time and didn't know it.} Thus, Duncan's excommunication from Blythe further isolated him from anyone but Mary. {Mary *and you*, which certainly wasn't my idea of a happy family.} Duncan's journal reached new levels of bathos {It was genuine sadness at the time, but even proper melancholy is worthy of scorn in retrospect} in listing those who had abandoned him, in pages and pages of affronted pride. I'll spare you all but a snippet of it.

Atriarch, Elizabeth—Assistant dean of student affairs, made a mock ritual
   of me dancing with her at school functions. Next to Bonmot, her support

was the most helpful in continuing my underground studies. She had once accompanied the famous Daffed on one of his odd specimen exhibitions into the Southern jungles, and she had learned to love the muck and mire of slogging through vegetation. I fed her a steady diet of harmless but exotic stories about the underground, and in return she looked away as my classes grew more and more esoteric. Now, I might as well be a shadow to her. {Everyone was a shadow to that woman. I should not have taken it personally.}

Balfours, Simon—One of the guards I used to evade while making my way to trysts with Mary; he liked to joke with me about the Hoegbottons. The one time I saw him in the street since, he barked out my name like a curse, and followed it with real curses. {Since dead, of a heart attack, falling while on duty. I can't blame him for his response—I made a fool of him.}

Binder, David—A stuffed shirt fool, head of Morrow Studies, who used to chatter on endlessly while I was trying to get to my next class. Now he's gone silent as dumb stone, as useless to me now as he was to my research. {I stand by my assessment, especially now that he, too, is dead, run over by a motored vehicle.}

Bittern, Ralstaff—The gardener! Even the gardener won't talk to me, won't look at me. Although, in truth, he never liked me much. But I thought he at least enjoyed matching wits with me in his efforts to uncover the scope of my midnight perambulations. It seems I was incorrect. {Now he's the gardener for the grounds around the Truffidian Cathedral, and his attitude is absolutely the same. He spits at me when he sees me.}

Cinnote, Fiona—Indigenous Tribes Studies. Beautiful in her own way. She used to laugh at my jokes. I used to laugh at hers. There was a world-weariness behind her eyes that made me think she had an interesting history. But she had an affair with Binder, for Truff's sake. How dare she judge me! {And how dare I judge her, truly. I actually thought about suggesting lunch, but she quit the Academy and mounted an expedition to the Southern jungles, never to be seen again.}

. . . and on, and on . . .

When it came to Blythe Academy, all Duncan could think of for several years was how he had been wronged by them. He couldn't see how he'd hurt the Academy, or his fellow professors. There was nothing in him, then, that was able to accept the guilt of his misdeeds. {Perhaps not on the surface, Janice. But

I've made up for it since. I think I've made up for it thrice over. But I guess *no one makes it out,* a line Lacond was fond of quoting from Tonsure.}

Even worse, these were people Duncan had never mentioned to me or hadn't known while at Blythe. He had never cared about them before, but their features came into sharp relief after he believed himself wronged by them. {I have no comment, no defense.}

So Duncan became absent from Blythe Academy, no longer roaming its halls, its gardens, its classrooms. The effect of Duncan's sudden removal on Mary, paradoxically, was an unlikely blossoming. Released from the constant "tutelage" and the equally lustful pressure of Duncan's ideas, she, Bonmot told me, had become one of the school's best students. With Bonmot to guide but not smother, Mary began to develop her own theories, the seeds that would eventually lead to disagreement and betrayal. {You find her theories totally without merit, Janice, yet claim that I constricted her intellectual freedom like some monstrous . . . monster. You can't have it both ways. I don't deny I made some mistakes, as I'm sure you'll soon demonstrate, but I'm not totally at fault. I'm not sure anyone is at fault.}

I can only guess how no longer having access to the Academy affected Duncan's studies of the gray caps. I imagine it hurt him to the core, if he could even register that pain above the intensity of his lust for Mary. {Wrong again! Wrong! You are setting new records for presumption in this account. By the time of my expulsion, I had nearly completed my experiments. There was little else I could set my students to doing that would not arouse suspicion. My classes had, by that point, become mockeries of classes, mockeries of studies. The students themselves sensed it. That the results were inconclusive does not mean the experiments were incomplete. I just moved my laboratory and studies to another location—namely, my own body. And quite a schooling that proved! As I began to live with my condition, and then find ways to control it, it became less of a disease and more of a transformation.}

❦❖❦

A WEEK AFTER DUNCAN TOLD me about his expulsion from Blythe Academy, the late afternoon brought not only rain and the murmur of prayers from the Religious Quarter, but also a knock on the door. Duncan stood on the porch in the rain, his hair plastered to his head and puddles around his booted feet. Gray as a mushroom dweller, and smelling of mildew. Eyes like phosphorescent green circles with dead black centers. For a startled second, I saw him as Mary would later—not of this world, but not having left it. Half-invisible spores, caught by the porch light, formed a hazy halo around his head. His hair had begun to thin and I noticed, with a pang of recognition, the emergence of gray at his temples. And yet, once again, he was fleeing the ruins of a self-made disaster. A part of me could not sympathize.

"This is becoming routine," I said.

"Can you find me a job?" he asked, grinning. "I'm broke." As matter-of-fact as that. With the old glow of fragile confidence you find in people held together by nothing more substantial than affection {and fungi}.

"Hello to you, too," I said, walking back into the apartment to find him a towel, vaguely happy that I would not be asked to scrape mushrooms off of him this time.

As I threw the towel in his face, I said, "Of course I can find you a job. There are lots of available positions for a paranoid, discredited, fringe historian with a fungal disorder who has recently been laid off for laying his students."

Duncan winced. "Student. Singular."

"Singular. Plural. Does it really matter?" I turned away from him. "So. Should I go or do you want to?" I asked. "Neither of us really has a choice. It's not like my gallery is going to pay your bills when it doesn't even pay mine."

"Go?" He stared quizzically at me for a moment, and then he understood. "You should go. What if he disapproves of me now?"

"You assume he knows."

"He knows everything. And what he doesn't know, he finds out quickly. You should go."

So I went. And that was the start of something altogether different.

❧

SIRIN'S OFFICE OCCUPIED PART OF the second floor of Hoegbotton & Sons' headquarters on Albumuth Boulevard. The dull mass of red bricks always smelled of packing sawdust and exotic spices. It had gained a kind of inbred notoriety due to a novel that had used the offices as a prop to its fading plot during its climactic scenes. The building had survived not only that malaprop, but centuries of other challenges—from the Gray Tribes, to Festivals gone bad, to fires set by outraged monks from the Religious Quarter protesting unsavory business practices. {Not to mention the ongoing assault on its editorial domains by a certain pair of increasingly toothless and shrill Shrieks.} "There are only

two times not to trust a Hoegbotton: when you're selling and when you're buy-
ing" was a common saying down at the docks.

Sirin's office—a haven for culture within the blunt instrument of greed that
formed the building proper—had a seasonal quality to it. In the winter and early
spring, Sirin's rosewood desk would be buried in contracts, manuscripts, propos-
als, financial information, and related books, all in preparation for publication.
{Not then, but soon—perhaps even within three or four years—one of those
manuscripts would be Mary's. She truly was gifted at one point. And prolific—
positively fecund—once she got started.} As the year progressed, his desk would
slough off much of the clutter, until, by autumn, all but the finished books had
vanished, and the magazines or broadsheets pregnant with reviews, both bright
and dark, had taken their place. Then winter would once again obscure the lovely
rosewood of his desk with the weight of things promised and things promising.
His office had the most wonderful smell: of parchment pages, of ink, of newly
printed books.

Remembering this as I type, I suddenly see not just one trip to Sirin's office,
but many, over several seasons, a pleasant overlay of memories as sensual as any
heated groping of bodies in the back rooms of a guest house. I see the perpetual but graceful aging of Sirin, which for him manifested itself solely in his
hair, which whitened and receded, while the rest of him stayed exactly the
same. I see the constant rush and withdrawal of the papers on his desk. I see the
sudden and inexplicable disappearance and reappearance of his legion of secre-
taries. The blur of colors and motion outside of his windows. The steady permanence of his smile, his desk, his butterflies. {It's difficult to shake off the
feeling, isn't it, Janice? Difficult because you don't want to. Neither do I.}

One of the more distinctive aspects of Sirin's offices, beyond the sheer ex-
pansive clutter on his desk {early spring, then, was it?}, and the lingering odor
of cigars and vanilla, were the tubular glass enclosures a Morrow glass blower
had made for him. They lay clustered on the table behind his desk, near an oval
window that overlooked Albumuth Boulevard. Each had tiny holes cut into the
glass and contained a caterpillar, chrysalis, or fully formed butterfly. {Certainly,
little bound his butterflies to the past, or the present. As they emerged glistening from their tight houses, they knew nothing but the moment. Sometimes I
envied them.}

I had often observed Sirin puttering over his charges as his secretary showed
me in, but this time he stood there lamenting a dead butterfly. Sirin looked

tanned and well-rested beneath his crisp gray suit and burgundy shoes, any graceful effect ruined by a glaring multicolored bowtie that a clown would have been ashamed to wear; it was his only vice, besides tricking people. His hair had by now receded to reveal more and more of his narrow, intelligent face.

I had known him for many years, and yet I knew little or nothing about him, really.

Sirin spun around at my approach. {Butterflies and moths lived inside his head, Janice, just as mushrooms lived inside of mine. This made it difficult to hear.} He fixed me with the famous stare that could pierce walls and bring confessions from even the most hardened Truffidian monk.

"Look at this," he said, gaze bright but disturbed behind the gold frames of his glasses. "My favorite sapphire cappan has been colonized by the emissaries of the gray caps. It's a sign, perhaps." His outstretched hands, smeared with fungal spores and bearing the crumpled corpse of his beloved butterfly, belonged to a piano player, not an editor and writer. {I often thought his piano playing was a step above his editing, to be honest.}

We met halfway between the door and his glass habitats. I stared at the creature in his hands. True enough—the dead butterfly was completely encrusted with an emerald-green fungus. The outstretched wings had sprouted a thousand tendril colonists, topped with red and resembling a confusion of antennae. It looked like some intricate wind-up toy covered with jewels. It looked more beautiful than it could have alive—not just a butterfly choked with fungus, but a completely new creature. Even the texture of its exoskeleton appeared to have changed, become more supple. I stared at it with sudden irrational fear. It was too similar to the process that had begun to claim my brother. {I am neither butterfly nor fungus, and I chose my fate, but I appreciate your concern.}

Sirin's voice brought me back to the present.

"It's a shame, Janice," he said. "A terrible waste. A tragedy of Manzikertian proportions. I should never have left." He had recently returned from a "vacation" in the Southern Isles forced upon him to avoid the backlash from his role in the Citizen Fish Campaign, about which the less said the better. {Even an aging historian such as I, Janice, must consider that statement a challenge: Senior members of the Hoegbotton clan had suggested Sirin temporarily disappear after it became known through a leak to the city's broadsheets that Sirin had been behind Citizen Fish, an effort to fill the recently vacated Antechamber position with a stinking, five-day-old freshwater bass.}

"You had no choice," I said.

A dismissive shrug. "We might have won the election. Anyone would have been better than Griswald. He'll last a few weeks, perhaps, before they tear him down. Figuratively, one can only hope. A shame."

"Yes," I said. "It is." But I wasn't sure if he meant the butterfly or something more elusive, more dangerous. The distance between us grew with each new utterance.

Sirin turned toward his desk, butterfly still cupped in his hands, and seemed startled by the cacophony of papers, books, pens, manuscripts, newspapers, and contracts that greeted him. Most prevalent were the manuscripts, which had been so thoroughly lacerated with red pen marks that they looked as if they were bleeding out. {Sirin the Invasive, I used to call him. Always trying to put his stink on a poor writer's immaculate style. Always intimidating people with his little red pen. I used to joke that if he had had to use his own blood to make his marks he'd have been stingier with his criticism.}

"Sit, sit," he said, gesturing to a chair piled high with books. "Just push those off."

Bent almost double by the burden, I did as he suggested. As I sat down, I could not help but notice a ragged piece of paper, in his handwriting: "Did the arrival of the Manzikert family in some way trigger a change in the gray caps? Did the arrival of M ruin our chance to understand them?" {That is another thing I will never forget about Sirin: his ragged notes, the emissaries of authorial destruction.}

So Sirin, too, had his finger on the pulse of a mystery {or simply a note mimicking or correcting some book he planned to publish}. I sometimes thought that should Sirin and Duncan ever sit down for a serious talk, all mysteries would be solved, revealed, undone. {No—not true. An altogether uglier scenario comes to mind.}

Sirin laid his tiny burden down on the desk in front of me, then sat back in his chair, arms crossed, and stared at me, an odd smile flitting across his face. Perhaps he was already contemplating his escape, or perhaps it was one last smile of pain for his sapphire cappan. An exotic jewel, the butterfly looked ever more beautiful in the light streaming from Sirin's window.

"I heard a rumor," Sirin said, "that Duncan has left Blythe Academy under peculiar circumstances. Is this true?"

"He has left, it's true," I said. "There is nothing peculiar about it, however. A difference of opinion, really. Nothing that would get in the way of his being hired by someone else."

"Janice. Is Duncan determined to destroy every career he makes some progress toward?" {Typical of the bastard.}

I gritted my teeth. "It was an amicable parting of the ways."

"I hear otherwise," Sirin said, but dismissed my nascent protest with a wave of the hand. "Not that it matters much."

I'm confused now. I can't remember if we had this discussion in his office or somewhere else, if I'm thinking of another conversation. As I try to imagine his office during our meeting, I see books that belong to other eras, other encounters. I'm fairly sure that *The Exchange & Other Stories* by Nicholas Sporlender had not yet been published, for example, and that that book of essays about Martin Lake wasn't published until several years later, either. Why, now that I really look, I can see a cane in the corner of Sirin's office, although he didn't use one. And over there—glimmering darkly, like some expanse of black lamp-lit water—a starfish Duncan never showed him. No, actually, it's a pair of the same glasses I brought with me to Lake's party. I can see that now.

Does that mean Sirin knew what Duncan knew? About the glasses? {You worry me, sister. The one thing you had going for you was a kind of grim, lurching linear progression. You seem to be losing that now.}

It's darker in here than before, but I can see better, if that makes any sense. The spores are thick. I shall ask the bartender to bring me a fan, or to open the window. I can't afford to leave again now. It's getting too late to rewrite. All I want to do is move forward. All I want is to look ahead. Typos will proliferate. Sentences will wind up nowhere. I don't care.

But we were in Sirin's office, attempting to throw off the weight of accumulated memory.

Sirin told a joke of some kind, but I didn't understand the punch line. We sat there uncomfortably for a moment before I said, "I came here to see if—"

"You came here to find work for Duncan, and possibly for yourself. Your gallery is failing. Duncan was indiscreet with a student. Tell me why I should help you?"

No respite from that uncanny knack he had for knowing things. I said the only thing I could say: "We've always done good work for you. Rarely missed a deadline. Our private lives have never affected Hoegbotton."

Sirin laughed at that—or perhaps I am again remembering some other meeting—and as his body shook with that not unsympathetic laughter, a strange black dust rose from his suit.

He sat forward, elbows on the desk, fingers templed. His features took on a sudden intensity. He said: "I am going to recommend you both for positions.

Temporary or permanent, who can tell? Something horrible is about to happen that will provide an opportunity for you both to find work. *The Ambergris Daily Broadsheet* will soon become the only reliable source for information. They will need reporters. Between the two of you, you should be able to supply that need and do a good job." {Just do a good job? Nothing was ever so simple with Sirin, which is why I kept well away from him.}

This information stunned me. "How do you know?" I started to say, but then shrugged. I had given up trying to understand how or why Sirin knew so much, or why it continued to surprise me. Someday, I was sure, Sirin would write a book that explained it all.

"It doesn't matter why, does it? I'm offering you employment." {Witty, yes. Clever, yes, with a core of hidden sadness, but also deadly in his way.}

He leaned forward, offered me a card from the end of his long fingers. I liked looking into his eyes, used to experience a tiny tremor from the effect of that gaze.

"Visit the editor at the *Broadsheet*," he said, "in about six weeks. When it all begins."

"Six weeks is a long time to wait," I said. Ahead, in those six weeks, lay a period of the doldrums—Duncan stalking Mary from afar, unable to get close, while I piloted the doddering skeleton of my ever-less-seaworthy ship of a gallery. At times, sitting at my desk with no customers on the horizon, I could actually feel the room begin to list from side to side, the gallery anchored to nothing more permanent than perpetual debt.

Sirin sat back in his chair. "Not as long as you might think." His gaze softened. "I cannot guarantee you anything, Janice. No one ever receives what might be called an ironclad guarantee. Now, I have another appointment, so you'll have to excuse me. If you're lucky, perhaps you can turn your work for the *Broadsheet* into a book for me. We'll see about that later, depending on whether or not Ambergris is still standing at the end of this."

And that was the end of my meeting with Sirin. As I left, he had returned to his butterflies, clucking his disapproval of the fungus that had swallowed up his sapphire cappan.

Two things stayed with me from that encounter. First, the name on the card: "James Lacond." Lacond—thick, stinking of cigars, rumpled, pinkish, rambling—would soon play a large role in Duncan's life. But as I stared down at the name and tried to understand that our lives would be changing in six weeks, he seemed nothing more than a bit player. This was when it first occurred to me that perhaps Sirin had not received his information about Duncan in quite as intuitive a way as I had thought. As I left, I could have sworn that I saw a manuscript with a title page reading "The Role of Chance in the History of the Southern Cities" pinned between two volumes of *The Lore of the Ancient Saphant*. Even now, the thought of that title, Sabon's first book, causes an involuntary shudder.

{Like those hallucinations you were having a few paragraphs ago, this is clearly impossible. Mary did not publish her first book for four years. For two of those years, I saw her drafts. Such marvelously light, sensual drafts. I would only reluctantly apply my red pen to them, for to edit her, often in the afterglow of making love, was almost to draw upon her skin, to criticize her very form—which I could not do, for she was perfect in every way.}

Within the hour, Sirin, that elegant man, would disappear from Ambergris for three years. Where he went, what he was doing, no one would ever know.

❧❦

A FIGHT BROKE OUT IN the bar a couple of minutes ago. As I typed, I listened to the raised voices for a few minutes before the screech of chairs and a heavy sound, like a table being overturned, marked its escalation to something more serious. For a moment, I wanted to go out there. I felt insular, removed. I wanted to talk to someone. Anyone. Instead of just "talking" to whoever is reading this account.

I have wondered, more than once, who will be reading this after I am gone. I am faced with the distinct possibility that the owner of the Spore will read it—or at least glance at it. {Wrong—I got here first.} If this is so, thank you for your hospitality. I wonder what you'll make of these spore-stained pages. {I wonder what he'll make of my notes. Except I'm not sure I'll leave the pages here when I'm done. I might move them somewhere safer.}

There.

The bar is silent now. Someone is breathing deeply. Someone is typing and breathing deeply. We're getting close to the end. I can see Mary at the bottom of that staircase, waiting patiently for me to destroy her world.

There's a hole behind me, you know. I may have mentioned it. They've filled it in, but on breaks from typing I've been reopening it. I've cleared away a lot of rubble in the last few days. Something also seems to be working at it from the other side. Maybe it's yet another indication of the Shift, or maybe it's just an old-fashioned intrusion. I guess I'll find out eventually.

❧

FIVE WEEKS AFTER MY TALK with Sirin, a man later identified as Anthony
Bliss walked up to the entrance of a Hoegbotton storage house near the docks.
He nodded to the attendant, who stood inside stacking boxes, and then, according to a witness, held out his hand with something in it. The attendant, John
Guelard, straightened up, nodded back, and took a step toward Bliss. Bliss
tossed the object to the attendant. Guelard caught it with one hand, cupped it
with his other hand, and then frowned. He tried to pull his hands away from
the object, but he was stuck to it. Bliss nodded, smiled, and walked away into
the crowd, while Guelard writhed on the ground, his skin turning rapidly
whiter and whiter while beginning to peel off in circling tendrils of the purest
white . . . until nothing remained of him but glistening strands of fungus. The
strands of fungus began to darken to a deep red, and then exploded into a gout
of flame. Within minutes, before water could be pumped to the scene, the storage house had burned to the ground, taking a considerable portion of Hoegbotton & Sons' imports for the month with it. The object Bliss had tossed to
Guelard had been a kind of spore mine bought from the gray caps: Frankwrithe
& Lewden's first overt action against their mortal enemy, Hoegbotton & Sons,
in what would come to be known as the War of the Houses.

Part 2

It is perhaps too cruel to think of Tonsure not only struggling to express himself, to communicate, underground, but also struggling aboveground to be heard as [historians try] equally hard to snuff him out.

—DUNCAN SHRIEK, FROM
The Hoegbotton Guide to the Early History of Ambergris

*"Let no man nor woman say
they crossed me and lived to tell
unless in grave discomfort ever after!"*

*"What ho! I see Sophia's Island
before me, weighted by the night,
as like an echo as a ghost."*

*"Might we shed our ghastly fate
and shed with it this war
that we never should have waged?"*

What do you most vividly remember about the War of the Houses?

Even as recently as six months ago, some brazen young reporter asked me that question, having taken the time to track me down in my apartment: a ruin crowded with the detritus of a lifetime of false starts. I can't even remember what broadsheet he represented, to be honest.

I was surly and morose after a long day of serving as a tour guide for the type of people I call the Ignorants and the Rudes, and I had begun to take on some of their less savory characteristics. Besides, he was *very* young; even as a child, Sybel had never been that young. I doubted this one had been alive at the start of the war.

"What do you most vividly remember about the War of the Houses?" he asked me.

You could see dust motes floating in the air behind his head, revealed by the sunlight of the open window. I rarely opened that window anymore. I didn't like what it revealed about my apartment: the worn red carpet, the sequined dresses half-hidden on hangers in a corner, draped over a dumpy old sofa chair; the dozens of paintings I'd rescued from my gallery, none of them worth a thing. I even had two ceremonial swords from Truff knew where—and dozens of picture albums I hadn't had the heart to pull out in years.

The place needed a serious airing out, although to the reporter's credit he didn't so much as wrinkle his nose, even when a plume of dust rose from the impact of his sinewy buttocks meeting the seat of the second sofa chair.

"What do I remember?" I echoed. Truff, his face was smooth and bare of worry, even in that light. Does every innocent share that look? "Why, the opera, of course," I said.

His eyes brightened and widened, and he began scribbling on a useless little pad he had brought with him.

"When we were reporters during the war—especially by the middle of it— we didn't have paper," I said in a helpful tone. "We had to jot notes on handker-chiefs using our own blood. Usually when the ink ran out."

He looked up, startled, his brown hair sliding down over his even browner eyes, then stared at his pad with an almost guilty expression until I cackled—a sound that startled me more than him—and he realized I was joking.

"Are you upset with me for some reason?" he asked, all semblance of reporter gone. Suddenly he was just a kid, the way Duncan had once been a kid.

I stared at this nascent reporter and sighed, sat back in my chair and said, "No. I'm not upset. I'm old and tired. Can I get you something to drink? Or eat? A friend made me some pastries. I think they're still around here somewhere." I started to look beneath the pillows assembled at my feet.

"No," he said, a little too quickly. "That's all right. I just want to know more about the war, about the opera."

He had lips that would always be full and yet empty of expression or inflection. A serious mouth, without even a hint of an upward or down-ward curve to reveal whether he was an optimist or pessimist. Because of that alone, he might someday become a good reporter, I thought. Or a good card player.

But now he was sitting there, waiting for my answer and sweating, the sweet young scent of him filling my apartment.

"It was a war," I told him. "A lot of people died. A lot of buildings were destroyed. It was hell—and for what? I don't think anyone knew *why* after a while."

He nodded as if he understood. But how could he, really? We'd been reporters during wartime and we didn't even understand it. As my father always said, a reporter is a mirror, not a window, which makes it doubly painful. You don't just let it flow through the glass of your perspective; you stare back at it.

Already a lump was forming in my throat. My apartment looked unbearable. My leg was heavy and inert and aching.

I rarely tell any reporter what I remember—to them I give platitudes, clichés, spirals of brave words that mean nothing. Because it's painful. Because we lost so much during the war.

"No one makes it out." Those were among Samuel Tonsure's last written words, according to what Duncan had uncovered at the fortress-monastery of Zamilon, and it's a good piece of life advice: *No one makes it out.* Enjoy what you can while you can.

I was tempted to repeat Tonsure's wisdom to the reporter, but I had already begun to feel self-conscious, and irrelevant. Besides, he had a question.

"And what about the opera?"

I smiled and leaned forward, staring into his pretty face and untroubled eyes.

"What I remember about the War," I said, "is that right in the middle of it near the very epicenter of the conflict, when hundreds of men, women, and children might be blown up or turned to spores in the next week, the creative powers that be in Ambergris decided to stage the most ridiculous folly in the city's entire ridiculous history: an opera."

❧≈❧

AND WHAT AN AMAZING ENTERPRISE *that* was, the opera described in advertisements as:

THE ROMANCE OF
AMBER & GRIS

◆- - - - - ●- - - - -→

AUTHORED BY

Anon

◆

SPONSORED BY

Concerned Citizens

◆

DIRECTED BY

Sarah Gallendrace

◆

STAGED AT

The Trillian Opera House—if still standing

◆

STARRING

Various & Sundry Talents—as available

◆

A Wicked "Mutual Satyricon" of Both Parties to the Current Conflict, whilst Containing a "Poignant Love Affair" Stolen Whole from The Distant Past, by way of Subterfuge and Subplot. An Opera—with what Music can be Spared From The War Effort—Overseen by Sarah Gallendrace, the Genius Behind the Production of Voss Bender's Opera *Trillian*.

Price of admission negotiable at the door.

In hindsight, no matter what happened, the opera would be the one great success of the war, the only sign that there might still be a city called Ambergris
afterwards.

The city at that time—after more than two years of conflict—had begun to
tear itself apart, like a beast that hates itself with a passion born of long familiarity. Every night, the deafening thunder of bombardment, the lights in the
sky—the purple, red, or green of fungal bombs—the continuous, monotonous
noise, so febrile, soaking into the very ground so that even the strange new
flocks of crows, come to peck at our dead, became married to it, their cries the
perfect mimic of fungal mortar fire. {No one knew whether they were about to
duck death or bird shit.} And in the morning: the self-inflicted wounds, buildings sliced in half or crumbled into dust, the great, slashing scars in the
earth . . .

In the weeks before the announcement of the opera—ragged hand-lettered
posters nailed to charred posts and crumbling walls—a fear had begun to overcome many of us: a fear that Ambergris, as a place or an idea, could not last,
that it might fall for the first time, and fall forever. With the fear came a terror
of our own mortality that we had put aside through the first years of the war.
With the evidence all around us that the city itself might die, we could no
longer ignore thoughts of our own individual fates. Now we all seemed to shine
with a clarity that imbued our forms with a figurative kind of light, a light we
had not had before. It shone out through our eyes, our mouths, our movements.
It made us all noble, I suppose, this fatalism, in a disheveled, unwashed way.
{Such a lovely way to put it, but all I saw was grime and dirt and blood and
death. The only real beauty lay underground, and it was a deadly beauty. How
strange to be caught between such extremes.}

When Hoegbotton & Sons and Frankwrithe & Lewden came together at
Borges Bookstore the week before the opera to announce a ceasefire, we all relaxed a little. We all let down our guard. If they could call a ceasefire for an
opera, then perhaps they might one day call a ceasefire for more important
things.

It had been a hard {not to mention dangerous} two years for Duncan and
me, chasing after this or that story. We needed the rest. We needed the comfort.
{The opera occurred, I felt later, almost out of the collective consciousness of
the city—an impulse toward a remembered harmony Ambergris had never really known. When I heard the rumors of the opera's impending production, I
thought of them as horrible lies, intended to make us hope. It never occurred to

any of us that one night House Hoegbotton and House Frankwrithe & Lewden would find themselves entangled in a temporary peace, and we would find ourselves in front of the Trillian Opera House.}

❦

THE NIGHT OF THE OPERA, we formed a party of five: me, Sybel, our employer James Lacond in the middle, Duncan, and Mary. Sybel, Lacond, and my brother served as an impregnable barrier to any potential unrest involving myself and the Lady Sabon. Sybel had recently reentered my life as a runner for Lacond and sometimes stayed at my apartment, just like old times.

"An opera?" Sybel had said when I told him. "Is there a building left standing to stage it in?"

Miracle of miracles, the Trillian Opera House stood conspicuously intact between two mounds of red fungi—seething rubble that had once been a bank and a restaurant. Granted, a huge wedge-shaped gouge {the classic indication of a fungal bomb} broke the opera house's skin, running from the roof down to the second floor and exposing the rough-hewn timbers that formed the building's skeleton. Such a minor wound, compared to so many buildings that had collapsed, unable to withstand the insidious veins of invading fungus.

It was dusk and the blood clot of a sun sawed through the opera house's wound, lit the street with a deep orange light that I had never seen before. We waded through this light, our party and many others approaching the opera house. A smell permeated the street that made us anxious to get inside—the all-too-familiar stench of mold, afterbirth of some fungal weapon, fired a week ago or a day ago or an hour ago. One could never tell.

The doors, unharmed, swung open on their rusty gilded hinges, ready to receive us all, whether Hoegbotton, Lewden, or neutral. No one would be turned away who wanted a seat, even though certain seats would require more bartering than others. {Tickets in such a context would have been too specific a madness. It was such an odd experience to enter the opera house that night, in that context, after so many years of stealing away at lunch for a performance, or taking students there for an assignment, or going with you, Janice.}

As I recall, Mary and I looked magnificent in our sequined dresses, perfumed and powdered. I had taken from a safe place the finest of my outfits from the height of the New Art's popularity. A curving neckline. An audacious black hat. Shoes made from lizard and mole skin. A handbag of a texture and design rare in any but the most southern of the Southern Isles. My hair was still a bit of a mess—that could not be helped; scarcely a mirror survived in the city, most fragmented by bombardment or wrinkled by filaments of fungi. For me, wearing such clothes reminded me of what had been, which made me sad—but also made me stand taller, for back in my glory days I had practically owned the opera house. I cannot remember what Mary wore, but whatever she wore, it could only presage future glory.

Mary and Sybel and I had one thing in common: none of us had succumbed to any of the fungal diseases that had so ravaged the general population as a side effect of the ceaseless bombardments. The same could not be said for many of those who surrounded us as we jostled our way through the door.

Toadlike James Lacond, ever-present cigar between his lips—his usual Nicean Reserve—had a patch of tendrils, a brilliant green, growing off the left side of his balding head. Nothing in his sour demeanor, however, revealed even the slightest discomfort. {As always, for a fat man he moved with surprising grace.} "Lie down with the gray caps," he was fond of saying, "and you make your peace with them, in one way or another."

My brother, however, tight-lipped and nervous {because I expected, with no truce yet spoken or implied, that you and Mary would fight the entire evening; why, the war was at times the least of my worries, even though I could sense the gray caps in the floorboards, their symbols and signs everywhere}, showed more of the strain. A silvery-purple "birthmark" writhed upon his forearm like a living tattoo. Who knew if his clothes hid some greater embarrassment? {They didn't. I could now maintain control, at least for a while. Had I manifested in my full fungal state, it would have cleared out the opera house.}

Some of those around us had even incorporated their misfortunes into their costumes. As we walked into the antechamber, stairs on left and right leading up and down, the gold-painted walls and somber red curtains unable to hide the gouges in the floor, the gutted, silent bar awash with signs of flame, we encountered these fashion marvels. The full extent of Ambergrisian ingenuity or insanity became clear. One woman had actually created a body-length trellis over which to cultivate the deep blue fungi ravishing her, the fronds forming a full dress, complete with train. Others had fashioned earrings or other accessories from their symptoms. {It says something that we had come far enough not to be shocked by what we saw that night. How quickly people adapted to such extremes; and how, secretly, I was glad of it, for it made me normal for a time, no more or less afflicted than anyone else, especially in Mary's eyes. Later, of course, it would help me not at all, once the "ordinary" citizens of Ambergris conveniently forgot the strangeness, the surreal quality, of the city during wartime.}

Mary gasped when she saw the woman with the trellis. Sybel and Lacond turned withering expressions of contempt toward her that she pretended not to see. Sybel had never been underground, but he had a way of adapting to each new situation as it presented itself. Lacond, meanwhile, had not gone as far belowground as Duncan, nor for as long, but he was marked for life by it, nonetheless: an encrusted blackness sometimes shone through his pores.

"You'd all better get used to it," Lacond muttered. "There'll be much more than that to get used to before the end."

Sybel scowled; I knew Lacond's pronouncements sometimes struck him as both vague and pretentious.

But you may wonder how, even with so great and ponderous a weight as James Lacond between us, Mary and I could walk so calmly into the opera house as members of the same group. The circumstances of war, as well as her keeping her distance and being eclipsed by the mushroom moon known as Lacond, didn't hurt, but you must also remember that the two semesters of Bonmot's ban had long since passed into history. The ban, along with much else from before the war, had become so remote that sometimes I could not find these details in my memory, or could not find them with a sharpness that made them real.

So I had, for the duration of the conflict, suspended my judgment of many things, including Mary. I had even become reconciled to the idea that Duncan and Mary might make a life together. Indeed, you might say that the war, for a time, created another kind of excitement for Duncan and Mary, an urgency to replace what they had lost now that they could no longer sneak around Blythe Academy. {Yet you were still so tense, your smile so forced, your politeness so impolite.} I did not speak to her, but we both laughed at Duncan's jokes, and made comments to each other indirectly, through Duncan or Lacond. Sybel, for his amusement, tried to create situations in which Mary would have to talk to me, or vice versa, but was never successful.

Through the sweat-stained, boot-scuffed antechamber we walked, all of us crowded together as we climbed the stairs to the balcony, having to ignore our own sour smell.

Then, a rush of stale air in our faces, followed by another, even staler, blast, as we walked onto the balcony and beheld the opera house!

We stared down at row upon row of worn gilt seats, rapidly being filled by the people sitting in them, saw the orchestra pit filled with the febrile scratchings of musicians tuning their instruments, and beyond that, the plain wooden stage, half-hidden by burgundy curtains that had great, gaping holes in them, revealing the scurrying singers behind the veil, the grunt and nudge of set pieces moving into place.

The more we looked, the more small details came into focus, the grandeur fading upon closer inspection. Plaster cherubim placed at the corners of the balcony, framing our view, had grown old, fissures of wrinkles aging them to appear wiser, and more malevolent than innocent. Every seat had a sweat stain from years of use. Every filigree and swirl of decorative paint on the walls or ceiling had a crack, a dent, a fault line. It had always been that way, and the familiarity of it comforted me.

Then Duncan gasped.

"Look," he said, pointing toward the ceiling. Only Lacond did not make a sound when he saw it. Even Sybel swore, under his breath.

It seems odd now that we had not seen it before all else, as if we wanted at first to deny its existence.

Looking up, as we walked forward to the edge of the balcony seats, we slowly came to recognize the source of the clear, clean, but undeniably *green* light that served as our illumination. {The rational mind can absorb only so much of the strange without damage.}

"What is it?" Mary whispered.

"The remains of a fungal bomb," Lacond replied.

"Half-exploded," Duncan said. "Fused to the ceiling."

The wound we had seen from the outside of the opera house had provided scant evidence of the damage suffered by the building. The center of its mosaic dome—a stylized scene of Morrow cavalry riding to Ambergris' defense during the Silence—had disappeared, the shards of its dissolution having simply vanished, assimilated, replaced by an intense green that shed its light in waves upon the stage. The green had eyes, or so it seemed, for it manifested itself as a series of circles or nascent fruiting bodies.

My breath caught in my throat. My neck grew sore from staring up at it. You could see through the green to the stars in the sky beyond, as if the green were no more substantial than gauze, than fog, and yet it sparkled and spun, each particle of it, as it shed the light that allowed us to see as we found our seats.

Lacond noticed that I could not look away from it, even as I sat down.

"Nothing you haven't seen from the outside in," he said as kindly as he could. His bulbous eyelids twitched, the cigar working up and down between his teeth, caught in his grouperlike lips. The sweet spicy smell of the cigar calmed me. "A fungal bomb that misfired, like we said. It hit the glass and stone of the dome and formed a substance . . . well, unlike anything I've ever seen. An interesting effect. And stable. It'll stay there for a long time, or at least for the next four hours." He laughed.

"Almost a piece of New Art all by itself," Sybel said, grinning.

"Beautiful," Duncan said, staring up at it. "Absolutely beautiful."

"Horrible and shocking, I would have thought," Mary said—a distant murmur, a whisper lost in a current of air.

"Quite a climb up there that would be," Sybel said. "I think I could do it, though."

"You'd climb a rainbow if you could," I said, earning a halfhearted scowl.

I tore my gaze from the ceiling. I had to. Otherwise my thoughts would have remained up there, trapped, during the entire opera. {It stunned me to see such a thing aboveground. It reinforced a thought that had come to me more and more frequently during the war: if that which belonged belowground came aboveground, why should I remain aboveground? I was like a sailor who falls overboard and reaches for the light, only to find that the light is false, and he has descended into even greater depths.} And yet, haven't we all seen things much stranger since the beginning of the Shift? Thinking of that ceiling now, I'm oddly unmoved. I've been undone by too many miraculous sights, both holy and unholy.

No one had tickets, but that didn't mean we had good seats. Even during the war {especially during the war!}, there remained hierarchies, and hierarchies within hierarchies. Lacond could have sat in the orchestra area with one guest, but that would have meant leaving the rest of us behind. Guided to the top row, we had to lower our heads for fear of bumping them against the balcony ceiling {a comforting white, that ceiling, at least}. The seats were hard wood—hard indeed for an opera that promised six acts and only one intermission. Above us, the dome; below, the fatal curving lunge down to the ground floor seats {which, from that perspective, seemed to go on forever}, then up and through them to the orchestra pit and the stage. The balcony smelled like old rotten books. No one had cleaned it for ages. That which from afar had looked both smooth and spotless was, up close, tawdry and sad. Only Sybel, with his lithe frame, seemed comfortable.

Perhaps I remember the opera so clearly because it was the last time anyone saw so many enemies occupying the same space without trying to stick a literal or figurative knife into one another. Agents from both sides of the conflict attended the opera that night, carefully guided through separate entrances, one of which consisted of a large hole in the wall. Anyone considered neutral had been positioned in the middle section of the ground floor, farthest from the exits. {Which made me laugh—should the two sides lose composure and attack each other, the neutrals in the middle would suffer greatly for their nuanced stance.}

Imperious members of the House Hoegbotton, already resembling scions of Empire in their somewhat presumptuous frocks and pleated trousers—if made a bit cadaverous, cloth sliding off elbows, from having to ration their food—made the forced march to their seats. Fixed stares. A few nervous smiles. Many of them wore medals they had awarded to themselves for wartime bravery.

The Frankwrithe & Lewden side was entirely different. They sidled in, wore mostly black, tried to stay in the shadows—except for their leader, L. Gaudy, who entered in what I can only call a "costume" of bright red, transformed by the green glow of the fungal light to a pulsating, brackish purple. He stood for several minutes, staring over at the Hoegbotton side, hands on his hips. A wide grin had seemingly paralyzed his face. {There was some discussion as to whether this bold figure truly was L. Gaudy, or one of the many actors hired by Gaudy to portray him at official events, the real Gaudy having developed an understandable fear of assassination attempts over the past two years. Regardless of whether it was Gaudy or pseudo-Gaudy, a healthy shiver of fear fled down my spine at his appearance.}

In the neutral section, we saw Martin Lake and his lover Merrimount take their seats, surrounded by the remnants of the New Artists, all looking rather tattered and downcast. {Their day was done. No opera could resurrect them.}

Martin and Merrimount had chosen to wear half evening gown, half formal suit, and I could almost smell the aggressive cologne that had become Martin's "signature smell," even though his sponsorship of it gained him no monies during the war. {You make it sound like an actual ceasefire, this opera. Janice, we were all armed to the teeth, like pirates sailing down the River Moth looking for a ripe place to build a city. You couldn't move through the hallway toward the restrooms without bumping into someone's concealed bulge of a gun or knife, or worse. And when you did get to the men's room, it was full of spies exchanging information.}

We took the sadly amateurish hand-printed playbills off our seats and sat,

Lacond still occluding all sight of Mary on the other side. In the expectant green light, the muted chatter of people still entering the opera house, the pauses in conversation as three or four times it appeared the opera was about to begin, I had a glimpse, an echo, of my former life. For an instant, sitting there, my buttocks rapidly beginning to ache from the hard seat, I had the illusion that I had conjured up the resources, out of full-on ruin, to create an opera. For just that period between taking our seats and curtain rise, I felt powerful again. An awful feeling. I could see Edward's slack face in the insane asylum, feel the ribbon of red rising from my wrist. I did not want that life back, not really.

Besides, the illusion was ruined anyway by a brief encounter on the way to the bathroom before the opera began. Narrowed and wrinkled by the years, Merrimount's jester face suddenly came into view.

He nodded and said, "Did you have anything to do with this opera, Janice?"

"No," I said. "Not me." Caught. Accused.

"Ah, right," he said. "I thought maybe you had." A pause, and then, "Do you think this is what the New Art has all been leading up to? An insane opera performed during wartime?" His smile was all teeth, and then he was gone.

I hated the elation that made my face flush, brought out a little shiver of happiness. Merrimount had talked to me. {Very sad, sister.}

I told Duncan about the encounter, across Sybel's thin chest and Lacond's broad belly, and before he could respond, out of the darkness I heard Mary say, "If so, it's been a waste. Everything leading up to this one performance. They should have saved it up for after the war."

I laughed, and Sybel, like a good former manager, said to Mary, "Merrimount means that except for him, Martin, and Janice, every member of the former New Art movement of any consequence is involved in this opera. It's the only thing they've been able to agree on long enough to bring to the public attention."

Mary nodded, held her tongue. She knew Sybel didn't like her, and she knew Sybel didn't like her because I didn't like her.

"Admittedly, a captive audience," Duncan said, "with nothing else to do except hunker down in their homes."

"True," I said. "I suppose there is a hint of desperation in it."

Desperation during those days could not be hidden at the opera. In such close quarters, the truth of our diets would begin to manifest as a sour smell of stale bread and vegetable broth and, oddly enough, doorknobs. Some enterprising individual had discovered that many of the doorknobs in the city had been made from sawdust and ox blood. If heated and distilled, a doorknob could be eaten, given an extremity of hunger.

"Martin and Merri are living on the kindness of friends and neighbors, you know," Sybel said.

"If he's painting at all," Duncan said, "it's with borrowed canvases and stolen paints. He'll get the odd job here and there, but work must be scarce."

"Yes it is, my dear Duncan," I heard Mary whisper, "but you don't need to worry."

He didn't need to worry because Mary's parents had conspired to acquire an apartment for her out of the way of both the local Hoegbotton and F&L militias, in an area that had not yet been the target of attacks or skirmishes. Mary, meanwhile, had yet to realize that, having taken Duncan in, she might have more worries than the average person where the gray caps were concerned. {She had less to worry about. Trust me. I protected her well.}

My gaze burned through the darkness that protected Mary.

"What are your plans after the war?" I asked Duncan.

Was that the hint of a smile on my brother's face?

Mary answered for him, making Sybel sit up and pay attention, as if he had a bet riding on the answer: "The same as now. To continue my studies. To write books, like Duncan's."

Well, it was true that she continued her studies during the war. In fact, the war often had no impact on her whatsoever, not emotionally. But she didn't want to write books like *Duncan's*. She wanted to write books *like* Duncan. That became clear soon enough.

A hush fell over the audience. The lights could not dim, but the curtain could rise. It chose that moment to do so. I could either stare into the now silent darkness or turn toward the stage.

The curtain rose. The green light was very much like the green light in this place, as I type this afterword. Here, I am on the stage. There, I was part of the audience. Not that there's much difference.

The opera began.

❧❧

DESPITE GALLENDRACE'S VALIANT EFFORTS, IT soon became clear that the opera would be a rather muddied affair. What more could one expect under the circumstances, hampered by lack of funds, lack of time, donated costumes and sets, and the shortage of many other supplies? But a certain unnecessary complexity also wreaked havoc with the production—too many parts and not enough actors. Further, men played most of the female parts and women played most of the male parts, which created a dissonant musical effect, tenors and sopranos popping up in the most unexpected places. It became increasingly difficult to keep track of all but the most major characters.

Still, the main storyline had the kind of familiarity that is difficult to lose in translation, especially when you're in the middle of the conflict in question. As in real life, the opera carefully related the particulars of a deadly war between merchant families.

To put it plainly, what hawkish Sirin had anticipated so accurately was an economic invasion of Ambergris by Frankwrithe & Lewden, the type of invasion that only coincidentally results in bloodshed. For years, the constant pressure exerted by Hoegbotton & Sons on F&L in their home markets around Morrow had hindered Frankwrithe's attempts to expand into Ambergris—although a tenuous toehold had been gained through influence on Antechamber book bannings and through bookstores large enough to ignore Hoegbotton intimidation. However, mere months before my enlightening trip to Morrow, F&L had managed to take over its governance from a failed monarchy, in the process issuing a decree banning all Hoegbotton agents and imports from the city. Hoegbotton found itself unable to mount an effective counteroffensive. {In part, F&L took advantage of H&S' temporary shift of attention to trains and railways, a fixation that emanated from Henry Hoegbotton, the hoary but clever patriarch of the Hoegbotton clan. Henry Hoegbotton—of whom not enough has been written; if not for my present circumstances, I would attempt the biography myself—had hoped for an era of economic domination over all of the South, to the very tip of the last atoll of the Southern Isles, and all of the North, including the frozen Skamoo in their spackly ice huts. Many experts speculated that Hoegbotton might then wage "a holy war of commerce" against the closed markets of the Kalif's empire. However, such a vision required Hoegbotton to overextend itself so much that it became unable to effectively respond to a threat like being banned from Morrow.}

This new vision on the part of F&L explained the large numbers of their operatives that had dominated my view from the window of my {comfortable, furnished} prison{-like} cell. Emboldened by victory at home, F&L sought to bring their trade downriver, staking their chances not only on their diversification into a superior brand of typewriter, the Lewden Model II—a version of which I am typing on now and which I swear and sweat by; if only this fungus would not keep nibbling on the accursed keys—and long distance telephone services. In fact, many infiltrations of Ambergris began as the result of F&L agents installing telephone poles: not only did F&L inject liquid explosives into hollow portions of these poles, but the installers themselves formed a secret army of espionage in the city. F&L also funneled more and more funds into Ambergrisian banks, hoping to create influence in those quarters.

Hoegbotton, naturally, resisted, and matters came to a head over Sophia's Island, a curling finger of an atoll located north of Ambergris in the middle of the River Moth. The "Sophia" of Sophia's Island was none other than the wife of Ambergris' founder, Manzikert I—they had used it as a summer residence many hundreds of years ago. Now, it occupied a strategic position in the northern trade routes: whoever controlled the island could levy all sorts of tariffs, and use the island as a storeroom to boot. An obscure lease on the island had been given to the rulers of Morrow, the Menite Kings, as a thank-you for their aid to Ambergris during the Silence. Despite the fall of the Menite Kings, the lease had never been withdrawn, and Frankwrithe & Lewden used it as pretext to lay claim to the island, with predictable results. The conflict that had begun on the island had spread to Ambergris, and had probably been an excuse to initiate open warfare.

The opera attempted to convey the entire origin of the conflict in song using a motley collection of servants, bankers, merchants, and soldiers—a chorus of voices that stumbled ragged about the stage—while a forbidden love affair between members of the Hoegbotton and Frankwrithe clans—a plot device old long before Voss Bender took his first, tottering steps—played out in the foreground. A subplot involved two servants, one from each clan, and the odd appearance of a man from the Nimblytod Tribes, who observed from on high {in this case, two boxes set atop each other}, and provided sporadic narration—much to the disgust of Sybel, who muttered to me about "stereotypes." The ghost of Sophia Manzikert also made many an appearance, fated to roam her beloved island as all manner of skullduggery occurred around her, and she unable to stop it.

A hail of catcalls and whistles abused the singers when Sophia's Island first appeared as a series of earth-colored potato sacks stitched together and held up by men dressed in black who were still, tragically, visible in the green light. As the island sailed toward the singers rather than the other way around, atonal booing drowned out the voices coming from the stage.

Pieces of the music had clearly been stolen from Bender's *Trillian*, as might be expected with Gallendrace in charge. The orchestra was short a flutist, his place taken by a rather aggressive whistler. {In fact, the entire orchestra sounded like the "scrittling, scratching brittlings of a skeleton crew," as one wag put it.} A few holes in the floor of the stage—apparently there had been no time to repair them—resulted in Sophia's ghost at one point pitching head-first into the orchestra pit, much to the delight of the audience, which stood and clapped. {We might have been glad to have an opera during wartime, but that didn't mean we had given up our essential nature as Ambergrisians.}

The {almost} corresponding holes in the curtain made scene breaks tantalizing, and scandalous, in that the audience could see the flash of thigh and buttock in the frenetic thrashing of costume changes. The set changes proved much less dramatic, as Gallendrace had chosen to use the set to suggest rather than illustrate, letting unpainted wooden boxes and other unconcealed objects serve as placeholders for the imagination.

Still, it was a passable attempt at an opera. The orchestra lurched on even after Sophia fell on top of them. The singers had good voices—they had convinced the great retired baritone Samuel Rail to make a short appearance. However, the hole in the ceiling, even clogged with fungus, changed the acoustics in such a way that sometimes those voices came to us profoundly curdled or twisted; at times, I felt as if I were hearing the voices of gray caps, not human beings at all.

Halfway through the second act, my legs beginning to fall asleep, I turned in my seat and looked back. Some ten rows behind us, I caught a glimpse of Bonmot with some of the teachers from Blythe Academy. I waved; he waved back. I was inspired for a moment to go talk to him, perhaps even join them—after all, Duncan had his Mary and Lacond had his Duncan, and Sybel was too busy being angry about the depiction of his people to be of much use to me. But it was then that Sophia fell into the orchestra pit, and as I turned back to watch the ensuing chaos, the moment was lost. By intermission, Bonmot had left for some reason {along with several others in the audience!}, although not before Mary had made a great show of going over and talking to him, abandoning Duncan for several minutes. {She didn't do it to *hurt* me, Janice, but to *help* me. She worked hard to try to repair the rift, thought that a ceasefire for the warring Houses might also mean a ceasefire for House Bonmot and House Duncan, but it was not to be.}

After intermission, the set design devolved even further, and the plot became ever more ludicrous, featuring a plethora of ghosts, and even an appearance by a wingèd fairy—a device so pathetic I thought violence might break out. The singers desperately tried to cover for these faults with stellar, sometimes over-the-top performances, voices drowning out voices, dissonant not in their individual talents, but as a group.

By the middle of the fourth section, I seemed to have missed some essential act of communication. I had lost the thread of the narrative, I suppose. Actors dressed in deep red uniforms identical to those favored by the Kalif's soldiers began to appear on the stage, to much clapping and cheering from all of us. Finally, some real costumes! Some spectacle to satiate our lust for pomp. They poured onto the stage in a tight pool, almost as if a bottle of wine had overturned and leaked across a table. In their midst, we saw the white turban of a Kalif's commander as he fired his guns across the stage with a great crack and recoil. The audience roared once more, for he presented a fine sight on that stage, singing or not singing, with his dark beard and mustache, his piercing gaze.

He aimed at a singer and s/he fell—Sophia again, poor Sophia, so fated to fall. The leak of blood, miniature mimic of the soldiers' progress, that spread across the front of Sophia's white dress, had the effect of renewing our love for the opera. Such melodrama! Such an authentic battle scene!

From the rising screams and shouts onstage, we naturally expected one clear soprano or alto would rise above, drawing together the threads of chaos. The Kalif's men would drop their guns and swords. They would become part of a great chorus of voices, or a powerful counterpoint. The lovers would reunite. The houses would reconcile. The curtain would fall, then rise again, that our applause might become more specific, rewarding our favorites.

But none of these things happened. Not a one of them.

Instead, the music began to lose its harmony, become discordant, and momentarily returned as strong as ever as a section of foolish woodwinds held their ground. It then dissolved into individual horns and violins before falling away into silence, leaving only the sounds of struggle.

Silence from the audience, for a moment. {Some of us were just glad the musicians had stopped playing.} Finally, we began to understand. We did not know it to be true all at once, and each of us reached our conclusions separately. But understanding did come to us, some with gasps, some with shouts or screams, others in a silence born of dread or amazement. Under the green light, anything was possible, even an invasion.

When the white-turbaned commander drew his sword and cut Sophia's head from his neck and held it, dripping and white, by one gloved hand, we knew any performance had ended minutes before. As we had sat there, watching the opera, the Kalif's troops had invaded Ambergris. {For me, it was a few seconds later, when Sarah Gallendrace appeared on stage, her belly cut wide open, her impossibly pale hands trying to staunch the flow. That's when I unfroze.}

The flag of the Kalif was unfurled on the stage. The moat created by the orchestra pit became so cluttered with the most unmusical of things—dead, hacked-apart people and the remnants of the set, cleared with methodical precision—that it was no great leap for some of the soldiers to bridge it and start firing into the audience.

Now, in the most orchestrated event of the entire evening, House Hoegbotton and House Frankwrithe & Lewden gave their reply. It was animal, guttural, and in almost perfect unison. With a great shout of both outrage and fear, out came guns previously hidden. Out came the knives, the swords. While the neutrals—I saw Martin and Merrimount running for an exit—tried to extricate themselves from their now utterly indefensible position, Hoegbotton and Lewden, Hoegbotton and Frankwrithe, came together in a unity of purpose. You could see it in their eyes, that, for a time, all differences would be laid aside to defeat a common enemy. They poured up toward the stage, firing, stabbing, while the Kalif's soldiers, under the calm command of their leader, laid down a murderous fire. Bodies fell in the aisles, cut to pieces. The smell of blood and gunpowder rose from the stage. Billowing smoke, caught and distorted in the green light. The utter panic and dissolution of those who had never thought their night might end like this, some in their distress running back and forth as if caged, unable to find their way out.

Those of us on the balcony seemed to have a better chance than most, unless the front entrance lay blocked. We began to make our way to the stairs and down. We were much calmer than those on the ground floor. Just as the stage had, during the performance, been remote from our rarefied location, so too the violence. We had the sense of it spreading slowly, the stain of the Kalif's soldiers like some natural force, one that had its own rhythm of invasion, one that would allow us to casually take our leave.

Lacond had pulled his pistols from their ankle holsters. Sybel wielded a particularly deadly-looking knife so long I wondered how he'd managed to conceal it. My brother had, in his protectiveness for Mary, let his fungal disease overtake him further, so that one eye lay clear and blue while the other had become overgrown with a green curling substance that magnified its intent and size. His right arm he had allowed to become a kind of fungus club, black and shiny. The look on his face told me he was ready to die for Mary, right there, right then. {And perhaps endure a minor maiming for you and Sybel.}

We took cover behind the battering ram of Lacond, who cleared a path for us by shoving people out of the way. My last glimpse of the stage showed that the Kalif's soldiers had advanced farther into the audience, the Ambergrisian resistance becoming more of a rearguard attempt to let the majority escape, rather than anything resembling an offensive.

Then down the cramped stairs, stinking of sweat, and out the front door into the night, running, all too aware now of the new sound of what would turn out to be the Kalif's mortars, set up to ring the city. Shells hurtled through the air, poorly aimed and indiscriminate. {We knew them as the Kalif's because the unique sound had no parallel to H&S weapons. And unlike F&L bombs, they did not become a writhing explosion of fungi and spores. They just smashed into things and sent shards of those things crackling across the space between, then lay inert. Why we feared those mortars more than the weapons of the Houses, I do not know. Perhaps the sheer unfamiliarity of them. We had grown accustomed to our other assailants.}

And that was our night at the opera, which I remember more clearly than all the rest.

❧

IT HAD BEEN A STRANGE, strange war long before the opera—two years of watching Ambergris, like some sun-drenched, meat-gorged reptile, make one of its random attempts to molt, to shed its skin, to become something new. All across the city, from the narrow alleys of the ruined Bureaucratic Quarter to the wide bustle of Albumuth Boulevard, we could sense it coming. Odd alliances formed under stark orange skies. The vertical invasion of telephone poles, for example, once a random dotting, had become a concerted march from the docks into the city's scaly white underbelly. Guns poured in with the telephones, both originating from the Kalif's empire {although often by way of F&L's agents, already gathering in the city, fly-thick and as black-swarming}. The guns came in every size and description, most of them oddly bulky and gleaming with the kaleidoscopic reflection of unknown metals. They smelled both new and old at the same time, smelled of far-off places, as if the metal had soaked up the essence of the foundries and factories that had produced them. The guns frightened me. They seemed like an emanation from some future Ambergris, some place that did not yet exist, but soon would.

Outdoor café life became charged with danger and interruptions. Shootings and stabbings became all too frequent. {The novelty of guns was too much temptation for the average Ambergrisian.} Motored vehicles began to reemerge—dark, dank metallic beetles long dormant—as new Hoegbotton resources brought barrels of sticky black fuel into the city.

The very air smelled different—it had a charged quality, as if we were all breathing tiny particles of gunpowder; our lungs burned even without the impetus of pollen in the spring, and, in the fall, even on days when the air wasn't cold and dry. {This was not your imagination—the spore content of the city began to change, to be transformed. The gray caps had begun the process of slow but inexorable translation/transformation that would culminate in the Shift.}

At the time, none of us thought much about these changes. Ambergris, for all its history, its secrets, its allure, had always been dirty, sickly, on the verge of crumbling back into itself—battered, babbling, incoherent in its design and intent. We all thought that, ultimately, the molt wouldn't take, and the reptile that was the city would sink back into the mud a little, its skin ever more mottled from the experience.

Into this strangeness, this bubble of trapped amber, in which everything and nothing was happening all at once, the war intruded. Suddenly, what had seemed random had form and structure: it was Us against Them: a Hoegbotton many of us could not tolerate against Frankwrithe & Lewden, an Other that was far worse: an invader, usurper, the likes of which we had not known since the Kalif's temporary Occupation generations before.

It was in this atmosphere that we became reporters for *The Ambergris Daily Broadsheet* under the guidance of the *Broadsheet's* editor and publisher, James Lacond.

Duncan, in the absence of Mary—still, in those early days of the war, imprisoned by the two-semester ban—decided to take it upon himself to visit Lacond and make the arrangements with him. I can't say I minded Duncan going instead of me. I had made some inquiries about Lacond and discovered a man of many vices—he smoked at a ridiculous rate, he drank, often while on the job, he swore constantly, and he sometimes participated in the dangerous fungal drug trade. {All vices you once possessed, Janice!}

At first, Duncan found Lacond to be cantankerous and irritating. He seemed unable to understand the value of adding us to his stable of broken-down journalistic nags. However, he had met Duncan before, read his work, and even reviewed one of his books in the past, and that made him warm to us. {Warm to me. I don't know if he ever really warmed to you. It certainly wasn't your fault—he was, without much doubt, a blustery old fart. The day I went to see him, James had already begun a downward spiral. I think this is why he wound up liking me when we got to know each other better. He saw in me a fellow lost soul, an underachiever, a candidate for an early reputational grave. As I was to find out, I had crossed his path as his expectations were decaying—journalism was as much a low point for him as for us. When I came upon him—bloated, red-nosed, squat, a cigar in his mouth—setting type for the printing presses that clacked and rattled and sobbed behind him, I sensed a stubbornness, a refusal as yet to acknowledge his fate. He was talking fast, his stubby fingers working the type in and out of position with an unexpected grace. The man liked plain shirts, over which would hang striped suspenders, holding up pants that he tucked into short boots. He often muttered to himself—always muttering to himself as long as I knew him, whether about the price of ink or the vagaries of typefaces.

{"What do you want?" he asked, never looking up from his work. He didn't need to look up. I could guess our connection from the faint black stippling around his chin, his ears. He had been underground. And when he finally did look up, he recognized the same in me. After that, any reluctance on his part was mere economics.}

For Lacond, by fate or fortune, or both, was the founder of the Ambergrisians for the Original Inhabitants Society, a historical organization known for its outlandish theories and high fatality rates. As Duncan wrote in his *Early History of Ambergris* several years later:

Never has membership in a historical society been so fraught with peril. Every two or three years, another few members succumb to the temptation to pry open a manhole cover and go spelunking amongst the sewer drains. Inevitably, someone gets stuck in a drainpipe and the others go for help, or the gray caps, presumably, catch them and they disappear forever. One imagines the helpful AFTOIS members waving their official membership cards at the approaching, unimpressed gray caps. When not conspiring to commit assisted suicide, the AFTOIS publishes *The Real History Newsletter.*

This newsletter would later become Duncan's eccentric flagship as he led a fearless crew of "fringe historians" into the uncharted and unclaimed waters of Oblivion. These hardy men and women subsisted at the far reaches of popular acclaim and derived what little sustenance they could from peripheral mentions in the lesser-known broadsheets and journals—lingering in the brackish backwaters of footnotes in papers by their more famous colleagues. {Mary's footnotes would eventually take on this preservative quality, often the only extant mention of any number of historians, myself included. Although some felt gratitude, for most living in the margins proved a grim and unfulfilling existence.}

Our dad loved historians, of course, but he had always hated journalists. He considered them the juvenile, larval stage of the historian, and as with certain reptilian or insect species that eat their own young, he believed they should be done away with for society's greater good. I remember he used to call journalists "Historians without the wisdom of perspective."

As Duncan used to say, though, after the war, "Father was wrong. Journalists are just frightened people with notepads who are trying very hard not to get killed." It was, paradoxically, a boring time, what with all the running around. All we did was skulk and hide, then run somewhere. Record what we saw—the aftermath of an explosion, an outbreak of illness, a battle—run somewhere else. Hide. Report. Run. Hide. Report. Run.

"Bring me the story!" Lacond used to bellow from his chosen spot behind the typesetting machine. "There's a story out there—find it now!"

Even as, some weeks, he was reduced to paying us for those stories with bread, vegetables, and milk.

Bring me the story! This command became our lives. Rather than a slow, bleary-eyed stagger down to the gallery, my day would begin—in the deepest part of the night—with the telephone ringing. I would fumble for the phone, offer a mumbled "Hello?" A voice, usually Lacond's, sometimes his assistant, would whisper "123 So-and-so Street—there's been a bombing." If the phones weren't working, it would be a knock on the door from a runner, usually Sybel, who'd taken the job because there was nothing else for him in the city. Where once Sybel had dressed outrageously, now he wore clothes that allowed him to blend right into the wall. "To each time and place its own apparel," he told me. "Not that I don't miss the bad old days." {Miss them? He was still *living* them. Acting as a runner for a broadsheet gave him a certain amount of neutrality in sections of the city critical for him to reach if he wanted to continue providing "substances to those who desire them," as he was fond of saying. It certainly made it more convenient for Sybel to slip me my "peace of mind," as he called the tincture I required. As for Sybel's wartime clothes, they hardly taxed his skill at camouflage. You should have seen what he wore while in his natural element, the trees. Except . . . you *couldn't* see him there.}

I would then rush into a shirt and trousers—the only practical clothes for a woman in such circumstances—shove big black boots over cold feet—and careen out the door, pen and notebook clutched in one hand. In my pants pocket, the dried mushrooms Duncan had given me. If a spore bomb exploded near me, I was to swallow them as an antidote. Of course, this only helped against F&L's unconventional weapons. I would still be vulnerable to the shrapnel bombs of H&S.

I cannot think—through all of our transformations of position, location, and function—of a change more bone-crunching than that which made us reporters. I had never counted physical endurance among my attributes, but now I had to call on hidden reserves almost every day. I kept spraining my ankles, too, whether running toward a story {or away from one that had proven too hostile}, walking across an uneven island of pavement disfigured by fungi, or fighting to avoid being trampled by a mob of fleeing citizens. Eventually, I wrapped both ankles in bandages before I went out, hoping that the extra support would help.

Considering the ease with which death had found our father, it can only be luck that saved us. Sometimes, as we stared at the smoldering remains of a grocery store, the clerks reduced to red ash, the stench unbearable, I wondered if I wasn't trying to kill myself all over again.

{If so, then the entire city was trying to kill itself. One of the strangest things about the war for me was the calm in the midst of violence that sometimes came over people—a state of grace, or denial, perhaps. I can remember watching from one end of a street as a fungal bomb blew up a few blocks away. It was one of those hideous creations that, dissolving into a fine purple mist, travels forward from the impetus of the blast and enters the lungs of anyone in its path, making of them brittle statues that disintegrate at the slightest touch or breath of wind. I ducked into a side alley, even though I was already immune—the purple mist would encounter and be neutralized in my lungs by the green mist already residing there—and watched as people ran by, screaming. There was no help for them, no help I could give. Across the street, though, I saw a man in a long overcoat standing calmly by a lamppost. He had on thick glasses and he had covered his nose and mouth with a mask of cloth. As the mist washed over him, bringing with it the usual, if incongruous, smell of limes and lemons, he did not panic. He just stood there. As others were brought up short in midflight, rendered motionless, their eyes rolling into their sockets, a light purple fuzz hardening on their lips and eyebrows, crawling up their legs, this man stood there for a moment, and then went on about his business. Over time, as more and more precautions were taken, you would see people going about their daily lives with a calm, with a sense of peace, that astounded me. Only in Ambergris! For, incredibly enough, very few people fled the city during the war. Stockton and Morrow combined received no more than a few thousand refugees.}

Poor Duncan, meanwhile, had different afflictions. His seasonal fungal diseases intensified under the stress, until he jokingly said to Lacond that at times he could lean against a fungus-covered wall and no one would see him. His trench coat grew oddly empty or full depending on the virulence of the attack, a hat hiding most of the tendrils that insisted on colonizing his scalp. Thick coatings of cologne helped disguise the reek of decaying mushroom matter—at least until the second year of the war, when so many people had contracted their own fungal diseases that disguise was no longer necessary. {Often, Janice, I was flexing my newfound control of my affliction. My changes in shape, in density, were but responses to the spores in my immediate surroundings. They were how I defended myself—and, not coincidentally, *you*. Although sometimes I was hiding an awfully big gun under my coat; some threats are best met with bullets.}

But this was not the full extent of my brother's handicap. The rest, in those early days, was expressed by his longing for Mary to return to him. I can remember the two of us running down a deserted alley, my swollen ankles killing me, Duncan's disease in full bloom—tendrils of bright green fruiting bodies shooting forth from his hatless head like flares signaling the enemy—while behind us, through the billowing smoke of an H&S grenade attack, some dozen F&L irregulars chased us, intent on making us pay for someone else's transgression . . . and as we ran, Duncan wrote a love letter to Mary—a jotted phrase or two at a time, scribbled on a thrice-folded piece of paper. One such "letter" ends, "Must wrap this up, my love! Would like to write more, but am late to an appointment." Truff knows how he smuggled them into Blythe Academy and, later, Mary's parents' house.

Blythe Academy stayed open for one and a half of the two semesters Mary needed to complete her degree, although the professors and priests continued to use it as a safe haven after the students had been sent home. For the coursework Mary and all the students in similar straits still needed to complete, Bonmot made weekly rounds to their parents' houses. Typical of him, he ignored the danger implicit in crossing barricades and encountering militia checkpoints. I imagine him, solid, strong, in his green robes, walking down the street, impervious to the bloodshed occurring all around him. To be a priest during that war required a certain amount of dissociation from the real world.

I knew what it was like to lead such a life—it conferred an illogical form of *immunity* by forcing you to become separate from your surroundings. You *had* to separate yourself, pull yourself out of the context swarming all around you. There was no choice. To allow yourself to become part of it would have meant a kind of death. {Odd you should think that, Janice, because most of the time, while not attending to my job, I was fleshing out theories of history at odds with that opinion. To me, the events of the war—the chaos—mimicked the worst qualities of my precarious relationship with Mary. My own body seemed able to express emotion through transformation. As I felt, so the world around me felt, or vice versa. I did not, of course, believe that my mental turmoil created the conflict—this was a metaphorical connection only, but no weaker because of it. Would it not be true, I began to think, that a historian could best explain those periods of history that most closely imitated the events or significant emotions of his own life?}

❧❦

I'M SURE SOME OF THE regulars here at the Spore of the Gray Cap remember the insanity of the war—there are certainly enough gray beards and grizzled voices among them. Even this green glass that provides my only light beyond candles—this glass that distorts the quick, rhythmic stride of walkers making floorboards creak, the random punctuation of a cane—has experience of the war: it was caused by clear glass fusing with a fungal bomb. The result is beautiful, if unintentional. {And since the glass seems to shift and re-form every so often, who knows if an end result has yet been reached? Perhaps it is transforming into something else altogether.}

But the intensity or scope of the conflict never gave me pause—it was the nature of the weapons. It was as if the gray caps had come aboveground in disguise and started to slaughter us. Guns now shot fungal bullets that, upon hitting flesh, burrowed deep into arteries and created thoroughfares of spores that hardened within seconds, making the victim as brittle as any coral from the Southern Isles. Certain special fungi could serve as bombs or mines or grenades, decomposing a body in seconds, or release spores that choked the victim to death. Telephones soon became dangerous, used as the emissaries of assassination—the victim would pick up the phone only to hear a high-pitched scream that burst the eardrums and the heart {said screams very similar to those attributed to the giant "gray whale" mushrooms that became common in Ambergris immediately prior to the Silence}. Henry Hoegbotton's brother Frederick died in this manner, as did several other merchants. {Did F&L realize what they were doing when they found a way to procure such weapons from the gray caps? Probably not. They probably didn't have a clue. They just wanted results.}

One of our first joint reports dealt with the issue of the new weapons.

BOMBS *ARE* BREAD
by D.J. Shriek

This past weekend, a disturbing new fact has come to light regarding the weapons being used by House Lewden: they can be eaten. In certain parts of the Merchant Quarter, which has sustained heavy bombing damage in recent weeks, citizens have been hunting through the rubble not for other survivors or the bodies of loved ones, but for the bombs themselves.

Dr. Alan Self, a physician employed by a House Hoegbotton militia, confirms this information. "I don't know how it started, but because of the food shortage in parts of the city, starving people have begun to eat the remains of House Lewden's infernal fungal bombs," he said.

The core of these bombs does not explode, but serves as the delivery system for the bomb—ballast, of a sort. The ballast is high in protein and appears to have no harmful side effects, as of yet.

Some kinds of fungal bullets appear to share these properties.

"They have a short half-life," according to Sarah Mindle, one of many Hoegbotton employees recruited to fight in the increasingly confused civil war. "After about five hours, most of them become inert, harmless."

High in nutritional content, these bullets are also being harvested by the poor and those cut off from food by the barricades and militias of the various warring factions. Of course, finding the bullets can be hazardous. Knowing when they have become harmless requires yet another set of skills.

"I wait until [the bullets] lose their purple tinge," Charles Jarkens said. Jarkens is a homeless man whose wife died in a bombardment at the beginning of the war. "I wait for that, and I wait until they get a little orange around the base of the bullet. That's when I know they're good to eat."

In an unverified and extreme case, a family whose son was killed by a barrage of such bullets resorted to removing them from the body and eating them.

What no one can as yet explain is exactly how House Lewden procured such weapons, nor why Hoegbotton & Sons have not yet deployed captured weapons against F&L. Some speculate that the blockade of Ambergris by F&L ships has led to such a reduction in food stores for Hoegbotton's various militias that the Lewden weapons are, in fact, being deliberately detonated for use as food.

As might be expected, such incendiary stories led to Lacond's offices being bombed so many times that he eventually moved his printing presses, under cover of night, to a secret location in the forests outside of Ambergris.

"Let them stop me now!" he would say, face flushed with defiance. "Those pompous, homicidal swine can blow me up as much as they like—the presses will keep churning out the pages!" {The war, I must say, revitalized Lacond for a time.}

While the fuel lasted, motored vehicles brought the broadsheet in every morning, and fast runners—usually boys and girls from ten to fifteen years of age, the only group with the stamina for the job who had not already been conscripted by the Hoegbotton militias—would distribute it to a few safe or neutral locations, where it instantly sold out. Distribution was dangerous, and sometimes our runners did not come back. Sybel kept at it for a time, but it wore on his nerves.

"I can't take it," he said one morning. Dark circles had formed around his eyes and he had developed a habit of blinking rapidly, his left hand subject to uncontrollable quivering no matter what his mood. "I can't take it. I can't take it." {What he couldn't take was working so many jobs at once. Although he did have several disturbing episodes involving either militia members who robbed him at gunpoint, or bombs.}

Lacond had come to love our work by this time, so he let us use Sybel for our personal missions, which didn't mean he was in any less danger—just a different kind.

"You must be doing a good job," Lacond said once, while all three of us sat on the floor of his office, sweaty and exhausted. "Both sides want your heads on a platter."

Thus, it became wiser for us to publish our reports under pseudonyms like Michael Smith and Sarah Pickle. I even began to sleep in different locations, seldom returning to my apartment for fear of a fungal bullet to the back of the head.

And yet, on certain days, in certain parts of the city, you could walk down a dozen streets and not even realize a war was going on—if you could rationalize the mortar fire as thunder. Markets were open, people walked to work, the telephones operated {even if few wanted to use them}, restaurants served what food they had. The Religious Quarter, for political reasons, remained largely safe, with both H&S and F&L doing a respectable trade in foodstuffs and clothing—sometimes while fighting raged only a few blocks away. {War was also an opportunity for the native tribes, the Dogghe in particular, to make a killing supplying food and collaborating with the enemy—either enemy.} A few times, I was even able to meet with artists and gallery owners, regaining a little respect from them because of my new profession.

This sometimes sense of safety was in part caused by a retrenchment by both sides following the first seven or eight months of the war. House Lewden's original probes centered on feints to the southeast and southwest, with the aim of control of H&S headquarters and the docks. But after several intense battles, F&L had been restricted to the northern third of Ambergris. They controlled part of the docks and a portion of Albumuth Boulevard, but they could not smash through to H&S headquarters. Recovering from the initial shock, H&S had found the morale and discipline to hold their ground. Thus, the "front" became relatively stable, except for some porousness due to spies, sneak attacks and, eventually, the Kalif's mortar fire. The regularity of it became a kind of comfort. {I was never comforted. The whole conflict had troubled me from the beginning. Just trying to guess the reasons for gray cap involvement bothered me. Never before had they backed one faction over another, or even seemed to recognize the difference between factions—or, if they did understand the difference, to care. Why now should they change tactics? Also, their weapons were everywhere, but *they* were nowhere to be seen.}

Still, it could not go on forever. The city was in real danger of becoming less than a city, of becoming rubble and black smoke and piles of bodies—of becoming twenty different cities that only loosely formed a country called "Ambergris."

Duncan sensed this, but could not really articulate it. {I anticipated it as a feeling deep in my ever-changing body, but could do nothing about it.}

"We're near the end," he said one evening eighteen months into the war, as we sat in the smoldering remains of the Café of the Ruby-Throated Calf. It was more or less neutral ground now that most of it had been destroyed by mortars. At least we could count on no one trying to kill us as we sat there, protected by overturned tables and a few strategically placed shrubs. The service was terrible, but, then, all the waiters were dead.

Duncan was pale but whole, face dark with dirt, a flurry of cuts rubbed red. We were drinking a couple of bottles of Smashing Todd's Wartime Stout, which we had found—miraculously whole under a fallen, splintered door—in an abandoned store.

"Near the end?" I prompted.

"Yes," he said, and took a long pull on his beer. "We're near the end. Something has to give. Someone has to blink. To change. It can't go on this way. It can't."

"It's done a fine job of going on this way for a while now, Duncan," I reminded him. I took a sip of ale. It was warm, almost hot, but the bite of it still tasted good.

"Maybe I mean *I* can't go on this way," he said.

"You mean, being paid in eggs, cauliflower, and milk?" I said.

He laughed, but I knew he was thinking about Mary, always Mary.

How to express the overlap between war and blissful domesticity? For this was the time of Duncan's purest happiness—when, for those few months before they began to tear each other apart, he had Mary's body, her mind, and the little apartment they shared. Mary had come free of her Academy obligations a couple of months before and graduated with honors. Bonmot had no hold over her anymore, except for the hold created by her gratitude. She and Duncan moved into an apartment off of Albumuth Boulevard. A nice little arrangement. In his journal he wrote of a contentment that served as a welcome respite from his aboveground and underground adventures, almost as if Manzikert had confessed to enjoying sewing.

I wake early to make a pot of tea and to cook up some eggs. We have matching placemats but the plates are all mixed up. A few I bought have some kind of whale motif, while others Mary stole from her father's house, and these have a tracery of ivy on them. I like mine better. But the forks are all the same.

It was almost as if he had lost his mind. Didn't he know the Family Shriek is condemned to wander above and belowground like the most transient of

Skamoo nomads? Or like the foraging armies of the doomed infidel Stretcher
Jones? {No, I most certainly did not know this, Janice. Until Dad died, we were
most assuredly stay-put people. Nothing fated us for a lack of domestic bliss.
Besides, without that fragile calm, I don't think we could have survived the
war. It's odd what stays with you. *I still* remember the tracery of ivy on those
plates she stole, and the pleasure she got from the theft, and the tiny and not-
so-tiny cracks that those plates acquired over time from the constant echo of
bombardment.}

What for me had always been like quicksilver, the intense heat of a caress
that faded from my memory over time, was for him long, and drawn-out, never
far from his thoughts. Another typical entry, from several weeks later, read:

> In the morning: sunshine and her. I'm not sure which I'm more enamored of.
> This freedom after so much heartache seems almost unreal. She's here, in
> front of me, sleeping. I can watch her as long as I like—catalogue the ele-
> ments of her beauty, from her rose-colored mouth to the fine down above her
> upper lip to the soft line of her nose to the long lashes that frame her closed
> eyes to the neck with its delicate glide to the lightly freckled arm that slid out
> from beneath the sheets during the night. I should wake her. I should. But I
> can't. She's so peaceful right now, and the world outside is not. I gain strength
> from watching her like this, and I hope I give it back to her as well when she
> is awake. I must cut this short—the mortars are going off again, and she is
> beginning to stir.

{That's a nice entry, if atypical for more than a short while. I almost feel as if
I was trying to convince myself with that entry, considering the horrors of the
world around us. I went home to her every night after hours of hard, dangerous
work. Under even the best of circumstances, I would hardly have made what
you would call a stable lover. But with bombs exploding everywhere, screaming
shells digging into the street only blocks away, and the random violence of the
militias, I was very unstable. There were times when the danger brought us
close together, when we didn't need words or other constraints, like it had been
back at Blythe. And then it was good. But the rest of the time, I struggled to
love her despite the tense, closet-like atmosphere. I admit it—there was no way
to preserve the allure of the forbidden, of having to sneak into her room at night.
Now I was the man who snored at night and sometimes, choking on the spores
in my throat, woke gagging. I think I began to scare her almost from the beginning.

This was everything she hadn't seen yet. She wasn't ready for me. She was brave in many ways, but not in that way. And I can't blame her.}

We sat there in the café and watched as, across the street, six Hoegbotton irregulars took up positions behind a stand of trees and began firing into the buildings, from which came spiraling the distinctive crimson bullets that had become known as "Lewden Specials." Two of Hoegbotton's men went down writhing and clutching their chests. An F&L supporter fell from the third story of one of the buildings and landed with a wet thud on the pavement below in a confusing welter of blood and bone.

And we just sat there, watching and drinking our ale. Really, it was tame next to what we had already seen. Really, it was expected. So we sat there for another half hour and talked while men killed each other across the street.

❧❦

THEN, OF COURSE, THE KALIF invaded during the night of the opera performance, and we suddenly had a new topic to write about.

KALIF'S MEN SURROUND CITY:
OCCUPATION, PHASE II? ONE MAN'S OPINION
D.J. Shriek

The Kalif has in the past given us telephones, guns, and a variety of delicious cheeses. Now, it appears that the current Kalif wishes to give us two things we already have in abundance: bombs and war.

Clearly, the Kalif has forgotten the essential lessons of history. During the first Occupation, before the Silence, the citizens of Ambergris set aside their petty squabbles long enough to thoroughly demoralize and defeat the Western Menace.

Now the Kalif has returned, bombarding the city with mortar fire from the outskirts. Despite a brief foray into Ambergris, apparently for the sole purpose of ruining our enjoyment of a humble but entertaining opera, the Kalif seems generally reluctant to send his troops into our streets. Apparently, he believes he will not need to enter Ambergris, that we will simply capitulate like some Stockton ne'er-do-well.

He may be wrong in this assumption, however. Instead, his actions appear to have united enemies whose only previous commonality was an ampersand.

Along Albumuth Boulevard yesterday, this reporter saw elements of House Lewden's Twelfth Militia and House Hoegbotton's Fifth Irregular Infantry {or the "Filthies," as they're commonly known} moving in concert toward the docks, intent on rooting out any of the Kalif's men unlucky enough to still be in the area.

Besides this circumstantial evidence, respected sources tell this reporter that Hoegbotton & Sons and Frankwrithe & Lewden may orchestrate a general ceasefire, the main goal of which will be to ensure the Kalif's defeat prior to the resumption of hostilities.

The broadsheets accompanying the Kalif's mortar fire haven't helped the Kalif win much support, either. These odd, half-shredded love letters to our great city indicate that the Kalif has come to "liberate the citizens of Ambergris from chaos and tyranny."

"Frankly," says the typical man on the street {at least typical among those who are still alive and not crawling with fungal bullets}, "I thought we were already doing a good enough job of that ourselves. This is our squabble. Between us and those bastards from F&L. The Kalif should stay out of it."

The broadsheets also indicate that "To preserve the rare antiquities and collective wisdom of the Religious Quarter, the Kalif has decided to stepped in and bring an end to the conflict."

"Stepped in," indeed.

Many of us wondered why Stockton, Nicea, and other Southern cities had not intervened in the conflict—after all, their trade was profoundly affected by this split between merchant houses. Now we knew—they had been calling on a higher power, and although it had taken almost two years for that august entity, the Kalif, to take notice, take notice he had. He would have needed little real pretext; after all, in each Kalif's heart must burn the desire for revenge upon our city for earlier defeats.

The scream of the Kalif's mortar fire—often indiscriminate or ill-timed—was a welcome contrast to the whine of fungal bullets, the garrulous chatter of Hoegbotton guns. {As the city was at war, so, by then, was my body. The rumblings of my belly, where fungus fought fungus—much remarked upon by Mary in her less charitable moments—matched the Kalif's invasion. The sharp pains that sometimes annihilated my chest hurt no more or less than the spiraling flight of bullets through the Ambergrisian air.}

Perhaps more insanely, no one paid the Kalif's troops much attention once we knew H&S and F&L had united against them. Even the day they came marching down Albumuth Boulevard on a daylight raid in a long, proud column of red, we ignored them. We had suffered through too much war. Either we could not digest this new threat, or we felt no need to.

This, then, is how things stood that year on the threshold of the Festival.

THERE CAME A NIGHT SO terrible that no one ever dared to name it. There came a night so terrible that I could not. There came a night so terrible that no one could explain it. There came the most terrible of nights. No, that's not right, either. *There came the most terrible of nights that could not be forgotten, or forgiven, or even named.* That's closer, but sometimes I choose not to revise. Let it be raw and awkward splayed across the page, as it was in life.

Words would later be offered up like "atrocity," "massacre," and "madness," but I reject those words. They did not, could not, cannot, contain what they need to contain.

Could we have known? Could we have wrenched our attention from our more immediate concerns long enough to understand the warning signs? Now, of course, it all seems clear enough. Duncan had said the war could not continue in the same way for long, and he was right.

As soon as Duncan and I saw Voss Bender's blind, blindingly white head floating down the River Moth two days before the Festival, we should have had a clue.

"There's a sight you don't see very often," Duncan said, as we sat on an abandoned pier and watched the head and the barge that carried it slowly pull away into the middle of the river. A kind of lukewarm sun shone that day, diluted by swirls of fog.

"It's a sight I've never seen before, Duncan," I replied.

F&L had cut apart a huge marble statue of Voss Bender that had stood in the Religious Quarter for almost twenty years and loaded it, piece by piece, onto the barge, displaying a remarkably dexterous use of pulleys and levers. There lay the pieces of Bender, strewn to all sides of his enormous, imperious, crushingly heavy head. About to disappear up the River Moth. As vulnerable-looking in that weak sunlight as anything I had ever seen.

"I wonder what the people who live along the banks of the river will think about it," I said.

"What do you mean?" Duncan asked.

"Will they see it as the demolition, the destruction, of a god, or will they be strangely unmoved?"

Duncan laughed. "*I'm* strangely unmoved."

In part, we had come to the pier to relax. We were both still a little rattled from a close call the day before, when we had arrived at what was supposedly the scene of a bomb attack only to find the bombs exploding as we got there. My hair was dirty and streaked with black from the explosion. My face had suffered half a dozen abrasions. Duncan had had a thumbnail-sized chunk of his ear blown off. Already, it had begun to regenerate, which I found fascinating and creepy at the same time. {Do you want a glimpse of something even more fascinating? The real problem was: it wasn't my ear. That had been blown off a long time before.}

"I think it's sad," I said. "They're carting off all of our valuables, like common thieves."

Until then, F&L had contented themselves with bombing us silly day and night. The steady northward stream of goods, art, and statuary had only started in the past week. It should have been a clear sign that the war was about to change again. After all, F&L, with their fungal mines, bombs, and bullets, seemed to have a direct line to a certain disenfranchised underground group.

"Actually, Janice," Duncan said, as he dipped his ugly toes in the Moth, "I hesitate to try to convince you otherwise, but I think the sight of Voss Bender's head floating vaingloriously down the Moth is very funny. So much effort by old F&L, and for what? What can they possibly think they will do with these 're-mains' when they reach Morrow? Rework the marble into columns for some public building? Reassemble the statue? And if so, where in Truff's name would they put it? We hardly knew where to put it ourselves."

"Maybe you're right," I said, "but that doesn't mean it can't be sad, too."

※

DID I ALREADY SAY THAT there came to be the most terrible of Festival nights? It burned down the Borges Bookstore. It stopped the war between F&L and H&S. It stopped the love between Duncan and Mary, too. Snapped it. Was no more. Never again. {It brought an end to many things, this is true. But the Festival had nothing to do with ending my relationship with Mary. I caused that all by myself.} There had never been a Festival like it, except, perhaps, during the time of the Burning Sun. There may never be another like it again. {Why would there need to be? Every week since the Shift began, some part of the city is as raw as during Festival time.}

As far as I can remember, our father had never had anything to say about the Festival. {Not true. In his essay "The Question of Ambergris," he wrote [I paraphrase from memory]: "At the heart of the city lies not a courtyard or a building or a statue, but an event: the Festival of the Freshwater Squid. It is an overlay of this event that populates the city with an alternative history, one that, if we could only understand its ebb and flow, the necessity of violence to it, would also allow us to understand Ambergris." Statements like this led me to my explorations of Ambergris. I remember trying to read my father's essays at an early age, and only understanding them in fragments and glimpses. I loved the mystery of that, and the sense of adventure, of the questions implied by what I *could* understand.} However, he did say one or two things about the gray caps. I recall that at the dinner table he would ramble on about his current studies. He had no gift for providing context. He would sit at the table, looking down at his mashed potatoes as he scratched the back of his head with one hand and pushed his fork through his food with the other. There was always about him at these times a faraway look, as if he were figuring something out in his head even as he talked to us. Sometimes, it would be a kind of muttering chant under his breath. At other times he was genuinely talking to us but was really elsewhere. He smelled of limes back then, our mother having insisted he wear some cologne to combat the smell of old books brought back from the rare book room of the Stockton Library. But since he hated cologne, he would cut up a lime instead and anoint himself with its juice. {I enjoyed that smell of books, though, missed it when it was gone—it was a comfortable, old-fashioned smell, usually mixed with the dry spice of cigar smoke. I came to feel that it was the smell of learning, which provoked the sweat not of physical exertion, but of mental exertion. To me, book must and cigar smoke were the product of working brains.}

At one such dinner, he looked up at us and he said, "The gray caps are quite simple, really. I don't know why I didn't think of this before. So long as what you're doing doesn't interfere with their plans, they don't care what you do— even if you cause one of them physical harm. But if somehow you step across the tripwire of one of their 'activities,' why, then, there is nothing that can save you."

{I remember that, too. "Tripwire." A word I'd never heard before he used it. Why did he use that word? It fascinated me. While teaching at Blythe, I used the term in connection with the Silence. Had the Silence been caused by some kind of triggering of a "tripwire," a set of circumstances under which the gray caps thought they could activate their Machine successfully? If so, what particular stimuli might have come into play? Could we predict when another such attempt might be made? And yet, even after the most minute study of ancient almanacs, historical accounts, the works of a number of statisticians such as Marmy Gort, and anything else we could lay our hands on, I still could not divine those finite, measurable values that might have created the ideal conditions. I concluded that the gray caps' extraordinary ability to collect information, coupled with their additional spore-based senses, made it unlikely that we would ever be able to know. This did not stop me from continuing to try. Or continuing to ask the most important question: why build a Machine? And what—exactly—did it do?}

We were to find out during the Festival of the Freshwater Squid that year just what happened when Ambergris collectively sprung a tripwire. For the bad Festival was like the antithesis of the Silence, sent to convince us that any semblance of law in the city was illusory, that it could not truly exist, whether we thought it resided in the palm of an obese, elderly Hoegbotton, a thin, ancient Frankwrithe, or the wizened visage of a Kalif none of us had ever seen.

※

THE NIGHT OF THE FESTIVAL, the sun set red over the River Moth. Most of the crepe paper lanterns that people had set out had already been crushed by rubble or by the motored vehicles of opposing forces. The Kalif's men had stepped up their bombardment of the city from without. They made no pretense anymore of aiming at anything in particular, their bombs as likely to crack open a hospital ward as a Hoegbotton sentry post. Really, it was as random as a heart attack. Why worry about what you cannot defend against? So we walked the streets as calmly as we had before the war, when we hadn't been hunkered down against threats like a fungal bullet to the brain from some trigger-happy F&L recruit.

No, gunfire couldn't get to me. What terrified me as I looked out from my apartment at dusk was the proliferation of red flags.

On the way back from our journalistic assignments that day, before we turned in our now infamous "The Kalif Yearns for Every Ambergrisian's Head" article, the flags of the gray caps had appeared in multitudes—rhapsodies of red that seemed, like the ever-present fungus, always on the verge of forming some pattern, some message, only to fall apart into chaos again.

As we approached Lacond's offices in the late afternoon, the wind picked up. It rattled the gravel on side streets. It brought with it a strange premature twilight, and a smell that none could identify. Was it a smell come up off the river? It seemed bitter and pleasant, sharp and vague, all at once.

The light, as Martin Lake might have said, had become different in Ambergris.

We left Lacond's offices tired and ready for rest, Duncan to his and Mary's apartment, me to my own place much farther down Albumuth Boulevard in the opposite direction. {Not even Lacond could demand we cover the Festival, not that year. The Kalif's troops were an unknown factor—they made us nervous, as had the uneventful Festival the year before.} Sybel had decided to take me up on my invitation and stay with me that night, just in case. Either we'd celebrate the Festival together or defend ourselves against it. {I left ample protections; I'm sorry they were not enough.} We had all been through many Festivals. We were old pros at it. We knew how to handle it.

I had thought about making the trek to our mother's mansion, but Duncan had assured me he could keep her safe. {She was quite safe, for several reasons, not least of which was her location: far enough upriver that the Kalif's men had not requisitioned the house, and far enough from Ambergris that she would come to no harm from the gray caps.}

Dusk had become night by the time Sybel arrived, breathless from running. After I let him in, I bolted the door behind him.

"It's not good out there," he said, gasping for breath. "The trees are too still. There's a silence that's . . . like I imagine what the Silence must have been like."

That was a thought. I felt light-headed for an instant, a conjoined chill and thrill. What if, tonight, we were to experience what the twenty-five thousand had experienced during the Silence, the city to become another vast experiment?

"Nonsense," I said. "It's just another Festival. Help me with this."

We pushed a set of cabinets up against the door.

"That should do it," I said.

Outside, a few dozen drunken youths passed by, shouting as they stumbled their way past.

"Death to the Kalif!" I heard, and a flurry of cursing.

"They'll be lucky if they survive the hour," Sybel said. "And it won't be the Kalif that kills them, either."

"When did you become so cheerful?" I asked.

He gave me a look and went back to loading his gun. We had pistols and knives, which Sybel had managed to purchase from, of all people, a Kalif officer. There was a booming black market in weapons these days. Some wags speculated that the Kalif had invaded Ambergris to create demand for inventory.

Meanwhile, the gray caps had spores and fungal bombs, and Truff knew what else.

"Do you think we're much safer in here?" I asked.

Sybel smiled. "No. Not much safer."

There seemed about him that night more than a hint of self-awareness, mixed with that rarest of commodities for Sybel: contentment. {It was only rare to you because you never saw him in his natural element.}

❧

WE DIDN'T BOARD UP THE window until much later, fearful of losing the thread of what was going on outside. The full moon drooped, misshapen and diffuse, in the darkening sky.

Through that smudged fog of glass, we watched rivulets and outcroppings of the Festival walk or run by. Clowns, magicians, stiltmen, and ordinary citizens with no special talent, who had put on bright clothes and gone out because—quite frankly—in the middle of war, how much worse could the Festival possibly make things? True, without the great influx of visitors from other cities there wasn't nearly the number of people that we had become accustomed to seeing, but Sybel and I still agreed it was a more potent Festival than had been predicted by the so-called experts. {Including us, Janice, in our column in the *Broadsheet*.}

Then the merrymakers began to trail off. Soon the groups had thinned until it was only one or two people at a time, either drunk and careless, or alert and hurrying quickly to their destinations. Every once in a while, something would explode in the background as the Kalif's men kept at it. The bright orange flame of the shuddering explosions was oddly reassuring. As long as it stayed far away from us, that is. At least we knew where it was coming from. {Yes, with all the force of His benevolent, if distant, love.}

Sybel and I sat there looking out the window like it was our last view of the world.

"Remember when we used to host parties in abandoned churches on Festival night?" Sybel said. He looked very old then, in that light, the wrinkles around his eyes and mouth undeniable.

"Yes, I remember," I said, smiling. "That was a lot of fun. It really was."

At least, more fun than the war. I didn't want to return to those days, either, though.

Sybel smiled back. Had we ever been close? I search my memory now, thinking of the glance we exchanged back then. No, not close, but *comfortable*, which is almost more intimate. In the preparations for countless parties, in seeing Sybel day after day at my gallery, a deep affection had built up between us.

"Maybe after the war, I can . . ." The words felt like such a lie, I couldn't continue. "Maybe the gallery can . . ."

Sybel nodded and looked away in, I believe, embarrassment. "That would be good," he said.

We continued to watch the city through our window: that fungi-tinged, ever-changing painting.

❧

FINALLY, IT BEGAN TO HAPPEN, at least three hours after nightfall. A stillness crept into the city. The only people on the street were armed and running. Once, a dozen members of a Hoegbotton militia hurried by in tight formation, their weapons gleaming with the reflected light of the fires. Then, for a while, nothing. The moon and the one or two remaining street lamps, spluttery, revealed an avenue on which no one moved, where the lack of breeze was so acute that crumpled newspapers on the sidewalk lay dead-still.

"It's coming," Sybel muttered. "I don't know what it is, but it'll happen soon."

"Nonsense," I said. "It's just a lull."

But a chill had crept over me, as it seemed to have crept over the city. It lodged in my throat, my belly, my legs. Somehow, I too could feel it coming, like a physical presence. As if my nerves were the nerves of the city. Something had entered Ambergris. {Creeping through your nervous system, the gray caps' spores, creating fear and doubt, right on schedule. I'd put the antidote in your food, but an antidote only works for so long against the full force of such efforts.}

The street lights went out.

Even the moon seemed to gutter and wane a little. Then the lights came back on—all of them—but they were fungus green, shining in a way that hardly illuminated anything. Instead, this false light created fog, confusion, fear.

Sybel cursed.

"Should we barricade the window?" I asked.

"Not yet," Sybel said. "Not yet. This might be the end of it, you know. This might . . ." Now it was his turn to trail off. We both knew this would not be the end of it.

We began to see people again on the street below. This time, they ran for their lives. We could not help them without endangering ourselves, and so we watched, frozen, at the window, beyond even guilt. A woman with no shoes on, her long hair trailing out behind her, ran through our line of vision. Her mouth was wide, but no sound came from it. A few seconds later, some *thing* appeared in the gutter near the sidewalk. It tried to stand upright like a person, tottered grotesquely, then dropped all pretense and loped out of sight after the woman. The roar of the Kalif's mortar fire followed on its heels.

"What was that?" I hissed at Sybel. "What in Truff's name?"

Sybel didn't reply. Sybel was whispering something in his native language, the singsong chirp of the Nimblytod Tribe. I couldn't understand it, but it sounded soothing. Except I was beyond being soothed.

Then a man came crawling down the street, shapes in the shadows pulling at his legs. Still he crawled, past all fear, past all doubt. Until, as the Kalif's mortars let out a particularly raucous shout, something pulled him off the street, out of view.

Silence again. I was shaking by that time. My teeth were grinding together. I'd never understood that your teeth could actually grind involuntarily, could chatter when they weren't grinding. Sybel made me bite down on a piece of cloth.

"The sound," he whispered. "They'll hear you." {If they heard you, it is because they "heard" my protections on the door of your apartment—my attempt to help you may have endangered you instead.}

The street lay empty, save for the suggestion of shapes at the edge of our line of sight.

Suddenly, the Kalif's mortar fire, which had been progressing in a regular circle around the city, became erratic. Several explosions occurred at once, quite near us, the characteristic whistle of destruction so banal I didn't even think of it as a threat at first. The ceiling lifted, the floor trembled, dust floated down.

Then nothing for several minutes. Then another eruption of explosions, farther away. On the outskirts of Ambergris, gouts of flame lit up the night sky, whiter than the moon. Slowly, as the fires spread, it became clear that the conflagration was forming a circle around Ambergris.

We watched it spread, silent, unable to find words for our unease.

After a while, Sybel said, in a flat voice, "Did you notice?"

"What?"

"The Kalif's mortars have been silenced."

"Yes, yes they have," I said.

Nothing rational told us that the Kalif's positions had been overrun, but we knew it to be true regardless. Someone or something had attacked the Kalif's troops. And yet not even H&S or F&L would have been foolhardy enough to launch an attack on so unpredictable an evening as Festival night.

That is when we decided to board up the window. Some things should not be seen, if at all possible.

❦

SHALL I TELL YOU DUNCAN'S crime during the Festival, in Mary's eyes? While Sybel and I boarded up my apartment window, Duncan was leading Mary to safety—just not a safety she had expected or particularly wanted. It was not the safety provided by a living necklace of acclaim and warmly muttered praise. It was not the kind of safety that reinforces trust or love. For where could Duncan possibly be safe with the surface in so much turmoil? I think you already know, my dear reader, if you've followed me this far. Some of us read to discover. Some of us read to discover what we already know. Duncan read Mary the wrong way. He thought he knew her. He was wrong. How do I know? His journal tells me so. It's all in there.

I took Mary underground as the Festival raged above. Truff help me, I did. Why I thought this might be a good thing for us beyond ensuring our immediate survival, I don't know. The Kalif's men were too close to our home, and I could sense the gray caps getting even closer. The spores in my skin rose to the surface and pointed in their direction. My skin was literally pulling in their direction, yearning to join them—that was how close to turning traitor my body had become. Besides, some F&L louts were five doors down, beating an old woman senseless. It seemed clear they'd reach our door before long.

"Do you trust me?" I asked Mary. She was pale and shaking. She wouldn't look at me, but she nodded. I don't know if I've ever loved her more than at that moment, as she left everything familiar behind. I kissed her. "Get your jacket," I told her. "Bring the canteen from the kitchen."

And then we set off. The place I meant to take her was underground, yes, but a place rarely inhabited by gray caps. The entrance lay halfway between our home and the F&L thugs. We had to hurry. We were scurrying to a rat hole before the other rats could catch us. I had my greatcoat on, which I had seeded with a few varieties of camouflaging fungi. I was carrying an umbrella for some reason—I don't even remember why anymore. Except I remember joking with Mary about it, to make her laugh, at least a little bit. But she was too scared, frozen. I really think she thought we were both about to die. Thankfully, I was more or less human right then, or she would have been out of her mind with terror. When you can't count on your lover to stay in one consistent shape. . . .

We beat the F&L thugs to the entrance by a few minutes—we could hear their cries and catcalls, the swish of their torches, smell the bittersweet decay that coated anyone who handled fungal weapons for too long—but they passed us by as we descended ever deeper into the hole, down a ladder.

"Where are we going?" Mary asked me. I don't know if she really wanted an answer or not. She smelled like fear, her perfume gone sour.

"Keep following me," I told her. To her, it was dark as we came to the end of the ladder and into a tunnel, but my eyes were different than they had been. I could see things she couldn't. I could see markers in the tunnel. I could see colors spiraling out of the dark. I held her hand—cold, and clutching my hand desperately—as we walked through the passageway. It was wet now—we were wading through thick, shallow water, the tunnel beginning to slope downward, so we had to be careful not to slip. Through the darkness, I could see the sightless eyes of certain mushrooms, the fiery green of creeping mosses. We could hear dim, dumb shudders above from some kind of bombing: I remember being, insanely enough, happy to hear that sound. Surely it would make Mary realize we could not have stayed aboveground?

Of course, as a corrective counterbalance, the smell coming from below us was rank, stifling. And then, as if to undo all of my reassurances, there came the sound of scuttling, of scattering. That's when I think her spirit really broke and she began to panic. She pulled away from me, to turn back, to run. I held on to her wrist, would not let go. I had to put my hand over her mouth to stop her from screaming.

"We're lost, my love, if you make a sound," I said. "We're dead. You understand?" She nodded, and I took my hand from her mouth. Her eyes in the dim light were white and wide.

The sounds came from below us, moving fast. Something wanted out. Something wanted to reach the surface. It wasn't my place to stop it even if I could, which I couldn't. There was no time to do anything but what I did: I pulled Mary inside of my greatcoat and pushed her into the side of the passageway, my coat covering both of us, and the coat itself covered with the protective spores. They had begun to take root and form fruiting bodies. I had to hope it would be enough.

The scuttling sound and the smell became more intense. I could tell Mary was still stifling her screams. She was shaking, her body tight against mine. Nothing at Blythe Academy, or in her relatively short life so far, had prepared her for anything like this moment.

Then they were all around us—gray caps, racing up the tunnel, speaking in clicks and whistles. One even brushed against my coat, but they were in such a hurry that they did not stop, and before long there was silence again, save for the echo of their progress to the surface. Something was going to happen tonight; my instincts had been right. It would be much safer belowground than above, because tonight even the gray caps would be on the surface. I shuddered, pulled Mary closer.

"Can you go on?" I asked her.

"I think so," she said, her voice calmer than before.

I've often wondered since if that was the point—if it was in that tunnel, as the gray caps passed by, that she made her decision. If she had decided then that she refused to believe any of it, no matter what she saw. If she was going to disown me, discredit me because of that moment. Or this moment. Or the moment after that. I'll never be sure, but I do wonder. For me, though, the moment was a sweet one: to smell her hair, to feel her next to me, to know we were both still alive, and together.

Meanwhile, in the darkness caused by the boarded-up window, Sybel and I awaited our own fate. We had no recourse to the underground, no thought that it might be safer there than where we were.

Sometimes we heard strange sounds that could not have been real— gurglings and shouts and screams, but oddly twisted, as if distant or distorted. At other times, it sounded as if soldiers fought with swords on the street below. The sound of leafy vines growing and intertwining at great speed. The sound of buildings collapsing—a dull, muted roar, then the sweet exhausted sigh of wood or stone hitting the ground. A smell, sharp yet musty, began to enter the apartment.

Sybel began to rock back and forth, holding his arms over his knees.

"We should leave," he said. "We should get out of the apartment. Find a high place."

"Don't say that," I said. "This is the safest place to be."

Sybel smiled and gave me an odd look. "The Borges Bookstore was the safest place to be, and they burned it down."

Sybel was beginning to scare me.

Something scratched at the outside of the door. A slow, tentative sound. It could have been anything. It could have been the wind. But the breath died in my throat. I realized every nerve in my skin had come alive in warning. I shut my eyes for a long time, as if willing the sound to go away. But it did not. It became louder, gained in confidence, precision. Scrabbling. At the door. At the window. I heard it sniffing the air. Reading our scent. I shivered, caught in the grip of nightmare. If we hadn't boarded up the window, it would have been looking in at us at that very moment.

Sybel moaned, took me by the arm. "Janice, I think we have to leave."

I held the gun tight, so tight my knuckles ached. "But where can we run to, Sybel? And how do we get out of here? I don't think it's possible now."

"Do you think you could slide out of the bathroom window?" Sybel asked.

A knock at the door before I could reply—but not at the height I'd expected; lower, much lower.

I stifled a scream. "It's too close. It can hear us right now. It can hear us talking. It knows what we're going to do." I held the gun like a club. I was no use to anyone. The fear had gotten too far into me. This wasn't like trying to kill myself. I could face the fear of that now, but not this fear—this was too different, too unfamiliar.

Sybel grabbed me by the shoulders, whispered in my ear, "Either we go through the bathroom window or we're dead. It's going to come in here and kill us."

"Yes, but Sybel," I whispered back, "what if there's already one at the bathroom window, too? What if they're already back there?"

Sybel shrugged. There was an odd, fatalistic light in his eyes. "Then it doesn't matter. We're dead. I'll go first. If they get to me, go back into the apartment and lock yourself in the bedroom, and hope dawn comes soon."

I hugged him. I've never been more terrified than at that moment—not even now, writing this account. I don't know what came over me. I'd seen the horrors of war, become clinical and precise in the cataloguing of them, but somehow this was more personal.

The thing at the door knocked again. Then it spoke.

In a horrible, moist parody of a human voice, it said, "I have something. For you. You will. Like it."

Was this the first time in Ambergris' history that a gray cap or a creature sent by the gray caps had spoken to a resident of the city? Most assuredly not—history is littered with the remains of those who have had such conversations; at least a dozen, two dozen. And yet, that night more than one hundred people reported having such contacts. What did it mean? At the time, no meaning would have penetrated my fear. {Mostly meant what a clever mimic, a parrot, means: nothing. A lure. Bait. A tripwire. A distraction. Delivered by their drones. Now I wonder if this was another harbinger of the Shift.}

❧

WE MADE OUR WAY TO the back of the apartment, to the bathroom. I helped Sybel clamber up to the window. Behind us, the creature with the wet voice was banging on the door like a drunk and making a low gurgling laugh. "Let me in!" it said. "Let me in! I have something for you."

"Quickly," I said to Sybel, as he fumbled with the latch. "Come on!"

Sybel undid the latch. He looked down at me.

"Open it," I said, bile rising in my throat.

I flinched as Sybel opened the window, gun held ready.

Fresh air entered the apartment. Fresh air, the distant sounds of battle, the roar of flames in the middle distance, over the silhouette of rooftops, but nothing else.

Sybel pulled himself through. Then it was my turn.

The creature began to pound on the front door. It began to laugh—great, rippling waves of laughter. Perhaps it was calling to others of its kind. {It was gathering its strength—it had nothing but a collective consciousness; it was but the sum of its spores.}

I stood on the toilet seat and pulled myself up to the window ledge by pushing off against the wall with my left foot. A narrow ledge, a narrow window.

The banging behind me had become splintering.

Sybel offered his hand and pulled me through.

The splintering had become a rending. The door would be broken down within the minute.

Sybel shut the window behind us. The night was glistening with stars masked by patches of fog; there was a chill to the air. The fires on the edges of the city raged on.

Shivering, pistol stuck through my belt, knives in my pockets, as much a hazard to myself as to others, I stumbled out onto the second-floor roof. There wasn't much room. I had to engage in a close shuffling dance with Sybel so we could both leave the storm drain for the roof proper.

Behind us, a muted roar. A shriek. Something I'd never heard before, something I never want to hear again. {No matter where you are now, I'm afraid you'll be hearing it again. What we all heard in that moment of the war was the first groaning, rust-and-flesh-choked stirrings of the Machine. It fed off of that energy. It needed it. Forever after, my finely tuned senses could hear that hum, that vibration, in the ground. It terrified me.}

How do you control your fear at a time like that? I couldn't. I could barely stop from wetting myself. Bombs are different. Reporting is different. This time, I couldn't get outside of myself. I couldn't get outside.

"What now, Sybel?" I asked. I was breathing hard. I think I might have been whimpering.

"Now, we go higher," Sybel said.

Looking at him, I saw a sudden confidence in him that I had not seen before. As a Nimblytod, high places were his birthright, no matter how long he had lived in the city.

So we went higher, following the curve of the roof to a point where we could pull ourselves up to the next level and the next, until we were on a real roof—a slanted, tiled affair a block away from my apartment. We couldn't see over the other side of it, and we didn't want to. On that side lay an unimpeded view of the street—and whatever had come through the door to my apartment.

We tried to be quiet, but the creature somewhere below had already heard us. Was tracking us.

Sybel knew this better than I.

"It's at the bathroom window. It's coming out onto the rain gutter," he said. He looked to our right. Three feet separated us from the flat roof of the next building. It was higher, but we could see the edge of a wall in the middle of that roof.

"We need to jump to the next roof," I said.

Sybel nodded.

He went first, so he could help me if I didn't quite make it. A smooth, grace-ful run; the leap up into the night; and then landing on all fours on the other side. I tossed my gun and knives over to him. I could hear scuttling sounds be-hind me. There was a smell now, like rotted flesh, but mixed with a fungal sweetness.

I ran toward the gap as fast as I could and jumped, the ground spinning below me, the flames to the west a kaleidoscope; came down heavily on the other side.

Sybel helped me up and we ran for the wall. Once behind it, out of sight if not out of smell, Sybel handed back my pistol and knives.

We could already hear it sniffing our scent from the other roof. We could sense its enjoyment. The sound of that thing slowly coming toward us will never leave me.

"It knows exactly where we are," Sybel whispered.

We could hear it getting closer and closer to the gap between the roofs.

I was babbling by then. Praying to Truff, to Bonmot, to anyone I could think of. Even now, in this afterword, with the hole in the ground behind me, my typewriter slowly turning into fungal mush, I am babbling, thinking of that moment.

We waited. We almost waited too long. Its smell came closer, came closer. It jumped onto the roof—we could hear it leap to clear the gap with an effortless stride, heard its claws scrabble to find purchase on our side. It couldn't have been more than twenty feet away.

"What do we do Sybel what do we do?" I kept saying, over and over again.

"Be calm and quiet, Janice," he said. "Just be calm. When I say, stand up and fire at it."

I looked up at the few stars through the moonlight, the clouds and the smoke that had begun to move in over the city. It was a cool night. I could feel the rough chill of the stone wall against my back. The seconds seemed to stretch out for a very long time. I had time to think about my gallery, to wonder if it would still be standing in the morning. I had time to think about Duncan and Mary, and to ask myself if I had been too harsh, if it had ever been my place to disapprove. I experienced a twinge of regret—that I had never married, never had children, never lived a "normal" life.

You understand, I hope: I thought I was going to die.

We almost waited too long. We thought it was farther away. But then it be-gan to run at us. It had played its game of Stalk as long as it wanted to—now it meant to finish us. It was talking as it ran at us: "I have something for you something for you something for you you will like it you will like it you will like it," like the chant of some senile priest counting beads cross-legged in the Religious Quarter.

That's when we rose, in our fear. We rose up, and we emptied our pistols into it. It was dark as the night and yet transparent—you could see the stars through it when it got close. It was thick. It was thin. It had claws. It had fangs like polished steel. It had eyes so human and yet so various that the gaze paralyzed me. It was indescribable. Even now, trying to visualize it, I want to vomit. I want to *unthink* it.

Our shots went right through it. It veered to the left, misjudged the distance, and struck the wall in front of us, reared up again. We shot it again—tore great holes in its fungal skull, its impossible body. It roared, spit a stream of dark liquid, and tried to come up over the wall at us. Sybel stuck the muzzle of his pistol under its soft-rigid chin and pulled the trigger. The recoil sent the creature screaming and stumbling to the edge of the roof, and then over—falling. Still talking. Still telling us it had something for us that we'd like.

We stood there, numb, for a moment. Some things cannot be described. Some things can only be experienced.

Gone was the fear. I couldn't feel it anymore. I just couldn't. I had no room for it; it had no room for me. It had other places to go, other people to visit.

"Come on," I said to Sybel. "We have to get off this roof. There might be others. They will have heard. We'll seek refuge in the Religious Quarter. It might still be safe there."

Off the roof and into the night.

And how did that feel, you may ask. It was terrible, I tell you. Terrible. It was an experience to inoculate you against horror forever.

⁂

MEANWHILE, DUNCAN AND MARY TRAVELED ever farther into the depths. . . .

So down we went, ever down, until the tunnel leveled off and an odd green phosphorescence that even Mary could see began to rise from the walls, the ground. Now we walked across a thick green carpet of blindly grasping tendrils. Soft and silent, so that our every sound was sucked into that which we trod upon. Ahead, we could see nothing but the continual wormhole of the tunnel, with no possible deviation, no other possibility.

"How much farther? Where are we going?" Mary asked, her voice flat and dull.

"Not much farther," I told her, heartsick at how every step seemed to make her more distant, even though we walked shoulder-to-shoulder. "We're going somewhere we can be safe." As safe as we could be anywhere, at least.

The fungi on my body had come alive the farther down we traveled. They pulled at my coat, they curled across my chest. They knew they were home. They wanted to return, but I wouldn't let them. If they returned, I would never leave.

At the same time, I could hear Mary next to me, her every sound magnified by my heightened senses. Her breath, the nervous movement of her hands, the tread of her shoes.

"I don't know why this is necessary," she said at one point, the fear gnawing at her face in the green light.

"We have to," I said. "If we'd stayed aboveground, we might be dead by now." The dim dumb hum and throb of explosives somewhere over our heads punctuated my point. The emptiness of the tunnel just confirmed it.

And yet we were not alone. Mary just couldn't see them, floating in the air around us, as oblivious to us as Mary was to them, conforming to their own rituals and needs. I still didn't know what they were, nor could I even describe the shape of them. Perhaps they were red-tinged megaspores, diaphanous, translucent. Perhaps they were some other organism altogether. I'd learned long ago not to wince when I walked through one.

"You trust me, don't you?" I asked her while all around us the tendrils swayed, and the green was not one green but a thousand shades of it, and the intensity of the voices in my ears made me want to shout to be heard, although I knew no one could hear them but me. The blind voices of the fungi, calling out. So beautiful. So unbearable.

"I don't know if this is about trust," she replied. "This isn't real, Duncan. I don't accept that this is real. You've fed me a pill. I'm having visions." It was odd to see her, usually so strong, so weak when out of her element.

I ignored her. The fungi were like pale hands beneath our tread. I had to carry her for a while. "We're almost there," I said.

"Almost where?" she asked, trembling in my arms. "Almost dead?"

What can I tell you about our escape to the Truffidian Cathedral? What, I wonder, will put it all in the proper perspective? I hardly know where to begin, but, then, that's not unusual. There's no balance between measured prose and raw experience that does not end in mediocrity or a slow burn into oblivion.

It happened like this: Sybel and I left the shelter of the roof and began to make our way through back streets and alleys to the Truffidian Cathedral. It was the only landmark I could think of that might be safe.

"What if the cathedral's been overrun?" Sybel asked.

"Then we go somewhere else," I said. "But we have to try."

Sybel knew as well as I did that we couldn't sit still—we couldn't stay on that roof and wonder what might be coming over the ledge next.

The world we found ourselves in was silent. In some places the lamps were on, and in others they were not. Where they were on, they illuminated everything in purples or greens. The purple and the green both came from spores. The spores were heavy in the air; so as not to breathe them, we tore strips from our clothing and put them over our mouths and noses.

Was it effective? I'm still alive today, but at the time I could not get over the uncomfortable feeling that I was breathing in thousands of tiny lives, that I was one step away from becoming Duncan.

I said that the world was silent. Do you understand what I mean by that? I mean that there was no sound anywhere in the city. The spores clotted the air, muffled noises, sucked the sound out of the world. We lived in silence. It was like a Presence, and it was watchful. As we sidled along a wall, keeping to the shadows for long moments, I felt that each spore was a tiny eye, and that each eye was reporting back to an unseen master. A heaviness grew in my lungs that I've never felt since. The air was trying to suck words as yet unspoken out of me, and snuff them, stillborn.

Silence and haze. The purple and green of the spores made the air heavy, made it hard to see more than two feet in front of us. It was a kind of fog, through which we could just make out the distant flames that signified the destruction of the Kalif's army.

But I don't mean to suggest that this silent haze was empty. It wasn't. As we picked our way through streets turned foreign, unrecognizable, hints of movement suggested themselves, almost out of view, always on the periphery. We did not turn to look at whatever walked there, for fear this would make it too real. That which watched there ignored us, went on past—saving energy for other, more important missions, no doubt. But this made it no less frightening.

Nor did it blunt the effect of the human catastrophe that came out of the haze and lingered for far too long in our vision. Some lampposts played host to bodies swinging from ropes, heads lolling, tongues distended, skin pulled back in caricatures of smiles. Other bodies crowded the street, stumbled over in the dark. Pieces of people that appeared to be carefully cut apart, not the victims of mortar fire, but in precise stacks: legs, arms, torsos. The moon overhead like the knuckle of a fist pressed against a dirty window.

And always the motion, so unnerving that at one point I fired into the dark, screamed into the shadows, "Come out! Come out, you bastards!"

Sybel didn't even try to stop me. He just stared ahead and kept walking. His gaze was haunted, his face vacant. Not all fears are the same. I met mine on the roof; Sybel met his on the streets.

We reached the outskirts of the Religious Quarter by taking two steps forward, a step sideways, a step back, two forward, always almost seeing the vague delineation of ghosts, flitting and circling.

The Religious Quarter rose out of the mire of night as an outline of domes and steeples, highlighted by the flames that lay miles behind them. In that light, it looked unearthly, bizarre, not of Ambergris. Still, we entered it, in the hopes that that way lay safety. We allowed ourselves to come under the influence of those spires, those outcroppings of alcoves, all silent, all dead, not a priest in sight. {Probably cowering in their basements for all the good it would do them.}

We were on a street called Bannerville. I remember that. The streetlamps there were bare of the terrible burden of death. Some of them worked. Glowed green. At the end of Bannerville, we'd turn to the right and we'd be a block away from the Truffidian Cathedral.

A strange surge of joy or recognition overtook us, all out of proportion to our reality. We began to run, to laugh, abandoning our shuffle through the shadows; with safety so close, it was agony to walk. The worst seemed past. It really did. I was already thinking about what I'd say to Bonmot. I was already thinking about that, Truff help me.

Sybel had stopped holding my hand. He was a little behind me at this point. We were almost at the end of Bannerville, not more than twenty feet from safety. Overhead, a street lamp flickered free of the green glow that pervaded the rest of the city.

We were both about to turn the corner. I could hear Sybel's heavy breathing as he ran. Then I heard an unfamiliar sound—a sound trapped between a gasp and a moan—and when I turned to look back at Sybel, all I could see was a mist of blood, floating out in streamers. I stopped running and stared. I couldn't breathe for a second. Nothing of him was left—not even his shoes. Nothing at all. His dissolution was complete. Utter. There was such a final and terrible beauty to it that I thought it must be an absurd magic trick, a horrible joke. But it wasn't, and the laughter caught in my throat, became a sob. Sybel had died, almost in front of my eyes, less than a block from the cathedral. A moment later, I realized it must have been one of F&L's fungal mines, but for an instant it seemed more deadly, more immediate—something personal.

When I tried to move—away from the blood mist? toward it?—I put pressure down on my right foot, felt a shock of pain, and fell to the ground. That's when I realized that the mine had also erased my right foot, shoe and all. There was now just a stump. Nothing else. I lay on the ground, panting, and watched the blood dribble out of the part of the wound that hadn't been cauterized. The silence had been transformed into a pounding of blood in my ears, a slow, aching pulse. It reminded me of the blood I'd let spurt from my wrists, and for a moment I was content to watch it leak out of me—all of this liquid that constituted me at a level more basic than brain or mind, soul or spirit. I almost let it happen. I almost decided to lie back and let it happen.

But then I thought of poor Sybel and something changed inside of me. We had come so far. We had almost made it. I started to shout or scream then, but not words, nothing as coherent as words.

I took the strip of cloth from around my mouth and made a crude tourniquet to stop the bleeding. Around me, the blood mist that had been Sybel writhed in strands of gorgeous crimson, already dissipating.

I got up, grit in my teeth. I began to hop around the corner, toward safety. I don't know how long it took, or even what was happening around me—all I could focus on was the sound of my remaining shoe against gravel as I hopped, pain in my left leg from balancing the weight of my entire body. At some point I fell and could not get back up. I remember crawling until I reached the great doors of the Truffidian Cathedral, rising long enough to shove those doors open, pushing my way inside, and then falling to the floor.

Everyone inside the Cathedral was dead. I lay where I had fallen, next to a corpse. We stared at each other, eye to eye, and it took me a while to realize that somewhere in the background, near the altar, something was moving.

Once we reached our destination, I set Mary down. We stood in a large, circular cavern. Green lichens coated the floor. The walls reflected red-and-green, spores floating through the gold-gray light. I had made a throne of mushrooms for her, lavender and silver. I had sent into the air perpetually twirling strands of emerald fungi, like shiny crepe paper. I had carved a table to appear from the ground, and upon it set a cup of pure cold water from an aquifer. And beside it, three mushrooms—orange, blue, and purple—that would not only feed her but leave her feeling strong and calm.

I had spent a long time preparing for that moment. And yet, I must admit, not everything in that cavern lay under my control. How could it? Something was laughing in a corner, at a pitch no ordinary human ear could hear. Something nonhuman. It almost sounded like human speech. Things crept and crawled through the murk. A smell like rotted mango permeated the cavern. But, still, this was as safe a place as you could find belowground. It was my laboratory, my refuge. I knew everything here, including the thing that laughed. I knew them all on the most basic of levels. I relaxed as Mary wrapped her arms around me. I thought she would appreciate all that I had given her. But she wouldn't talk to me, and she refused to look around. I couldn't talk to her, either. Instead, I turned away so she wouldn't see the veins of emerald creeping up my face.

They stayed for hours in that secluded cavern, sitting or standing. They spoke, if at all, in whispers, and sometimes not even whispers because some new threat would approach every few minutes, requiring utter silence.

"I was happy," Duncan wrote in his journal. "I thought we were reaching a new closeness, one beyond words. That the extremity of our situation would make us as one. Instead, we were growing further apart with each passing minute. Now, I am confused by my happiness that night. Was I blind?" {Was there a moment when I switched from the epiphany of discovery to the weight of discovery? I don't know, except that one day I realized that knowledge— especially secret knowledge—had become a burden.}

❧

MARY'S ASSAULT BEGAN FROM THAT moment, from the moment when her mind refused to accept what she had seen, for she maintained her distance all the way back up to the surface the next morning.

From that moment, it was only a matter of time until the flesh necklace, until I would confront her at the base of the stairs. It smoldered in her eyes, as indelible as the mottling of fungus on Duncan's body. All of her scholarship, all of her will, would be focused on making what she had seen as unreal, as distant, as possible. Who could blame her? I could, and did, even if Duncan lacked the nerve. It was a failure—a failure of love and of imagination.

While they waited underground, I lay on the cathedral floor, gray caps walking among the bodies, me dead and yet not dead, seeing yet sightless, staring up at a ceiling that depicted the glory of the Truffidian cosmos. It almost might have been a premonition of Sabon's flesh necklace. It too was incongruous to its surroundings. It too was dead and yet not dead, blind yet had eyes. But mostly I had not a thought in my head as I tried to survive by playing dead next to such a weight of bodies. I had no room for grief at that moment. I had no time for tears. In that moment, I began to relax. I began to give up my self. I had no choice. I had nowhere to hide, nothing to hide with.

That is the night I stopped being a reporter and became something else entirely.

❧ 3 ❧

THE CLOSER I GET TO the end, the closer I get to the beginning. Memories waft up out of the ether, out of nothing. They attach themselves to me like the green light, like the fungi that continue to colonize my typewriter. I had to stop for a while—my fingers ached and, even after all that I have seen, the fungi unnerved me. I spent the time flexing and unflexing my fingers, pacing back and forth. I also spent it going through a box of my father's old papers—nothing I haven't read through a hundred times before. Drafts of history essays, letters to colleagues, perhaps even the letter he received from the Kalif's Court, if I dig deep enough. On top, Duncan had placed the dried-up starfish, its skeleton brittle with age. {I kept it there as a reminder to myself. After your letter to me—which, while reading this account, I sometimes think was written by an entirely different side of your personality—I wanted to remember that no matter how isolated I might feel, separated from others by secret knowledge, I was still *connected*. It didn't help much, though—it reminded me how different I had become.}

I've put the starfish on my table here, as something akin to a good luck charm. Perhaps it will help me finish.

Next to the starfish, I found sea shells, dull and chipped—the last remnants of our most noteworthy vacation. I was ten, Duncan six. Our dad had gone on sabbatical from his position as a history professor at the Porfal College of History and Advanced Theory {or as Dad called it, "Poor Paul's Collage of Hysterics and Advanced Decay"} in Stockton. I cannot recall ever taking a weeklong vacation before or since. Dad had bought berths on a river barge for us. Mom was relaxed, happy. Dad was as calm and at peace as I've ever seen him.

I remember one habit he picked up during that vacation. He liked to take a stalk of sedge weed and hold it in his mouth like a pipe, gnawing on the end, a wide-brimmed hat shading his face. We'd sit in the deck chairs and read, or watch the countryside go by.

In those days, the west side of the River Moth was almost entirely uninhabited. We saw strange animals come to the water's edge to drink; they would look at us with curiosity, but no fear. Once, we saw odd, short people dressed in outlandish clothes, staring across the water at us with a peculiar intensity. The water formed a mirror in which our images reached out to theirs across the waves—stretched, unreal.

We took the barge down to the Southern Isles, where we spent four days on the beaches. We couldn't afford to go farther than the northernmost island of Hathern, with its black sand and the melancholy ruins of the long-dead Saphant Empire, but we still had a good time.

Mom refused to go *in* the water, so she had to put up with Dad splashing water *at* her. Dad loved to swim—although "bob" or "float" might more accurately describe what he looked like when he took to the waves. Mom loved to watch the sunrises and sunsets from our little rented bungalow. During the day, she would walk along the beach for hours, and always brought back shells and shiny rocks for us. Sometimes Duncan and I went with her, sometimes we stayed with Dad.

At dusk, we sat on a blanket together and Dad would make a fire, cooking fish over the flames. I can't remember if he bought the fish or caught them. I don't remember him being much of a fisherman.

Then Dad would lecture us in a teasing way about the mighty Saphant Empire.

Pointing to the black-gray nubs and jagged walls drowning in the sand and sea, suffused with the orange of sunset, he would say, "Those are the result of war. A naval conflict and then the survivors fought on this very beach. There used to be a city here. Now, just what you see. And then . . . and then!" And then he would find a way to bring pirates and adventures into his history lesson.

I didn't give his words about war much thought at the time. The ruins were just great rocks to climb on, tidal pools to explore. That men had fought and died there hundreds of years ago seemed too remote from our vacation to be real.

Another time, Dad presented me with a tiny hermit crab in a white coiled shell.

"Don't hurt it," he said, "and leave it on the beach when we go."

"I will," I said, marveling at the feel of its tiny legs against the skin of my palm.

The sand crunching between my toes; the heat and breeze off the sea, the lights of boats far offshore.

Mom looked after Duncan for most of the trip, because he was young and needed constant attention. {I remember only the vaguest flash of sunlight, the most tenuous thread of a memory of water—it was all too idyllic for me to retain, I suppose.}

It is one of the only times I can recall the full attention of my father upon me. Five years later, he would die. Eight years later, my mother would bring us to Ambergris and the house by the River Moth. Twenty years later, Duncan would feel the first twinge of the fungal colonization occurring within him. Twenty-five years after our long-ago vacation, I would try to kill myself. Thirty years later and the War of the Houses would almost kill us all.

⁂

HOW CAN SUCH A PLEASURABLE memory as a childhood vacation coexist comfortably with memories of the war? How can the world contain such extremes? I thought about such things as I lay among the bodies in the Truffidian Cathedral. Each question begat another question, so that soon the questions seemed to contain their own answers.

I lay there for a very long time, gazing at nothing and no one while the gray caps rummaged all around me, each syllable of their clicking speech a knife slid between my shoulder blades. I do not know what they were looking for, nor whether they found it. I could hear them rolling bodies over, rifling through the pockets of the dead. Once, a clawing hand brushed against the side of my face. I could feel someone or something looking at me; I refused to look back. I could *feel the breath* of one of them upon me, smell the spurling tangle of scents that clung to them like their skin: must and mold and funk and dust and a trace of some spice.

And then, finally, the stained glass above me refracted the light of the sun, and it was dawn, and the gray caps were gone, and I was still alive, surrounded by hundreds of the dead, the blood upon them dark and caked.

Stiffly, like an old woman, I propped myself up, struggled to raise myself onto my foot, stared around me at the carnage.

The dead did not look peaceful. The dead did not look planned or purposeful, or *at rest,* or any other combination of words that might signify comfort or the rule of law. Legs and arms lay at unnatural angles, torn or contorted or dislocated from torsos. Mouths were caught in extremes of pain and fear and surprise. Dried blood and gathering flies. Skin a pale yellow tinged with blue. Great wounds, like vast claws, had cut into chests leaving dull red furrows.

A row of heads disembodied. After a while, I had to stop looking. I had to stop myself from looking.

I wish I could have told you they looked beautiful.

That is when I resolved I would never become one of them. I had to find a way out. {Even if it meant typing up an afterword in bad light, on a limited budget, for a potential readership of thousands or none?}

Painfully, hopping, I made my way through the bodies, pushed open the double doors with a supreme effort, and walked out into postwar Ambergris.

⁂

AFTERWORD, AFTERMATH. I'M SHAKING NOW, and I don't know if that means I'm hungry or that I'm afraid of what might come out of that hole in the ground behind me. Or if I'm upset thinking about the aftermath of that catastrophic struggle between Houses, gray caps, and the Kalif. Between me and my now traitorous leg. Between Sybel and the fungal mine he never saw. Between Duncan and Mary.

As I hobbled through the city that morning, still in shock, using a stick as a crutch, it became clear that we had been having a bad Festival for many, many months. Buildings reduced to purple ash. Corpses still unburied, but frozen by needlings of fungus, which, mercifully, took away any smell. I marveled at the number of people who walked through the city with a blank look in their eyes; I was one of them. A look of sadness, yes, but beyond sadness—a sense of dislocation, of desolation. We were encountering Ambergris as survivors and asking a question: is this really our city? Is this really where we live? {I thought it went deeper than that—the listlessness, the fatigue. It seemed to indicate a confusion, a mental flinch, an inability to understand if we'd won or lost. How could we tell?}

Collapsed buildings lay impaled on their own columns, which still reached toward open sky. Streets strewn with garbage and bits of torn-up flesh. Relics of past ages splintered into unrecognizable thickets of wood and metal. The Hoegbotton headquarters, which had survived any number of F&L attacks, had been brought low on that last night—looted and gutted, the stark black of extinguished fire racing up the interior walls toward the lacerated ceiling. The ever-present smell of smoke and of rot, which we had grown accustomed to over the last few years, but which, on this particular morning, had a sharpness, an intensity, that we had not experienced before. The Voss Bender Memorial Post Office had been ransacked, and little metal boxes, some of them melted and deformed from fire, littered the cracked steps. Elsewhere, whole neighborhoods of people worked to tear down barricades erected to keep out the Kalif's men, or F&L's men, or the gray caps. If I could have flown crowlike over the city, I would have seen it as a crumbling eye pierced through the center and smoldering at the edges where the abandoned mortars of the Kalif lay surrounded by the bodies of the slain.

It will sound odd, but I realize now that if I had looked closely enough, I could have seen physical evidence of the beginning of Mary's attacks on Duncan's books. Stare long enough, hard enough, with the appropriate intensity, and Duncan's theories were all there, woven into the brick, the stone, the wood, even inhabiting the wind that came down and whispered through narrow streets backed up with rubble. And, in the sheer remembered violence of bloodstains, burnt wood, crippled brick: Mary's retort, her refutation of him. As Mary walked through some other part of the city that day, through some other aftermath, what did she see? What could she see but the embodiment of her father's Nativism theory? Everything catalogued as the most natural of disasters. {Truly a stretch, Janice, if ever there was one!}

I understand now, remembering *my* walk through the city, that the glittering flesh necklace surrounded a neck that supported a head filled with maggoty ideas. Filled with images that do not connect, and which will always make it impossible for Sabon to recognize the truth in Duncan's theories. She has found her own personal history; she has written it to drown out the truth.

In a sense, almost every word, every sentence, every paragraph she has written about Ambergris since the war has been an attempt to undo my memories—what I saw during that war, what I saw that night with Sybel beside me, what I saw afterwards, walking through the city. And, of course, everything she saw belowground. {This is nonsense. Mary reacted no differently than many other Ambergrisians. A deep sense of denial pervaded the city, but how can you blame any of its inhabitants? They still had to live on in the city. It must have been much worse after the Silence. Imagine your loved ones being spirited away one night and you unable to do anything except go about your daily business and hope that you, too, would not be subject to the same fate.}

⊰❊⊱

EVENTUALLY, ON THAT FIRST MORNING after the war, I found myself at Blythe Academy. I had hopped and hobbled my way there after an hour or two, my journey aimless and funereal. An ache and an emptiness had begun to gnaw away at me. A glimpse of the familiar acted like an anchor.

For some reason, I had assumed that the desecration of the Truffidian Cathedral would have extended to Blythe Academy as well, but this was not the case. I saw a few broken windows, two overturned benches, an area of burnt grass, and a singed section of roof, but the willow trees remained the same as always. Priests and teachers bustled across the lawn, cleaning up the debris. The air of activity, of honest labor, gave me hope.

I sat down on a bench, hoping that somehow the memory of those long-ago conversations that had so calmed me then might calm me now.

Instead, a shadow fell across me. I looked up, and there stood Bonmot, staring down at me with a grim smile upon his lips. His face was grimy with soot or dirt. He had a long, shallow cut running down his left cheek. Bonmot, in that moment, looked invincible, even though he had become more vulnerable than I could then know. {Whose faith wouldn't falter for at least a moment in the midst of such inexplicable carnage?}

His grim smile softened to concern as he saw the condition of my foot—or, rather, the lack of a foot.

"You're alive," I said, in wonder. By now, the lack of sleep, the terror of what I had gone through, had taken me somewhere else entirely.

"You need to see a doctor," Bonmot said. He crouched down beside me, gently cupped his hand under my calf to better examine the wound.

"Not really," I said. "There's nothing to be done now. It's mostly cauterized. I washed the rest of it. The flesh is clean. I spent all night with a mob of corpses in the Truffidian Cathedral. You may wish to investigate."

He bowed his head, looking at my stump. "I know. I've heard. You were there?"

"Yes," I said. "Pretending to be dead. Please, don't worry about the leg."

He stared at me. "Janice, you need to have it looked at anyway."

I laughed, an edge of bitterness in my voice. "I suppose," I said, "but who will look at it? I've been limping around this broken old city of ours all morning. And I've seen little that isn't mangled, mashed, cracked, twisted, or dead."

"It won't take long to rebuild," he said. "You'll be surprised. All of this will be behind us someday." A pause. "Have you heard from Mary?"

This, then, was the closest he could come to asking about Duncan.

"No, I haven't," I said.

{And you wouldn't, not for a few days. I had returned Mary to our apartment, which had been ransacked but not ruined, and we took up again the unhealthy non-bliss of our domestic lives together—a little more silent around each other, a little more reserved, a little more distant. She became fond of saying I was "suffocating" her in those first few days after the war. I had no response. I needed comfort from her. I *needed* her.}

I started to cry. I was still talking, my face still set in a half-grimace, half-smile, but I was crying. "Sybel's dead," I said.

And then, even though he had a thousand responsibilities that day, Bonmot pulled me to him and held me as, sobbing, I told him about all of the dead.

—❧❧—

THE LOSSES KEPT PILING UP. When I visited my gallery, I found the inside had been gutted by fire. All of my inventory had disappeared yet again, taken by looters or flames. The artists blamed me, even though I was convinced some of them had stolen their own work off my walls. I wasted time. I wasted money. I thought I could resurrect the gallery, but without Sybel, I was lost. I did not have the requisite number of "friends with money," as he had liked to call them. I reopened for a short time, but I could no longer attract even mediocre talents. I was left with a half-dozen elderly landscape oil painters as clients. Clearly, I was doomed.

Looking back, the war signaled the end of so many things that the dying throes of my gallery must be considered no more than a buried footnote in the history of that period. For example, the war certainly ended my right foot—there's no doubt about that. I'm tempted, whenever someone asks me what I remember about the war, to point to my grainy toes and say, "Ask my foot."

As a hidden perk of so many people having lost limbs, the art of wooden limb construction had reached new heights. I personally picked out the wood for my replacement from the very best strangler figs on the west side of the River Moth, near where Sybel had grown up. My foot might even have been made from a tree Sybel had once climbed. Maudlin, I know, but I don't care about the sentimentality of that thought.

I had Judith Aquelus, a sculptress, collaborate with the wooden limb experts at Similian's Arm & Leg Shop, to create the unique artifact that is my right foot. I had Judith carve a miniature, stylized version of the opera house stage on it on which the Kalif's soldiers could be seen, making their acting debut.

No amputee should be seen in public without a Judith Aquelus creation. A foot and a cane: the perfect accessories for such necessary tasks as walking to the grocery store for a loaf of bread! With my cane and my new wooden foot, I have attained a whole new level of eccentricity. Why, I've become my own work of art—my only option, considering that creating art and selling art had proven so unprofitable for me.

The funny thing is, the green fungus that has colonized my typewriter and makes it harder and harder to complete this afterword has also begun to infiltrate my wooden foot. I am becoming a rather small forest. In my own way, perhaps I'm experiencing what Duncan went through. {Dead wood does not equal living flesh. There's nothing to compare to that heart-choking prickle of another life entering your skin and flesh.}

Since that first foot, I have found it hard to resist having more made when I can afford it, or carving them myself. In my more whimsical moments, I'm tempted to leave a trail of feet through the city. One day a foot may be all that is left of me.

"Do you like it?" I asked Duncan the first time I showed it off to him.

"It's very much you," Duncan said. {I'd had too many strange experiences with my flesh to be too empathetic. The sloughing off of flesh, the losing and regaining of it, had become too normal an experience.}

"It itches," I told him. And this is still true now. The foot, with its lithe straps and silver clasps, itches like hell at the oddest times.

"I itch all the time," Duncan said, not to be outdone.

On that particular day, down by the docks, watching the ships come in, Duncan was very pale. You could see, if you looked closely, that the hair on his head was not really hair ruffled by a breeze, but a black fungus lazily swaying back and forth. There was a further suggestion of movement under his coat. I doubt anyone else saw it—or wanted to see it.

"Do you miss him?" I asked Duncan.

"I miss him terribly," he replied. {I missed the everyday normalcy Sybel had brought to my life. Dealing with you, Janice, was an up-and-down experience, often full of melodrama. As much as I loved Bonmot, my conversations with him had always had some religious subtext. But speaking to Sybel was so natural and effortless and free of judgment that I didn't even miss the experience until it was over.}

"If it itches really badly," he said, "I could probably find a way to grow you a fungal replacement."

I ignored him and asked, "How's Mary?"

He didn't answer.

✖

I HAD TO STOP TO clean off the typewriter keys. The green fungus had become too insidious. The keys weren't striking paper, but bunching up in emerald moss, the paper itself reflecting a series of ever more vegetative marks. I couldn't get it all off, but enough of it is gone that I can continue typing for a while. I'm not sure when I will run out of time; there are so many factors to consider. When will the patience of the Spore's owner run out? When will I tire of what increasingly seems a pointless exercise? When will something crawl out of the hole in the ground behind me and put an end to my speculations?

I think it's morning outside, but I haven't bothered to check. I had thought it was lunchtime earlier, but it turned out that my stomach had it all wrong. If it is morning, the sky is probably gray and undistinguished, flecked with rain. It's that time of year when sudden showers appear and make of the city stark outlines, robbing it of color and texture. A welter of umbrellas appears on the streets and people walk quickly to their destinations, with no appreciation for anything around them.

⚜ 4 ⚜

AFTERWORDS. AFTERWARDS. AFTERWAR.

The war had been jarring, numbing, senseless. In its aftermath, the balance of power remained much as it had before all of the bloodshed. The Hoegbottons controlled Ambergris and F&L controlled Morrow and Sophia's Island but lacked the military and political will to enforce their ridiculous tariffs. The Kalif's mauled troops retreated across the River Moth even as their merchants advanced to secure deals with the Hoegbottons to rebuild the city and import new products. {Oddly enough, the Kalif's troops could be said to have ultimately achieved their goal, if not in the preferred way. For, after all, hadn't they liberated the citizens of Ambergris from chaos and tyranny through their sacrifice?}

After the war, Ambergris forgot the real enemy—Hoegbotton & Sons still railed against Frankwrithe & Lewden or the Kalif, but provided no warning against the gray caps. People gratefully went along with this mass denial. Wasn't it easier to blame F&L than an amorphous, faceless enemy that hid underground and attacked seemingly at random? {To be fair, the still unknown way in which F&L had acquired fungal weapons confused the issue—F&L did look like the sole instigator. After all, didn't the gray caps periodically erupt from their hidey-holes during the Festival anyway?}

The terrible, cold beauty of the truth appealed to no one. Every few weeks, for several years, one or two, or three or four, people were killed by a left-over fungal bomb or a new one planted by someone—the gray caps or F&L, I assume, but who could tell the difference? H&S did nothing to prevent this, and tried hard to stop Lacond from reporting it. We were a city and a people unable to face our coming annihilation, incensed over an enemy that posed not a quarter of the threat. In a way, we lived in a fairy tale, convinced that someone else's actions or inactions might save us. As day after day passed without Ambergris being invaded, we flinched less and less, let down our guard. No one was going to destroy the city—only rumors could do that, the thinking went, only idle talk. If we pretended otherwise, the enemy could not creep out at night and make us all disappear. Permanence had become a thing from the past.

{I didn't think much had changed, but if it had, it had changed for the reason most eloquently put by the historian Edgar Rybern: namely, that barbaric institutions and individuals can benefit society, while "civilization" can, in its most benign forms, prove barbaric. This led me to two conclusions germane to the war. First, that the very act of F&L coming into contact with the gray caps and then into contact with H&S had irrevocably changed all three parties; and second, that stated goals aside, all three of these institutions have been thrown off-kilter by the war. Now, whether they realize it or not, each new decision pulls them slightly further away from their original purpose. What effect this might have, I could not tell you.}

❧

FOR DUNCAN PERSONALLY, THE END of the war meant two things: that Lacond was available to help him limp back into a shadow career in print—it became apparent at war's end that Lacond could only keep one of us on, and, even if I had wanted to stay, it wasn't going to be me—and that Mary's patience with him was almost at an end.

The slow withdrawal, the retreat from love, went on at the same time Lacond began recruiting Duncan for his eccentric obsessions. {No more eccentric than my own obsessions, Janice. Lacond and I understood each other in a way that made me no longer feel quite so alone.}

How did Mary withdraw? Let me count the ways. She no longer tolerated my brother's erratic schedule. She no longer found his eccentricities endearing. She no longer found his fungal diseases tragic, his endurance of them brave. {I'm not sure she *ever* felt that way about my fungal diseases. It was more that she put up with their side effects to be with me.} The small apartment they shared became claustrophobic. Duncan's journal skirts the reason behind the feelings:

> I cannot find my inspiration in this place—I have to go down to the Spore or Lacond's apartment to write, or I just stare at the page. I don't know why my apartment has become so stifling, but it has. There's nothing in it to spur me on to create. Except Mary, of course.

But Mary spent more and more time with friends. Sometimes she even stayed at her parents' house. Duncan had no chance, no choice. How could he? He didn't have the experience to combat it, to see the signs. To Duncan, sadly enough, the only way to get her back was to keep showing her the truth, even though it was clear to anyone with any sense that he'd need to start *lying* to her if he wanted to keep her. {A cynical view that would only serve as a short-term solution. And I was neither so naïve nor Mary so experienced as you make out.} Every time he showed her the truth, she pushed him farther away. Duncan wrote in his journal:

> I feel as if I am living by myself again. She isn't really here anymore. She's a husk or a shell. Her eyes are dull. Her hair is dull. Her words are weighted and slow. She doesn't listen to me. I am killing her.

But the truth also meant accepting that the day-to-day domesticity didn't suit him either, especially for long periods of time. I will spare you the contrast between the journal entries that detail with a silly kind of joy the beauty of her snores early in their relationship and the dull snarl of his comments on those self-same snores near the end. Or, take this terse entry only a month before disaster: "another night of odd smells." Sometimes he would be almost apologetic: "She could easily have complained about the frequency with which I spored. Or how I tracked in strange green mud from time to time. But she didn't."

Even then, I think he wanted to stay with her. I don't believe he ever understood that he might actually lose her. {I couldn't, back then, imagine a tolerable moment without her—and, in all honesty, tolerable moments since I lost her have been fewer and less intense.} After all, he'd never been through a breakup before—unlike me, who had been through dozens. I had become an expert on broken relationships. It had become ritualized with me, each battle with its own histories, its own decorum, and its own rules of disengagement.

Duncan and Mary managed to stay together in their little apartment for a few more months, but like the starfish that rapidly became brittle, their love had died long before they acknowledged the fact. The bond between them had broken, snapped, and although Duncan was still in love with her—even though I don't know if he *liked* her anymore—she was not in love with him. Their situation frayed, unraveled. They had screaming arguments, tearful reunions. Duncan would seek refuge at my apartment, only to go back, over my objections.

He wrote in his journal at some point near the end:

I feel as if she is made of clay or wood or stone. There is no longer any of the
lovely fluidity that made me lust for her, although I lust for her still. I keep
thinking that it will just take time—that, in time, she will reconcile herself to
that night and to what she saw. That she will understand the strange beauty
of it. That her understanding of it will lead her to an understanding of me.
Until then, she complains about the amount of time I spend away from her,
with Lacond and "that stupid society," as she calls it, and then, when I do
spend time with her, she complains that I smother her. She cringes in distaste
when my fungal disease flares up. I must keep myself wrapped in a bathrobe,
away from her critical eye, when I feel it coming on. I cannot relax around her.
My love for her is making me old. I keep thinking back to that night. The
rush of joy I felt because she would finally see what I had seen, that we could
finally share it. And I wonder how I could have been so naïve.

Duncan never thought of disavowing his findings, of putting the underground
behind him, denying what he had found. He was, however, capable of self-blame:

How could I expect her to believe what I myself scarcely comprehended at
times? Sometimes I wish I had been able to find another way. Sometimes I
wish I could undo it all, start over. But I don't think she will let me.

Soon, they barely talked to each other . . . then, one day, he came home from
Lacond's offices and she was gone. He thought that she had just stepped out for
a moment, until he found the note. He left it with his other notes. It is right
here beside my festering typewriter. It reads:

My Love:
    I *do* love you, but I am not in love with you anymore. You want me to see
things that aren't there. You want me not only to see the impossible—you
want me to think it beautiful, a revelation. That night was a terrifying experience for me, Duncan. And with your insistence that I believe, you have begun
to frighten me.
    There's no way to rescue us. I can't keep living with you. I hope that in
time we can become friends, but for now we must be apart. Besides, we both
have books to write, and neither of us can be creative in this situation.

Do you know how hard it is for me to leave not only my lover but my teacher? But I have no choice.

Thank you for everything you have taught me, everything you have shown me about history and about the world. I'll never forget that.

I'll end here, for now, because, as you know, too many words can be a trap.

Love,
Mary

P.S. I'm leaving you the apartment until you can find your own place.

The difference between what we need and what we want can be an abyss. For example, I want more light in this accursed room, but I need lunch because my stomach is grumbling. Duncan would always want Mary, but did he need her? In a way, he didn't. In a way, like the writer who pursues his art above all else, Duncan did not need anything other than access to the underground. {You make me out to be a theorem in search of expression, rather than a human being.}

Next to Mary's note is a letter she wrote to a friend. I don't know how Duncan came by it. I don't like to guess in this instance. {It was a low point for me, intercepting her mail. It was a brief insanity, a madness created by love. I only did it once or twice. I'm still ashamed of it.} The letter explains the situation much more baldly, and must have driven Duncan a little crazy when he read it.

Duncan has become ever more himself. I left him because I couldn't take any more of his ravings about the gray caps. Everything is focused on the gray caps. Even if he did love me, I'd never be more than ancillary to those damn gray caps. It didn't help that my parents hated him for, as they saw it, spoiling the innocence of their little girl. And because he was impossible to live with, and because he was like a child—he always wanted to be in love, so when he wasn't in love with me, he was in love with his studies. He wore me out. He was so intense. How can anyone be so intense all of the time? I couldn't breathe, or think. And his opinions on my research! Always picking at it, always so sure he was right and I was wrong. I don't think that I would ever be more than a student in his eyes, so I had to get away from him. Yes, I loved him, but, sometimes, as I am discovering, you need more than love.

{A mental shudder. A sudden moment of self-awareness—was I like that? Yes, I probably was. But I don't know if Mary ever understood the great strain I was under, how what I sought was of the utmost importance. That it meant nothing more or less than safeguarding the fate of everyone who lives in this city, perhaps in the world. And still. And yet. I knew she had taken something from me, that I had been valuable to her. I had given nearly as much as I had taken. I'd been her mentor and she'd been my student, no matter what grief I had caused her. I took some small comfort from that.}

And that was the end of it. Or so I thought. For although Mary was free of Duncan, Duncan would never really be free of her, or her flesh necklace.

❦

AS DUNCAN'S ROMANTIC FORTUNES WANED, his fortunes as a historian waxed again: a flowering in miniature, given the heights he had ascended to in his youth. Although those who did speak a kind of truth about the gray caps and Ambergris' past were condemned to the fringes, they did have their own organization: the Ambergrisians for the Original Inhabitants Society. Most of Duncan's postwar hopes of self-expression reached fruition through AFTOIS.

AFTOIS had once again become Lacond's passion—and in its limited way, it flourished for a time after the war—so that the *Broadsheet*, which paid the rent, often suffered from his neglect. {Indeed. It never quite failed when he was in charge, but some years after I took over production of the *Broadsheet*, I would have to put it out of its financial misery, much to the delight of our many enemies.}

"The important thing," Lacond said to me once, "is that we get the truth out in some form, that we document what is happening. So that at the very least, there will be a record that someone knew about it."

This struck me as an absurd statement. "Why?" I replied. "So that when the abyss opens up you can stand on the edge and shout down, 'I told you so!'?"

Lacond looked at me as if I hadn't understood anything he'd said.

When I told Bonmot about this exchange, he said, "Yes, but without Lacond, how much more mischief would Duncan get into?"

A good point, I had to admit. Because Lacond spent much of his time in those years after the war making Duncan his second-in-command. Without Lacond, the loss of Mary might have hit Duncan harder than it did. {How much harder could it have hit me? I hardly left my apartment for months. Lacond had to drag me out of my bed to get me to work for him. For years afterwards, I would feel this hollow space in my stomach, in my lungs. Sometimes, I would think of her and I couldn't breathe.}

⁓❧❧⁓

LACOND HAD A PERVERSE EFFECT on Duncan. Lacond made Duncan want something he thought he had given up on long ago: the restoration of a measure of legitimacy. {I might have reconciled myself to living without respect, but that didn't mean I didn't fight hard against it. Years would pass between a chance at even the most minor legitimate publication opportunity, but I never gave up.} Lacond kept telling Duncan that if he published enough essays in the AFTOIS newsletter, he would eventually get noticed again.

"Enough essays in a marginal journal read by a couple thousand fellow crackpots?" I said to Duncan when he told me. "A path to greater glory? I don't think so, Duncan. I really don't. You should attempt another book—you might find a publisher."

Duncan shook his head. "Not now, not yet. I can't even think about a book—my thoughts are too fragmented. But essays—yes, I could do essays. And Lacond might be right, you never know."

Ridiculous! Yet Duncan believed it. As he wrote in his journal:

> Sometimes I read through the letters I kept from my glory days, when readers could acquire my books easily and in quantity. There were people back then who understood me, who realized I told the truth. I can't imagine that all of them have died in the twenty years since, or that there aren't new readers who might appreciate my books. I just need to find a way to reach them again. And if I can't reach them, perhaps I can reach Mary again. It's easy for Mary to dismiss Lacond, or AFTOIS, but it might alter her perception of me if . . . but it is too much to hope for, to think about.

{I did believe this then, perhaps naïvely, but over time my emphasis would shift. I no longer thought books would be my salvation. I no longer thought in terms of publication, really, but more in terms of accumulating knowledge and making as much of it public as the public could stand.}

Didn't Duncan see that Lacond had been trying for years—decades—with less success than my brother? Not any more than he saw that, for all the time he spent in the shadow of the huge oak tree outside her parents' house, hoping to catch a glimpse of her, Mary was traveling along a very different path. How could someone so smart be so foolish? But Duncan persisted. {I had no choice. I thought Mary and I could eventually be friends. I justified my hauntings of her by telling myself that I was watching over her, protecting her. The truth? My heart, caught between hope and pain, could not bear never seeing her, even if seeing her meant only the slightest glimpse of her through a window—a silhouette that, for many months, could still transfix me.}

Bonmot used to say that "The limits of our imagination are the limits of our free will." Duncan could not imagine a life that did not include Mary and the gray caps. I sometimes wonder how different it would have been if he could have wrenched himself free of Ambergris and set sail for the Southern Isles, lost himself in the waves and the wind, adopted a different obsession.

{Janice—*all* obsessions are the same. They vary little in the essential details. You refuse to believe that my search for knowledge wasn't so much personal, wasn't so much for myself, but out of a fear for the future of our city. I pursued Mary out of a fear for the future of Duncan Shriek. There wasn't much holding me to the city besides Mary, to be honest. As I continued to change, I needed to make up reasons why I shouldn't just venture underground and stay there. I could have planted myself in a dark, moist corner of the gray caps' world and taken root. I could have allowed the fungi to colonize me, taken in the breath of their sleep and woken in a thousand years to a far different fate. So was it love, after a certain point in time? Probably not. It was probably just a grasping for some kind of normal life. But can you blame me?}

If only Duncan could have apologized to Bonmot in a way that Bonmot would have accepted. But he wouldn't. I think Bonmot was more fragile in his faith than he let on—I think he believed that if he let Duncan back into his life, it would affect his character, would erode his integrity. Duncan could have used Bonmot for balance during those times. He could have used someone other than a sister with one foot who had nightmares about being buried alive in a pile of corpses. Because Lacond really did have him convinced—they'd go to those lunatic meetings of their lunatic society, and Duncan would think that because three hundred people showed up and listened to him he was making progress. {Lacond was enough for me. Lacond never made me feel as if I were damaged or deranged, the way Bonmot could even during the best of our conversations. There's a whiff of righteousness in the most humble servant of Truff that is a terrible, terrible thing. But Lacond taught me confidence and endurance. Every year of his adult life, he had written down his bizarre, unpopular theories and, through his society, made them available to the public. And every year, most people rejected his work, or feigned indifference, or found his theories an unkind reflection or comment on the man himself. Yet he never stopped, never gave up. It's more than I could have done.}

I went to one AFTOIS meeting. That was enough for me—one glance at the agenda handed out by a portly woman with a purple scarf wound endlessly around her neck, as though a purple constrictor had a choke hold on her—one glance convinced me I would not be coming back:

THE AMBERGRISIANS FOR
THE ORIGINAL INHABITANTS SOCIETY
WEEKLY MEETING NO. 231

– As Presided Over by Society President James Lacond –
– Minutes Taken by Linda Pitginkel –
– Incidental Music Provided by "George the Flutist" –
– Refreshments Baked by Lara Maleon –

ORDER OF EVENTS

(1) Recital of the Society Motto: "In pursuit of truth, for the truth, by the truth. Against inertia, against ease, against the false."

(2) Introduction of Speakers [James Lacond]

(3) Rebecca Flange reads an excerpt from her book *The Crimes of Tonsure: The Role of Poison*

(4) "What Is the Truth—How Shall We Approach It and Its Importance to Our Understanding of the Gray Caps"—speech by Sarah Potent

(5) "Channeling the Dead—Its Impact on Our Understanding of the Gray Caps" —speech by Roger Seabold

(6) "I Am the True Descendent of Samuel Tonsure" —speech by James "Tonsure" Williams

(7) "Evidence for the Existence of a City-Sized Fungus" —speech by Frederick Madnok [as read by Harry Flack in Mr. Madnok's absence]

I think the agenda alone should give some insight into the kinds of buffoons with which Duncan had aligned himself. He had gone from writing legitimate books to writing legitimate articles to teaching at a legitimate school to scandal and heartbreak, and now lived a sad existence at the very fringe of his chosen field.

{Again, unfair. I appreciate your protectiveness, but the truth is often so strange that one cannot, at the outset, discard even the most ridiculous of theories, the silliest of suppositions. Remember how I let my students do my research for me? This was a similar situation—I was always searching for the sliver of truth in the outlandishness presented at those meetings. Even the most absurd theory might have in its core details, its foundation, some hint of information about the gray caps, something to be salvaged or redirected. I attended those meetings for that reason, not because I *believed* everything I heard, or even wanted to be associated with all of them. But who else, Janice, would publish my "crackpot theories"? No one after the war except, ultimately, Sirin. And even *he* didn't do it properly, as you—my benign, self-chosen executioner—well know.}

Certainly, I was used to dealing with strange people—I've never met an artist who wasn't at some level a deeply strange or estranged person. But this was different. These were people on the edge of the edge of sanity. Oddities. Carpenters who, in their spare time, developed paranoid theories about House Hoegbotton that grew to full fruition in the dark, glistening spaces of their imaginations. Stay-at-home wives who, bored, had bought into the more lurid broadsheet headlines. Self-hating bank clerks making a pittance who had curdled inside and defended the gray caps because they would have cheered if the gray caps had risen up and taken over the city. People who believed they were the reincarnation of historical figures like Tonsure. And, on the fringes of those fringes, homeless people who used the meetings to take shelter. The mentally challenged who had been discharged from the now-destroyed Voss Bender Memorial Mental Hospital. I even thought I spied a gray shape that resembled my former fellow inmate Edward at one point, although when I looked again, he was gone.

And those were just the audience members.

How the spittle flew during the meeting I observed! The sour taste of vitriol! The sad, lonely, pathetic, nervous, neurotic, psychotic, exposed underbelly of the city.

"In my opinion, Tonsure was a gray cap disguised as a priest."

"The grace with which the fungus leapt from tree to tree astounded me."

"I didn't realize I had the gift to channel ghosts until I was twelve."

"In the vast, empty spaces beneath the city, this huge fungus has taken over and means to envelop us in its clammy grasp."

"Being a woman, I am more attuned to the feelings of inanimate objects."

And Duncan wanted to become their leader: the Lord of the Disinclined.

Disinclined to work. Disinclined to hold a job. The Disenchanted who had never been enchanting, except, perhaps, as children. No wonder Mary hated that group. *I* hated that group. We could have taken an oath of solidarity on that much, at least. {And yet, they, and I, are much closer to the truth than those who scoffed at our organization, regardless of the sometimes illegitimate evidence provided at those meetings. I sense a certain amount of snobbery in your remarks, Janice, as if the only people worth a damn are artists or writers or playwrights—but look back on your own description of the New Art and the New Artists. Were they really any different, except that the results of their obsessions and imagination were more forcefully inflicted upon the world? Sometimes a theory or idea is as strangely beautiful as that expressed by any painting, even when it's articulated by those who are not articulate.

{Let me tell you what I saw that day, at that meeting. I saw a woman trying to come to terms with the death of her sister by inexplicable means. She did so by taking what facts she knew about Samuel Tonsure and bending them to a theory that attempted to reconcile the irreconcilable. In that forced assimilation of fact and fancy, Janice, there might have been a fragment of truth, even if only a psychological truth. Perhaps by seeing Tonsure in a different light than I, she advanced my understanding of him one tiny increment.

{Sara Potent's diatribe about the truth, taking as her basis Stretcher Jones's rebellion against the Kalif and expanding it to include many of the unanswered questions about Ambergris' past—wasn't she, in disguised form, asking the same questions we all have asked from time to time? Does she deserve vilification for trying to think her way through all of this?

{Could you have missed the beauty of Frederick Madnok's theory that Ambergris is "shadowed" from below by a giant fungus, wide as the city and deep as the city is tall, through which catacomb the tunnels of the gray caps? Could you not see the utter precision and craftsmanship of his many diagrams? The humor of the labeling—a sense of humor that tells the reader that Madnok *knows* how outlandish his theory may sound.

{There is an art, Janice, to being an outsider, a skill to being a good crackpot. Some people decide to become writers of fiction and this is considered a legitimate endeavor. Others decide to make their expressions of the imagination more personal. I, for one, gained more from that meeting than from any novel I have ever read!}

But the fact is, Duncan didn't see them as they really were, only as he wanted them to be: a society of visionaries, of dreamers, revolutionaries. Apparently so enthralled by them that he lost his wits for a time, Duncan became anti-social and avoided me. {Who could blame me, considering your attitude then? So similar to your attitude toward Mary. Oh, the irony, considering her attitude toward AFTOIS.} As these crackpots began to take up more and more of his time, he began to forget to bathe. He didn't change his clothes for weeks on end. He babbled to himself. {I missed Mary terribly. I missed her so much, Janice. I don't know if you can conceive of how much I missed her.}

Worst of all, Duncan assumed more and more responsibility for the AFTOIS newsletter, as Lacond became sicker, meaning that Duncan wrote less as his increased editorial duties ate up his time.

Like Lacond, Duncan did not censor theories in conflict with his own. Duncan believed, given the inability of most "experts" to absorb the truth about the gray caps, that all outlandish theories should be given an airing, regardless of their validity. He thought that this would make minds receptive to the unusual and improbable, "softening resistance," as he used to mutter, "to reality. A kind of general insurrection against the complacent surface of things." {For all the good it did me.}

To this end, the journal, which he edited more and more "in the name of" the still-living Lacond—even writing essays under Lacond's name—became even more eccentric, and thus ever more dismissed, unread by a populace living in denial. {But some of these theories were beautiful and elegant, no matter how wrong-headed. For example, "morelmancy"—divination of the future from mushrooms . . . or, as you called it, much to my amusement, "a flowering of spores, long dormant, a colorful array—of insanity." Not everything beautiful has to be true to have value, you know.}

At least Duncan had seen the truth, or a kind of truth, firsthand. All the rest of these people sitting in their glorified clubhouse listening to why intelligent mushrooms were going to rise to the surface one day and kill everyone—and, in some cases, why they were going to enjoy the experience—these people hadn't seen the truth. They just didn't know any better—they were guessing. They were lonely and screaming out for company, or for something to keep out the darkness. Even a crackpot theory is better than no theory at all. Than nobody. Than an abyss.

Like the hole that lies behind me, leading Truff knows where. {Truff may not know where it leads, having more important things on His mind, but you and I both know it leads into the underground. Let me evoke Truff in a more appropriate context: for Truff's sake, stop being so melodramatic!}

❧❧

WHAT WERE MARY AND I doing while Duncan decided to go slumming? I'm so glad you asked. Mary was establishing the beginnings of her brilliant career, which would eventually result in the creation of her stunning flesh necklace. Meanwhile, I climbed further down the ladder of success. I said goodbye to my gallery one murky spring day.

I stood there alone on the street, and Sybel said, "It had a good run. You accomplished a lot. You shouldn't be too sad. How much longer could it hold together anyway?"

"Once, you said this was just the beginning, Sybel."

"Did you really believe me? I just told you what you needed to hear."

"No, you're right. You're right."

I turned to look at him and he was gone, of course. I had to collect my thoughts for a moment after that. Then I walked away without looking back, for fear of bursting into tears.

❧❧

ESCAPE, ESCAPING, ESCAPED. I'D DONE it. I was no longer in even the most remote danger of being considered a success. I would have to begin again, in a city I did not entirely trust to help me. I loitered in the same circles, lounged in the same antechambers of vice on occasion, but it was only pretense—a kind of fading afterglow that did not warm the face.

I threw myself on Sirin's mercy once more. Sirin had taken up his long-ago position at Hoegbotton, with nary a whiff of rumor as to what skullduggery he had involved himself in while he was gone. {I don't know what he knew about the Hoegbottons to provide him with such protection, but it must have gone beyond mere evidence of embezzlement, adultery, or vice.}

But while Mary received from Sirin first-class treatment in the form of her first book contract, I got a job as a tour guide to Ambergris, my "office" on the first floor of the newly-rebuilt H&S headquarters building. Although we rarely saw each other, Sirin and his rosewood desk lay directly above me. Sometimes I would look up at the ceiling tiles and imagine I saw butterflies fluttering out from between the cracks. There were days, I admit, when I seethed, ground my teeth, floated silent curses toward that ceiling. {The worst admission of all, I suppose, is that I introduced Sirin to Mary a few weeks before the war. It was largely on my recommendation that Sirin, upon his return, inquired with Mary as to the possibility of a book. I didn't tell you for the obvious reasons.}

To be fair, without my gallery and the tattered, faded cloak of respectability it had conveyed, I could no longer command a prestige position—and Sirin had found younger, cheaper writers for the article assignments that had once gone to Duncan and me. So, five days a week, a trickle of tourists would find their way to my office and sign up for such ridiculous tours as "Gray Cap Haunts and Habitat"—which consisted of showing them where various famous people had been "disappeared" or killed by the gray caps, then descending into the basement of the newly rebuilt Borges Bookstore, a place in which no gray cap had ever been seen. Another favorite tour was the dusk-to-midnight "Haunted Ambergris" expedition, to which I had to bring a measure of acting skills I did not possess, and a ream of notes to read from, since the stories all blended together otherwise. {I imagine I might have been good at this kind of work, if you'd ever given me an invite.}

But the worst tour, over time, was "Literary Highlights of Ambergris," since, as Sabon's popularity grew, I would be forced to take them past whatever expensive hovel she was currently renting, where they would gawk and circle, certain they would soon catch a glimpse of the author peering out from behind a curtain.

"This is the home of the controversial and talented Mary Sabon," began the official spiel I was made to mutter and cough to tourists who may or may not have cared very much.

"It is in this house that Sabon wrote much of her book *More Banal Banalities,* which disproved many of the more paranoid theories about the gray caps." And so on and so forth.

Sometimes, Sybel stared out at me from a nearby tree, sporting a not-unsympathetic smirk on his face and dressed in his most familiar outfit: the woodland greens and browns of his youth.

"Gently, Janice," he would soothe. "It's not so bad. It could be worse. I know all about worse."

"Worse? How much worse could it get?" I would ask him, but by then he was already a mote of dust spiraling at the corner of my eye, and me having confused myself and tourists alike by having spoken aloud.

The more I reflect on it, Sybel had it right: I was, considering the condition of my foot, lucky. My status as Old Relic counterbalanced the crippling whorls of my wooden toes and the grain of my soles. I could diverge from the script to tell stories about the places we visited with a knack for detail and intrigue and personal panache that few other guides could match. I truly had been there when *that* happened, or *this*, or *this*. To pay for my past crimes against public decency, against modesty, I would even sometimes have to guide people to the site of my poor gutted gallery, there to recite a history of it and the fabled New Art. {Do you really believe that Sirin didn't experience a shiver of perverse satisfaction from forcing you to go back there? I'm sure he did; how could he not?}

I didn't mind the job too much in those early years, if I'm to be truthful, especially when I didn't have to do the "Haunted Ambergris" tour, and before I had to stand outside Mary's home like a fool. At least part of the time a horse and buggy would be employed so I didn't have to drag my leg around. And business gradually became more robust: the cessation of hostilities soon brought a new wave of the curious—not curious enough to venture over for the Festival, but curious enough to explore during the daylight of other seasons.

Besides, I often contrived to arrive at the Blythe Academy right before lunch, so I could allow those bright-eyed travelers from Morrow or Stockton or Nicea to wander as they would, within reason, while I sat down for a sandwich with Bonmot. At a stone bench. Under the fabled but now considerably more wizened willow trees.

"Tough crowd today?" Bonmot would almost always say, making me smile.

"I'm not a comedian or a juggler, Bonmot. I don't have to entertain. I just have to lead them around to interesting places."

"You are such a kind tour guide," Bonmot would say, trying not to laugh. "To teach them the responsibility of finding their own entertainment."

"Why not? That's what *I* have to do."

I wish I could say my lunches with Bonmot felt the same as before, but they did not. Yes, a similar sense of contentment, of ease, lingered over those conversations, but it became a more fleeting thing; it did not last as long or affect me as powerfully. Our discussions had limits; we had acquired scars. Bonmot never discussed Duncan, and I, not wishing to give up even the faded pleasure of those lunches, never pressed the point.

If the situation had changed, so had Bonmot. The war had changed him.

"You're hesitant sometimes now," I said to him once, during an uncomfortable silence. "You halt on the verge of saying things."

Bonmot nodded. "You're right. I halt because I am not certain anymore. The things I thought I knew do not always seem *right* when I say them, so I say them first in my head, and then speak. Otherwise, it's as if I were mouthing sawdust. And I miss people who have died, and sometimes when I speak, I see them, because this priest or that priest who has passed on had taught me the truism I was about to say."

He stared at me with a knowing sadness. "I liked it better when I knew everything."

A barking laugh. And an echo from Sybel, standing in the willow tree, whispering to me: "I liked it better when I knew nothing."

For my part, I found it odd to sit there watching the current crop of fresh-faced students make their way across the courtyard—lithe, flushed with success, seemingly innocent—and know that it was just a few years ago that Mary and Duncan and Bonmot had played out their appointed roles of lust, love, secrecy, and discovery. The war lay like an insurmountable black wall between then and now.

❦

I SHOULD HAVE MENTIONED BEFORE that the beads of Mary's flesh necklace actually did have faces and names. As I stood at the base of the stairs, the scarlet imprint of my hand still warm on Mary's face, about to respond to her hateful words, I remember turning away from her for a moment to stare at them. Let me identify them for you as they come into focus in my memory, that you may know them if you see them: John Batte, Vice-Royal under Bonmot, rose to the post of Royal following Bonmot's death, and is a staunch supporter of Sabon's work, even going so far as allowing her access to previously closed Truffidian archives. Sarah Cryller, currently the ambassador to Ambergris from the House of Frankwrithe & Lewden, is a newly risen star still bright-burning who at one time hoped Sabon might defect to her publishing company. The oft-mentioned Merrimount provided Sabon's "in" to the creative community at large and appeared at many of her book release parties. Jessica Hoegbotton, scion of the House of Hoegbotton, main liaison between the public and Sabon's words, is the one who laughed loudest at Mary's joke about Duncan. Daniel Griswald, Antechamber of the Truffidian Church, has teeth that glint like fangs when he grins, which is more often than a stone gargoyle, and who, in his infinite wisdom, has failed to ban any of Sabon's books, instead embracing them and recommending them to his congregation. And, finally, Mathew Daffed, one of Duncan's colleagues at Blythe Academy, is now among his most outspoken critics.

And others, still others, whose faces blur even as I conjure up their names. Why did I invite them? Because I had to—Lake demanded it. Even as I condemned them with my gaze, I found that I was surprised—surprised that they should have so disliked my brother, surprised at the fear rising from their faces like steam. {Some of them have been scoundrels at times, but most of the rest of them have caused me no harm, even as they continue to send Mary to her triumph.}

⤜⧉⤛

AT FIRST, I RECEIVED UPDATES on Mary's progress through Bonmot.

"Mary has sold her second book," Bonmot told me one fall, the willow trees impervious to the change of seasons even as, across the street, oaks became an indignant red-and-orange, and then bald, and a strange whisper of flame spread through the city.

"Her second book," I said.

It was almost unbearable to receive such information from Bonmot, when every day I could hear the creak and shift of timber above me as Sirin walked between his desk and his precious butterflies. {Worse, worse—I found she had taken up with another man, her own age, the son of her father's best friend, someone she had known for years. Someone comfortable. Someone safe. Someone with a "III" in his name. I could tolerate the books, because I knew they contained a little piece of me in them, but I could not tolerate that relationship.}

"Yes. It's called *The Inflammation of Aan Tribal Wars*. I've had a look at it, and it's excellent. Very well researched. She's a credit to the school."

As Duncan was not, went the tired old, silent old refrain. {Bonmot never forgave me, not even at the end. I couldn't understand that. I'd have forgiven him had our situations been reversed, but, then, I am not a priest. I did see him sometimes, in the last few years before he passed on. When I took walks in Trillian Park, I would discover him sitting on a bench as I turned a corner. He would look up, and our eyes would meet before he could turn away. Those few times, I would see a peace within him that faded as he recognized me. I wouldn't stop to talk—it was too painful, too maddening, to understand that he could not move past my lapse of judgment. Later, back in my apartment overlooking Trillian Square, I would sit on my balcony drinking wine, analyzing the moment in the park, searching my memory of our brief encounter for some hint of recognition on his part that did not include bitterness or rancor. Sometimes I convinced myself, sometimes I did not.}

Bonmot—to his credit, or perhaps not to his credit—never realized that I might prefer not to hear such details, such confirmation of Mary's success. Later, when he better understood the humiliation of having to stand outside of her various residences and tell tourists about her, Bonmot stopped telling me. He must have realized by then that her ascent was self-evident.

"That's nice," I mumbled. "I am sure it is a very interesting book she has written." Through a mouthful of my chicken sandwich, looking out of the corner of my eye for my bumbling tourist charges, to make sure they had not gotten into too much trouble.

We studied Truffidian religious texts at lunch sometimes as well. I found them soothing. *My God, keep my tongue from evil, my lips from lies. Help me ignore those who slander me.* Although I could no longer bring myself to attend services in the newly renovated Truffidian Cathedral or any other enclosed space, I took some measure of comfort from the hymns and sayings. *Guardian of happiness, in whose presence despair flees, with Your great compassion grant me the ability to welcome what may come with calm and grace, to experience happiness and joy.* When I read them aloud before sleep, the nightmarish images would recede, the red mist of Sybel's death dissipate. *May You find delight in the words of my mouth and in the emotions of my heart.* The sensation, when I went to bed, of lying down amongst a row of corpses would lessen, become tolerable. *The wise must die, even as the foolish and senseless, leaving their possessions to others.*

"Do you like being a tour guide?" Bonmot asked me at one lunch.

"I do," I said, before I could think about it. If I'd thought about it, I would have said no.

"Why?" he asked, no reproach in his voice, just a genuine curiosity. He had hinted more than once that he could find me a comparable job with the church, but turning my religion into a daily chore, complete with choir, didn't interest me.

"Why?" Why did I like working as a tour guide? In those early years: "Because I get to be outside a lot. I get to see the city afresh, from the perspective of those unfamiliar with her."

Because it took me away from Duncan's world. Because it allowed me to relive, in daydream reveries, my past successes week after week. Because I met interesting people, some of them men, though I had learned to be more discerning than in the past. Because those who I guided saw me not as a failure but as part of the heritage, the history, of Ambergris. And there was something to be said for not trying quite so hard. I arrived in the same place, I had begun to notice, regardless of the amount of effort.

※

BUT I COULD NEVER TRULY escape Duncan, just as Duncan could not escape himself. And ultimately I wouldn't have wanted to. Except for my father's writings, Duncan is my only link to my father. Duncan is still here, I hope, in the flesh, while Dad speaks to me in shards of meaning gleaned from the fragments Duncan kept of his journals, his scribblings and essays. All of it is work-related; Dad appears never to have written anything that was not related to work, or, at least, such writings weren't found when Mom catalogued his things.

I've gone through all of it twice before lugging it here along with anything else I wanted to salvage from Duncan's apartment. Most of Dad's papers are so dry, so dusty, that I've begun to understand that he lived in his own little specialized world. His work galvanized and, perhaps, electrified, other historians with its sense of rarefied knowledge, but there's nothing for the rest of us to hold on to. Sometimes I think Duncan took it upon himself to "translate" our dad's work into a form that might be palatable to the public. {I thought maybe he knew, maybe something in the papers would solve my mysteries. It never did.} Sometimes I think that Duncan would have been better off becoming a plumber, a carpenter, a blacksmith, a merchant, a missionary.

Nothing of our personal history made it into Dad's work, even though that history had some relevance. Some said, not without a hint of mockery, that you could trace our family's history on my mother's side all the way back to the founding of Ambergris by John Manzikert—that one of the anonymous, unremarked-upon members of the ship's crew, George Bliss, had been our distant great-to-the-umpteenth-power grandfather. Over the years, among our shadow relatives—aunts, uncles, grandparents, cousins, "shadow" because they lived in far-off cities like Nicea and we saw them rarely—an entire mythology had grown up around Bliss. Stories of Bliss fighting off gray caps, of his friendship with Samuel Tonsure before Tonsure disappeared, vague references to the underground—all apocryphal, of course. {Apocryphal? Maybe, but I enjoyed those stories growing up. Those stories reaffirmed my birthright to crawl around in dimly lit places.}

Dad used to joke that he had married Mom as part of his research into the history of the city.

"Your mother, children," he said once, "figures prominently in my current research. She's fodder for my essays. Certain experiments, certain experiments cannot be conducted without her—or, if conducted, do not"—and he stared pointedly at Mom and then back at us—"yield the same results."

Sometimes when he said this, he would hold her close from behind, nuzzle her neck. Mom would give a sly, quick smile then, before pretending to be offended as she pulled away from him, and I remember that smile, because it gave me the first clue that there might be an adult world existing above or on top of the one in which we dwelt as children.

Mom had a problem laughing at herself; she never knew if people were laughing with her or at her, so she never fully gave herself up to it with other people—Dad was the only one who could make her laugh in a way that seemed effortless rather than forced.

As for whether first-generation Ambergrisian blood flows through our veins, I don't know, but I think our dad believed it did. {And if it didn't before, Janice, the city probably flows through my veins now, in altered form, whether I want it to or not. An entire world flows through my veins these days.}

❧❧

WHILE UPSTAIRS SIRIN WORKED ON making Mary the flavor of the decade and downstairs I labored at scraping out a living, Duncan fleshed out his theories and his articles, which would one day culminate, or dissolve, in his *Early History of Ambergris* tour guide book. {Or at least culminate in the unexpurgated version that has still never seen print.}

In those days, sentences crawled out of Duncan's skin, paragraphs exhaled with each breath. On a winter's morning, you could almost see them forming in the white smoke of his speech. {For all the good it did me—most of the sentences and paragraphs didn't coalesce into longer works, or if they did, I sacrificed them to the AFTOIS newsletter.}

Sometimes I thought the Spore of the Gray Cap made him prolific—that in a space neither above nor belowground, he felt in the most perfect balance—and thus balanced, ballasted, he could write without self-consciousness. Certainly, the owner loved his presence—"fringe" or not, they'd never had a historian use their tavern as a work space. Of course, Duncan brought more business with him than I ever did, in the form of his fellow crackpots. Lacond even indulged for a time, before his illness made that impossible.

The following note in Duncan's journal exemplifies his approach:

Should the historian's personal life happen to coincide in some way with the history he has chosen to write about—if the personal history "doubles" the public history—then an alchemy occurs whereby the historian, in a sense, becomes the history. That is, once rendered in all the signs and symbols at the historian's command, the history he has written becomes, for him, the story of his own life. This fact may not be obvious to the reader except in flashes and flickers of reflected thought, where the passion of the historian for the story peers out, naked, from the page. There, for a flicker of a moment, we find the historian exposed, if only the world decides to correctly interpret the clues. {I didn't write this. I was quoting another historian. I can't even remember which one.}

In expressing this theory—a theory that calls for the historian to internalize a selected portion of history as part of his or her life; or, more specifically, to map historical events to personal events—Duncan was deeply influenced by the work of the idiosyncratic Nicean philosopher-historian Edgar Rybern. Rybern believed that the personal politics of each individual distorts their view of history. As Rybern wrote in his book *Approaches to History* {a book Sabon violently disapproved of, even during her days at the Academy}:

Such a person never merely traces the outline of the past. Texts do not sit side by side on the shelf, but intermingle, entering into conflict and confluence with one another until the probable emerges from the impossible. Reduced to rubble, such sources provide the raw building material for a theory of greater import and durability. However, the story that emerges from this process does not interest such a historian. The tale told is mere preamble to explanation, preamble to a more personal theory. In such a process, the chronology and lineage of the acts depicted in the narrative depend on the prejudices and experiences of the individual's psyche, and the subconscious impulses embedded therein.

Based on Rybern's musings, Duncan began to ask himself—in countless articles published in the hapless AFTOIS newsletter, and in countless conversations with Lacond—"Why not *consciously* distort history by focusing on those portions and patterns that have the most relevance or resonance to one's own life?"

Such a slant would, presumably, intensify the empathy that the historian has to those particular historical events. For example, I, as a historian, would be most at home describing the history of various mental wards and the effects on the psyche of mass slaughter witnessed up-close.

If every individual mind can be said to exist within a lively morass of prejudice and subjectivity, then the pursuit of the objective becomes a futile, laughable goal—in effect, a lie; especially in a field such as history, where every day, every hour, every minute, the historian becomes more distant from the core occurrences under observation.{A simplification, true, but essentially accurate. Not that it matters to anyone anymore. History is about to catch up with us, and what I've really learned is that anything connected to the printed page becomes a kind of tombstone, marking the death of the past.}

Lacond, for all of his faults, understood this about Duncan. {After all, he, like me, had been underground at least once or twice, and came away from it having paid a physical price.} In one issue of the newsletter, Lacond wrote:

> When Duncan Shriek writes about the Silence—as he has been known to do within these very pages—he quite literally, in my opinion, writes also of his personal silences over the years, the way in which he has been silenced—by others, by his own mistakes—and all the similar silences, suffered by us all. In a sense, he has made Ambergris' history personal. He may be too good a historian to invade his text, but certain parallels emerge again and again— allusions to Tonsure's descent into silence and despair and subsequent reemergence in the form of a book being especially prevalent.

Those experts who bothered to refute Duncan's theories—mostly Sabon— pointed to the dangers of the personal history approach. Sabon wrote an essay for the H&S collection *Impersonal Perspectives: Objectivity in Ambergrisian History* {which probably sold about five copies}:

> The irrefutable fissure in any theory of "personal history" lies in the impulse to find a plateau far above sheer fact, to reveal a lesson or universal "truth" that can be mapped to an individual life and intertwined with a complicated intellectual distain: contempt for accuracy, rejection of contradictory evidence, confusion of conjecture with truth, resistance to correction.

Sabon had a point, of sorts. Not that Duncan's theories were flawed—no one ever dared to test their veracity through underground research. But when Duncan began, a few years later, to write his *Early History,* he looked to what he was writing for some indication of how to live his life, so that instead of finding what in history could become personal, he let the personal become history. {You might be right, but the reading public never had a chance to discover the truth or falsehood of it, either in the book or in reality.}

Unfortunately, in my opinion, the parallels that Duncan sought did not always exist. As I told him once, "Nothing in your studies will ever explain the death of our father." I don't think he believed me. He would have believed me even less if I had told him Bonmot and Truffidianism might be able to help him with that mystery. {Of all your incarnations, your transformation to the cause of organized religion baffled me the most. I certainly didn't begrudge you your conversion, though—all I envied was the time you spent with Bonmot.}

❦

I'VE FINALLY FOUND SOMETHING PERSONAL of Dad's in amongst all the dry discourse—tucked away inside a box inside another box. A canvas sculpture of a mushroom, about twelve inches tall. Part of his personal history, you might call it, and the symbol of a rare hiccup in the respect my parents showed each other.

That respect manifested itself in the way our father avoided invading Mom's space. Our parents were as separate and yet together as any two people could be, and I've often thought that when Dad died, the reason it took Mom so long to create again is that Dad created the space for her to be able to make her art.

Dad did not enter some rooms of our house in Stockton—in particular, Mom's studio. There, she would relax and sketch, paint, or even work on sculptures, her studio window providing a magnificent view of the forest. She knew that Dad would never enter, not even for a quick visit or to remind her of some dinner party they had to attend, not even when she was out of the house. And she did the same for him—his office formed a country forbidden to all of us.

Some days, they would be in their separate spaces and the house would seem quiet, but Duncan and I could sense a kind of tingle or hum in the silence, a potent energy. Because we knew that, in their separate spaces, in their own different yet specific ways, both of our parents were *creating*. That feeling of applied industry, of work, permeated our awareness in those years before Dad's death.

Which is not to say that our parents didn't take joy in their creations, or want to share them. But there was a space to work and a space to share their work. The living room served as that latter area. If either wanted to share in the flush of post-inspiration, out the pages or painting would come to the living room.

On that neutral ground, they would present their findings and receive their praise. Dad would read from the loose-leaf pages crumpled in his hand while Mom would murmur, "Lovely. Inspired. Very original." Or Mom would unveil a sketch or study or painting and discuss the spark that made it coalesce into being, while Dad would say, "Wonderful use of color. I love the way you've drawn that figure. Beautiful." {Such compliments would be tenfold in intensity, Janice, should you or I share our early experiments. I can still remember how much praise they lavished on you for your first paintings. They loved your work unconditionally.}

In that separate space and that shared space, I think I can see the secret of their happiness. Each could feel the other's presence in their separate spaces as powerfully as in their shared space.

But the living room also served as a place to seek assistance. If stuck, if faced with conundrum or puzzle, dead words or dead paint, one would stomp out into that middle ground and, by certain signals, make it clear the other was needed to brainstorm possible solutions.

On our dad's part, the signal involved much crinkling of papers and long, deep sighs {I perfected my own sigh listening to his}, perhaps even an artificial propensity to make noise by banging into furniture. On Mom's part it was more direct, because to get to the living room she had to pass Dad's office. A quick slap of the palm against his door on the way to common ground usually got his attention.

What always surprised me is how quickly the other parent would halt in his or her own labors and come out to the living room. Sometimes it was just to listen to the other vent, sometimes to offer practical suggestions.

Only once, to my knowledge, did one or the other cross a boundary. Our dad one day decided to try his hand at sculpture, but not just any sculpture. He wanted to use wire and canvas, to combine sculpture and painting, in a sense. I could see from the expression on Mom's face what she thought of this idea, but she loaned him the supplies and for a week he worked on his own New Art. You could hear him bumping into things in his office, cursing sometimes, coming out to beg more supplies from Mom. Duncan and I both expected great things. {Or, at least, *something*—or, as Janice put it at the time, some *thing*.}

Finally, Dad had finished, and we all gathered in the living room for the unveiling. The sculpture stood on a table near the couch, covered by a bedsheet. Mom stood to the side, arms crossed, while Dad explained the concept.

"I wanted to reveal the true shape of everyday things. This is the first of a series of studies that combine painting and sculpture into a new hybrid," he said.

With those words, he pulled the sheet away, to reveal . . . a canvas mushroom, wires under the canvas giving it a shape.

"A mushroom. Made of canvas," Mom said.

"Well," Dad said, "I haven't painted it yet."

Mom went back into her studio.

I went back to reading.

Only Duncan had the decency to walk up to our dad and tell him how much
he liked it.

Dad never crossed the line into the arts again.

I DON'T THINK I WAS fated to be granted the kind of connection our parents
often had, and I don't know if I learned enough from our parents' example. The
dynamic changed too much after Dad's death, and our careers took us too far
apart to allow it, but I imagine this connection, this understanding, is something that Mary and Duncan shared before they grew apart. {All too briefly, I'm
afraid. Some months it was there, some months it wasn't. You need to know a
person for a long time to develop that kind of trust. We didn't have enough
time.}

"NATIVISM," DUNCAN SAID TO ME once, "is like a prolonged case of mass suicide."

I mention this because History and my reincarnation as a tour guide continued to intersect in a number of ways, against my wishes. For example, evincing
a cruel kindness, Sirin managed to finagle me a nonpaying position on the
toothless horror that is the Ambergris Tourism Board, in a nod to my past status as an "iconic figure in society in general, etc., etc.," as one of the other board
members greeted me before slumping back into a kind of half-drool, half-
reverie that looked quite pleasant.

I joined the board at the perfect time: it seemed to be trying to make itself
obsolete. The first day I reported for service, the board decided to mount a
rather muddled campaign to discourage tourism in the city because, as one
gout-ridden veteran of many a real or imaginary war put it, "These fools. Must
protect them. Too many deaths. At Festival time. Darlings deserve better." I

almost pointed out that fewer tourists meant more of a chance, statistically, that local residents would be the targets of violence or "odd events," as the broadsheets now sometimes termed encounters involving gray caps. But I kept my mouth shut. After all, it was only my first day on the job, and I wasn't yet sure I wanted to burn any bridges. {If you'd taken your duties more seriously, perhaps some of AFTOIS' positions would have received a sympathetic hearing from those old bastards. As it was, I can't recall you doing anything at the public meetings of the board but taking up space.}

As a result, for two years, in the months leading up to the Festival, the board paid for posters to be put up that depicted dead dogs in a variety of unkind and teeth-grimacing positions, complete with titles such as DEAD DOGS. DEAD TOURISTS. IT'S ALL THE SAME TO US. STAY OUT OF AMBERGRIS AROUND FESTIVAL TIME.

The posters appeared to result in insulted—but not fatally insulted—tourists, if the large number of people letting me lead them around the city and babble about dead people and old buildings was any indication. I certainly didn't mind this change, but posters or no, a more profound and negative transformation had begun to change Ambergris. The invisible yet necessary buffer between the professional and the personal slowly eroded, and for this I blame Nativism.

I'm sure that blaming Nativism for *anything* will be seen as blasphemy by many readers, but then, you've made it this far—you can't give up now. So, if you haven't become irrevocably jaded, perhaps even revolted {or revolting}, by the preceding pages, I dare say you'll hardly even twitch when I say: *I blame Nativism.* Not the specific form of insanity displayed by Sabon's father—not that brand of Nativism. No, I refer to the form that Duncan called "the final outcome of the war": an attempt to become blind, deaf, and dumb as a most peculiar and pathetic method of semi-survival. {It allowed people to function in their day-to-day lives, rather than boarded up, gibbering in fear, in their homes. I'll give it that much.}

As Sabon's kind of Nativism spread throughout the Southern cities by way of her books and essays, it infected the tourists who subjected themselves to my tours. Over time, I no longer needed Bonmot to give me updates on Mary's progress. Instead, her flock of black crows feasting on the carcasses of Duncan's investigations could be clearly seen in the eyes of the visitors I guided from one banal site to another.

I can't say I minded these intrusions into rote routine at first. As I told Sybel when he accompanied me on these jaunts—and he was always there in some form—each recital of the same information became more stale than the last, until I was like some crippled, half-senile goat or sheep, chewing and rechewing the same yellowing stalks of grass. It was a relief when the replies to my jaded bleatings began to change from polite nods or the obvious questions or the occasional attempt at wit, to observations such as "Mary Sabon wrote about this place in her book on Nativism. You should mention that next time."

"What a good suggestion!" I would reply. "I'll be sure to do that," and try to carry on as if nothing offensive had been said, if they would let me.

Sometimes they also came seeking wish fulfillment: "Do you think we might see Sabon on this tour?"

To which I would reply in a clipped but neutral tone, "Not on this tour." Not even if we stood for a week in the shade of the large oak tree outside her ancestral home.

Even more jarring, though, were the questions out of nowhere—broadsides I was in no position to absorb, meant to torment me—that opened a door where no door should exist.

"Are you any relation to the Duncan Shriek mentioned in Sabon's books?"

Most of the time, my interrogator exuded a naïve good humor as natural as sweat when asking the question—wanted only to know that I was not just an expert but intimately *involved* with the information I imparted, whether we stood inside the old post office or outside of some tavern with "Spore" in the title.

I had no problem providing graceful answers in such cases, although each time it did surprise me—and more than surprise me, it changed the world so that I saw my brother's influence in everything.

"Nativists are like Manziists or Menites or any other religion," Duncan said once. "Just as righteous, just as right." No wonder their questions changed my worldview.

As Nativism conquered the city and the entire South, I found the door to my misery widening and darkening, so that a belligerent quality entered the voices of those asking the questions.

One particularly grueling and hot summer afternoon a few years before the Shift began in earnest, I heard the words, "Are you Duncan's sister?" delivered in a tone somewhere between fervent eagerness and bloodlust.

My surroundings, which had faded to the usual blur—my mouth spewing a stream of familiar words while my mind went elsewhere—came back into sharp focus.

The tour group and I stood in the middle of Voss Bender Memorial Square, in front of a fountain depicting Banker Trillian's victory over the rival banker-warriors of Nicea. Around the square stood the ancient buildings that had once served as Trillian's headquarters. In between, a pleasing and aromatic mixture of green-and-red blossoms signaled not only the arrival of the summer's wildflowers but House Hoegbotton's crass attempt to memorialize the struggle that followed Voss Bender's death. I had set the tour group loose on the square for a few minutes, and they currently wandered here and there, staring at everything with a freshness I could not understand.

I faced my interrogator, who doubled in an instant. A woman had spoken, but her husband stood beside her, just as resolute and nervous. Both of them had reached the far end of their fifties, the woman gray-haired and stuffed into a formless flower-print dress, matched to white stockings and blocky wooden shoes.

"I can't say I much cared for the mad glint in her eyes, or the thick red smile she gave me," I told Duncan later, relaxing in his apartment.

In fact, I looked at her as if she were a huge mushroom that had erupted through the courtyard tiles.

"That was no mad glint," Duncan replied. "That was the spark of righteous purpose."

Her husband, stocky muscle half-turned to fat, wore spectacles and, bizarrely, the kind of trousers and tunic that had gone out of style long before Old Fart had capitulated to New Fart—close to the kind of museum pieces I spoke about during the tour.

Helpfully, their jaunty name tags, affixed to the continents of their chests, disclosed not only names but locations. Mortar and Pestle, as I came to think of them, hailed from my birthplace of Stockton. Somehow, this did not reassure me.

"Are you Duncan's sister?" Pestle asked again. This time it felt as if she'd poked me in the ribs with her finger.

"And what if I am?" I asked.

Mortar remained impassive while Pestle gave me a blank look, as if she hadn't expected a question in return.

"We'd have a message for him if you were his sister," Mortar said in a gravelly baritone, shifting uneasily. I could tell that this conversation hadn't been his idea, but that he'd decided to make the best of it.

"Really? You'd do that?" I said. It wasn't really a question, and I'd like to report that I delivered those words with the appropriate amount of withering scorn, but that's not true. I was truly caught wrong-footed by the idea that two tourists could walk up to me and *presume* in such a way.

Mortar balanced on one leg for a second while Pestle hesitated; she definitely hated being asked questions.

"Absolutely. Absolutely that's what I'd do," Pestle said, finally.

"And what would the message be?" I asked her. I shouldn't have bothered. I could have ignored her. I could have moved on to the next part of the tour.

Pestle frowned and her face achieved a certain narrow intensity. "Why, I'd ask you to tell him that he's wrong and that the Nativists are right."

"And that he should stop trying to scare people with his theories," Mortar added.

Mortar and Pestle stood there, waiting for my response while the sun baked us all. My gaze fled to two swallows chasing insects through the searing blue sky, and I wondered how it had come to this. Had I misjudged how far I had fallen, and was falling still? Where will it end? Can it end? Should it end? My fingers are green with spores. That cannot be a good sign.

❦

I COULD HAVE TOLD OLD Mortar and Pestle—for whom I now feel a mounting affection where no such affection should exist—that Duncan was closer than they might have thought, and perhaps they would like to meet him? But I don't think they really would have wanted to meet him. That the person they had pictured in their minds actually existed would probably have confounded them. Unlike Nativism, which existed precisely so people could avoid being confounded.

Nativism, to my mind, had become the next "phenomenon," like the New Art before it, except in a different discipline. You didn't have to paint anything or enjoy art to join it. You didn't have to react or interpret or express yourself. Nothing so active. You just had to believe in a theory and mindlessly recite it to others with any minor variations you might have added to it in the meantime. {Not much different from the chants some of the imprisoned Truffidian monks used to drive the fear from their hearts.}

Nativism would become so popular that not long after Mortar, Pestle, and I had our enlightening conversation in Bender Square, the Ambergris Tourism Board, against my sole and emphatic "No—hell, no," vote, added a Nativism tour to my busy schedule.

What did this new tour consist of? Our standard "Gray Cap Oddities" tour combined with a few extras, like a view of Sabon's family home, Blythe Academy, and some carefully selected and cultivated fungus-infested walls—"Ooh, very pretty, very awe-inspiring," most tourists would coo—and a lot of extra propaganda that made my teeth hurt. I never thought that I would ever be required to repeat the name "Sabon" so many times to so many strangers.

❖❖

"AM I DUNCAN'S SISTER?" I finally replied. "Yes, I am. Do you know him?"

"We know of him," Mortar said, almost cleverly.

"But you don't know him?"

"No, not personally," Pestle replied.

"They didn't even know you, Duncan," I told him later. "Hadn't met you even once. And yet it was as if they thought they did know you—personally."

"Oh, I see. I thought perhaps, given your use of his first name, that you were old friends of his."

"The price of reflected fame, I guess," Duncan said, staring out the window into the courtyard. "It's enough to have read about you."

At least I got the courtesy of an embarrassed look from old Mortar. Pretty Pestle, though, went right on pounding away.

❖❖

EVENTUALLY, I MANAGED TO RESCUE myself from the Nativism tour, but it took almost a year. People liked the irony of a Shriek, any Shriek, narrating that tour—at least the ones who had read Mary's book, and too many of them had read Mary's book. {Even me. I'm surprised you make no mention here of the time *I* took your Nativism tour. I've never seen anyone have to hold in so much irritation for such a long time. I only did it because for a time I contemplated joining the fray. If they wanted to use my life for their mass hallucinations, then I should at least have made a little extra money off of it. Can you imagine the furor if *Duncan* Shriek had become a tour guide?}

Cinsorium: Rethinking the Myth of the Gray Caps was a book we needed during those reactionary rebuilding years as much as we'd needed Sabon's pig cartel book a few years before. It was the book that made the rift between Duncan and Mary permanent. As Duncan wrote in his journal after reading it, "For the first time, my body understands what my mind accepted long before: Mary is never coming back to me."

In her book, Sabon alternately refuted Duncan's theories about the gray caps and cribbed from them—as if she had ground Duncan's ideas down to specks of glitter and then used them to decorate her own creations. {Perhaps it wouldn't have hurt so much if I hadn't given her a copy of my own *Cinsorium* when we were at Blythe, inscribed "My dearest Mary—here's the heart of me. Treat it gently. Love, Duncan." She couldn't have treated *my* Cinsorium more ruthlessly in *her* Cinsorium if she'd honed the book's boards to a fatal sharpness and then stabbed me with them repeatedly. I can forgive her for most things, but not that.}

"So that is the message you would like me to relay to Duncan?" I asked Pestle, to make sure.

A triumphant look from Pestle. "Yes, thanks. That would be wonderful. But we have more to tell him."

"I rather thought you might."

⊰✤⊱

AS EVERYONE KNOWS, NATIVISM CONSISTS of two major ideas, but most people do not realize that only one of them is unique. The other has been around for centuries. Sabon's innovation consisted in how she put the two together and then slapped her father's crowd-pleasing title of "Nativism" on top of it all like the final slice of bread on a particularly messy sandwich.

What was the first part of this magnificent theory? To start with, Sabon floated the thought—I can't even credit it with the term "idea"—that the gray caps were the degenerate descendents of a local tribe similar to the Dogghe or the Nimblytod {without asking either tribe how they felt about being lumped in with the gray caps, and without consulting their extensive oral histories}, but a tribe that had been colonized and then subjugated by several variations of fungus found in both above- and belowground Ambergris. She claimed that the mighty city that had existed before Manzikert I razed it had housed a Saphant-type civilization predating the gray caps. She even went so far as to suggest that the gray caps had been a servant class to this hypothetical other race. {I found it highly ironic, given the fate of my books at the hands of reviewers, that by postulating this "other race" and leaving that question as the book's central mystery, she so captured readers' imaginations that no one thought to cry out, "Where's the proof?"}

Pestle said, "Tell Duncan that he doesn't need to worry about the gray caps."

"They say you don't need to worry about the gray caps, Duncan."

"Ah, but I know that they worry about us, and that worries me."

Duncan did a rather unconvincing imitation of a shuffling gray cap. If I hadn't seen him do it before, I wouldn't have known what he was trying to do.

"Half -wit."

"Unappreciative pedant. But what else did they say?"

"Also tell him," Mortar added, without a hint of threat, "that he might want to go into another line of work."

"Ho ho! Haven't you said the same to me sometimes, Janice? So how can you complain?"

"Do you want to hear the rest or are you going to be difficult?"

"I'm sorry," I said to M & P, remembering a valuable bit of advice from Sybel about how it's never too late to correct your course so long as you've not yet run aground. {Because Sybel was, of course, an *expert* on sailing metaphors.} "I'm sorry, but I was joking. I'm not really Duncan's sister. I just like to claim I am sometimes, you know, because it makes things more interesting. My apologies."

I turned to the rest of the tourists, who had regrouped in front of me and had become a little too interested in my conversation with M & P.

"Now, as we continue, notice the telltale Trillian period details in the building across the square—in particular the fluted archways, the broad columns, the fine filigree. Also note—"

"I don't believe you," Mortar said, with the kind of earnest emphasis that can be interpreted as sternly polite or quietly angry, depending on your inclination.

Not for the first time, I remember thinking that perhaps it was time to change careers again.

<hr />

THE SECOND PART OF NATIVISM reflected an odd prejudice that Duncan had tried to refute in his own book: most historians {and laypeople} thought of and wrote about the gray caps as if they represented a natural phenomenon, as immutable, faceless, and unpredictable as the weather, and, therefore, best understood in the aggregate, like the change of seasons or a bad thunderstorm. {Would that the Nativists had treated the gray caps like weather and tried to divine, from certain signs—a lowering of the temperature, a particular type of cloud, a strange hot wind—what the gray caps had planned for us.}

As Duncan wrote in his book so many years ago:

Looking back at all of Ambergris' many historical accounts, the answers to three basic yet profound questions are always missing: (1) in the absence of a

strong central government, how does Ambergris manage to avoid fragmen-
tation into separate, tiny city-states? (2) What cause could there possibly be
for the fluctuating levels of violence and personal property damage experienced during the Festival? (3) Given the presence of members of over one
hundred contradictory religions and cults in the city, what prevents occurrences of holy war?

For Duncan, the answers always returned to the gray caps, who, by use of hidden
influence {the first physical manifestation being Frankwrithe & Lewden's use of
fungal weapons} and a multitude of carefully engineered "spore solutions," kept
the population balanced between anarchy and control. To Duncan, this meant that
it served the gray caps' interests for Ambergris to lurch ever forward, never truly
disintegrating or cohering, but instead always on the edge, teetering.

However, Mary and her Nativists refused to believe in conscious gray cap
machinations. In an article for *Ambergris Today*, Mary wrote:

Time and again, apologists blame the gray caps for our own follies and misdeeds. Such a position abrogates personal responsibility and is as irresponsible
as those religions that attribute deeds to the sun, moon, or sea. We are, ultimately, responsible for our own actions, our own history, and our own happiness. I do not refute any claim that the gray caps are vile and degenerate
creatures, or that they have not influenced our city in a negative way. But they
have not done so with *intent*. Their story is not that of an overarching conspiracy, of careful control over centuries, but instead the pitiful tale of a subjugated race that acts with the same instinct and lack of planning as any of
the lower animals. For us to confer intent upon them—or to seek intent from
them—turns us into victims, unable to fashion our own destinies. I reject
such crackpot ideology.

Mary mercilessly picked away at any attempt to prove that the gray caps had ex-
hibited conscious thought or causality, no matter how minor. For example, in a
letter to the editor for a broadsheet, Duncan wrote about what appeared to him
to be a side effect of the gray caps' efforts: {I did not. I considered these effects
to be as intentional as all of the overt harm done to us by the gray caps.}

The very spores that keep the population in thrall also undertake many
beneficial tasks. For example, Ambergris has stayed relatively disease-free

throughout its history, with no documented plague as has occurred in Stockton and Morrow. Whether intentional or not, these benefits should not be overlooked.

Mary skewered this idea, writing in a subsequent issue, "Does the absence of disease lead one to the immediate conclusion that some force other than common sense and hand-washing is protecting us?" {I am ashamed to admit that her letter to the editor, in response to my own, sent a little thrill down my spine. I know she wasn't responding to me personally, but it was still direct communication of a kind.}

※

"IT ALL SOUNDED SO LOGICAL in her book," Duncan complained to me as we looked down at Trillian Square from his apartment window. Below us, M & P and the rest of the tourists were milling about, not sure what to do. "It doesn't matter that her proof is as insubstantial as mine."

"Yes," I said, "but can't you provide proof, Duncan? Can't you do something?"

"How? With another article for AFTOIS? All the mentions in the world in Mary's books do me no good. I'm offered a few interview opportunities, but only if I play the role of clown or eccentric. Anything I said to them would be tainted and instantly discounted. Better not to speak at all."

※

EARLIER, I HAD SIGHED AND turned back to Mortar and Pestle.

"You're right. I wasn't joking," I said. "Duncan is my brother. So I'll let him know what you said next time I see him. Now can we—"

"And give him this letter," Pestle said, pulling a sealed envelope out of her pocket and handing it to me.

I took it from her as if she had given me a dead fish. What further surprises could the day hold? How patient should I be? It was difficult not to see them, on some level, as Sabon's personal emissaries, sent to torment me.

". . . and give him your letter," I continued, lying. I threw it away, unread, at the first opportunity. "But I have a favor to ask in return. I need you to relay a message for me."

That surprised them, but Mortar nodded and said, "That only seems fair."

※

THE MAIN APPEAL OF NATIVISM to Ambergrisians was that it freed them from any responsibility to think about or do *anything* about the gray caps, while reassuring them that this was the most responsible thing they could do. And, in my opinion—I can already hear the howls of outrage, but I am unmoved— it absolved Ambergrisians from any guilt over the massacre perpetrated by Manzikert I.

"Not to mention that it saved them from having to worry about another Silence," Duncan said. M & P had disappeared from view. The square below was relatively quiet.

"Not to mention," I said.

Perhaps the speed with which House Hoegbotton and House Frankwrithe & Lewden embraced Nativism proves Duncan's theory. What better way for the gray caps to protect themselves than by convincing the Houses? {I think this enters the far reaches of that land known as the Paranoid Conspiracy Theory, Janice.} Meanwhile, those of us not as devoted to blind ideology have had to suffer through the Nativists' huge rallies, their righteous speeches, their letter-writing campaigns when anything the least bit threatening to their worldview has the audacity to step out into the light. I would imagine that even Sabon never realized that Nativism would become so popular, or that it would drive her book sales for so long. {Although, you must admit, the mechanics of the Shift have put a stop to her momentum.}

I had personal reasons for rejecting Sabon's theory. Sometimes, during my tours of duty, I would see Sybel standing in the nearest available tree behind some mob listening to a Nativist speaker. He'd look back at me and shake his head, sadness in his eyes. After all, he'd been killed by a very specific deployment of the gray caps' weapons. I'd lost a foot. It was hard to blame either outcome, ultimately, on the random, the unexplainable. At least, I refused to do so.

"But how can we pass on a message from you?" Pestle asked.

"Easy," I said. "It's for Mary Sabon. She is, after all, the leader of you Nativist types."

Mortar had already begun shaking his head, about to protest that they didn't know Mary, that they'd only read her books, but I waved these objections aside, pulled them both close.

Before the war, before Sybel's death, before I became a gallery owner, this is what I would have said to them, either in a whisper or a roar: "First, let me point out that if you don't deliver this message for me, I will have Duncan bring the gray caps down upon you like a plague so you can see for yourself just how motivated they are. So I suggest that as soon as I stop talking, you start search-ing for Sabon. I want you to tell Mary to stop misleading sycophantic morons like yourselves. To stop making it seem like everything in our lives is under our control, to stop undermining everything my brother has ever worked toward. To stop killing him by degrees, in public. To stop wasting your time and his time with these ridiculous theories of hers that only apply to her personal demons. To stop to stop to stop to stop to stop."

But I didn't say that. I was Janice Shriek, former society figure, and I'll be damned if I let any two-bit tourists just off the slow boat from Stockton get under my skin.

❦

WHAT DROVE MARY TO THE cruelty of showing her "affection" for Duncan as mentor by tearing down all he had built up—and doing so after he had al-ready become comfortable as a ghost—I do not know. Perhaps it was not just fear. Perhaps it was out of envy. Perhaps it was to show she could do it all better.

The practical effect of Sabon's resurrection of discussions initiated by Dun-can was that Frankwrithe & Lewden bought the rights to his books from Hoegbotton & Sons and proceeded to publish them in a badly edited, hideously expensive, horribly abridged omnibus entitled *Cinsorium & Other Historical Fa-bles* {Dad would have punned it as *Sin-sore-ium & Other Hysterical Foibles*}, an edition intended solely for the library market so that scholars could peruse it as part of their primary text exploration of Sabon's books. The rights Duncan had sold to Hoegbotton were all-encompassing and he could do nothing but accept a trickle of royalties from publication of the omnibus. He could not stop the butchery of his original texts. {Nor could I afford to object anyway, my income having dropped off precipitously since AFTOIS could not sustain me by itself.}

The omnibus received scant attention from reviewers—it was considered a historical curiosity, reflecting the "hysteria and ignorance of a less enlightened time," as one of the few notices put it—meaning that kind readers like Mortar and Pestle only encountered Shriek through Sabon's filter. One hates to think of Duncan struggling to express himself while F&L and his beloved Mary struggle to snuff him out, but that's exactly what was happening.

Despite Sirin's assertions from time to time—rebutted by Lacond at many a furious AFTOIS meeting, where according to Duncan, the issue came up continually—that Sabon meant no harm by her actions—perhaps even the opposite—and that neither did Hoegbotton in selling the rights to Frankwrithe

& Lewden, I'm certain she resurrected him merely to more effectively destroy him. Whether she meant to or not. Nativism, as it turns out, was an excellent descriptor for Mary's own actions.

What made me angriest, though, is that Duncan didn't even seem to mind, as if accepting her right to take advantage of him. {I couldn't hate her for it. And even as the sight of butchered chapters and paragraphs cut me to the quick, part of me thrilled to see *any* of my words back in print, in any form.}

❧

NO, WHAT I SAID TO Mortar and Pestle with sincerity and with hope, as I handed them my cheat sheets for the rest of the tour was simply, "If you do ever see Mary, tell her that Duncan sends his love." It's a pity I couldn't maintain my composure later, on a certain marble staircase, but I've never claimed to be consistent.

Then I put my arms around Mortar and Pestle and turned all three of us to face the tour group.

"I'm afraid there's been a change of plans. These two fine upstanding citizens from Stockton will be leading the rest of the tour. Enjoy!"

I left them without regret, Mortar and Pestle speechless, and climbed the steps to Duncan's apartment overlooking Voss Bender Memorial Square, where we talked for quite some time, while below, through the open window, we witnessed the slow disintegration of the tour group.

The Ambergris Tourism Board—caught between their dead dog slogans and their sense of profit, between my protestations of being "confused" as to the message we were trying to convey and their certainty that I'd known exactly what I was doing—contemplated firing me, but couldn't quite summon the nerve.

Most days since, I've been glad they didn't.

5

SOMETIMES—ONLY SOMETIMES—I WONDER who I am writing this account for. Who will read this? Will they care? I am past the delusion that I'm writing an afterword for Duncan's *The Early History of Ambergris*, and I suspect that you, dear reader, if you've come this far, are past that delusion as well.

Sometimes, I think I'm writing out of anger and sadness, out of a sense of injustice—a sense that my life, that my brother's life, should have been easier, that we should have been more successful. At other times, I think I'm writing this account to preserve some part of me after I'm gone. Or that I am in some sense trying to write past those bodies in the cathedral, or my red ribbons for wrists, or Duncan's heartbreak.

There are certainly those who would prefer I not write this account—they'd prefer to have the same image of Janice they've always had, the same thoughts about Duncan. A more full-bodied likeness would ruin all of the stylization they've spent years accreting to both of us. {Who are these people, so intent on our ruin? Your oft-mentioned flesh necklace? Janice, no one *cares* enough to create an image of us—and they haven't for years.}

Then there are those who simply hate what Duncan represents, those who cannot accept the truth and thus must reject the messenger along with the message. It's common enough in life, isn't it? Mary is a prime example. She's still waiting there, at the party, but I honestly don't want to write about that yet. There are more important things to discuss first, and it's possible I won't have time to finish this account, but I'll soldier on because there's nothing left to do.

A gate. A mirror. A door.

Somewhere there's a door, surely?

ONE AFTERNOON, AFTER I HAD guided a family from Stockton on a tour centered around Trillian the Great Banker, Sirin appeared at the head of the stairs leading to the second floor. He beckoned to me with one long, graceful finger, and disappeared up the steps.

His office was the same as it had always been, down to the butterfly paradise residing in glass flasks at his back.

"I have a job for Duncan," he said, without preamble, smiling from behind his desk.

At the time, Duncan hadn't yet begun to "benefit" from the pittance Frankwrithe & Lewden would pay him for the infamous omnibus and still made his marginal living editing the AFTOIS newsletter for a Lacond whose health had begun to fail. So the money would come in handy. But I couldn't imagine that Sirin, whose current fortunes depended on the continued publication of the great Mary Sabon, would have anything of value for Duncan.

"What sort of job?" I asked, sitting down heavily. My stump was throbbing against the strap and wood of my artificial foot. If Sirin had been a kinder man, he would have met me on the first floor.

"A writing kind of job," he said, and smiled again. "The sort of writing job I think might appeal to Duncan, if presented to him in the right way."

I already didn't like the sound of it.

"What is it?"

"We have a pamphlet we need written. The original writer proved unreliable and it's scheduled for publication in less than three months."

"Unreliable how?"

"He was blown up by a stray fungal bomb."

"Oh."

"But," Sirin hastened to add, "it had nothing to do with his assignment. Wrong place, wrong time. Strictly."

"What's the title of the pamphlet?"

"*The Hoegbotton Guide to the Early History of Ambergris.* Do you think Duncan would do it?"

I didn't know how I felt about this proposition. Sirin had more or less abandoned us after the war. On the other hand, he had gotten us a job during it. He had helped Mary more than us of late, but no one could say his choice didn't reflect good business sense.

"A travel guide?" I said.

"Yes. A travel guide. Duncan will have to understand that up front. There will be no place for his outlandish theories in the piece, unless they add an element of entertainment. We don't want to upset the tourists—think of the effect it would have on your own business." Again, the smile, the upturning of the lips as his eyes acknowledged the debt I owed him for my position.

He named a compelling price for completion of the project.

"I'll try," I said. "Thanks for thinking of us."

I don't really know how I felt. My expectations of influence and power had decreased so rapidly and so monumentally that I believe at the time I felt Sirin was bestowing a great honor on Duncan. I believe I thought that Sirin was attempting to usher us back into the ranks of the Privileged, the Chosen. I was mistaken, but can anyone blame me for hoping?

At the door, I turned and asked, "Why didn't you give the assignment to Mary Sabon?" {And if not Sabon, surely a member of her flesh necklace would have welcomed the opportunity?}

"She's busy with other things," and then, catching himself, "but more importantly, she's not the right person for this. Your brother is somewhat unique in that regard."

❦

IT DID NOT TAKE MUCH convincing—by then Duncan had begun to chafe under the restrictions and limited audience of his AFTOIS soapbox. He welcomed the opportunity to do something different. {I welcomed the promise of money.}

"It'll be like old times," he said in this very room. "It will be like before the war."

His right eye writhed with gold-green fungi. His left index finger had formed a curled purple tendril, like a fern. His neck was encrusted with a golden patina that pulsed like the skin of a squid. His smell was indescribable. Yes, it would be like old times.

For two months, Duncan lugged thousands of pages of books, magazines, and old papers down here. For weeks, he labored on this very typewriter, creating his early history of the city. I believe he thought he might be creating a Machine of his own, made from the city's leavings. {The assignment came at the right time—it came as I was attempting to synthesize and explain all that I had learned over the years. It took two months, yes, but also thirty *years* to write that account. My findings might have been destined for a travel guide, but that didn't mean I had to make them shallow or incomplete.}

I left him to it, after a while. I stopped in every few days to see how it was going, but that was all—I had my own life to lead, and an ever-growing list of tourists to exhume the city's highlights for. . . .

When Duncan showed me pieces of his essay so that I could report to Sirin on his progress, he did so by reading selections of it to me aloud.

"The importance of squid to the Ambergrisian economy cannot be overstated," he would say.

"Not squid again," I would say, and he would make a hushing sound.

"Certainly the rebel Stretcher Jones learned to appreciate the freshwater squid, as it sustained his army for long periods of time when they were relegated to the salt marshes on the fringes of the Kalif's empire," he would intone.

I would catch Sybel's eye and he would fold his arms and shake his head, while I nodded in agreement. {How like you to conjure up a dead man to agree with you.}

"The type of cannonballs used by the Kalif during the Occupation proved useful in the creation of walls during the rebuilding efforts." {A very interesting fact that many a tourist would have found useful, if it had survived Sirin's sword.}

And on and on. It didn't sound much like a tourist guide, based on my experience guiding tourists around, but at least Duncan was making progress toward completion. I didn't think it productive to give him advice until he had finished it.

❧

BUT, AT THE END OF two months, Duncan bypassed me completely and sent his finished manuscript to Sirin via courier. It was six hundred pages long. Of those six hundred pages, two hundred and fifty pages consisted of long, convoluted footnotes, some of which had their own footnotes and additional annotations. I think he knew what I would have said had I read it first.

Sirin called me up to his office, where we could both contemplate the green-stained pages that lay in an awkward lump on his desk. Some of the pages looked like dried, veined lettuce leaves. Others had the consistency of moist glue. Still others had a dark phosphorescence to them. I could have sworn I could hear a low hum coming from the pile.

"What," he asked, "am I to make of this?"

"It does look a bit long," I said.

Sirin spluttered. "The length? Are you looking at the same pages I am? The length is not really the issue. I mean, certainly, the length is an issue, but not *the* issue. Have you read it?"

"Only the parts Duncan read aloud to me."

Sirin sat back in his chair, a look of disgust on his face.

"Everything I hate about AFTOIS is in this manuscript, and then some, Janice. Every old wives' tale, every fear, every paranoia. He even tries to tie your father's death into his web of gray cap conspiracy theories."

"Is it really that bad?"

"Janice, not only that, but he attributes any number of insane theories to James Lacond that sound beyond the pale even for that old rogue."

I didn't bother to tell him that this was intentional. Duncan had disclosed to me that Lacond's reputation had been so compromised by his obsessions that he found it useful to let others use his name as cover for those theories that might discredit them, while he wrote under his own pseudonyms. {"James Lacond" became a house name at the newsletter. It got out of control, but it felt good, too. A kind of self-destructive impulse embedded in it, a way of acknowledging our own irrelevance, but reveling in it. It embodied Lacond's self-deprecating manner. I merely played off of this in the *Early History*. Ultimately, Sirin ignored it and left it in, much to our delight.}

"You can't edit it into shape?" I said instead, already knowing the answer.

"No, I can't," Sirin said. "I can't save this." A pause, a calculating stare. "Why? Do you think you can?"

"Maybe," I said, knowing the real trick would be to get Duncan to agree to change even one comma of it. {How little you understood me, Janice.}

⁍⁌

I MET DUNCAN AT THE Spore again, in this room. As I approached the door, the flickering light within played a trick. I thought I saw his shadow, impossibly vast, curled around the edges, *snap* into a more human shape. A gurgle and whine that coalesced into a human voice.

"Janice," came a throaty greeting, then, "Janice," in my brother's true voice.

I hadn't entered the room yet. He couldn't have seen me. {Not with my own eyes.}

When I did enter, I found him pale and shrunken, folding and unfolding his arms.

"You've come from Sirin," he said. It was not a question.

"Yes."

"So you've seen . . . you've seen my early history?"

"Yes."

"And he has read it."

"Yes."

He looked up at me, his gaze suddenly desperate.

"Does he like it?"

"Does he like it?" I echoed. "No, Duncan—he loves it. He absolutely loves it. He asked for a travel guide version of an early history of Ambergris and you gave him a tome large enough to contain every Truffidian hymn ever sung—and half of it in footnote form. He absolutely despises it."

Duncan began to mutter to himself. It was a habit he'd developed in the years after the war. It did not endear him to many people.

"But I've finally gotten it right," he said. "I've finally documented all of it."

Sirin had let me read some of the manuscript in his office. It was riddled through with strange symbols, strange characters. It contained much that was personal to Duncan's life. It rambled. It made sense only in spurts. I felt, reading it, that several different people had collaborated to write it, only two or three of whom were sane or had consulted with the other writers. {I agree. It was a bad time. I could not control my shape. I could not get my bearings. Keeping myself cooped up in that room, working on the essay, I let other parts of me infiltrate the text with their opinions. From hour to hour, my body changed, making it hard to concentrate on my task. In the end, it all *seemed* right to me, but there were so many of *me* then.}

Duncan frowned and looked away {to hide a mushroom blossoming on my cheek}. "So he doesn't want it."

"Duncan," I said, "I'm not sure even AFTOIS will want it. It doesn't make all that much sense."

Duncan stood, pasted a smile onto his face, kept to the darkness.

"What about you, Janice?" he said. "You could edit it. You could give Sirin what he wants. At least some of what he wants. And I'll save the rest for something else."

This response shocked me. The old Duncan—or at least a Duncan who wasn't this vulnerable—would have taken his manuscript back from Sirin. But I remember making excuses for Duncan as I stood there. The times had passed us by. Duncan needed money to pay for his tiny apartment and his space at the Spore, so we had to take what we could get. But I never really understood why he didn't fight for himself more, why he gave in so easily. I'm not sure I ever will. {Because, Janice, I was *becoming* what I believed in. I was *becoming* it. And it might have been strange and unknown, never to be recognized, but it meant more to me than words on a page by then.}

"I can try," I said.

"Thanks! Thanks," he said, so pathetically grateful he even gave me a hug. "That'll work out fine then. Go tell Sirin," he said. "Go tell Sirin. Make Sirin happy." {I needed you to leave. I was getting ready to change again, and sometimes now when I changed, I would *assimilate* things around me.} So I went to tell Sirin.

⊷⊶

WHAT HAD TAKEN DUNCAN TWO months to write took me three days to edit. I simply discarded anything that didn't make sense and tried to keep anything that hinted of a chronological history. Duncan read over the result mournfully, added a few more footnotes, changed some of my line edits, and gave me his approval in such an offhand way that I was even madder at him for the ease with which he had given up.

Perhaps I should have been more empathetic, though. In his journal from the time, I find this entry:

> How will I die? Not that way, not me. For me it will be the slow decay, the failure of my senses, the graying of the world, the remaindering and misunderstanding of my books, followed by the very forgetting of my words, the pages wiped clean of all marks, and so too the wiping clean of me, my brain sinking into slow senility, utterly alone, no vestige of past family and friends left to me until, finally, when I am dust, I shall unleash a sigh of forgetfulness and leave not a trace of my existence in the world. . . . But until then, if the black bough taps against the windowpane, I shall ignore its brittle invitation—and in all ways and in all things I shall not dignify the name of that which will one day take me.

Rather vainglorious melancholy, and contradictory, too, but clearly indicative of the depression Duncan sometimes fell into during this period. {Janice, that whole quote is from one of the Kalif's genealogists, who wrote potboilers on the side! Context, Janice, context. Or is my handwriting so bad you couldn't read the attribution?}

⊷⊶

WHEN I BROUGHT THE REVISED essay to Sirin, he still didn't care for parts of it, but with his deadline approaching, he had little choice.

"Besides," he admitted, "a little eccentricity will probably seem quaint to the tourists."

Among those eccentricities, in that first edition, were entries in the appended glossary for both Duncan and for Sabon, alluding to what no longer existed:

SABON, MARY. An aggressive and sometimes brilliant historian who built her reputation on the bones of older, love-struck historians. Five-ten. One-fifteen. Red hair. Green, green eyes. An elegant dresser. Smile like fire. Foe of James Lacond. In conversation can cut with a single word. Author of several books whose titles I quite forget at the moment.

SHRIEK, DUNCAN. An old historian, born in Stockton, who in his youth published several famous history books, since remaindered and savaged by critics who should have known better. His father, also an historian, died of joy; or, rather, from a heart attack brought on by finding out he had won a major honor from the Court of the Kalif. I was ten. I never died from my honors, but I was banned by the Truffidian Antechamber. Also a renowned expert on the gray caps, although most reasonable citizens ignore even his least outlandish theories. Once lucky enough to meet the love of his life, but not lucky enough to keep her, or to keep her from pillaging his ideas and discrediting him. Still, he loves her, separated from her by the insurmountable gulf of empires, buzzards, a bad writer, a horrible vacation spot, and the successor to Aquelus/Irene.

. . . this last bit of cuteness a reference to the entries for the Saltwater Buzzard, Samantha, the Saphant Empire, Scatha, and Maximillian Sharp that lay between his entry and Sabon's. Even here, toward the end, he could not give up on Mary, no matter how much he should. And no matter how I begged him to delete it—to delete both of them. {I also left numerous clues to the fact that I was fronting Lacond's various misshapen theories, but I doubt the reading public caught them, butchered as they'd been by the editing process.}

❦

THE EARLY HISTORY HAD BEEN saved, but the effect was minimal. Serious journals do not review travel guides and tourists rarely remember who wrote them. More importantly, no new work was forthcoming from Sirin for Duncan or for me. And Duncan, for the first time, I think, clearly understood that there was no way back for him. He would continue to haunt the fringes of his former career, and I would be an apparition that appeared as a warning to travelers and passersby.

It was almost like a joke. Me, living on as a ghost. Do you know how ghosts manifest themselves in Ambergris? They haunt you as travel guides. They lead you to old buildings. They educate you on the history of the places they haunt.

Once I realized I was a ghost, I became much happier.

⁂

SOMETIMES, AS I MAY HAVE mentioned, I go outside at night, just for a break. Night is so different from day for me. I cannot keep the ghosts out as easily at night, and the cot I have had brought in here is somewhat uncomfortable. My leg grows cold from the fungus that enraptures it, but I don't mind the feel of it.

On a good day, I have been averaging several thousand words. It's true I return to certain paragraphs and pages and revise, but mostly it's ever forward. I can't hope to create something perfect, but perhaps I can create something that's *alive*—assuming I can finish it. Right now, I see no reason to imagine I will ever stop typing this afterword. The hours float by so quietly and without event that there seems nothing else worth doing. What would I want to do? And what will I do when I'm done?

But we *are* getting closer to the staircase, the party, the necklace, with each word. I can almost *sense* the ending, even if I can't see it yet. I'm so prolific I surprise myself—I keep filling up pages. I keep creating new sections, new chapters.

All the same, I'm tired. My prose, I've noticed, becomes by turns more plain, more linear, only to jump out into time as if in a desperate attempt to maintain momentum. Even if it doesn't feel like it, I cannot be far from the end, even if I end too abruptly. It may be that my fatigue will outweigh my momentum, that it will rush the ending and send you, dear reader, out of this riveting true-life account far sooner than necessary or proper. If this should occur, I refuse to apologize. This is an afterword or an afterwards—I can't remember anymore—and no one reads them. No one cares what they contain. By the time the afterword appears in a book, the story has already ended. Why, if I wanted to, I could write one hundred pages on obscure Truffidian rituals to offset my fear. It is not without precedence. It has happened before.

What's left to tell? Many years passed, in much the same way as they had passed before. Sabon's star continued to ascend. I was forgotten, although I continued on as a tour guide and cantankerous member of the Ambergris Tourism Board. On rare occasions, they called upon me to make short speeches at the rededication of certain historical buildings, or to make appearances as one of several fossils at various dinners mummifying the War of the Houses.

Duncan was forgotten, except for Sabon's continued cruel resurrections. Bonmot died—in the long view of things, one moment he was there and the next he was not—much to my ever-growing sadness. I would sit at the old stone bench with my sandwich at lunchtime and try to conjure up the image of those wonderful conversations, that gravel voice, but it was never the same. Memory may be all we have, but it's a poor substitute for flesh and blood.

And still, even as he seemed to make little progress regarding his theories, Duncan was changing, becoming other, the process always ongoing. He never recovered fully from Sabon {or AFTOIS, for that matter}, rarely expressed interest in other women, never took enough of a break from his work to notice them, really. Sometimes, Duncan later confessed to me, he would still haunt Sabon from the shadows outside her current house, or her current lover's house. {I went a little crazy at times. Late in the game, I set traps for Mary in the AFTOIS newsletter, using Lacond's name for crazy theories that I thought she would be forced to refute, wasting her energy and, at the same time, unknowingly engaging me in a kind of dialogue. It never happened, to my knowledge.} Between his obsession and my tour guide job, we were a veritable team of stalkers, me during the day, him at night. {The only thing that comforted me: she never married. Surely that meant something?}

Somewhere along the way—I don't know exactly when—we grew old, Duncan and I. Old and yet defiant; if not wise, then wizened, at least. Exactly as we had always been, only more so. *No one makes it out.*

Even as we stayed the same, the city changed again and again, as it always would, its grime-smeared head, its soiled towers, its debauched calls to prayer the same, and yet always it changed. I grew to love and appreciate it more than I ever had before. It was all I knew, and I knew it almost too well by now. {Yet neither of us ever found out if it loved us back.}

Then, some four or five years ago, the Shift began to affect Ambergris, disrupting the flux and flow of the city. All became unpredictable, save for one constant: as once it had become colder, now the city seethed with heat, even in the winter and spring. With this heat has come the rain, sliding down in oily sheets, or mumbling to itself in little gusts and flurries, or dissipating into a fine gray mist.

In a *Broadsheet* article Duncan cut out and stuck into his journal, the strangeness of the rain is remarked upon in detail:

> This rain behaves oddly sometimes. It forms funnels in the sky. It falls one way on the left side of Albumuth Boulevard and at a different angle on the right side of Albumuth Boulevard. It delivers a puzzling bounty: fish and tiny squid and crabs that are not native here. They lie struggling in piles of seaweed as alien to the city as we are to them while crowds form around them, or do not; many among us try to ignore such happenings.
>
> Over the River Moth, the rain behaves as if with a conscious will, for there it will sometimes form columns on two sides with no rain between, and the air there, as one eyewitness put it, "turns to darkness with a weight and smell unlike the rest of the sky." {A door, Janice.}
>
> With the rain has come, again, as in the old days, a proliferation of fungus, so that the business of mushroom culling and cleaning is once again very profitable. And yet the gray caps have become absent even during the deep night.
>
> That no one knows what these signs mean may be more troublesome than the signs themselves.

Even House Hoegbotton, in the past three years, has looked askance at the weather, seemed oddly humbled by an enemy it can neither predict nor defeat.

With the heat and rain have come the agents of House Frankwrithe & Lewden once again, infiltrating Ambergris, although this time with no discernible gray cap support. And yet, with murder on the rise and rumors of war constant now, our nerves have once again become as frayed as they were on the eve of conflict so many years ago.

None of this has helped the tourist trade. The number of people attending my increasingly rote tours has dropped off. Incidents such as having to walk around a three-foot crimson mushroom suddenly erupting from the pavement near their feet, or ducking a torrent of tiny silver fish delivered by a thunderstorm, has positive novelty value to only a select few.

I know that even these simple statements of fact about the Shift will outrage some readers, most of them Nativists. To them, there has been no Shift. To them, the continued "strange-ification of the city," as Duncan once put it, has no pattern to it, no rhythm or cause. Some still deny anything odd is happening at all, pitiable fools. I suppose, in our usual way, even those amongst us who admit to the Shift have begun to become accustomed to it. {We shouldn't become accustomed to anything anymore. We are beginning to live in our own future, and it *should* feel strange.}

Perhaps this will make it more personal, more real: at the beginning of the symptoms of the Shift, James Lacond fell ill. When I say he fell ill, I mean that his fungal disease finally overwhelmed him, as it had sometimes threatened to overwhelm Duncan. {Alas, he hadn't traveled far enough underground, or for long enough. Which is worse than going too far. I told him more than once that he needed to experience more, to know more, inside his body, to survive it. He refused the advice.} He was forced to retire to a back room in his own offices while Duncan ran everything in his name, instead of just part of it. After a while, he couldn't hold on any longer and almost literally faded away.

{No one knew how ill he was until after he passed away. Janice, you should have visited him toward the end. I was there every day, hunched over a chair beside his fungus-riddled bed, trying to pry an intelligible word from between the rotted teeth of the poor feeble wreck, to no avail. "Hmmmm bwatchee thoroughgard stinmarta," he would say to me with the perfect clarity of those beyond hope. I would nod wisely and continue to work on my own diatribes against Nativism and all the other dangerously deluded theories.

{He smelled of the rum I gave him to soothe his agony. He smelled musty, like rooms not opened to the air since the Silence. It's true I loved him dearly and I helped him as best I could, but you could never say he was a substitute for Bonmot—that would be unfair to both of them. More correctly, when I looked at him, I saw a mirror of my own future self: gray-bearded, addlepated, a half-century's study of history dribbling out of my brain through a mum-mumbling mouth. I cannot say it comforted me much, and yet how much more tenderly I cared for him because of it!

{There might have been no coherence to his speech, but Lacond could still write at times. Once, he drew me close and showed me some words scribbled on a scrap of paper: "I am concerned that disintegration and ensuing death will blunt my ability to continue to coherently put forth my usual arguments with the customary vigor." It made me laugh, and that made Lacond smile, as much as he was able. I nodded, to let him know I understood. When he did pass away and I assumed the editorship of the AFTOIS newsletter, it seemed natural to continue, to dig up an almost endless series of "newly discovered" papers by the old rogue, as if he still mumbled nothing-nothing-nothing in my ear.

{Early one morning, I entered Lacond's room to find a fine misting of glistening black spores clinging to the white sheets, and no sign of a body. The sheets smelled vaguely of lime. I knew what had happened. It had taken so long to happen that I didn't feel grief in that moment. I just felt a sense of purpose.

{I rolled up the sheets and walked with them down to the River Moth. As I walked, I scooped up black spores in my hand and let them fall. On Albumuth Boulevard. On the cobblestones of the Religious Quarter. Smeared them along the walls in the abandoned Bureaucratic Quarter. Abraded the bricks of H&S headquarters with them. Dropped them on bushes and on park benches.

{When I got to the river, I tossed the sheets into the water and watched them drift and unwind, the last spores, drunk with moisture, disappearing from sight.

{Of course, I saved a vial of the spores to spread underground. No part of Ambergris was going to get rid of James as easily in death as in life.}

✦

SOMEWHERE, SOMEWHEN, IN THE LAST year, my {our!} mother also died, out in her mansion by the river. Her neighbors found her sitting in a chair, staring out at the water. She looked happy, they said, but no one likes dying, so I don't see how that could be true. She looked as if she understood everything, they said. Or, at least, understood more than I ever did, despite my restless searching.

The strange thing is, the night before she died, the telephone rang at about three in the morning. When I answered it, there was no voice on the other end. Maybe it was a wrong number. Maybe she had decided there was nothing left to say. Maybe she just wanted to hear my voice before the end. I don't know.

This was in the spring. The trees all around her home were in bloom—white-and-pink blossoms that drooped heavily from the branches. The lawns strewn with petals. It didn't seem like the time for a funeral. The scent of the flowers drove out the scent of death.

Duncan and I accompanied the casket back to Stockton, over the River Moth by barge, and then by mule-drawn carriage. We buried her next to our father in the old communal cemetery next to the library where our father had spent so much of his time. There weren't many people there for the ceremony: a few relatives, the Truffidian priest, an old friend of Dad's—an ancient fossil of a man, stooped, bent, and a little confused {throughout the ceremony, the clasps of his suspenders hung over his shoulders, where he had flung them up while using the gents' room}—and a couple of young people whose parents had known Mom. Standing there, surrounded by tombstones and bright green grass, it didn't quite seem real. It didn't seem true.

We didn't stay in Stockton long—we had no connection to it any longer. It seemed like a foreign place, somewhere we'd never visited before. {Ambergris will do that to you—it becomes so central to your life that any other place is a faint echo, a pale reflection, a cliché in search of originality.}

When we arrived back at her mansion, we realized how much of a storehouse it had become—she had so filled it up with things, made by her, bought by her, and placed by her, that it almost didn't seem as if she had left. {And yet, as it turned out, most of it had been stored on behalf of other people, the house emptying with each new relative who stumbled inside.}

"She was always so distant," Duncan said, as we stood in the hallway looking at all of the portraits and photographs of family members she had collected over the years. We had an entire constellation of relatives we could seek out—some we'd met at the funeral—but, really, why bother now? It was too late. We'd been taken to a foreign place, and since then all the old bonds had snapped like rotted rope. The people we'd met in Stockton were just polite faces now, and I only resented that a little bit. Part of me was relieved to excuse myself from all the work it would have taken to hold on to those relationships. Better that they remain photographs, vague smiles and handshakes and fondly remembered hugs from childhood. We had been cast adrift by father's death, and we had taken to it, in our way.

"She was always so distant," Duncan said again. It took me a while to hear him, in that empty and cavernous place, surrounded by the images of so many dead people. There were as many tombstones framed on the mantel in that place as puncturing the earth in the Stockton graveyard.

When I did hear him, I turned toward him with a look of irritation on my face.

"*She* wasn't distant. *We* were distant. We were odd and surly and *distant*. We crawled through tunnels and we didn't talk much and we were always alone in our own thoughts. Not much of a family, if you think about it. We never knew how to be there for anyone else. So *how do we know?*" I said, and by now I'd raised my voice. What did it matter in that place? It would just echo on forever, the sound captured in the swirls of the staircase, floating down into the flooded basement. "How do we know it wasn't *us?*"

Duncan's face scrunched up and turned red, and I could tell he was fighting off tears. It was difficult to know, though, because most of the time he couldn't produce tears anymore—or if he did, they were purple tears, semi-solid, that hurt as they slid out of his tear ducts. It's a measure of how accustomed I'd grown to Duncan that this didn't seem odd to me.

"I hardly ever visited her," he said. {I meant I hardly ever saw her. I did visit her, but I never saw her. I tunneled up through a dry corner of the basement and left her gifts from the underground—things I thought she might appreciate. I'm sure she knew they came from me.}

"She didn't mind. She was a solitary person. That was her choice."

Before Dad Died, she had been as sunny and well-adjusted as the rest of us. {We were never well-adjusted, Janice.} But that death had killed us all as surely as it had killed our father. How could we deny that?

Surrounded by the awful weight of Mom's things—the rugs, the paintings, the sculptures, the books, the bric-a-brac of collecting gone wrong—it seemed all too apparent. While the river, oblivious, gurgled and chuckled to itself outside the window. {Everyone always tells you that you become more alone as you get older. People write about it in books. They shout it out on street corners. They mumble it in their sleep. But it's always a shock when it happens to you.}

⋙⋘

WE COULDN'T KEEP THE HOUSE. {How could we keep the house? We made all the inquiries, but it was impossible—Mom had been too much in debt, her money so ancient it didn't really exist except as run-down property.} And we couldn't keep much *from* the house {because it wasn't ours!}. But I couldn't bear to lose the hallway of portraits and photographs. Somehow, to lose the only tenuous connection between ourselves and those people we should have known felt as wrong as seeking them out, trying to enter into a relationship with strangers. {Those polite protestations of "we should make plans to get together," which no one really ever believes, as we stood there by the gravesite in Stockton. Why did I make that effort for strangers and not for my own mother? I truly don't know. Unless I had truly believed that she would outlive me. Or that she had died a long time ago.}

"I'm not coming back," Duncan said as I closed the door behind us and we walked out into the glorious hot spring day, the sun lithe and yellow above us, the River Moth smooth and light and glistening beyond the mansion.

In the sun, he had a diaphanous look to him. He seemed like an avant-garde sculpture, a person from a myth or fairy tale. The light slid through his face. In the sudden glow, I could see the white hairs at his temples, the gray-and-white of his beard, the lines that had sculpted his mouth, his forehead, the way his eyes had sunk a little into the orbits. He was old. We were old. Prematurely.

"Not coming back?" I said. "Back here?"

"I'm not coming back," he repeated, but he wouldn't meet my gaze.

And he didn't. He didn't come back. I saw him only one more time.

❧

THE OWNER OF THE SPORE came in here again, muttering about unpaid bills. I gave him a smile and tried to fend him off with a couple of coins I'd hidden in a sock. Apparently, he has realized that he has begun to let me have this room for free. I wonder if he would understand if I told him I am standing vigil for Duncan. There is an old Truffidian ritual where you wait for a dead loved one out of respect. For three days, you wait as if for a resurrection, but what you are really waiting for is your own grief to subside, just a little. But the fact is, Duncan might crawl out of that hole in the ground behind me at any moment. {True enough. But you shouldn't have waited for me.}

The owner liked Duncan, but if Duncan came crawling out of the underground, the owner and his friends might have set upon him with clubs. I will have to leave soon, one way or another, so it strikes me that now might be a good time to tell you about the last time I saw Duncan. The very last time, three weeks before Martin Lake's party. Surprise, surprise—this is the last time Mary saw Duncan as well, although she didn't mention it to her flesh necklace while vilifying my brother at the party. I guess she didn't think it important. Perhaps her fear had become too great by then.

The reason Mary saw Duncan at all was because Duncan, throughout everything that had happened, had never given up on her. He was still trying, right up to the end—although the end of what, I don't know, and may never know. {I hardly know myself, Janice—I don't even know where you are now. I finally "creep out of that hole" as you put it so eloquently, and you're nowhere to be found—just this profane, infuriating, opinionated account.}

❧

DUSK OF A SPRING DAY, and I sat at my desk in the Hoegbotton & Sons building on Albumuth Boulevard. The weather had been strange as usual. The sun shone hazy through a layer of fog: a faint shedding of light through glass doors festooned with flyers and broadsheets proclaiming the restorative virtues of various Ambergrisian tours.

I had put a lamp or two near my desk, and since the weather had scared off my fellow tour guides and, apparently, any potential customers, I was spending my time paying off my bills and writing letters of circuitous regret to the artists who blamed me for losing their artwork during the war. Yes, I still owed money to a lot of people. I don't believe most of them are going to get anything, though—I've given all my money to the owner of the Spore.

I was in the middle of calculating how much I could give to Roger Mandible and also pay my rent, when *it* dropped from the ceiling, onto my desk. I suppressed a scream, internalizing it as a long, violent shudder, but backed away from the desk, holding my pen like a knife.

Anticlimax. It took me a second to identify what had dropped onto my desk, because the desk was so cluttered. The only unfamiliar object proved to be a pair of peculiar glasses, right side up atop a program from an old Voss Bender play. A red triangle of fabric had been knotted around one arm of the glasses. I circled the glasses slowly, looked up at the ceiling once or twice, my impromptu weapon still raised above my head. Still nothing there. Anyone observing from the street would have thought me crazy.

My heartbeat began to slow. I lowered my pen, set it down on the desk, and sat down, chuckling at my own fear. Glasses. Stuck to the ceiling? Falling onto my desk? I still could not grasp the chain of events. Had a colleague or tourist stuck them to the ceiling months ago and they had finally succumbed to gravity? At least I seemed to be in no danger. It would make a semi-interesting story to tell my fellow tour guides in the morning.

I picked up the glasses. The metal was warm to the touch, almost sinewy, but eyelash thin. A strangely golden, pinkish hue suffused the frames, the texture both rough and smooth. The lenses shared the thinness of the frames, but of a different order: thin as a dragonfly wing. The lenses too were hot, and my questing finger recoiled when the minute translucent scales that comprised them almost seemed to move under my touch, though it must have been the texture of finger and lens combined that produced the sensation.

I laughed when a hum rose from the glasses. I had the sense of a practical joke, of a whimsy that was almost within my comprehension, not of any danger. A vibration mixed with a sound, I thought, but I could not at first tell if this was simply the shaking of my own hand, a ringing in my ears.

I tapped the glasses against my desk. A sound tinny and fine, like the sound of a tuning fork, emanated from them. Out of the same sense of curiosity that pulls the wings from flies, I first tried to bend the glasses, and when that failed, break them against the side of the desk. Fully engaged in a series of experiments now, perhaps glad to turn my fear into aggression, I took a pen knife from the drawer and tried to scratch the lenses. I could not.

Then I set the glasses down, more confused than before. What should I do with them?, I wondered. Outside, the fog had deepened, come hard off the River Moth. No one had entered the office during my explorations. No one would. The fading sun had shrunk to a feeble white point outshone for brilliance by the luminescence of the fog.

I took a closer look at the red swatch of fabric. It did not look as if it belonged with the glasses. It did not have the same elegance or precision. With a slightly trembling hand, I unknotted it from the glasses. Now it looked familiar. The shade of red, the triangular shape. Where had I seen it before? I remembered a moment before I saw words written on the fabric in a familiar hand:

Put on the glasses. Follow the red path.
Do not be afraid.
Remember BDD.

Duncan. The red swatch was a piece of a gray cap flag, most commonly seen atop a wooden stake driven into the ground near any gray caps that had not returned underground during the daylight. Suddenly the flag and the glasses seemed very connected indeed. My mouth was dry, my heartbeat rapid again.

Put on the glasses? The thought had never occurred to me. I held the glasses up to the lamplight and looked through them, but did not put them on. Up close, they smelled like lavender and brine. Although the "scales" of the lenses distorted my view of the fogged-in window, I suffered no change of perspective, no clarity or fuzziness. These were not prescription lenses.

The scrap of red cloth on my desk stood out from all the mundane, colorless bits of minutiae that had begun to take over my life—the bills, the relentless letters from angry artists, the descriptions of various tours of the city, all the awkward geography of my daily life. And in the middle of it all, a scrap of color, a scrap of blood, a scrap of message.

What harm, after all, could there be in putting on a pair of glasses?

I stared out at the fog-shrouded sky. I walked to the door. I opened the door and walked outside. The fog clung to my skin. The faint tinkle and chime of distant conversation. The melodious roar of a motored vehicle. The smell of flames. The taste of metal. Could these glasses allow me to see through the fog? Could they undo the mist? I still held them in my left hand, away from my body, as if they might explode and shower me with shards.

Before Dad Died.

I hadn't seen or heard from Duncan in months.

I put on the glasses. They fit snugly against my nose, the arms sliding neatly over my ears; again they pulsed, as though alive.

For a long moment nothing happened, and in that moment I grinned. My poor brother had me staring through distorted dragonfly lenses into a world of mist. What was new?

But then the frames tensed, tightened around my ears. For a moment I experienced an intense heat, but so briefly that I did not have time to make a sound.

Then the glasses began to fill up with blackness. The blackness oozed from the top of the frames and, with a methodical precision, filled first one distorted scale and then the next. Slowly, as I stood there fascinated and horrified all at once, the liquid occluded my vision, replacing it with its own reality.

When the blackness was complete, the fog no longer existed, swept away, banished, along with all things unclear, diffuse. . . .

My world now consisted of two . . . levels? Layers? The world I knew had become subservient to a second world. It is not so much that the world I knew disappeared, but that it, still sharply in focus, became the translucent background to a new world. I could distinctly see the street, the stores opposite my office, the street lamp on the corner, the two women standing under the street lamp, the pigeon asleep atop the lamppost, the facade of store fronts that extended down the street—every solid brick or stone of it.

What stood revealed, however, made my reality seem very poor indeed. How to explain it? I was never a very good painter—how now to paint with words a picture that few if any have ever seen? {Start with color. Start with symbols. Start with texture. Start with hue. Start anywhere, but start!}

Example: across the street, the printer's store front . . . it was "painted over" with a living swath of minute, glowing red fungus. In amongst this fungus moved slow accumulations of emerald light, harvesting it. How can I describe it when I couldn't even paint it for you? The vision defeats the pen. It would take a better writer than I to begin to describe the least of it.

Every building—*every surface*—had symbols and words written upon its sides: glowing and bold, in phosphorescent greens, yellows, reds, purples, blues.

Arrows and road signs in a foreign language. The etched equivalent of clicks and whistles. Like the difference between the city before and during the Festival of the Freshwater Squid—when the lights festoon every balcony, every flourish of filigree. Now I was looking at the city as the gray caps saw it, I began to realize. Conveniently portioned out and mapped and described for their benefit. This was their city, still—this overlay the skin of their control. It was like a dream and a nightmare all at once. On the edges of my vision, I could see things moving in ways that seemed unnatural. In the air, a million spores leapt together, suffusing the sky in a vermilion orgy of renewal, the sky itself more dusk than dawn, the stars pale ghosts, larger and more opalescent than in our world. "Scents" hung in the air, in clouds and yet not-clouds, ripples and veins of texture that were not ripples or veins of texture.

BDD. BDD. I repeated the acronym over and over to myself. I tried to be calm. What had Duncan written? *Follow the red.* I should follow the red, and trust in Duncan.

Follow the red. There, before me, appeared a red path composed of tiny writhing tendrils. If I took off the glasses—could I take off the glasses?—I knew I wouldn't see the path, wouldn't see the fungus. Did I want to try to rip off the glasses and leave Duncan to his own devices? For a moment I hesitated, and then I followed the red path through the transformed city.

My self dissolved into . . . something else. How do I describe? How do I begin? Where do I begin? {Oh for Truff's sake, Janice! Start at the beginning. Proceed to the middle. Finish with the end. Muddle through.} The city darkened to black, with people like quicksilver flashes against that background, each composed of a thousand brushstrokes of individual whorls of activity. The red path erasing itself behind me, urging me on by erasing itself more quickly if I slowed.

Perhaps I should start with color. Perhaps I should try to paint it for you. The way an artist layers paints, these glasses layered information. Or, as an artist layers paints to reveal, to accentuate, some facet, some theme, some previously unknown truth, so these glasses revealed a different city, a city which the gray caps had returned to, recolonized, without our knowledge. {Never left, Janice, dear sister. They never left. The glasses didn't reveal what was hidden. They merely showed what had always been there throughout the centuries.}

Everything had become a negative of itself so that the fog snuck in like coal smoke and the dark, hard brick of buildings became as light, as insubstantially white, as glass. Burned into this real world, the world by which we are assured of our own foundations, our own existence—by which I mean our bedrock; assuming, of course, that the world interpreted by our senses has any objective reality—burned into it, I tell you, were all the signs and symbols of the gray caps.

Superimposed. A nice word, but not the one I'm searching for, because this might imply some ethereal, unreal attribute for something that was all too unbearably real.

What I am trying to say is that the real world, the world I had known for over fifty years, no longer held true when confronted by this other world that existed on top of it and yet also within it.

But what, really, did I see as I walked that red carpet toward the Spore of the Gray Cap? I saw a phosphorescent cloud of green spores dancing in the midst of the fog, the glistening, swooping fullness of them almost that of a single, sentient entity. I saw a wall of brick covered—clotted?—with insect-harsh letters and symbols, in a welter of colors so diverse it destroyed the imagination. I saw long, centipedal creatures rippling and undulating, blending into the translucence of the brick. I saw stretching out before me, threading its way through a street littered with clumps of glowing yellow, blue, green spores, a continuing trail of red splotches, etched into the street as if by a painter.

As if in a dream, I followed the path. I had no choice.

The trick was not to flinch at the suddenly mobile, unlikely things that might sputter and lunge into the corner of your vision. The trick was to imagine it was all a dream, to lie to yourself as much as possible. Sometimes I felt as if the skin of the city had been torn away to reveal another place—a parallel world that shared only a few points of similarity with ours.

{Ah, well, perhaps no one could have done it justice, or injustice. How to describe something not so much seen as observed through some sixth sense, some place between eye and brain that should not exist. Some who see it for the first time go mad. A monk living in the fortress at Zamilon saw it and jumped from the fortress walls. It didn't drive Tonsure mad only because so many other revelations overwhelmed his senses. You did well, sister. Very well. Better than Mary.}

⋯

DUNCAN WAITED FOR ME IN this very room. He sat on a chair near the hole in the ground, table in front of him. He couldn't be seen from the doorway. I sat down in the chair opposite him. With the glasses on, the entirety of the room shone in shades of violet and gold; things floated in the air, things like clear jellyfish.

With the glasses on, Duncan's body was transformed. Fungus moved across the outlines of his bones, reshaping him, slowly, patiently. Or was it fungus? I caught a glimpse of brown-gold cilia, of protrusions eerily reminiscent of a giant starfish. He smelled of stagnant wine left out overnight. He smelled of sewers scoured clean with an essence of honeysuckle and sandalwood, with the sewer smell still lingering in the background. Rotting flesh. Cinnamon. Blended into a smell, a vibration, never intended for a human nose.

❦

"CAN I TAKE THE GLASSES off now?" I asked Duncan. I didn't like seeing him this way.

"Don't you wonder?" he said, his voice throaty, harsh. "Don't you wonder what you're looking at? I would if I were you."

Something about the way he held his head—his head an oval of incandescent light, his neck a slab of mottled darkness—made me think he was drunk.

"Are you all right?" I asked him. Something told me to run away from him, to get away, to wrench the glasses from my head. {Those were good instincts.}

"I said—don't you wonder?" he replied, and smashed his fist down against the table. Orange spores rippled from his fist and across the whorled grain of the table. For an instant, it looked as though the table had burst into flames. Then it dissipated and the orange evaporated into nothing.

"Yes—I wonder. I wonder about the way you look. I wonder why you chose this way to bring me here. But I asked—are you all right?"

A rough laugh. "Have I ever been *all right*? In your experience."

"Yes. I've even seen you laugh on occasion."

Duncan held out one hand and I could see that it was engulfed by the pointed translucent pseudopod of some creature.

"Remember your letter?"

"Which one?" I asked. There had been so many letters. Letters litter the floor of this place even now.

"Golden strands of connections. No one is alone. Everything is joined. When someone dies, there is a keening across the lines. Something of that nature."

He was definitely drunk, or not himself. {Oh, I was myself—the self I'd been suppressing for years.}

"I remember," I said. "What does it have to do with this, now?"

Duncan laughed. "Everything! Because you were more right than you knew. What you are looking at, my dear sister, is the starfish I showed you so many years ago. It never died—it just shed its skeleton and its corporeal presence: Skeletonless and invisible, it has expanded to encompass my body. It feeds off of my disease."

I didn't know what to say, so I said nothing.

"In the gray caps' world nothing ever really dies—it just *transforms*. To other flesh. Other spirit. Other vessels. Look at it from their perspective and it's quite beautiful. It flenses me of disease, but at a cost. It brings me closer and closer to the world you see through those glasses."

You'll doubt me now, dear reader, even if you didn't already, even though this is all true. I doubt myself. I doubt the evidence of my eyes. Doubt was a great friend to my father. To Jonathan Shriek, it was the Great Ally. "Doubt," he would say, raising a finger, "is what will see you through. It is a great truth." Dad doubted every word he'd ever written. He told me so once, in the living room, at the end of a long, exhausting day. Every word. I thought he was joking, but now I can see that he wasn't.

So you can choose to disbelieve if you wish—whatever part you want to disbelieve. But don't disbelieve my intent: to set the record straight, to explain Duncan to you, to explain myself.

"Take off the glasses," Duncan said.

"I'm not sure I want to now," I replied. I had begun to understand that there could be worse things in the real world than what I saw through the glasses. Even as the invisible starfish made its slow orbit of Duncan's body, feeding off of his disease, cilia rotating madly.

I took off the glasses. It was no surprise to me when they scurried to the middle of the table and crouched there, waiting. Waiting for what? Me to put them on again?

Without the glasses, Duncan came into focus as . . . assimilated, made over in the image of some gray cap's imagination. A camouflage that seeped into the flesh so that it became entity, identity. He was slow and fast in that attire, that disguise, that incarnation. Swift and slow. He formed runnels of himself, the "particulate matter" of his left arm shining and purple, studded with the hoods of thousands of tiny mushrooms. The arm extended like a trickle, a slender stream, ending in a formless puddle of flesh. The strands of his other arm coalesced, recombined, came undone, came back together again.

Of his body, the less said, the better. {It was definitely not my best day.} There was nothing left to him that was Duncan, except for his eyes and a wry smile like liquid gold with a vein of granite running through it.

"What happens when it begins to infiltrate my brain?" Duncan said, though I'd said nothing. "I don't know. Maybe I'm no longer Duncan. Maybe I begin to know all there is to know about the gray caps."

But by now I was not afraid. I really wasn't, I was surprised to find. He didn't scare me. He was my brother, no matter what. I'd become accustomed. I realized now that even from the first time he'd stumbled into my apartment, covered in mushrooms, I had known it would come to this one day. {You weren't scared? Maybe because it wasn't happening to you. Me, I was fascinated and terrified at the same time.}

I reached out toward the shimmering, simmering writhing of his arm and touched him lightly.

"Tell me what happened," I said.

"We were both drunk," he said.

"Who?"

"Mary and me." He choked out the words.

"Where?"

"At a gallery opening. This afternoon. I happened to be there and she happened to be there. We had both had some wine before we met, and I guess that's why she didn't ignore me. She seemed in a good mood. She'd just finished a new book. She wanted to talk about it. I didn't mind. There was something about both of us, and the day, that allowed it. Everything from before had become ancient history."

I didn't believe him. That they had met by accident? That they had happened to attend the same gallery opening? Unlikely, knowing my Duncan. But I let it pass. {It's true. You're right. I planned it, down to the last detail. One last chance. I wanted to show her everything—all of it, from root to root, cavern to cavern.}

"Did you . . . did you look like you look now?" I asked him.

Duncan scowled. "No. I had control. I was keeping it all in. She didn't see any of this. I'm sure I looked a little fatter than when she'd last seen me, from everything I was keeping bottled up inside. But that's all."

"What happened?"

Duncan looked over at me, his frown enough to tell me before he said anything.

"We went outside. I began to talk about my theories. I had the eyeglasses in my pocket. Like I said, we were both a little drunk. We'd shared some pleasant memories from the Academy. I'd made her laugh. Now I think she was taking pity on me. At the time, I thought I saw in her face, her movements, a willingness to be friends again. And I couldn't help myself. I just couldn't. I pulled out the glasses. I told her to put them on. She giggled and said, 'What's this?' and then she put them on. She looked so beautiful then. I could not bear it. I think at first she thought it was a kaleidoscope, or some sort of party trick. At first, she laughed in delight. She let me take her by the hand and walk down the street. But somehow . . ."

"What?" I asked.

"Somehow, she guessed what she was looking at—she saw something that frightened her, something that made her so frightened that she got mad. She flung the glasses into the street. She began to curse me. I think she would have hit me if I hadn't backed away. I followed her for a while, to make sure she got back to the gallery safely. And that was it. I left her and came here. Then I sent my glasses to find you."

"That was it," I echoed.

After a pause, I said, "What did you think would happen?" Duncan shrugged. "I don't know. I guess I thought she would finally see, that if she could see as I saw, then I could make everything all right."

Instead, in her fear and his distress, he had finally realized that he would always be alone, that he would never have the luxury of a normal life.

He winced at the look on my face.

"Janice! I didn't think it would make everything like it was before, but I thought it would make her see that I'm not a crackpot, not a liar, not crazy. At least that . . . I spent a long time making those glasses for her, so she could experience it." {Ten years. It took ten years of research to make them. But no one wanted to see through them when I was done, except you, Janice, and you already believed me.}

"Did you really think that it could end well?" I asked.

The look of grief he gave me made it hard to judge him.

"Do you know how long I've protected her, looked out for her?"

I began to wonder whether Duncan's madness lay more in his inability to put Mary behind him than any of his more outlandish obsessions. {I had to try. I had to make the effort. Even if I knew how useless it was from the moment I entered the gallery.}

"Anyway," he said, "it's over now. I don't think I'm long for Ambergris, at least not aboveground."

"Going on another trip?" I asked.

"Not a trip. I wouldn't be the first. There are others down there. In the dark, rejecting the false light, as Bonmot liked to say. It's a choice. We all have a choice. So I think I'll travel there again."

"For good?" A panic threatened to overcome me, a panic that at first had no source.

"Probably. There isn't much left aboveground for me."

Which is when I realized, dear reader, that there wasn't much left aboveground for me, either. What would it mean to be a tour guide for the rest of my days, fated to point out landmarks that would always be personal for me, signs of success and failure? What kind of life would that be? Would I wind up like my mother? Perhaps I would try to kill myself again at some point, when the loneliness of it got too bad. Or perhaps I would let it happen to me, go through the same routines day after day, allow myself to fall into repetitions that masked the truth. And some days wonder, *Did Duncan make it? Did he find some kind of final truth? Did he find some kind of final happiness? Could it have worked for me?*

It might seem more like surrender to you, but right now it feels like defiance.

"You should join me," Duncan said. "They've moved the Machine. I have to find it before they bring it aboveground. Because when they do that, they'll be coming with it." He gave a little laugh, almost a yelp, as if something had stung him. "So it really doesn't matter where we are—above or below. It really doesn't."

"Coming aboveground?"

"The Machine is a door, Janice. But the flaw in it wasn't about the door itself. It was the location. They have to bring it aboveground. They have to reclaim the city. To use the door, to get back to wherever they came from. I've studied it. I've gotten close to it. It could take me to a new place."

As he had written in his journal:

Ghosts of images cloud the surface of the machine and are wiped clean as if by a careless, a meticulous, an impatient painter. A great windswept desert, sluggish with the weight of its own dunes. An ocean, waveless, the tension of its surface broken only by the shadow of clouds above, the water such a perfect blue-green that it hurts your eyes. A mountain range at sunset, distant, ruined towers propped up by the foothills at its flanks. Always flickering into perfection and back into oblivion. Places that if they exist in this world you have never seen them or heard mention of their existence. Ever.

"It's great detective work on my part, Janice," he said. "I just had to wait long enough and be patient. I just had to let the fungus eat me alive. The door is opening. The gray caps are almost ready. There will be a green light in the sky and between the towers another world will arise. Something Tonsure wrote in his journal put me onto the trail, of course—something about the fortress of Zamilon. So why not go to meet it? Why wait? No matter where it leads me."

It was at this point, even with all that I had seen, all that I knew, that I thought for a moment that my brother *was* crazy, that Mary was right, that everything he had ever told me was a lie; that he was more insane than Lacond had ever been; that Mary had been fleeing, as she'd written to her friend, a madman; that I had been living a life fueled by reports delivered from the insane asylum of Duncan Shriek's brain. It has certainly occurred to me that the readers of this account may have reached that conclusion many, many pages ago.

"Are you sure?" I asked. "Are you *sure*?"

Duncan had been steeped in decades of alternative history, discussing his theories with the dead by way of their books, and with the living, yes, but an assortment of crackpots and eccentrics such as to make the Cult of the Lord's Botches look positively mundane. He had developed a skin as tough as oliphaunt hide. {Yet it occurs to me now that I've never really wanted to be a historian, let alone a journalist. I've always wanted to create history, even if no one ever realizes what part of it I helped create.}

But I saw the look when I said that. The sudden, unexpected, hurt look. Was I going to second-guess him? Betray him?

"Yes, I'm sure," he said.

"Then that's good enough for me," I said, and smiled.

When he rose to hug me with his fungal arms, I let him, and I hugged him back and tried not to shudder. {That moment saved me. If you had stopped believing in me too, I would have been lost.}

Then I took the glasses and left, not knowing that I'd be back soon enough.

❧❦❧

I RECEIVED ONE LAST POSTCARD from Duncan before he disappeared. It had lodged on the doorstep, caught in a crack in the wood, as if it were an errant leaf. It read: *It's time*. That's all, just: "It's time." And it was true. Everyone we cared about was dead or lost to us. Why stay above?

Worried, I visited his apartment, where I received partial confirmation that he had left: the door stood open a crack, and inside, other than a large trunk, it was empty of anything important to him. As I walked through those bare rooms, I remembered something else I said to him, when we had finished talking about the Machine.

I told him, "No matter what you do. No matter how much you publish. No matter how much you transform yourself, you're going to die. Aren't you?"

He laughed, even though his eyes weren't his, and gave me a grin that showed his teeth.

He said, and it sent a shiver through me and a calm such as I had never felt before, "There may be a way."

Sybel and Bonmot stood there like ghosts, gazing over that empty apartment. We were all wondering what was in the trunk, I think.

⊰⊱

THERE MAY BE A WAY. I've thought about Duncan's words for a long time now. I have pondered what he might have been suggesting, and I think I know what he meant. I just don't know if it could really be true. Do I believe deeply enough in everything he's shown me?

I thought back to Duncan's account of the Machine and the underground. To him, it was another aspect of his quest, his obsession, no matter where it led. For me, it looked like a way out, a door, as Duncan had described it, or an open window into blue sky. What had it looked like to Tonsure, I sometimes wonder.

⟿ 6 ⟾

I FELL ASLEEP FOR A WHILE. I couldn't help it. I've been pushing myself to the end ever faster, taking fewer breaks.

I dreamt while I slept. Edward was in my dream. Neither of us had really ever left the insane asylum. We sat there in matching straitjackets in uncomfortable chairs, facing each other. We were surrounded by huge orange-red-and-black mushrooms. The sight of their amber gills above us, slowly breathing in and out in a sussurating mimicry of conscious life, was strangely calming to me.

"Where have you gone?" I asked him.

"Underground," he said.

"What did you find there?" I asked.

"Acceptance, everlasting life, and mushrooms," he said, and smiled. It was a lovely smile. It radiated outward to suffuse his entire face in a golden light.

"Is that all?" I said. "Was it worth it? Did you have to give up anything?"

"My fear. My consciousness. My former life."

"What was that like?"

"Do you remember those trust exercises they made us do? Where one of us would fall into the arms of the others, and you just had to fall and keep falling and believe that they would catch you?"

"It was like that?"

"It was like that. Except imagine falling for a hundred years before you're caught, looking at a black sky full of cold dead stars in front of you, and the abyss at your back." {I think you were absorbing a line or two from my journal entries in your sleep.}

"You're dead," I said. It wasn't an accusation.

"Probably," he replied.

By then, we had shed our straitjackets and we stood in the lonely dull courtyard that the asylum had swallowed whole. At the far end, twelve elegant emerald mushrooms on long stalks were being guarded by two round rolling puffballs that glistened with sticky sea-green spores in an odd approximation of the asylum's lawn bowling facilities.

"I'm sorry," I said, although I didn't know what I was saying sorry for.

"It's okay, Janice," he said.

Then he walked away from me down the alley, getting smaller and smaller until he disappeared into the cluster of mushrooms.

Isn't that odd? I remember thinking in my dream. Isn't that odd? And I don't even know what it means.

When I woke, I thought I saw Sybel standing over me, but I was wrong. I was quite alone in my cot, in this dismal back room.

❧❧

I HAVE LEFT OUT SO much, and yet there is no time now to go back and put it in its proper place. I've had no time to explore my {brief} conversion to Truffidianism under Bonmot's guidance after my unfortunate accident. I've not dwelt on my two miscarriages. Or that I was a drug addict for most of my adult life. That I loved Sirin, for many years, in secret, and that we slept together a few times four or five years ago. That—and I am so sorry for this—that I am the one who told Bonmot about Duncan's relationship with Mary. {I suspected. At the time, I would have been beyond furious; I never would have talked to you again. But now I see that that isn't what destroyed my relationship with her.} That I stole Duncan's journal from his apartment months before he left for the underground, long before I acquired the trunk. {Again, I had a suspicion it was you.} That there are definitely things walking up and down the tunnel at my back. That not everything I have told you is the truth as Duncan saw it. That my typewriter glows so brightly that I no longer need a lamp to see. That Duncan's glasses are in my shirt pocket, dormant, waiting for me to put them on.

None of that is important next to what I *do* have time to share with you, because I think I finally made Mary Sabon see—really *see*. It wasn't Duncan. It was me who did it.

How? A stroke of good fortune, and Truff knows I deserved one. About two months before Duncan's final disappearance, I led a group of insufferable snobs around the city—the type who sneer at anything genuine and delight in the false; the less truthful the better. Yet they turned out to be falsely snobbish themselves, once I saw them in another light—one was Martin Lake's new agent, David Frond, and two were his friends, visiting Ambergris for the first time. It was truly a miraculous intervention. When David found out who I was, the look he gave me made it clear he had thought I was dead. The thrill rising in my chest was because he knew my name at all.

After we talked for a while, David offered me a job rounding up Lake's old artist friends and getting them to display their work at a gallery show doubling as a party for Lake's fiftieth birthday. With any luck, he'd let me coordinate the party as well, he said. It was certainly a better offer than anything Sirin had brought my way in quite some time.

"It will be a regular parade of ghosts from Martin's past," he said, smiling.

It would be a parade of ghosts from my past, too, and I wasn't sure I liked the thought of that. Still, I needed the money if I wanted to keep my apartment. The tour guide business had been bad of late.

And, oh, the dead, the ghosts, catalogued but never accounted for among the living. The people I have known who thought they knew me. Each astonished face I tracked down vied more seriously for the winner of the most-startled-Janice-is-alive contest. Each astonished face would be a way to shore up Lake's ego by showing what a mediocrity Insert First & Last Name had turned out to be.

Most of them were people who had been oddly absent whenever I'd been in any kind of real trouble, coincidentally enough. During the ceremonial slitting of the wrists. During the gallery's financial woes. While I was in the hospital reconciling myself to the empty space where once five toes had cavorted like penned-up rutting pigs.

No, if it were to be a party of my peers {of veneers and sneers, more like}, then it would just be my luck that I uncovered "acquaintances" or "not quite friends" or outright enemies. Most of my lovers had vanished during the war—they'd survived *me*, but, still, somehow, the sight of bloodshed scared them—seeking out less eventful lives in Stockton, Morrow, or Nicea. Bonmot and Sybel had both died, of course, and Sirin—through his writing—had ascended to a place where he was, in a way, untouchable. Sybel, of course, was by my side throughout all of the planning for the party; how could I possibly plan a party without him?

When I think of the people I knew back then, I realize that each of us had such private, personal, and immediate experiences that discussion with anyone about them, let alone achieving some kind of joint catharsis, would be meaningless—like a Blythe Academy reunion that invited only strangers from different years. The jargon used might have some kind of similarity, but beyond that, an aching void. That had been the whole point of the New Art—pour all of that empathy into the work, leaving only the surface as a connection to other people. I wonder now if any of it was worth it to any of us.

Still, despite reservations—and, trust me, I had reservations about many of them—I managed to exhume enough of Lake's long-dormant, sleep-tinged, hibernating friends and their dusty, packed-in-storage-for-decades artwork to earn my salary and be kept on for the party.

My main duty at the party? To herd the ruminant artists, to keep them happy. In the background, I would also help with the invitations, and in return, I would not only receive more money, but a promise of a position at a gallery— a promise I'm sure I must have known would never be kept, no matter what happened at the party. I was beyond that kind of respectability, and some part of me may even have been proud of that.

Four artists showed up for the party that night—any more and I wouldn't have been able to handle them, or their egos. After all, I was getting close to an age when women of much greater strength than I had retired to an early dotage on some pleasure barge or houseboat sailing idyllic down the River Moth. I was also worried about my brother, and therefore not in the best of moods. I cannot say that I cared that much about party preparations or "reparations," as I used to joke in the days before the party—with the cook, a sardonic man of my age who lifted my spirits and tried to lift my blouse on more than one occasion.

Lake had decided that the party should be held at the refurbished and renovated Hoegbotton Hotel. It had previously served as a glorified safe house, most active during Festival days, and thus had to be taken apart almost brick by brick to become a "hotel." For example, such features as iron bars on guest room windows did not convey the right message. Nor, for that matter, did the "safety crawl spaces" that led to tunnels, that led to the River Moth. No, it had all been stripped away as if the gray caps and the Festival were now some remote happening—remote in time and space and even remotely unbelievable, from some period of ancient history that could not be verified by even the most reckless historian. A kind of silly rumor—a scary story told to children before bedtime by unenlightened parents. {I blame such innovations as the telephone. Such prosaic devices make it difficult for people to believe in the *other* until it stares them in the face and takes a swipe at them.}

To replace such outdated structures came wide staircases of marble bought from the Kalif at ridiculous prices and large glass windows that any lout with a plank of wood would find irresistible come Festival time. They had scented candles and handmade bedsheets made by the few Dogghe tribesmen who hadn't been slaughtered by our ancestors, and chairs and tables crafted by carpenters from the Southern Isles. Every floor had its own telephone on a pedestal, conveniently located near the staircase. The smell of new stone, new furnishings, and clean sheets was so un-Ambergrisian that as soon as I stepped into the place, I knew no locals would be checking in for a night's rest and relaxation.

The party would take up the ground floor, centered around the banquet hall, while the artists' gathering/gallery would be located on the second floor, in a smaller room.

❧❦

THAT NIGHT WAS CALM BUT for a steady drizzle and drip of rain, the moon missing, but the street lamps making up for it. A breeze blew into the reception area. It felt cool as I waited for the Four Ghosts of Lake's Past to arrive for the party.

I stood in the doorway, smoking a Smashing Ted's Deluxe cigar and nursing a glass of cheap red wine from the kitchen staff's stock. I intended to enjoy my evening by indulging myself early on, so if things went hideously wrong, I would still have a memory to look back on with fondness.

I watched the night as it passed by me on Albumuth Boulevard, one of the last times I had a chance to just relax and observe, as it turned out. And yet, a feeling of peculiar intensity came over me. I saw it all with such precise detail, in a way that I cannot put into words. It was not that the world slowed down or that I saw anything hidden in it, although I knew there was more in front of me than I could see—I had the glasses in my pocket to remind of that. It was more that my gaze *lingered* for once. It lingered and held, as if I was parched for that little glistening of light off water in the gutter as a motored vehicle rumbled past. As if I was hungry for the exact way a street vendor cocked his head while rattling off a list of his offerings. The quiet syncopation of conversation half-heard and then gone as people walked by. The lamppost opposite the hotel, illuminating the facade of a closed bank door. The quick-low cry of a nighthawk circling somewhere above. The feel of the street through my shoes. The grit of the doorway against my shoulder as I leaned on it. The bliss of the cigar's trembling surge of flavor, the biting smoothness of the wine.

I think I already knew then that I was not long for such sights.

❧

THE FOUR ARTISTS ARRIVED ON time—two by an old-fashioned carriage, another by hired motored vehicle, a fourth on foot. Sonter, Kinsky, Raffe, and Constance were their names: a motley rabble of ragtag talent, and none of them had ever so much as scaled a small mountain of acclaim except through the long-ago benevolent influence of Lake's hand upon them.

Sonter looked ancient and creaky, like a narrow, withered boat with bad caulking—on the verge of a watery death, perhaps. A decade spent on an island in the middle of the River Moth had done him no favors. Kinsky had become broad and looked defeated but brave, the gray circles under his eyes negated by an animation lacking from the others. Constance maintained a look of perpetual outrage that made me roll my eyes before I could help myself. Only Raffe, though aging—and, I realized with a shock, probably my own age—appeared in any way serene or accepting of Fate.

I greeted them. They were polite. That was all I expected from them.

Raffe said to me, "You look tired. Can we help with anything?"

Which comment, for some reason, made me want to cry.

I took them upstairs to the temporary gallery—a room converted from its original function as a bar. The lighting was all wrong and I hadn't been able to hang the paintings the way I would have liked due to an incompetent helper, but at least a small throng had gathered there already. I don't remember my welcoming speech, I just know that, for a moment, an emotion welled up in my throat that came close to affection for those I was introducing. After all, they were survivors just like me. They were also artists, and for twenty years of my life all I had done was introduce artists. Was there a sad twinge for my lost gallery? Of course, but these days there is a sad twinge about everything—to the point that I begin to wonder if it's my heart that's gone bad, rather than anything to do with my memories.

Besides, it can't be avoided. Bonmot once told me, "If you don't feel a certain sadness toward the past, then you probably don't understand it."

After my introduction and short speeches by the artists, the adoring if small-in-numbers public pushed forward to engage the Obscure, Sonter somehow evading the crush and coming up to me.

"I heard Mary Sabon will be here tonight," he said. "Is that true?"

The peace I had been experiencing left me.

"I don't know," I told him. "I didn't see her on the guest list."

That had been my one petty triumph—I'd managed through sleight of hand to get Mary Sabon uninvited from Lake's party, said sleight of hand involving an unmailed invitation and a sidewalk gutter leading to the nether depths. Somewhere *down there* a gray cap might be clutching that invitation as I write this account. It might be its most treasured possession.

So I hope you will understand in advance that my later actions were spontaneous, perhaps even unplanned. I did not go to the party, as some claimed in muttering whispers afterwards, to confront Mary. I had done my best to make sure she would not be there at all. {I believe you.}

Sonter opened his mouth to question me further, but I shut it with a well-aimed appetizer delivered on raised foot, the appetizer rescued from a passing waiter's tray with an ease I almost never experience. Sonter turned away immediately.

There may have been an expression on my face that made him turn away. It may have had nothing to do with the appetizer. I would not rule it out if I were you.

⚜

FOR THE NEXT TWO HOURS, I attended to the artists, explaining their paintings to those who required an explanation. It was hard work. Some of the paintings came from the kind of obscure symbolism that either baffles me or brings out my inventiveness, but the old potent phrases from the past came back to me from the void of memory soon enough.

"Vibrant use of color."

"Brave application of the oils."

"The composition accentuates the face, for nicely subtle symbolic effect."

This part I enjoyed, I admit. It made me feel free. For a brief time, while pointing out the detail of a sudden azure thrush in the dull emerald undergrowth at the bottom of one of Raffe's paintings, I could pretend Lake was still my client, that my gallery still served as the nexus of the New Art. I even caught the eye of a former lover from across the room, and he smiled. You could say I was happy.

Then they pressed me into duty helping downstairs, in the banquet hall. David Frond's idea of a menu included lark's tongues and frog's legs, fish eggs and lemon pie, squid soup and oliphaunt kidneys. It was quite an ambitious spread, worthy of the obese gastronome Manzikert III himself. It wasn't hard to imagine another time, another place, in which this would have been a party for Duncan, had luck been on our side. A string of alternate scenarios in which we rose to the top and stayed there, instead of being diminished by time and our own enemies. {Would it have been so much better that way, Janice?}

Ill-suited for such work, I hobbled back and forth past the extravagantly costumed guests as they cavorted across the dance floor—half hunter, half flushed rabbit—escorting notables with polite conversation about the weather—there was quite a drumming of rain outside by then—or about the history of the fluted archways in the lobby that the Hoegbottons had stolen from some ruin down south.

Some of the people I escorted, I remembered coming into my gallery as children or young adults, but none of them remembered me. Scions of Hoegbotton's mercantile empire, officials from foreign cities, even a nervous-looking emissary from Frankwrithe & Lewden {more than likely a hostage}. I don't know why I had to escort them, and I didn't much care. {Lake's agent probably feared they would get drunk and cause a scene.}

Then followed a period of rest for this old woman, where I just stood in the gallery room on the second floor and smiled at patrons of the arts as they glided by, drinks in hand. The artists had all joined the reverie on the ground floor, but I welcomed the respite by then.

The party had reached that unfamiliar point where, in contrast to past events, I stood outside of it, looking in. I was far away, and very tired, remembering with regret the cigar I had had to abandon when the artists showed up. Remembering that my brother was missing and feeling powerless to do anything about it.

There is, I have to say, a perfect anonymity at a party like that, in the role chosen for me. You can pretend by remaining silent that you are invisible and yet all-powerful. The way the conversation intermingles so that you do not hear any words, just a kind of spiraling hum, or babble, or crescendo—and you can then, if you listen hard, hear the individual words and phrases, but not in a way that makes any sense. Duncan was hundreds of feet below me by then, working his way to the heart of a mystery. I know he had to be because he was nowhere near me anymore {although closer than you think}, and it seemed to me in that moment that he really wouldn't be coming back.

And, also, I was thinking about how you can bring the hum, the babble, the crescendo low—bring it all low with a single accusation, a shout, a scream, perhaps even, yes, a shriek.

I might have stayed in that trance forever, enjoying a measure of melancholy contentment, if I had not heard someone, probably Sonter, say, "Mary Sabon is here" as he walked by the doorway.

The party jolted into focus again.

Sabon? Here? But she hadn't been invited. . . .

I surveyed the thinning gallery crowd. No sign of her. So she must be downstairs. I don't know why my first thought was to hunt her down, but I got up, pushed through a wedge of drunk people, and escaped to the top of the marble staircase.

At the bottom of the steps, surrounded by the glittering necklace of flesh that always surrounded her now, stood Mary Sabon. My attempts to keep her away had been useless. She was like an apparition to me, an apparition that had manifested itself in flesh and blood and makeup. Sabon transcended any attempt to ward her off. She had risen above that.

I had not seen her in years, except in newspaper photographs or granular dust jacket likenesses. She looked younger than she had any right to be, and there was a glow to her skin, and a sheen to her hair, as if she were feeding off of the heat and light given off by her swirling necklace of admirers. Admittedly, I almost couldn't see her, surrounded by that necklace. But such perfect poise. Such caked-on rouge. Such hypocrisy. There she was, telling her flesh necklace a series of stories to beguile them with her charm, to make them unrealize what the war and Duncan had been warning them about for years.

I couldn't banish her, so I decided to punish her instead. {You could have left the party. Would that have been so hard?}

I was, admittedly, a slow, deliberate stalker; anyone could have evaded me, had they been able to see me over the tall individuals who kept blocking my path. It took me ages to reach the last step, what with my cane and my wooden foot. What would I do when I reached her? What would I say? Perhaps, I thought, in a moment of panic, I should take off my foot and throw it at her and retreat to the gallery. But that was absurd, and she hadn't seen me yet. She was too busy talking about herself.

I had reached the last step when I heard her remark about Duncan.

"Duncan Shriek? That old fake? He's not a human being at all, but composed entirely of digressions and transgressions."

I laughed for a moment, out of surprise more than anything, but also out of affection for my brother, because it was true—except her tone made it obvious she didn't mean it affectionately.

Mary heard my laughter because it was out of place with the rest of it—an echo too remote from the original sound. She looked around and saw me just as I finished hobbling down the stairs, making a mockery of their convenience. I suppose if they'd had a dumbwaiter I could have winched myself down instead.

Thus I descended to the foot of the stairs. The marble shone like glass, like a mirror—my face and those of the others reflected back at me. The assembled guests slowly fell apart into their separate bead selves. Blank-eyed beads winking at me as they formed a corridor to Sabon. Smelling of too little or too much perfume, of sweat. Shedding light by embracing shadows. A series of stick-figures in a comedic play.

I walked right up to Mary. Red hair she still had in abundance, although I would not like to conjecture how she kept out the gray. She wore a dark green evening dress with brocade straps. Her gaze was contemptuous, perhaps, or merely guarded.

Ignoring my presence—something she would have done at her peril in the old days—she repeated, "Duncan is composed entirely of digressions and transgressions. Assuming he's still alive."

As she said this, she took a step forward and turned and looked right at me. We stood only a foot or two apart.

I stared at her for a moment. I let her receive the full venom of my stare. Then I hobbled forward and I slapped her hard across the face. She grunted in surprise, seemed stunned more than hurt.

She wasn't that much taller than me, really. Not as tall as she'd seemed while I was coming down the stairs. And not as young as she had seemed, either. My hand came away covered in makeup.

The imprint shone as red as her hair, as flushed as the gasp from the necklace of flesh. It lit up her face in a way that made her look honest again. It spread across her cheek, down her neck, swirled between the tops of her breasts, and disappeared beneath her gown. If the world is a just place, that mark will never leave her skin, but remain as a pulsing reminder that, at some point in the past, she hurt someone so badly that she wound up hurting herself as well.

"Once upon a time," I said, "no one knew your name. Someday no one will again."

The wide O of the mouth, the speechless surprise, the backward step, the hand raised toward her cheek, the fear in her eyes as if she saw herself already as dust. That slap would tease a thousand tongues in a dozen cafés that week, until even the swift-darting swallows that so love our city repeated it in their incessant, insect-seducing song.

To her credit, she waved back the guards. She waved back the onrush of beads from her flesh necklace. They retreated, gleaming and muttering.

"What is it you really want, Janice?" she said, smiling through her pain. "Would you like the past back? Would you like to be successful again? Would you prefer you weren't a washed-up has-been with so few prospects you had to agree to assist to help out with a party for an artist you used to agent?"

But I had nothing to say to her.

Instead, I turned to look at the assembled fawners and sycophants, the neophytes and the desperate, to make sure they were watching. Then I took the glasses from my pocket—and flung them at Mary's face. I didn't know I was going to do it until the instant it happened, and then it was too late to un-wish it.

In midair, the glasses opened up and, like some aerial acrobat of a spider, attached themselves perfectly to her face, the arms sliding into position around her ears, the bridge settling on her nose.

Mary was staring at me as the scales of the lenses filled with that amazing blackness—and she began to scream as soon as the top half of her pupils disappeared, a scream that grew deeper and more desperate as it continued, and continued. It was as if she had forgotten she could close her eyes. All she had to do was close her eyes, and, after a time, I began to hope she *would* close her eyes.

She stumbled, caught herself, blinked twice, stopped screaming—but, no: she was still screaming, it was just soundless. A look had come over her that destroyed the unity between mouth, eyes, forehead, cheekbones. Before me, she became undone looking through those glasses.

She fell to her knees, now grappling with the glasses, but they did not want to come off. Her precious flesh necklace didn't know what to do—it dithered, came forward, retreated, unable to reconcile this moment of Sabon's life with the last.

Raffe and Sonter were the first to recover from their shock, pushing through the crowd to come to Mary's aid. Sabon was slack-jawed, moaning, and saying a word over and over again. It sounded suspiciously like "No." Sonter tried to pry the glasses off while Raffe comforted Mary. But they still wouldn't come off.

Finally, mercy flooding back into me, I stepped forward and plucked the glasses off from her face; they scurried across the floor and rolled up into a ball. Sabon's face went slack, and I saw a momentary flicker of pain—the ghost of regret, perhaps?—and then it was gone. Her eyes rolled up into her head and she fainted.

The flesh necklace, now adding their cries to the growing cacophony, parted to let Raffe and Sonter carry Mary away, Sonter cursing my name. Even in unconsciousness, a look of utter terror and helplessness marred her face.

No one else wanted to pick up the glasses, so I did. After all, they were mine. I folded them and put them back in my pocket. They were still warm.

I was trembling and exhausted; watching Mary struggle had taken all of my energy. I still cannot decide if it was relief or horror that drained me. I still can't decide if what I did was right or wrong.

What had Mary seen? I don't know. I had stopped wearing the glasses more than two weeks before. Released from Duncan's expert guidance, they had become stranger and stronger somehow, as if they now pierced through layers of reality deeper than even the gray caps were meant to see. But whatever she saw, it was the truth—in one massive dose.

I've thought about whether I should put them on again—I've thought about it the entire time I've been typing up this account. Might I see *all the way through*? Might I see through the golden threads, if they exist, to something else entirely? Or would I just fall, and keep falling?

I do know this—sometimes, afterwards, I've had a daydream in which I seek Mary out once the glasses come off, and I find her weeping in a corridor in the bowels of the hotel, and I sit down beside her and I hold her close and I say, "Please—forgive me." But sometimes in the daydream I'm also saying, "I forgive you, Mary. I forgive you."

❧ 7 ❧

I BOUGHT A FEW NEWSPAPERS after I came here, but all they can tell me is that "Sabon is recovering from a bout of exhaustion." None of them mentions my role in her exhaustion.

And that is all I know, and all I want to know.

❧❧❧

I HALTED ON THE EDGE of an abyss when I left Mary, I think. I halted on the edge of a kind of Silence. I needed to write it down, try to make some sense of it outside of my own head. Draw the poison.

But I've shed my last skin. I've no more skins to shed. I can't start over again—I've started over too many times before. You won't believe me. *I* won't believe me, either.

Maybe all of this was prevarication and excuses and not an afterword at all. Not an essay. Not a history. Not a pamphlet. Just an old woman's ramblings. Maybe I don't want to think about that hole in the ground behind me and the decision I have to make. But if so, at least it's over now. I have told you everything I meant to tell you, and more.

As I sit here in the green light and review these pages, I see what Duncan saw when he wrote in this room—the sliver, the narrowness of vision, the small amount we know before we're gone—and I realize that this account was a stab in the dark at a kind of truth, no matter how faltering: a brief flash of light against the silhouette of dead trees. This was the story of my life and my brother's life, my brother and his Mary. {How could you think to tell such a story without me by your side, Janice?}

And, somehow, I have kept separate, hidden away in my mind, one single image of joy before disaster: my father, running across the unbearably green grass. And not what occurred after. Not what happened after.

I want that kind of joy, that epiphany, or a chance at it, at least, even if it kills me. {Must I echo to you your own words? That we are all connected by lines of glimmering light. How many times those words kept me alive, made me see approaching light in unending darkness? As Bonmot used to say in his sermons: "We are vessels of light—broken vessels, broken light, but vessels nonetheless." Fragments across the void. It's time to find you, Janice, and see what you've gotten yourself into.}

But you're free now, regardless of what this was—afterword, afterwards. I release you to return to what you were before. If you can.

As for me, it is time to abandon even this dim green light for the darkness. I've put as many words between myself and this decision as I can, but it hasn't worked. There's a space between each word that I can't help but fall into, and those spaces are as wide as the words and twice as treacherous.

A shift of attention. Another place to go. That's all it is. I'm not afraid anymore. I'm not frightened. Everyone is dead or disappeared or disappointed. I ask you, *who* is left to be afraid of? This is After Dad Died. This is After Mom Died. This is an entirely new place.

I think it is time for one last walk outside. One last look at this crazed, beautiful, dirty, sad, glorious city. Sybel and Bonmot and my mom and all the rest are waiting for me out there in some form or another—a whisper on the breeze, the rustle of the branches, a shadow across a wall, and, perhaps, there will be time for one last lunch under the willows, my glasses safely in my pocket. Then I'll come back and decide whether or not to seek out Duncan, whether to put on these glasses and face whatever Mary saw.

No one makes it out, Samuel Tonsure once said.

Or do they?

A (BRIEF) AFTERWORD
by Sirin

MY ROLE IN ALL OF this is complicated and compromised because I know or knew almost all of the people mentioned in Janice's manuscript, not least of whom was Janice herself. I was always fond of Janice, perhaps more than I should have been, but confronted with her typewritten manuscript, I felt much as I had felt several years before when confronted by Duncan's six hundred pages of early history: overwhelmed, irritated, fatigued, intrigued, and perplexed. I've always thought Janice had the best intentions, but also that her biases and her own obsessions sometimes led her to suspect conclusions. Many of these suspect conclusions had made their way into the afterword she left behind, and this explains, or helps to explain, my actions with regard to it. I hope.

⸎

I FOUND THE ORIGINAL TYPEWRITTEN pages in the back room of the Spore of the Gray Cap. I had gone there searching for Janice, as she had not shown up for her job in over a month. Since we had a professional history, I felt an obligation to find out what might be wrong. In fact, given our personal history, I felt more than an obligation—I was worried about her.

Given the events that had taken place at Martin Lake's party—events accurately described in Janice's account—I thought it likely she was "hiding" from a sense of shame or embarrassment. I never realized she might be writing a highly inflammatory, perhaps even actionable, history of her life and her brother's life.

When I found the manuscript, it lay in a disorganized mess of pages beside her typewriter. The typewriter had become clogged with a green lichen or fungus; the entire shell overtaken by the spread of this loamy green substance.

If I had arrived only a day later, the manuscript also might have succumbed to this same affliction.

I examined the pages briefly—long enough, however, to ascertain who had written the text and to note the comments added by Duncan, whose handwriting and attitude are familiar to me from our association over the years.

Beyond the desk, on the floor near the wall, a series of loose boards partially covered up a hole that led down into the ground. Once I saw the hole, I left quickly, pausing only to gather up the manuscript pages.

After I returned to my office with the manuscript and read through it, I was baffled as to what to do next. While many of the sections dealing with Ambergris' recent history had a general ring of truth to them, these were inextricably interwoven with sections that contained the most outrageous accusations and assertions. What was true and what false, I might never know.

Figure 1: Janice Shriek's typewriter. As the reader can see from this photo, the typewriter keys had been infiltrated by mushrooms. Many of the keys were brittle and fell off within weeks of taking the machine out of its room at the Spore of the Gray Cap. The typewriter disintegrated entirely within five months.

Neither could I corroborate any statements made about Janice's family—despite the mention of family papers and Duncan's journal in the manuscript, no such documents had been in evidence at the Spore of the Gray Cap. Worst of all, the manuscript did such a disservice to the reputation and character of my author Mary Sabon that from a purely professional point of view I was disinclined to attempt publication. However, paramount above all other concerns, I sincerely believed that Duncan or Janice would walk into my offices at any moment to reclaim the manuscript. So, for several years, I held on to it. I could not bring myself to destroy it. Nor could I bring myself to let the public have its way with the account.

However, it gradually became clear that Janice and Duncan had disappeared, possibly forever. Oddly enough, the owner of the Spore still swears that Janice never left his establishment on the day she would have finished her account—that she simply disappeared from the room, presumably through the hole in the floor. Similarly, the owner claims he never saw Duncan during the time Duncan must have been adding his comments to the manuscript.

That Duncan had been missing for several weeks before Martin Lake's party is supported only by the unsubstantiated statements in Janice's manuscript. As he was unemployed at the time of his supposed disappearance, no one, not even members of AFTOIS, noticed his absence. Still, it is true that he has not been seen in Ambergris since commenting on Janice's manuscript. It has been almost four years.

As for Janice, not much more is known about her whereabouts. The current rumor is that a person fitting her description fell (or was pushed—we will never know) into the path of a motored vehicle on the same day Janice seems to have finished her account. Supposedly, a wooden foot was found near the scene, but the body was too badly mangled to be identifiable.

⬦⬦⬦

ONCE IT WAS CLEAR THE Shrieks would not be coming back, I pulled out the manuscript again and reread it. In the three years that had passed, many strange things had happened in the city, so that even the most bizarre parts of the account no longer seemed quite so ridiculous. But there was still the issue of its portrayal of Mary. I decided to show Mary the manuscript and let her decide its fate. It may seem that I abrogated my responsibility in doing so, but I felt I had no choice.

To my surprise, Mary told me Hoegbotton & Sons *should* publish it. She was quite adamant about it, and further instructed me not to delete or soften any references to her, regardless of how unflattering. She became very emotional on this point, and I had the impression she wished I had shown her the manuscript the day I had found it.

Obeying Mary's wishes, I did not make many edits of substance in preparing Janice's account for publication. I did, in some instances, smooth out the text—for example, fixing the grammatical errors in those sections written in exceptional haste. Likewise, I corrected all spelling errors. Where Janice had alternate versions of a page or scene—which occurred with some frequency—I chose the more polished of the two. I also untangled Janice's handwritten corrections from Duncan's comments, deciding that placing the latter in parentheses and removing parentheses from Janice's text was the most elegant solution to a potentially wearisome problem. Where she spent too long on a subject, or lost focus completely, I did excise text, but the entirety of these deletions constitutes only five or six paragraphs in total. I may have erred too far on the side of preservation in this case—some of the discussion of Duncan's theories strikes me as tedious—but better tedium than claims I was overzealous in my editing duties.

I also deleted Duncan's final comment on Janice's manuscript, which he wrote on the page following her last chapter. I did this not because I wanted to, but because I *had* to. The comment was illegible. I had several handwriting experts examine the sentence. None could come to any agreement as to how it might have read. The most coherent interpretation? "Confluence of light between towers and being there at the right time leapt forward." I include the phrase here despite my best instincts to do otherwise. My sole addition to the text consisted of fleshing out one or two scenes where Janice's descriptive powers deserted her, but only in cases where I had been privy to the same information.

A further complication concerned the fungal contamination of the pages, coupled with the haphazard way in which the pages had been stacked on the table at the Spore. On some pages, the words were barely legible, and many pages or sections were out of order, several lacking the page numbers that might have allowed me to easily sequence them. I erred on the side of chronological order—even though Janice did not always adhere to such an order—but it is possible I made a few errors in my sequencing.

PART VIII.

Nothing was the same when I came back.

It's night here, as I type, and hot. Something is gnawing away at the wood between the ceiling of this place and the roof. In this context, I find it almost relaxing to listen to the chewing. It reminds me of our father's absurd mouse-catching inventions.

I'd rather listen to that than to the sounds I sometimes hear coming from below me. It does not bear thinking about, what may be going on below me. Really, this afterword has been the only thing saving me from too many thoughts about the present. The green light is ever-present, but the clientele is not. It's late. They've gone home. It's just me and the lamp and the typewriter...and whatever is chewing above me and whatever is moving below me. And I feel feverish. I feel like I should lie down on the cot I had them bring in here. I feel like I should take a rest. But I can't. I have to keep going on. Despite the heat. Despite the fact I'm burning up. I have some mushrooms Duncan left behind, but I'm not sure I should eat them, so I won't. They might help, but they might not.

So, instead, to stave off burning up, I'll write about the snow. I'll write about all of that wonderful, miraculous snow that awaited me on my return to Ambergris. Maybe the gnawing will stop in the meantime. Unless it's in my mind, in which case it may never stop.

I returned to an Ambergris transformed by snow from semi-tropical city to a body covered by a white shroud. Every street, alley, courtyard, building, storefront, motored vehicle had succumbed to the mysteries of the snow. Ambergris was not suited to white. White is the color of surrender, and Ambergris is unaccustomed to surrender. Surrender is not part of our character.

At first, the city appeared similar to dull, staid Morrow, but underneath the anonymous white coating lay the same old city, cunning and cruel as ever. Merchants sold firewood at ten times the normal

Figure 2: A reproduction of a sample page from Janice Shriek's manuscript. Despite Duncan's admonishment about the unimportance of Janice's description of a transformed Ambergris, I did not delete the text as he requested; nor did I delete anything in the manuscript that Duncan edited out. After careful consideration, I did, however, delete a half-dozen paragraph-length oddities that bore no discernible relation to the rest of the text, since I felt that these digressions would distract from the text more than they added to it. The careful reader will note that the page reproduced above contains one of these deleted segments.

Therefore, I have clearly made editorial decisions with regard to Janice's manuscript which some may consider to be too invasive, no matter how slight. But what is not true, despite the rumors, is that *An Afterword to the Hoegbotton Guide to the Early History of Ambergris* represents an elaborate deception on my part. Not only is the manuscript genuine (see the reproduction of a sample page herein), but I had nothing to do with writing it. Nor is Hoegbotton &

Sons only publishing it now due to the sharp upturn in sales of Duncan's books.[1]

❧❧

I HAVE NO DOUBT THAT the publication of this book will generate fierce discussion about the merits of Nativism, about the aims of the gray caps, and about the nature of the Shift that has increasingly disrupted life in Ambergris. Some will feel that Duncan is about to be vindicated in the most dramatic of ways.

In preparing the manuscript for publication, I have, for that very reason, experienced fresh doubts about making it available. We live in a very volatile time and I would not want this book to be a catalyst for extremism. Nor, I would hope, will readers jump to unsupportable conclusions having read it. I know that many people are clutching at whatever they can to make sense of the odd events that, on certain days, seem destined to overwhelm all of us. My sincere hope is that this book will not push anyone over the edge.

As to the current whereabouts of Duncan and Janice, I must fear the worst, although rumors,[2] as rumors will, continue to flourish in the current atmosphere of paranoia and fear.

And yet, despite the strife and violence chronicled and presaged by this volume, the enduring image I have of Janice and Duncan is a peaceful one. It is, oddly enough, of Janice in that room in the Spore, calmly typing away—from the bar folks' perspective, in a sliver of green light between the doorway and the corridor as once they saw Duncan, but farther and farther away, across green glass and green grass, and fading, fading as the light fails once more.

THE END

---

[1]Some on my editorial staff have suggested that we should include an unexpurgated version of Duncan's *Early History of Ambergris* as an appendix to this edition. However, I cannot acquire that text, as I returned my only copy to Janice and do not know what she did with it. Moreover, an edition that combined Janice's manuscript with the complete *Early History* would put even Hoegbotton's hardbound edition of its seventy-five Southern Island travel pamphlets to shame for sheer size and verbiage.

[2]No evidence exists to support supposed "Duncan Sightings" at Zamilon and Alfar, for example.

Acknowledgments

Thanks to my wife Ann, my first reader, who has provided invaluable comments on and support for this novel over so many years. My most sincere and heartfelt thanks and gratitude to Liz Gorinsky, my editor at Tor, who has worked so hard to make this novel as perfect as possible with her general, specific, and structural edits. This novel would be a pale shadow of its current self without her efforts. Special thanks to my other beloved *Shriek* editors Peter Lavery (U.K.) and Hannes Riffel (Germany), as well as the indomitable Jim Minz.

Thanks to everyone who read all or part of this book in manuscript form and offered their comments, including Matt Cheney, Clare Dudman, Richard Hutchinson, Jason Lundberg, Mark Roberts, Eric Schaller, Jonathan Stephens, Anne Sydenham, Anna Tambour, Jeffrey Thomas, Juliet Ulman, Robert Wexler, Elizabeth VanderMeer, Neil Williamson, Tamar Yellin, and Zoran Zivkovic. Thanks to Jonathan Edwards and Mark Roberts for wonderful forgeries. Special thanks to my agent, Howard Morhaim, for his guidance, advice, patience, and friendship; to Danny Baror of Baror International; and to Claire Weaver, for her tireless efforts.

Finally, huge thanks to all of the people at Tor whose meticulous attention to this book I very much appreciate, including copyeditor Robert Legault, proofreader John Yohalem, designers Peter Lutjen and Nicole de las Heras, production editor Meryl Gross, publicist Leslie Henkel, and other behind-the-scenes contributors in the sales and marketing, art, and production departments.

Music Acknowledgments

Over the seven years during which I wrote *Shriek*, I listened to music—an unofficial soundtrack that helped me stay focused and on task through the most difficult parts. Much of the soundtrack I listened to is listed below.

Afghan Whigs—*Gentlemen*—Mary and Duncan's relationship
The Cure—*Mixed Up*—transitions
Dead Can Dance—*Aion*—general
In Flames—*Soundtrack to Your Escape*—war scenes
James—entire catalog—general
Murder City Devils—entire catalog—war scenes and general
Muse—entire catalog—opera scene
The National—entire catalog—Mary and Duncan's relationship
Nick Cave—*The Boatman's Call*—the sadder parts of Mary and Duncan's
   relationship
Nick Cave—*Henry's Dream*—war scenes
Pleasure Forever—Compilation—Janice's dissolute parties and Festival night
Radiohead—*OK Computer*—general
Scott Walker—*Tilt*—Duncan's underground adventures
Songs: Ohia—*Magnolia Electric Co.*—general
South—*With the Tides*—general
Spoon—entire catalog, including *Gimme Fiction*—war scenes and general
Thursday—*War All the Time*—war reporter scenes
Tindersticks—*Tindersticks*—general
Scott Walker—*Tilt*—Duncan's underground adventures

Special thanks to The Church, whose music I listened to throughout the writing of *Shriek*—so much of it that I hear it in my head when rereading the novel.
—Tallahassee, Florida, May 1998–August 2005

Mia Hanson

WIDELY REGARDED AS ONE OF the world's best fantasists, bestselling author Jeff VanderMeer's book-length fiction has been translated into fourteen languages, while his short fiction has appeared in several year's best anthologies and been short-listed for *Best American Short Stories*. His most recent books have made the year's best lists of *Publishers Weekly*, *San Francisco Chronicle*, and *Los Angeles Weekly*. He is also the recipient of an NEA-funded Florida Individual Artist Fellowship for excellence in fiction and a Florida Artist Enhancement Grant. A two-time winner of the World Fantasy Award, VanderMeer has also been a finalist for the Hugo Award, the Philip K. Dick Memorial Award, the International Horror Guild Award, the British Fantasy Award, the Bram Stoker Award, and the Theodore Sturgeon Memorial Award. In addition to his writing, VanderMeer has edited or coedited several anthologies, including the critically acclaimed *Leviathan* fiction anthology series and *The Thackery T. Lambshead Pocket Guide to Eccentric & Discredited Diseases*. He also coedited the inaugural edition of *Best American Fantasy*.

VanderMeer grew up in the Fiji Islands and spent six months traveling through Asia, Africa, and Europe before returning to the United States. These travels have deeply influenced his fiction. He now lives in Tallahassee, Florida, with his wife, Ann, and three cats. He keeps a blog at http://vanderworld.blogspot.com and can be reached at vanderworld@hotmail.com.

For more information on *Shriek: An Afterword*, visit the *Shriek* Web site at: http://www.shriekthenovel.com. The site features a short film based on *Shriek* with an original soundtrack by rock band The Church, the "Rough Guide to Ambergris," video, and audio clips of readings, and much more.